Pursuit

Rod McFain

2022 White Bird Publications, LLC

Copyright © 2022 by Rod McFain

Published in the United States
by White Bird Publications, LLC, Austin, Texas
www.whitebirdpublications.com

Paperback ISBN 978-1-63363-592-0
eBook ISBN 978-1-63363-593-7
Library of Congress Control Number: 2022936570

PRINTED IN THE UNITED STATES OF AMERICA

Dedication

For Linda—

❧

And those who daydream.

Pursuit

**White Bird
Publications**

"For the great day of His wrath is come;
And who shall be able to stand?"
Revelation 6:17

PART I

1874 The Big Horn Mountains

Chapter One

Some say he cheated death as if the Grim Reaper were a gambler to be bested over a faded deck of cards in a sawdust-floored saloon. His wanderlust lasted twenty years. His rowdy character haunted him the entire time.

Gray Wehr stood a raw-boned six feet tall with piercing green eyes framed by heavy sideburns. Wavy blond hair danced along the top of his collar, giving him a bit of a roguish look. Women considered him a dashing figure.

Now, urging his bay mare to cross a murky little stream, the reputation was as distant as the dusty Kansas town where he first fired his pistol at another man.

"Step off and walk her across," his younger partner Trent Thaxton said. "She must not be much of a mudder."

Gray's bay balked again at crossing the muddy stream. "Come on, Lena; you're fine." He squeezed his heels against her flanks. She stepped up to the edge of the murky water flowing over blackish-green silt and mud only four feet from one bank to the other. Tossing her head and jerking at her bit, she tried to gain the advantage of a loose rein.

"Come on, Lena; get over there."

The mare crouched back.

"No, no…you're not going to jump. Walk across."

Again, the bay tensed, struggled back before Gray pulled her head around and let her take a few steps from the water while he patted and scratched the side of her neck. "Come on now; nothing's going to hurt you," he half-whispered before turning the horse back toward the stream, where she again tightened up.

"Kick her and slap her with those reins," Zach Joseph, the third member of the group, said. "I'm tired of watching you dillydally with her."

"And I'm tired of listening to you," Gray said back, nudging the mare once more toward the edge of the muddy creek. Again, she balked, shuffled before coiling back on her hindquarters.

"Well, jump the blamed thing," Gray muttered, giving into the bay. "I'm not gonna make a fight of this," he said, letting the reins go slack and making a kissing sound.

Without warning, the horse uncoiled. Life slowed. Every detail of the murky water passing underneath him was distinguishable. As the crown of the high bank caught his eye, Gray realized she meant not to jump only the stream; she intended to make the top.

The rain-softened dirt collapsed under her force and weight when she hit two feet below the crest. For a tick in time, the whole adventure stopped or slowed down. Lena sank chest-deep in the muddy bank, leaving Gray no time to react before throwing her head back, lurching, and twisting to free herself.

Gray lost balance before squaring himself back into the saddle. Icy fear shot through him while he and the horse tumbled backward, falling ten, twelve feet to the streambed.

The distance made the fall ferocious. But the bank's height also gave the mare time to twist herself enough for them to take the impact on the horse's side rather than straight back, driving the saddle horn into Gray's chest, killing him. Still, they hit with brutal force.

Their momentum sent the horse rolling over on her back with all four feet flailing. Gray feared the bay crushing him underneath her. For an instant, she caught her balance. She jerked and lunged in a frantic attempt to stand. Halfway up, the mare's feet went out from under her, slipping across six or seven birch trees some fool used trying to construct a footbridge. The saplings rolled, shot out from under her, again sending her down hard on her side.

Gray's stirrup twisted in the fall, pinning his foot under the animal at a severe angle. His anguished screaming blocked out all other noise as the bay tried a second time, with no greater success, to regain her feet, halfway up, down again. Hearing bones snapping like the popping of a pistol, life as an invalid flashed through his mind. What a burden he would be to his family—a useless, middle-aged cripple, no longer able to walk.

Lena lunged again, splashing mud and frigid water on her gnarled rider, wild anxiety shooting from her eyes. Nostrils flaring with each shot of hot breath, she finally made her feet, but Gray lost his seat, perhaps due to his will to stay with her. As the bay bolted to a standing position, Gray fell to the ground, his right foot wrenching in a brutal twisting motion.

Everything happened with such force, jerking him out of the stream, flipping him off his back and on his stomach, coming to a stop in the tall wet meadow grass. Hung up in the stirrup, he would never free himself before being dragged, perhaps to death, by the terrified animal.

However, the bay mare did not charge off. Instead, she stood almost statue-like until she turned her head, looking down at her fallen and broken rider.

"Damn," Gray groaned, stretching to make a second futile attempt for the out-of-reach reins. A sharp burning pain shot from his foot up the entire right side of his body.

He lay back on the damp ground, giving up, trying to

hold on to consciousness, as Trent eased toward the frightened animal.

"Whoa, Lena." Trent slipped down the bank and reached for the reins. "Easy girl," Trent kept repeating. His eyes darted back and forth across the soggy stream bottom. If the horse did bolt, grabbing her without being trampled would be difficult. With the silty ground so damp and slippery, getting out of her way, much less freeing Gray, would be tricky at best.

"Are you alright?" the younger man asked as he slipped along next to the mare.

Gray tried to sit up but failed.

"Are you hurt?"

"What do you think?" Gray bellowed, struggling again to grab hold of the stirrup. "Lena, you broke my foot," Gray complained, trying to slide forward, only to be rewarded by another knifelike pain shooting through his wrenched foot and leg. "Aww, kick my butt!" Out of sheer willpower, Gray twisted himself free.

"Kick my butt," he growled a second time, lying back down on the damp, cold ground, breathing fast and shallow. Squeezing his eyes shut, he tried to take deeper, slower breaths, hoping for a calming effect. Gray pictured serene meadows, something the town doctor once told him would help take a person's mind off his pain. Horse crap! What kind of fool would lie in mud pondering fields and flowers with his foot shattered?

When he opened his eyes again, Trent stood over him, bent at the waist with his forearms on his knees. "Is she hurt?" Gray moaned, glancing up at the bay mare.

"Is she hurt?" Zach Joseph mumbled, thinking that worrying about a horse when you are all busted up is plain stupid.

"I don't think so." Trent took hold of Gray's arm. "Can you stand?"

"I'm not sure. Give me a minute."

As Gray lay in the grass along the stream, his skin

turned pale; his light coat and shirt soaked up dampness from the marshy ground.

"Pull me up easy. It's wet down here." Gray still sounded groggy.

Trent bent down to help Gray to his feet.

Gray tried to put pressure on his right foot, hoping to gain balance. The effort caused yet another flash of burning pain, this one shooting clear to his shoulder. "I may be able to stand here," he sulked, "but I can't walk. Help me to the top." Trent ducked his lanky six-foot-three frame for Gray to put his arm around his neck. "Easy," Gray snapped when the young man started up the bank.

The slippery slope proved quite an adversary to their climb. "We're like a couple of drunks." Gray chuckled. They slipped and pawed their way up. Once on top, Trent and Zach held him until Gray's sudden faintness subsided.

After his head cleared and he regained his balance on one foot, Zach led Gray's mare and his horse up the bank to join the other two. "Are you hurt anywhere else?"

"I don't think so."

"How are we going to get you out of here? We must be three hours back in here."

"I'll ride Lena."

"You're not going to be able to ride."

"Well, I sure as the devil ain't walkin'." Gray took hold of his bay's saddle and, following an ungraceful struggle, shifted his weight to the horse. He started experiencing the same queasiness he suffered after his one trip on a sailing vessel. Seamen warned Gray about seasickness, but seasickness didn't afflict Gray in the least. Not while on the ship. He would have been better off staying on the boat because, for a week after returning to land, stomach-turning dizziness overtook him every time he tried to lie down. The world spun again, only faster.

Gray clenched his teeth, trying to keep his stomach down while leaning against Lena for several minutes, waiting for his nausea to pass. Hoping for relief, he took a series of deep breaths, trying to clear his head. It didn't work, at least not much. "Help me up on her." He took the saddle horn with both hands. "I don't want to be caught back here after dark."

"Well, we can't avoid that," Trent said. "I'm not sure we shouldn't build a fire and spend the night here. Your foot might be better by morning."

Gray glared at his young partner. "You want to scare Annie and Millie half to death? We don't come home; they'll make every man in the valley tear through these mountains looking for us. One of those storekeepers might fall off his horse wanderin' around on some dark skinny mountain trail and break his fool neck. Now, help me on here."

Trent did not doubt Gray's wife and his own would send out a search party. Trent thought it was an excellent idea. But, knowing Gray as he did, Trent accepted arguing with him would be pointless. They wouldn't be spending the night around a campfire. They would ride home, regardless of Gray's condition.

Both Trent and Zach took hold of their injured friend. Once, twice, three times searing, stabbing pains shooting clear to Gray's hip prevented their getting him on the horse. Disgusted, Gray pushed them away and, out of sheer stubbornness, stepped in the stirrup, cussed the whole situation, and threw his broken foot over the saddle.

"Go around to the other side and slide my boot in the stirrup." Gray directed the order more at Trent.

"What?"

He turned toward Trent. "Stick my foot in the stirrup."

"You can't do it yourself?"

"No, I can't! Go slip it in."

Trent went around the bay's rump, muttering something about how he didn't understand how someone planned to ride four or five twisting miles down a mountain if they couldn't put their foot in a blasted stirrup.

"Ah, we're not that far away," Gray said, trying to

sound less irritated. Trent took hold of Gray's boot heel and slid his foot in. "Be careful." For a moment, he again became so light-headed he thought he might fall off. Falling off would be humiliating. A rank horse might throw him off, but, by hell, he had never fallen off one.

"You sure you're all right?" Trent asked.

"Fine," Gray sighed as he took another deep breath. "Mount up and catch up." He nudged Lena away.

"He's a tough old rooster, ain't he?" Zach grumped. Trent shook his head as he stepped up on his tall chestnut gelding.

The longer the mare walked down the mountain, the angrier Gray grew. Mad at himself for not working the ranch, doing something worthwhile, instead of letting Zach Joseph, who lacked any lick of sense, talk him into a pleasure ride into the backcountry to test a young colt's behavior.

Now, the result of foolishness, he would be a useless cripple for the rest of his life.

They spoke little as they rode into the isolated valley. The only conversation occurred when Gray requested Trent to slow down the pace.

The sky turned from dusky cinnamon to complete dark as they made the trip to the Wehr home.

9

Chapter Two

Annie Wehr no longer worried much. The woman suffered through too many sleepless nights back when Gray had the wanderlust. Back when months would go by without knowing if the man she loved was alive or dead. She fretted herself sick, wondering when Gray would come home—or if he'd come home.

Annie and Jean once puked for three days after killing two whiskey bottles over a rumor about Gray being murdered in some bar room. Those awful times drained her of worrying and taught her to live only in the present. She learned to lock out fears. Someone being an hour late, a half-day overdo no longer mattered, no longer vexed her.

Besides, she doubted the accuracy of Gray's statement when he told her they would be home before dinnertime, expecting instead it would be dark or at least dusk by the time her husband returned. He might fuss up a little speech about too many responsibilities to be going off to test out a two-year-old colt, but Annie never for a minute doubted he would ride off for the day with his two friends. Next to her, horses were the passion of the man's life.

"Upstairs," she called out when Zach hollered her name.

"Gray's hurt. You better come down here."

Annie and Gray grew up in High Meadows, their families among the first to settle in the wild valley. Until a few years ago, Annie's family operated the general mercantile, while Gray's and their partners, the Josephs, flourished in the cattle business. Both found satisfaction in their endeavors.

Annie Laurie loved the wild-natured Gray Wehr for as long as she remembered. Yet, their marriage was delayed. First, by Gray's wanderlust, later by his reluctance to marry while haunted by a gunman's reputation, something he feared might make Annie an early widow.

The Lauries and Wehrs were close friends. The Lauries never mentioned it, didn't even hint at it, but Annie's family, especially her mother, opposed Annie marrying the Wehr's oldest son, a man who either couldn't or wouldn't stay home.

At last, six years ago, with a promise never to leave the valley again, Gray proposed on a bright Saturday morning, heading off on a picnic.

"I declare, you are the prettiest thing."

Annie walked right on past him. "Come on, Romeo, you can saddle my horse."

Gray stepped up his pace to catch her. "Annie, I think a woman as beautiful as you, on a day as gorgeous as this, needs a man to ask her to marry him."

She stopped and gazed into Gray's eyes. "And when do you think this marrying should happen?"

They decided on a September wedding. The ceremony turned out the grandest affair ever staged in High Meadows. Two years later, their only child, a son they named Kenyon, came along.

By the time Annie got down the stairs, Zach was back

outside, helping Trent slide her injured husband off his horse. "What happened?" she asked, hurrying over.

"Lena fell on him," Trent said, while Gray wrapped an arm around each of the two men. "I think he broke his foot," Trent said as they approached the porch with Gray hobbling gingerly between his two friends.

Annie tried to help as they started up the five steps but realized she would only be in the way. For a moment, seeing how white her husband looked, Annie thought she, herself, might pass out. She brushed her long, dark hair back from her face and took two deep breaths. "Let's lay him on the couch," Annie said. She didn't want the man she loved put through the agony of the long staircase to their upstairs bedroom. "Be careful," she snapped at the men when Gray cried out halfway across the sitting room, off to the left of the foyer.

"We're trying to," Trent said, sounding sheepish about being corrected. "Should we try to carry him?"

"I don't need carrying. I'm not a blamed baby."

"No. But you're not heading for a dance either." Annie shot back in that wifey tone, meaning she was in no mood for any nonsense. "Lay him down easy." She moved a green decorative pillow off the couch. "Have you had his boot off?" she asked, once the men had Gray as comfortable as possible.

"No, we didn't figure we'd be able to get it back on." Trent stepped back to give Annie room enough to kneel by her husband.

She took off his hat and ran her long fingers through his damp blonde hair and down across his face. "You have a fever," Annie whispered. "Bring him some water, would you, Trent? Go for Doc Hollins," Annie said, turning to Zach. "And go tell Millie Trent is over here, and you better tell Jean what happened too," she added, realizing Gray's two years younger sister would be more than angry if not told about her brother's accident.

Almost an hour—an agonizing hour for Gray—passed

before the valley doctor knocked on the front door. In his late fifties or early sixties, Doc Hollins, a small-framed man, provided medical care to High Meadows residents.

"What happened to him?" A shaggy white mustache drooping from his upper lip muffled his words.

"His horse fell on him," Trent said.

"Well, take his boot off so I can examine his blame foot," the doctor said in a flat, emotionless voice. "People oughta do things like this at a decent hour of the day, not after I'm in bed." His grumbling drew a disapproving glare from Annie.

Gray lurched off the couch and cried out when Trent gave his right boot the first pull. "If you're going to holler like a schoolboy, we'll cut the blame thing off," Hollins said. "Nobody can examine your foot with it on."

Annie got a huge pair of scissors from her sewing basket and handed them to the Doc. "Aw…kick my butt." Gray clutched at the overstuffed pillows on the dark green couch hard enough his knuckles turned white.

"And call me Charlotte," the wiry little doctor cracked, finishing the ridiculous phrase Gray used.

The afternoon ride down the mountain had hurt. But nothing like what Gray experienced later in the night and almost nightly for the next month. Gray considered himself a "man's man," but his crying out in the night interrupted Annie's sleep many times during the first three weeks.

After word of the accident got out, church women kept telling Gray, "God holds some purpose in mind." Some called the injury a "blessing in disguise." Others proclaimed his not being more severely injured or killed a miracle. Gray didn't consider himself an expert on blessings or miracles, but he would not have drawn such a conclusion.

Add to Gray's other aggravations, Doc Hollins, a quack in Gray's mind about as helpful as his ridiculous notion of thinking serene thoughts about meadows and flowers. On the night of the accident, Hollins pronounced the foot "busted all to hell." He told Gray he broke all five long bones running along the top. The good doctor dispensed the opiate, Laudanum, in liberal abundance but otherwise proved of little use. A month after being injured, when the pain subsided enough for Gray to be interested in a prognosis, Hollins would only say, "I can't give you one," a not only curt but useless answer.

At the end of the seventh week, the Doc allowed Gray to try getting around on a pair of crutches. Despite his lingering discomfort and swelling, Gray welcomed this news. In two weeks, the country would be ninety-eight years old, and Gray wanted to participate in the festivities, an idea Annie opposed.

"How on earth you think you're going to stumble around after dark watching those fireworks is a puzzlement to me," she said, her brown eyes flashing. "You can watch them from the front porch, and you wouldn't be taking a chance on falling."

"I don't want to sit on the veranda," Gray groused. "I'm tired of being laid up. The time is here to go out and mingle with people."

"People?" Annie laughed. "You don't even like most people."

Gray responded with a bit of a grunt before slouching down deeper into the couch. Slouching in the couch was his way of surrendering to Annie's point of view.

"I like some people."

"Humph. Jean, Millie, Trent, Kenyon, and me." A mischievous glint bounced across her eyes. "Anyone else?"

"Well, it's like livin' in a blame cave. The summer will end with me cooped up in this house. By the time I'm well, we'll go into five or six months of winter. This foot is going to cause me to miss an entire year of my life."

"Oh, you won't miss a year," Annie tried to sound light-hearted. "I'll bet you'll be off those crutches by August."

August? Gray thought about how far off August was. What Annie meant as encouragement had the opposite effect, sinking him into a deeper state of melancholy.

PART II

Bismarck, ND

Chapter Three

Bismarck blistered on the fourth of July, and the widowed Susan Carlyle fanned herself with a cheap starched fan while pointing to the buggy carrying her grown son and two of her three grandchildren. "Jenny is scared to death; I told Danny she's too little to be in the parade," she said to her best friend, Laura Reed.

Laura waved at the Carlyle carriage, trying in vain to elicit a laugh or smile from the younger child as the buggy passed in front of the Bismarck Tribune, one of the finer establishments in a town made up of little law, numerous saloons, and a dance hall. A few women were cracking the heads of respectable men for a school and a church.

"Where's your husband this morning?" Danny hollered to Laura, pulling back on the reins to slow the matched blue roan horses enough for Laura to answer before they passed by.

"He plans on coming this evening for the cookout and fireworks. He didn't think he could afford an entire day away from the ranch."

"Don't you let those girls get sunburned," Susan warned her son.

"They'll be fine; stop worrying so much," Danny called back at his mother before snapping his buggy whip to encourage the horses to pick up the pace again.

"You'll think 'fine' when you 're up half the night pouring vinegar on blistered babies."

"You're getting to be an old worrywart." Laura laughed, taking her friend by the elbow.

Firecrackers popped as two cavalry sergeants rode by, carrying the US flag and the Seventh Calvary banner. Susan and Laura placed their hands over their hearts before scolding two youngsters who tossed some small pebbles at the horses.

As the rest of the parade passed, the women talked about the army entering the Black Hills. "I guess Custer left Friday. This trek may start a war." Susan started brushing ants from the front of her faded blue skirt. "I've never seen as many red ants as this summer." She gave her dress a final brush. "Do you suppose the easterners are fools enough to believe the government's tale about going in there to survey land? They're looking for gold, as sure as we're standing here."

"I don't know what difference it makes," Laura said. "Either way, they're breaking the treaty. The Sioux won't stand for it, and those of us living out here will be the ones to pay." More firecrackers popped as the end of the parade came along.

"I better check on Gabe. It's almost lunchtime, and of course, he's not capable of making his own." Laura picked up a package containing a tan shirt and four pairs of socks she bought at the general store earlier in the morning. "We'll see you about dark, I guess."

"Don't let your husband work too hard in this hot sun."

"He ought to stay home until it cools down, but he's determined to put up a new fence line, so there's no point in arguing with him."

Gabe was asleep on the sitting room couch snoring like an old bear when Laura got home. She checked the kitchen before taking the shirt and socks up the narrow back stairs. The cupboards were closed, the counter and table were clear. "I swear, that man would starve before fixing a meal."

The Reed home had four bedrooms and a sitting room on the second floor. Dark-colored hardwood floors and heavily varnished mahogany-trimmed doorways gave it a museum-like quality. Laura put the new clothes away and headed down the front stairs to wake her sleeping husband. "Gabe? Gabe?" she said as she shook his shoulder.

He sat up and scooted forward on the overstuffed green couch to change the position of his aching back. "Good parade?"

"Too hot to enjoy anything. And all the carriages and wagons stirred up enough dust to choke a person. Did you eat anything?"

"Not since breakfast. I didn't feel like poking around the kitchen."

"Well, do you want me to fix you something?"

"Nothing much. Maybe a small sandwich; I'm too hot to be hungry."

Chapter Four

Dusk settled over the Bismarck city park as Gabe and Laura Reed pulled their canvas chairs into a circle with Susan Carlyle and her family. "Still sweltering," Gabe said as he eased down into the squeaky chair.

Susan fanned herself with a starched laced folding fan. "It's too hot to sleep. I wish it would cool down a bit, at least at night."

Tom Gibbs, a part-time newspaperman with the Bismarck Tribune, sweet on the widowed Susan Carlyle, showed the group the headline of the next day's edition: CUSTER SAYS "MISSION OF NATIONAL IMPORTANCE."

"So, the General's headed to the Black Hills." Gabe took the paper from the reporter and squinted to read the first couple of paragraphs in the remaining reddish light of the setting sun.

"A month late, but they're on their way," Gibbs said. "They say he took over a thousand men with him, a bunch of those new Springfield rifles, three Gatling guns, and a six-pound cannon."

"He must figure the land will be hard to survey," Gabe laughed, right before the first explosion of the town's Fourth of July celebration shattered the still of the evening.

The citizens of Bismarck gasped and applauded for thirty minutes as fireworks lit the night sky and the Fort Lincoln band filled the air with the strains of "The Battle Hymn of the Republic," "Garryowen," and other lively military and patriotic tunes.

"Laura Reed! Laura Reed!"

Hearing her name, Laura scanned the crowd, seeing Libbie Custer waving a handkerchief or some sort of scarf over her head. Laura stood and waved back as Libbie slipped through the gathering in their direction.

Libbie Custer was an attractive woman, thirty-two years old, with dark wavy hair pulled back behind her head. She kissed both Laura and Susan on the cheek as she joined the group.

"Did the general get away with no problems?" Tom Gibbs' question sounded more like a journalist's official inquiry than a friend's concern.

"He did," Libbie, who long ago learned how to deal with overzealous reporters, said. "I miss him already."

"How long do you expect him to be out?"

"As long as two months," Libbie said, thinking a competent newspaperman would know such details. "My heavens, I believe they took half of the United States with them." She sat down between Lara and Susan and directed her comment to them rather than to the reporter.

"He may need them if the Sioux catch him in breaking the treaty," Gabe said offhandedly, drawing a grimace from his wife.

"The general is not in violation of the treaty," Libbie said.

"Not in violation?" Gabe snarled. "What do you mean? White men are to stay out of the Black Hills. He's traipsing around out there with at least a thousand men. Sounds like a violation to me."

Wounded by Gabe's persistence, Libbie sat for a few minutes without speaking. After the awkward silence, during which Laura Reed threw Gabe a couple of evil scowls, Libbie stood and told the others she was going to head back to the boat so she would be there when they crossed the river to Fort Lincoln.

She had walked only a few yards when Laura got up and started after her, turning back only to mouth the word "Ass" at her husband. "Libbie! Libbie!" Laura called, catching up to the general's wife and slipping her arm around her as they both continued walking. "I apologize, Libbie. Gabe's been like that all summer; he's been wearing himself out on the ranch. Gabe didn't mean anything. He's grouchy because of the heat, I suppose."

Libbie's resignation regarding her husband's popularity, mixed at best, caused Laura to feel sorry for her. "Why don't you stay the night with us?" Laura suggested. "We can shop together tomorrow. You should spend a couple of days with us. There's no reason for you to sit in the fort with no one to visit."

Libbie's eyes widened in surprise. She glanced at Gabe. "Are you sure I'm welcome?"

"Quite welcome!"

Both chuckled. "I'd love to spend time with you," Libbie said. "Let's go tell your husband."

They found a repentant and much friendlier Gabe when they got back. He appeared pleased, or at least put up a noble front, about the idea of having a house guest for a few days, even asking Susan and Tom Gibbs to stop by for lemonade before going home.

Openly thrilled about the opportunity to spend added time with Susan, Tom almost fell over himself, trying to grab her picnic basket before she picked it up herself.

"How's your son and his family?" Libbie asked Susan as they settled around the kitchen table.

Laura set a fancy pitcher of lemonade in the middle of the table. She watched as Gabe grimaced when he took a sip. He was not yet back in her favor, so she'd made it sweeter than he liked.

"They're fine," Susan said. "The girls are the cutest things, and Dylan, their youngest, is growing into a handsome boy. I keep telling Danny how lucky he is to have three such beautiful children—and a splendid wife, I might add. Lucy's a wonderful mother, and she treats Danny like a prince."

"Having a loving spouse is a divine thing," Libbie said. "Autie and I have had ten fabulous years together," she said, calling her husband by his childhood name. "I believe I love him more than the day I married him, if that's possible," she added.

The five friends talked for two hours before Tom Gibbs got the chance to escort the widowed Susan Carlyle across town to her home.

Chapter Five

On the fourteenth of August, the stifling midmorning sun started a stinging sweat rolling into the eyes of Laura and Gabe Reed's sixteen-year-old son, Del, blurring his vision as he tried to stitch up an injured calf. "You better learn to stay away from those coyotes, or you ain't gonna last long, little fella." Satisfied with his doctoring, he untied the young bull, soon to be a steer, who, as payment for the stitching, shot a stream of crap across the boy's feet.

After giving the animal a brief cursing, he spread his arms to stretch the kinks out of his back before wiping his face with the old blue bandana hanging out of his hip pocket. Del picked up his canteen and poured water over his sand-colored hair.

As the water washed the sweat and dirt from his tanned face, he saw smoke east of the ranch, nothing but a wisp, so Del assumed Danny Carlyle, whose small farm was the only thing in that direction, must be burning a few stumps or perhaps some weeds along a ditch bank.

Del poured the rest of the water in his canteen on his handkerchief before tying it loosely around his neck. After scuffing his boots back and forth through the dry grass to rid them of the calf's going away present, he started to the pump to refill his canteen. Almost there, the smoke again caught his attention. Huge black billows now darkened the eastern sky. Del yelled for his father.

The raiding party attacked fast, right after sunrise. They were on Danny Carlyle before he could run. The arrow hit him an inch below the knee, shattering his shin. He fell sideways, stunned enough not to see the bare-chested warrior. The painted brave straddled him, grabbing his hair and jerking Danny's head up and forward.

Danny Carlyle lurched when the first burning, biting, cutting of flesh ripped around the top of his head. The hacking and sawing took little time, and the young man heard a loud snapping sound when the scalp tore off. Consciousness faded as the Indian stood over him, screaming and wildly swinging his trophy through the air.

At first, Gabe lost in the mindless job of saddle-soaping tack, didn't realize what Del was hollering at him. "Come out here. You better see this!" Del screamed again from outside the barn door. "I think Danny Carlyle's place may be burning."

"On fire?" The older Reed jumped up, tripping on a pile of latigo at his feet but righting himself before hitting the dirt. He bolted for the door and studied the sky toward the Carlyle Place.

"Laura!"

"Laura!" Gabe broke into a sprint toward the house. "Go into town and tell people Danny Carlyle's place is burning," he hollered as Laura came out on the porch. "Ride over and help them out," he barked at Del. "I'll come as soon as I can throw a saddle on a horse."

"Take Shorty!" Del rushed his saddled gelding to his dad. "Go! I'll catch up."

Gabe stepped up on the sixteen-hand horse named Shorty, one of Del's jokes. Gabe charged him toward the Carlyle farm while Del ran back into the barn, grabbing a bridle and bridling the first horse he came to in the corral. He led the horse, a paint gelding, out the gate and swung up on him bareback.

Gabe slapped the reins back and forth across the hips of his son's tall chestnut as the horse tore across the east pasture of the Reed ranch in long, flowing strides. When they crossed a shallow creek and came upon the rise of the other side, flames licked at the roof of the clapboard Carlyle house.

Black smoke heavy with the stench of coal oil burned his eyes and nose. The horse panicked. Snorting and fighting the bit, he reared up, spinning away from the heat and noise of the fire. For a moment, Gabe did not think he'd be able to stay in the saddle. The terrified animal whirled and bolted back for the creek.

"Whoa! Whoa!" Gabe screamed at the now out-of-control gelding. The reins stretched taut in his clenched fists; he fought the horse back under control and headed back toward the burning farm.

When Reed stopped the nervous horse, flames engulfed the house and barn, still a hundred yards away. There would be no saving any of the structures; now, only lives mattered. "Dear Jesus," Gabe mumbled, "What do I do?"

Running back and forth in front of the infernal hell, Reed kept screaming the names of the Carlyles. The rampaging blazes and dense, pungent smoke blocked his vision and choked off his breathing.

Del rode up and swung off his horse. "I've never seen

anything like this! Where are they?"

"I don't know!" Gabe yelled back over the noise of the fire. "You check around the barn! I'll go around the house!"

What Del found behind the collapsing barn horrified him. He froze. His stomach contents came up into his mouth. Del fell to his hands and knees, violently throwing up. The puking shamed him; real men didn't puke. They acted.

Despite the acrid smoke burning his eyes and throat, Del forced himself to move closer to the charred body. He squatted and took hold of the shoulders, yelping and letting go as the scorched body blistered his hands. He flopped backward, landing on the seat of his pants when the body let out a terrible moan. Again, he screamed for his dad. Not knowing what to do, he started throwing dirt on the burnt figure. Del rolled him over, grimacing as his hands burned from the heat of the charred body.

The burns were not as bad on Danny Carlyle's face or chest, but what he saw was ghastly, worse than anything Del ever dreamed about in a nightmare. They scalped Danny Carlyle. The white bone of the young man's skull shone through the blood and torn flesh.

"They took everyone," Danny uttered in a pain-filled, hoarse whisper. "They stole my family." His words were heartbreaking, but his eyes, his emotionless eyes staring at the smokey sky, were terrifying.

Del Reed scrambled clumsily to his feet and stumbled back around the burning structure, screaming. He found the older Reed on the far side of the house. Unable to put the horror into words, he pulled his dad with him, this time running back toward the barn. By the time they got back to Danny Carlyle, the young man had, mercifully, died.

The next thirty minutes were an eternity. Gabe and Del watched the Carlyle place burn. Ear-shattering crashes filled the dead morning air as the timbers collapsed, sending up sparks rivaling the recent Fourth of July fireworks. The heat, which intensified as the barn and house crumbled into piles of red-hot coals, forced the Reeds further from the crumbling dreams of the Carlyle homestead.

Tom Gibbs was among the first to arrive from town. "Good Lord, Gabe, you ever see anything like this before? Where are the Carlyles?"

Gabe stared at Gibbs impassively. "Danny's over there, dead," Gabe muttered as six more men arrived in an old buckboard. The manner of Gabe's speech was singsong, "He's burned and scalped."

Tom waved for the other men to follow and started toward the body at a run. Gabe Reed wondered why the hurry. Nothing will help a dead man. Gabe did not bother to go; he sat on the ground, with his head between his knees, gawking at the dirt. Del stayed next to his dad before wandering off in a half-daze around the barn ashes toward Danny Carlyle.

He found Tom Gibbs kneeling beside the body while others milled around in a semi-circle, staring down at the burnt corpse. The townsmen's behavior offended Del. Why didn't somebody do something? Why didn't someone take charge?

Gibbs rose. The reporter's ashen gray face made him appear ready to pass out and fall right on top of Danny Carlyle. "Who found him?"

"I did," Del said, "He was face down." The boy wanted to turn away, escape. But he didn't. He held his ground, determined to stare this death in the face while fighting back the urge to be sick again. He stood rigid, resisting the growing desire to run to the creek, dive in the cold water, and let the stream clear his head and settle his stomach.

"Was he dead when you found him?" one man, although Del didn't know which, asked in a quiet voice, almost a whisper.

It took Del a moment to realize they were questioning him. "No. No, still alive."

"I can't believe that. How could a man live through this?" one of the other men wondered, tossing a somewhat disbelieving scowl at Del.

Tom Gibbs peered at the younger Reed. "Did he say anything?"

Again, it took a little time for the question to sink into Del. The boy glanced around at the men, down at the body. "He, uh, he said, they took everyone. I think he said it twice." It was hard for him to remember. The horror of Danny's condition overwhelmed him. "He did; he said it two times." The meaning of the dying man's remark started sinking in.

"They burned the place and kidnapped his family," Del said, looking at Tom Gibbs. "Why would they do that?"

"The Sioux took 'em!" Red Holsten, a gigantic man with bright orange hair and a dark red beard, screamed in a voice ablaze with anger. "The damn Sioux done this!"

Tom Gibbs looked up, first at Del and around the small circle of men. "We've got to do something. We've got to go after them." Gibbs pulled a kerchief out of his hip pocket, coughed into it, and wiped his burning eyes. "Where's Gabe?" he asked, looking at Del.

Del forgot about his dad. "He must still be around on the other side."

The men circled the collapsed barn, finding Gabe Reed sitting with his head between his knees.

Gabe peeked up when the men approached. Several shook their heads but did not speak. "The Indians took Lucy and the children," Tom Gibbs said, in a voice Del thought calm and reserved. He admired Gibbs for his ability to maintain his composure in all situations. Del remembered seeing him act under control when questioning witnesses to a killing in town. He never flinched when General George Custer rudely took him to task over a story he wrote criticizing two Seventh Cavalry officers. Here, Gibbs stood, unshaken, directing two men to ride back to Bismarck and round up a posse to pursue the Sioux.

"We've got to chase them down and retrieve the captives before the savages hurt them," Gibbs said.

Hurt them? It's likely too late to stop that.

"Don't forget horses!" Red Holsten yelled as a couple of men jumped in the worn old wagon and whipped the four-horse team back toward Bismarck, leaving a trail of dust to mark their path. "Those Sioux will pay for this," Holsten growled. "By damn, they will."

By the time the two men returned with eight more men and mounts for everyone, Tom Gibbs had overseen wrapping Danny Carlyle in a blanket from the back of his saddle.

"You take this man back to town," Holsten ordered one of the older men. "Let's head after these savages," he grunted as he climbed on the back of his tall, stocky brown horse.

Two other men mounted before Gabe spoke for the first time.

"Wait, a minute. We need to go back to town before rushing after those Indians. Half of us aren't armed, and we have no food or bedrolls. We need provisions, or we'll have no chance."

Red Holsten, an impatient, ill-tempered sort, hated conceding that Gabe was right. They would need to be better armed to kill the raiding party and bring back the captives. As a result, the men agreed to meet in front of the Bismarck Tribune as soon as possible.

Laura Reed rode up with Josiah Park right behind her as the men mounted.

"What's your woman bringing that crazy old fool out here for?" Holsten asked Gabe in a hateful tone.

Josiah Park, an old buffalo hunter, had been wandering the northern plains and Rocky Mountains since the early forties. In the fifties, Park disappeared for several years, claiming to have lived with the Blackfeet. Most people assumed he had been a captive. When he came back, he was moonstruck. Harmless, but insane.

Bald and so skinny that people wondered what kept a stiff wind from blowing him away; he climbed down from his horse, an old roan, not much better fed than Josiah. Without speaking, he pulled the covering back from Danny Carlyle's head. The old man shook his head and folded the blanket back in place, much more carefully than done initially.

"What did you bring him out here for?" Gabe asked his wife.

"I didn't. He followed along on his own," Laura said defensively. "What was I supposed to do, shoo him home like some old dog?"

"I wish you had. He's in the way. And that damn Holsten'll blame me for the old goat being here."

Josiah eyeballed the burnt buildings and the group of men whose attention he was, for some reason, commanding. "Who did this? Who would've wanted to do a thing like this?"

"Get this old fool out of my way," Holsten snarled, bumping his horse up against Josiah. "Git the hell out of my way, old man." Holsten kicked his horse into a lope after ordering the others to find supplies and meet at the newspaper office.

The old man staggered through the ash and rubble. "Who did this? Who set all this fire?" He shook as he yelled the words out, "Who did this? Who did this? Who would want to do this?"

Tom Gibbs took Josiah by the arm, leading him back to his horse.

"The Sioux did, Josiah; the Sioux did."

The frail old buffalo hunter stopped, gawked at Tom, then around at the others. "Why the Sioux never done this," he said. "This is white man's work."

"Help him back home," Gabe said to his wife as he tried to assist the old man back on his horse.

"I don't need no help; I can git on my horse jist fine."

"Let me ride home with you, Josiah," Laura said. The old man smiled at her from atop his old roan.

"I'm going to eat some cornbread for supper, Miss Laura. Cornbread and beans. Would you like to eat some with me? My chef used to work in a high-class restaurant. Came to me from Philadelphia."

Chapter Six

Susan Carlyle sat at her maple kitchen table when the knock came on the front door. Two women from town put their arms around Susan. "We're so sorry."

There was no color in Susan's face other than in her swollen, bloodshot eyes. She spoke in a craggy voice, no louder than a whisper. "I lost my brother and both parents before turning twenty-one years old. At thirty-two, my husband passed. Now, my only son is dead, possibly, his whole family." Laura Reed wept as she sat across the table from her friend, but Susan Carlyle didn't cry. All the death squeezed her dry.

"The men left a few minutes ago," one woman said as she cradled Susan in her arms. "They'll find them, Susan; they will find them." Susan didn't respond. She couldn't gather the strength to thank them.

Chapter Seven

Red Holsten appointed himself head of the search party. Four days out and no sign of any Indians, a fact that irritated Holsten and raised doubts about his leadership.

"Where in the hell are those savages? They can't vanish into thin air."

"Thin air? I doubt they vanished into thin air," Gabe said to Holsten. "But how do we expect to find them when we've got no proof which direction they went. None." Gabe's rancor, building since leaving Bismarck, spewed out. "Four days heading north. Why? Not one of us has any idea why we're not going south or west. We didn't find any tracks to follow; you, all on your own, announced we were going north. I, for one, have no inclination why."

Holsten, an uncouth sort, resented Reed's criticism and let go with a barrage of vulgarity. Both worn out and weary of Holsten's guff, Reed pulled his horse right up next to the blusterous Holsten. "You'll not talk to me like that," Reed snapped, anger flashing across his face. "We've followed you four days, and you with no idea where you're going. I don't think you give a damn whether we find those children. I think you only want to find Indians to kill."

Holsten never dodged a fight. Coming to blows with Holsten would be disastrous for Reed. Except for Tom Gibbs and two other men intervening, Reed would have been in for a dreadful thrashing.

"Fighting among ourselves will serve no purpose," Gibbs pleaded.

"Reed, best shut his mouth," Holsten barked. "Else, I'll close it."

Reed wouldn't gain anything arguing with someone thick-skulled as Red Holsten, so Gabe pulled his horse away and said nothing more.

"Three more hours of daylight," Tom Gibbs said once the confrontation passed. "Let's not waste them." He pulled his gelding away from the group. "When we make camp tonight, we should discuss the details of the search a little more."

As soon as he spoke, Tom wished he had held his tongue. His mouth often caused him immense tribulation, twice getting him fired from jobs. Red Holsten's jaw set tight at Gibb's words. Turning his horse up the Missouri river, he kept quiet.

In the time between Gabe's argument with Red Holsten and the end of the day, the search party found no sign of Sioux or anything else. Gibbs and Red headed toward the river as the other men dismounted and made night camp.

"I wanted to ask you, Red." Gibbs chose his words, hoping not to provoke his burly companion. "Why did you go north? I mean, I'm sure for an excellent reason," he added, "you should tell the men what you 're thinking—to clear their minds."

In pure fact, Holsten did not have a reason. Not a good

reason, not a bad one, none at all. Not that Red would admit such a thing. "I suppose you think I'm wrong, too," he said in a voice both irritated and insecure.

"No. No, I don't, Red. Hell, you're more experienced with the Sioux than any of the rest of us." Gibbs hoped he was diplomatic enough; otherwise, the hulking man might tear his throat out. "I mean, no one wants to argue with you; we want to understand what you're thinking."

Thinking of an answer stumped Red. Many things stumped Red. There was no reason for heading north. He knew they should, yet he couldn't say why. Red plopped down along the river bank and pulled off one of his old boots. "By damn, we're all startin' to stink. I guess we oughta get a bath here tonight." He sat for a minute, scratching his beard and head. "Hellfire, Gibbs, I can't tell ya why I went north. My gut led me."

For a moment, the man sounded thoughtful, even insightful. But he turned menacing, plain mean, spitting a stream of tobacco juice, the tail landing on his shirt.

"Any of them loafers don't want to follow me; they can head off wherever they're pleased to," he said, profanity salting his words. "Straight to hell for all I care."

Gibbs sat a short time, hoping Holsten would simmer down. Finally, he raised his hand and patted Red on the back. "I understand how that is, Red," he said, nodding and trying to sound sincere. "Sometimes we're positive we're right. We can't explain why, but we are." Before heading back to the campfire, the newspaperman got to his feet and brushed leaves, grass, and a few small twigs off his ill-fitting plaid pants.

For another half-hour, Holsten sat on the Missouri River bank, pondering his situation as dark settled over the Dakota Territory. Thirty minutes was more than enough. Red wasn't much of a ponderer.

One man pulled a quarter section of the rabbit off the spit, handing the greasy bunny to Red when Holsten returned to the fire. "We thought you fell in."

"Not likely," Red snorted.

Tom Gibbs scooped another ladle of beans on his plate. "I told the boys, Red, you're sure we're heading in the right direction."

"I guess sometimes you follow your gut," Gabe said, attempting to pacify Holsten. "For sure, none of us have any better ideas."

Chapter Eight

Thunder rumbling in the west woke Del Reed from a fitful sleep. The boy rolled over and pulled the blanket higher over his shoulders. Ten days out of Bismarck, seven of them rainy, the search party had yet to find any signs of Indians. Several men doubted they were on the trail of the captives.

Someone on the other side of the campfire stirred and sat up, stretching out his arms and yawning. "Anybody awake?" he asked, pulling his wet boots on.

"I am," Del said, relieved someone else woke. "The sky is ugly. I bet we get more rain."

"I swear, I'm tired of being soggy," the other man grouched.

For the last three days, unseasonable rains soaked men and horses. Short tempers shortened more because of the severe conditions. Several men made their sentiments clear; they were worn out by the fruitless search. Starting now and riding in a straight line, they would be a week making the ride to Bismarck. Almost no chance remained Gibbs or

Holsten could keep the men out more than a day or two more.

First, they had homes and chores, and second, being shopkeepers and small farmers, the search was in vain. Succeeding had always been unlikely for such inexperienced men. Picking up any distinguishable trail now appeared impossible. Hope now lost, most likely, in the next day or two, the beleaguered group would head home.

Del stood and shook the grass and dirt off his blanket. "You awake?" he asked his dad.

Gabe sat up. "Sleep gets shorter every night. Anybody started the coffee?"

"Ain't got none," a heavy-set man said, scratching his growth of beard. "We drank the last."

"I'm done," another man declared. "The rest of you can tramp around up here, but I'm going home."

Long awake, Tom Gibbs laid quiet, loathing, hearing some men planning to head home. Everyone else would likely go along. Not close friends with any of them, this bunch would tell him to go alone if he wanted to keep hunting. What might keep the men searching would be Red Holsten getting so enraged the others would be afraid to go against him. Several of the men feared Holsten. They might give in to his bullying. Biding his time, hoping for an ally, Gibbs stayed under his bed role, wishing Holsten would wake up.

Gabe shook the dirt and grass from his blanket. "What are we going to do if the others head back?" Del asked his dad in a quiet voice, looking around.

"I hate to give up," his father said. "I suppose we'll go along."

Del Reed wasn't proud of being afraid; he worked hard

at hiding it. Still, since leaving Bismarck, he'd been scared half to death. The boy didn't belong on the search, and he doubted if many of the other men could handle themselves either should they stumble on a band of hostile Sioux. He wanted to go home.

He wanted to escape the nightmares, becoming more terrible every night. In every one, the scalping knife of a grotesquely painted Lakota warrior sliced through his flesh. In many of the dreams, his scalp crackled while ripping and tearing off his head. Repeatedly, the screaming savages beat the Carlyle family. While guilty about his fear, he wanted the safety of his bed.

Red started to snort and toss around on the wet grass, where he laid his black and gray plaid blanket. After a loud passing of gas, the 250-pound man sat up and spat out the remains of a wad of tobacco.

"This ground is rocky as hell." He groaned as he got to his feet. "I doubt I slept more'n two hours." He started toward a clump of brush, untying the rawhide lace fly on the front of his pants as he went.

Del wondered who would inform Holsten of the planned retreat. Not him, for sure. There were some advantages to being a boy.

The rest of the men were awake and stirring around, looking for half dry clothes and something to make a decent breakfast when Holsten stumbled back from his morning constitutional.

Tom Gibbs confronted Red with the issue on everyone's minds. "Red, several of the men want to head back home."

Del thought the expression on Gibb's face indicated he hoped Red would fly into a rage. Holsten disappointed him. Red sat by the fire. He opened his possibles pouch, stuffed full when they left, but now containing only a few scraps of jerky, some hardtack, and a dwindling plug of tobacco. He cut off half his jerky, stuck in his mouth before taking his last swig of whiskey.

"What do you think we should do, Red?" Gibbs muttered, his voice whiny.

"We've done our best," Red said. "No man can fault our effort." He bit off a chunk of the jerky and started putting his gear together.

Tom Gibbs acted as disheartened as Del earlier imagined him to be. He shifted from one foot to another and clenched and unclenched his fists. He glanced around at the other men, as if hoping to find one who might be a brother in a fight to continue the search.

"Oh, hell, Tom, she'll know you tried," one of the others said when Gibb's eyes moved over to him.

Gibbs's face flushed deep red and his hands clenched. "What do you mean?" His words shot back at the man like bullets.

"Just what it sounds like," the man said, without looking at Gibbs. "We can only do so much. Susan Carlyle can accept things as they are. If she gets pissy, too bad."

Red Holsten interrupted before Gibbs screamed back at the man. "Time to give up, Tom. Reed was right when he said I didn't have any idea of where I was going out here." He paused. "And if I don't know where to search, it's damn sure none of you do."

Old Red might not be quite as thick-headed as several of the men assumed, or perhaps this was Holsten's genuine character when not drunk or drinking. "We've done our best, Tom," Reed said, shifting his attention from Holsten and looking over at the newspaperman. "Let's go home where we can be of some comfort to Susan."

Within the hour, the search party packed their gear and headed back toward Bismarck, where they would deliver the terrible news of failure to Susan Carlyle.

Del wondered if Susan expected any better results.

Well past midnight, eight days later, Gabe and Del started

up the front stairs of their home, dirty, tired, and hungry.

"I can't wait to get a sound, peaceful sleep, safe from scalping knives, and in the morning, have one of Mother's fine breakfasts, perhaps with an apple dumpling." Del yawned, his shoulders drooping.

Gabe squeezed his son's shoulder. "Night, son."

Laura stirred a little as her husband closed the bedroom door. "Laura, you awake?" Gabe whispered, not wanting to startle his wife as he slipped into bed. Laura?" he repeated.

"Gabe? You're home!" she exclaimed.

"Sorry to wake you, but I wanted to tell you we got home." Sitting on the bed, he pulled his boots off. "We didn't find anything."

Laura closed her eyes and lay back down on their deep feather bed. "I didn't think you would." she sighed. "I'm glad you're back home." She sat up again and put her arms around him. "I'm happy you're home safe."

"I sure dread tomorrow," Gabe said. "I told the others I'd tell Susan." Gabe hesitated. "I don't understand why Tom Gibbs can't, or won't, but he sure didn't volunteer."

Laura squeezed him. "I'll go with you," she said. "I'll go with you." Gabe's stiff, scratchy shirt stank of dust and soured sweat. But she didn't care. Having her husband in her arms resolved everything.

As Gabe came down the back stairs, grease popped in an iron frying pan. Brown sugar was melting into the salty smell of sizzling ham. Life was palatable again. "Del been down?" he asked, taking a cup of coffee from his wife.

"Not yet. The sun's only been up for about half an hour." She sat across the table from her husband. "I wanted breakfast ready. I thought you would want to go over to Susan's house before she finds out from someone else."

Reed rubbed the back of his neck and took a long drink of coffee.

"How did your back behave on the hard ground? I worried about you constantly."

"My back did fine," Gabe said as he sat the cup down and put his face in his hands.

Years of marriage taught Laura Reed when her husband didn't want to talk. She turned a thick slice of ham before putting the sizzling meat on one of the china plates they received as a wedding present from Gabe's aunt. She added three scrambled eggs with a piece of bread from the loaf she baked two days earlier. She set the plate in front of her husband. "I'll go up and dress," she said.

Susan Carlyle was brushing her hair when the Reeds knocked. Her back barked when she rose from the dressing table to start down the stairs. Without warning, Susan was old beyond her forty-four years. The oak door stuck at the top. An aggravation she pestered her son to fix, but somehow, he never got around to it. Now, he never would.

All hope disappeared when she saw Gabe standing at the door with Laura. Her family was dead.

Her hand trembling, Susan unhooked the weathered screen latch, pushed the squeaking, sticking door open. Laura stepped in first, with Gabe following.

Gabe's eyes dropped to the floor. He stood there ghost-white, shaking his head. "We didn't find anything, not as much as a trail to follow. I'm sorry," Gabe said, his voice not much above a whisper.

A stronger woman would have taken optimism in their not being found. But Susan's hope had blown away in the hot winds that killed everything green, everything living. "You did your best," Susan said. "It was always hopeless."

"Don't give up, Susan." Laura put her hand on her friend's shoulder. "General Custer is in the Black Hills. He might find them. Most people think that's where they headed with Lucy and the children."

Susan sat in the straight-backed rocking chair. She didn't say anything. She rocked back and forth without looking at either of her guests. After an awkward period of silence, Gabe spoke. "Susan, if you want us to, some of us will go back out. Head east or southeast, or west. We spent only ten days looking and always heading to the north." Reed surprised himself by volunteering to go searching again. He hoped Susan would not say yes. Hoped she would understand the effort would be fruitless. He studied her face for a clue what her answer might be.

Laura shook her head to tell him not to say anymore.

Susan slouched in the chair, giving up. "No, Gabe, there's nothing else to do. And you have a ranch to run and a family of your own to care for."

After another moment, Laura put her hand on Gabe's arm. "Go on home, Gabe. I'll remain with Susan a while longer." Reed bore an awkwardness as he turned and started toward the front door. He went through the door and down the porch steps. Each one creaked, adding to his sense of sneaking away.

"Can I get you anything?" Laura asked. "A cup of coffee or something from the kitchen?"

Susan managed a slight smile. "No, I'm fine."

Laura pulled a chair close and took Susan's hands into her own. The two women sat for another hour.

Still asleep when his dad got back to the house, Del was far from easy to wake. "Roll out of bed!" Gabe yelled. "We've got a lot of work to do." The boy took another fifteen minutes to dress. Dawdling, Reed thought, plain stalling. "Come on! I'm tired of waiting on you," he hollered up the stairs.

"Aw, quit your bellowing; I'm on my way." The boy came down the steps with his hair sticking out in fifty different directions.

"I want those fence posts we left set today. We can run the wire by the end of the week." Reed headed out the front door and over toward the barn, not waiting for any response from his son. Del pushed his hair back under his floppy tan hat and followed his dad.

"Damn, it's going to be a hot day for setting fence posts," he said as he went toward the corral for a couple of horses.

Chapter Nine

Lucy Carlyle spat on the dirty old rag, trying to moisten the cloth enough to wipe some blood from her younger daughter's arm. "I know it hurts, Jenny, but you mustn't cry. They'll hurt us more if you do. Shush, sweetie, try to be quiet." She turned her attention to Maddie, her older daughter, and tried to smile. "Did you get enough to eat?" she asked her blonde child. "You can have a little more rabbit."

"I'm not hungry anymore," the six-year-old said. "I don't want to sleep here. It's dirty."

Lucy put her arm around the little girl. "Hush now. Don't say anything to make them come over." Slipping closer to her five-year-old son, Dylan, she studied the left side of his face, so swollen he would be unrecognizable to his Bismarck friends and neighbors.

His little lips were split open and almost three times their size. Lucy inched his hair away from his face. She wanted to examine the deep cut over his right eye. A terrible kick to Dylan's mid-section turned his entire abdomen and side dark purple. A spur rowel left a trail of blood caked along his rib cage. Dylan took far more abuse than the two girls. A boy held less value to them than a female.

Chapter Ten

The tapping on the front door was soft. "Where are you going?" Laura asked Del when he pushed his chair back and stood at the dinner table.

"I'm going to answer the door."

"I didn't hear anything," Gabe said.

"Well, somebody's knocking," Del said, a bit too curt for his mother's liking, as he left the room. Susan Carlyle was standing outside the screen door in a faded calico dress and looking haggard and worn out. "Come on in." Del pushed the door open before stepping back to let Susan pass.

"Are your folks home?"

"They're in the dining room. Come on back."

"I didn't think you would be eating," Susan said. "Let me come back later."

Unlike his awkward father, women did not intimidate the boy. He took Susan's arm. "Don't be silly. Come on in."

Gabe stood when Susan entered the room. "I'm sorry to interrupt your supper," she apologized.

"We sat down late," Laura said, standing and pulling a chair out for her. "Gabe and Del didn't come in 'til after seven. Can I get you something?"

"No, no, I've eaten."

"How about coffee?"

"Yes, thank you," Susan said, despite not liking coffee.

"Another hot day," Gabe said, playing with his fork.

"That's hot," Laura said, sitting the cup in front of Susan. "Do you want sugar or cream?"

"Both, please." Susan put two full teaspoons of sugar in, followed by a long flow of cream.

She stirred the coffee for the next minute or so, watching the cream first swirl a light brown streak through the cup before turning the dark brew pale tan. Susan drew a sip and a longer one. She sat the green china cup down and stared for a moment at the table. "I hate to ask you this, but I've no one else to turn to," she whispered, still not looking up.

"Susan, we'll help you any way possible," Laura said in a quiet but empathetic voice as she reached out and touched Susan's hand.

For a moment, Susan sat with her head down, her eyes downcast or closed.

"Are you praying?" Del asked.

The innocence of the boy's question made Susan chuckle. "I should be," she said, patting Del's arm. She turned toward Gabe. "There's someone who can find Lucy and my family." Tears rolled down her face; she didn't hide them. She dabbed at her eyes with a napkin Laura handed her. "Would you take me to him? I wouldn't ask," she said with her voice now trembling, "but I can't make the trip alone. I thought maybe Gabe and Del would take me." Susan forced a smile.

Susan's watery eyes glanced around the table at each of the three Reeds. "I believe in my heart they're still alive." She sounded beaten. Yet her voice rang with determination.

Gabe leaned back in his chair. "Who do you want us to

take you to?"

Susan was stiff, emotionless. She whispered the name, sounding almost afraid to say it out loud; reverence soaked her voice. "Gray Wehr."

"Good Gawd, Susan," Del exclaimed, his eyes bugging out. "Gray Wehr!"

"You know Gray Wehr?" Gabe showed more composure than his son.

"I grew up with him. He and my brother were best friends."

"Who's Gray Wehr," Laura asked.

"Ma," Del crowed. "He's as famous as Wild Bill Hickok or Buffalo Bill. He killed Harvey Kehn and Crow."

"And a lot of other people, as I understand," Gabe said.

"Is he a sheriff or a marshal or something?" Laura asked.

"He's more of a gunman," Gabe said. "He's killed a dozen men or more. He's a real pistoleer," he added, looking over at Laura.

"How long since you've seen this man?" Laura asked, turning toward Susan.

Susan closed her blue eyes and sighed. "Over twenty-five years. Danny, my brother, died before my fourteenth birthday. I left High Meadows three years later." Susan stared at them. "Time doesn't matter. He was Danny's best pal. He'll help me."

"Still, such a long time, Susan. He might not remember you." Laura cautioned her.

"We grew up together, Laura." Susan glanced at her brown-haired friend. "I was a barefoot little pest. But Gray wouldn't let Danny pick on me." For a moment, Susan was again the skinned kneed nuisance trailing after her brother and her hero. Laura smiled and stroked Susan's hand. Any woman who had ever been a girl understood.

"Did he become a gunman?" Laura asked.

"No, not a gunman or a killer," Susan said, pushing her hair back away from her face, wondering how to explain

Gray Wehr to the Reeds. She remembered him silver-tongued with biting eyes and a sweet and disarming smile. "When he was nineteen, Gray wandered down into Kansas. He always wandered. He got into a bar fight. Not his fault," she added empathetically. "Some rough cowhand slapped a girl around. Gray stepped in, and the puncher pulled a gun on him." Susan paused and focused on Laura. "Gray killed him." She said it—there was no point trying to hide the truth. "The shooting got him a reputation."

"I guess so," Del declared.

"He also scouted for the army," Susan said. "He and Bill Hickok did some scouting together, along with Bill Cody," she said, looking at Del, "Gray never liked Cody much. Gray became a hero in the war."

"Where do you think he is?" Gabe asked.

Susan's thoughts slipped back through the years to the valley where she spent her childhood. She remembered spectacular tree-covered peaks, sparkling trout-filled rivers, and lush green meadows filled with sweet-smelling wildflowers. She also remembered death. "In the Bighorn Mountains."

"Clear the other side of the Sioux land?" Laura asked, eyes stretching wide open.

An uneasy amount of time passed before anyone spoke. Susan assumed the silence meant they were trying to think of an excuse not to make the trip. They did not need a reason. Refusing such an outrageous request required none.

Gabe glanced first at Laura, then at Susan. "When would you want to leave?"

"As soon as possible," Susan answered, starting another period of almost unbearable silence.

"Well, would you give us two days to finish some work?"

"Yes! I can't thank you enough, Gabe."

Laura Reed remained quiet and reserved for the rest of the evening. When Gabe crawled into bed, he took his wife in his arms.

"We'll be alright, Laura," he hesitated, "but if you don't want us to go, we'll stay home."

Of course, she didn't want them to go. No woman wants her husband and child to go off chasing danger.

The trip would take them not to, but clear across Sioux land, from which a treaty banned all whites. Assuming they made it, they would go after a bloodthirsty Sioux raiding party. Yet she thought of Susan Carlyle and everything the poor woman lost. *This is such a cruel place we're trying to make a life in.* She often wondered if it was worth the sacrifice, the dying. After tossing and turning for hours, she drifted into a fitful sleep, surrendered to what needed doing.

Chapter Eleven

Two days after making their promise, Gabe and Del rode up in front of Susan Carlyle's home at daybreak. Reed almost changed his mind about the trip over last-minute worries about leaving Laura. He would have if Libbie Custer had not agreed to stay with her.

As they stepped from their horses, Gabe spotted Tom Gibbs riding down the street from the other direction, leading a roan packhorse carrying a pack stuffed to near bursting. He was wearing a bowler hat and ridiculous green plaid pants.

"Has Susan been out yet?" Gibbs asked as he rode up to the hitching post in front of Susan's whitewashed home.

"We just got here ourselves," Gabe replied. "Go around back and see if she saddled her horse," he said, motioning to his son. "Tom and I will go up to the door."

Stung by Susan approaching the Reeds for help, Tom Gibbs

wanted to beat the Reeds to Susan's front door. He missed his chance. Although Susan and Gabe enthusiastically accepted his offer when Tom volunteered for the trip, not being initially asked still frustrated him.

This morning, he wanted a few minutes alone with Susan to declare his dedication and concern, perhaps taking her by the hand, one of her soft, beautiful hands. Because of his packhorse romping around the pasture, Tom arrived late. He would now need to find another opportunity to express how he would care for her, be whatever she asked.

Hair bedraggled, Susan met the two men at the door, wearing a pair of dark gray trousers and tugging the shoulders of a pale-yellow shirt hanging on her like a sack. Her eyes were bloodshot, and her face flushed. "I'm ready, and my horse is out back." She walked out on the porch, closing her stained-glass door behind her.

"How are you doing this morning?" Gabe asked, slipping his arm around Susan's shoulder, giving her a slight hug.

Tom Gibbs thought he should be the one hugging her, the one offering affection, affection more appropriate coming from him than from a married man.

"Not much sleep," Susan confessed. "Nightmares full of babies crying haunted me all night."

"We're going to find them," Gabe said as they went down the front steps and toward the hitching post, where Del returned with Susan's brown gelding. They started their horses west, away from the rising sun.

PART III

Pursuit

Chapter Twelve

Despite being located in a valley high up in the Bighorn Mountains, High Meadows was swelteringly hot and uncomfortable most of the summer.

Trent Thaxton's wife, a dark-haired, young beauty named Millie, tapped on the Wehrs' screen door before coming in. "Annie? Annie, are you home? Jean and I are here."

"In the sewing room."

Millie and Jean found Annie putting the finishing touches on a powder blue dress.

She broke the thread and tossed the spool into her sewing box. "Well, that's the best I can do. Come over here, and let's find out how this fits," she told her sister-in-law as she gave the dress a shake to straighten out some wrinkles.

"You finished in a hurry," Jean said, admiring the white lace cuffs. Annie held the dress at arm's length to check for the proper fit. "I hope I'm small-waisted enough," Jean laughed.

"If you're not, we'll tighten your corset," Millie said. Jean slipped her dress off and stepped into the new one. "The moment of truth," Millie chuckled.

"Wonderful," Annie said, half-admiring her work and half-thinking how the shade of blue highlighted Jean's tanned face and blonde hair. Hearing the front door open and close, Annie called out, "We're up here. Your sister's trying the dress on."

Gray and Trent Thaxton walked in with Gray, still limping from the horse accident.

"I swear, Jeannie, you clean up right nice." Gray grinned.

"She's a beautiful woman," Millie said. "I hope I'm still as pretty...when I'm her age." She added, mocking Jean's comment about being small-waisted.

"You may be lucky to be our age," Annie said, taking a mock jab at the girl with a needle. The three, despite Millie, only twenty-three, being twenty years younger, were inseparable.

"Town is burning with news today," Trent said. "Custer is in the Black Hills with more than a thousand men."

Shocked, the three women turned and stared at the men. Annie's eyes burned into Gray, looking for verification.

"Are you sure?" If accurate, fear of retaliatory Sioux raids would scorch across the plains' dry grass.

The people of High Meadows would be safe in their valley. Most of them grew up childhood playmates with local chief Paints His Horse and his band of Lakota. High Meadows residents provided kindnesses like giving the Indians cattle, helping them through the winters. The Lakota, the name the Sioux preferred, would bring warm buffalo pelts to the whites. They also gave horses captured in their raids on the Crow and Blackfeet. The mutual friendship benefited everyone.

Despite being safe in their valley, the people of High Meadows would be afraid to leave their mountain sanctuary and venture out on the plains for much-needed supplies, with the American government violating the treaty of 1868. Sioux bands under the command of chiefs and leaders hostile toward whites would not be reluctant to take the life of any Wasichu.

Gray shrugged. "I remember someone in this room once telling General Sherman the Army would never keep faith with the Sioux."

Jean and Millie thought back to their trip to Ft. Laramie in '68 when Annie denigrated William Tecumseh Sherman's dealings with the Sioux. Both stared at Annie. "I guess you were a prophet," Millie said, smiling.

"Well, this will start a war." Jean's expression soured. "I hope Custer rides right into Crazy Horse."

"I suppose riding into Crazy Horse is unlikely," Gray said. "Quint Swain and his oldest boy went hunting over on the east slope last week and ran into Paints His Horse. The rumor among the Sioux is," Gray continued, "Crazy Horse and Sitting Bull are along the foot of the Bighorns. They may not be aware of Custer's being in the Black Hills."

Annie walked over next to Gray. "How long have they been over here?"

I don't know," Gray replied. "I don't think Paints His Horse knew for sure they're over here."

"More of a rumor, I believe." Trent sat in a wing-backed chair next to the window. "Quint also said Paints His Horse is moving his people down along the Powder for the rest of the summer and fall."

"If he's going to the Powder, I'll bet he's certain Crazy Horse is over here," Annie said.

"Well, I guess I don't care who scalps him. Crazy Horse or anyone will do," Jean said.

"You're mighty set on old Son of the Morning Star getting his scalp lifted," Millie laughed.

"I can't believe the Army is going into the Black Hills breaking another treaty," Jean said, her voice full of exasperation.

"I doubt Custer traipsing through the Black Hills will

affect us." Annie tugged the bottom of Jean's skirt. "Is this too short-waisted?" She asked her sister-in-law as she gave the skirt another tug. "I mean, our relations with the Lakota are warm and friendly," she said, turning back to the subject at hand.

"I think the waist is fine," Jean said, rising on her tiptoes to check how much the dress came up off the floor.

Chapter Thirteen

You're a gorgeous woman in the morning light," Gray said, wrapping his arms around Annie's waist.

"You'll make me break this yolk," Annie said and laughed.

The tall, dark-haired woman, indeed still beautiful at forty-six, slipped the eggs on the china plate.

"It's sausage this morning. We're out of bacon."

"Is Kenyon awake?" Gabe asked.

"Not yet. I'll wake him in a little while. Millie's bringing the twins over here today. She wants to go with you and Trent when you separate the weanlings."

"Separating them is going to be a time-consuming job," Gray said. "A lot of those mares are on the upper slope. I suspect we'll take more than half a day getting them back down here."

"Why don't you ask Zach to help you?" Annie asked, sitting coffee in front of her husband. "A fourth hand would make things easier."

"I talked to him yesterday. He wanted to come, but Paxton pitched one of his fits. Said Zach's got enough work over at their place."

"Paxton." Annie shook her head. "Your brother can be a horse's hind end when he wants to."

A smile passed over Gray's face.

"When he wants to? When does he not want to?" Gray's face furrowed. Annie, not a coffee drinker, made the stuff too strong. "I thought I might send Trent over to find out if Jean wants to go. Like you say, the work would be easier with a fourth hand."

"Well. Paxton won't stop Jean." Annie grinned while looking out the kitchen window. "Here come Trent and Millie now."

Gray met them at the front door, where Trent agreed to go for Jean, saying they would be back in half an hour. Millie came in mischievously putting her hands over her face in mock guilt over being the one to spend the day working with the horses.

"I'll tend the kids tomorrow, and you can go with Gray and Trent to move the mares to the north pasture," she said to Annie as she got a mug from the cupboard and poured herself a cup of coffee. "The air is cooler this morning; I hope the hot spell is going to ease up."

"The nights are too sticky to sleep," Annie said.

"You should sleep naked. I do."

"How do you know we don't?" Gray asked, grinning at Annie, intending the grin to tease both women.

Millie flushed and turned back toward the window without noticing the cupboard door. "Ow!" she exclaimed. "Ow!! Who left the door open?"

"You did," Annie chuckled.

Millie sat at the table next to Gray, holding her fingers to her eye. "I'll bet I end up with a black eye. I think I cut my eyebrow off."

Gray raised Millie's chin and brushed her dark hair away from her face. "What a terrible gash! You're gushing blood. I better sew you up."

"No, thanks! I've seen your needlework," Millie said, referring to a scar high on Jean's thigh, the result of Gray's stitching up a wound she took.

"How bad is your eye?" Annie asked in a more earnest tone. "Let me see." She took the girl's chin in her hand and raised her face toward the light of the kitchen window.

"I'm fine," Millie protested.

"Let me look," Annie demanded in motherly authority. "The cut is right in the brow. Hardly a gash," she added, scowling at her husband. "You are bleeding, but I don't think you'll have any noticeable scar. I'll put something on your eyebrow." Annie headed toward a drawer where she kept household cures.

"Don't you be getting any iodine. You're not setting me on fire."

"You hush; I'm getting some salve to keep the skin soft and speed up the healing."

"Well, you can dab salve on me, but you're not going to iodine me."

"I'll iodine you if you don't quit whining," Gray said.

"I'm not afraid of you," Millie said, "I'll box your ears."

"I'll spank your butt."

"Oh, both of you, be quiet. Now raise your face." Annie dabbed the salve into the split skin and smoothed the excess with her finger. "Now, let it stay on, and don't be poking at it."

"Yes, mommy, I'll be a sweet little girl,"

"I'd like to live to see the day," Gray cracked. "And I still may sew your eye up. Fifteen or twenty stitches ought to do the job."

"You're too slow to catch me, you old gimp." The girl wrinkled her nose at Gray as she headed into the formal living room to check Annie's salving work in a mirror hanging over a velvet couch. "Good Lord, Annie, you've got enough goop on me to heal a stuck pig."

"And you leave that goop alone!"

Before Millie realized he was coming, her dad landed a fly swatter on her butt, starting a wild, noisy chase through the sitting room, dining room, living room, and back to the kitchen.

"Will you two stop! Go outside if you want to act like two weanlings," Annie laughed, swinging a dishrag at them both. Instead, the two scoundrels sat down to the rest of their breakfast. Gray finished as Trent and Jean arrived.

"What is on your eye?" Jean asked.

"Doc Annie's cure for scratches."

"What did you do?" Trent asked, putting his hand along the girl's face.

"I banged into a cupboard door, but I doubt it's fatal."

Jean and Gray rounded up twenty-six mares and their colts by mid-afternoon, heading them down the south side of the upper slope behind the Wehr/Thaxton horse pastures. Trent and Millie had another twenty working their way down the center of the hill. "Did you see Tenino or her colt?" Gray called out to Trent and Millie when they got within earshot. Tenino, a broodmare, foaled many quality colts over the past five years.

"Not her or Rickashay either," Trent yelled back. "Rickashay was with this group day before yesterday."

"Kick my butt and call me Charlotte. Where do you suppose those horses are?" Gray muttered at his sister.

"I'll bet they're up in those higher meadows," Jean said, waving her coiled rope at a dun filly wandering too far behind her mother.

"I hope not. That'll be an aggravation."

Trent and Millie came down first, and Millie counted the mares and weanlings as Gray and Jean drove the rest into the meadow. "Sixty-two."

"Eight more are in the back pasture, so we've got four

missing," Trent said.

"You sure they couldn't be over along the river behind your house?" Jean asked.

"I went back there yesterday," Millie said. "I found some of the two-year-old geldings but no broodmares."

Gray slipped his right boot out of the stirrup and let it hang free.

"Is your foot hurting?" his sister asked.

"Throbbing like Satan stuck me with his pitchfork and swollen up some."

Patting her brother's knee, Jean's affection for him was apparent. "You better elevate it back at the house."

"How many calves has that cougar killed?" Trent asked, looking over at Jean.

"Five. Alan and Ethan hunted him four days last week, but they never picked up as much as a sign." Along with their brothers Zach and John, Alan and Ethan Joseph were partners with Jean and Paxton Wehr in a sizable cattle ranch. Gray had been a partner until he sold to Jean when he married Annie.

"Well, we need to find those horses," Gray said. "If they're up into the high pastures, those weanlings will be easy prey for a mountain lion."

"I'll go along with you tomorrow. We'll find someone to take the kids, so Annie and Millie can both come," Jean said.

"Let's push these over into the south pasture. Annie will have dinner ready by the time we're back at the house," Gray said.

The smell of fried chicken greeted the group as soon as they opened the front door.

"Did you gather them all up?" Annie asked.

"All but four," Gray said. "I'll bet they're up around the falls."

"Those meadows are where Alan thinks the cat is?"

"We're going up tomorrow," Jean said. "After we eat, let's you, Millie, and I go over to Alan and Martha's and find out if she'll babysit. If she will, you and Millie can both go."

Martha Joseph became the matriarch of the Wehr/Joseph ranch when Gray and Jean's mother died. The task might have fallen to Jean, except Jean wanted no part of herding children or cooking at family gatherings. Martha, much more the "motherly" type than Jean, reveled in the role of *ranch mother*. After a few minutes, the women came back from picking up the kids.

"Martha said she'd be glad to watch them," Millie said. "I'm going to stop by the house for some extra clothes for the twins in case we don't find the mares tomorrow and decide to camp overnight."

"I'm not planning to," Gray said. "My guess is they'll be in those flats above the falls."

"I hope we find them in one of the meadows," Trent said. "It'll still take all day to go up and back."

Chapter Fourteen

"I don't want to be captured anymore, Mommy, not anymore."

Lucy Carlyle was almost numb from beatings. Wrapping her arm around her child, she winced from the pain in her left elbow, swollen twice its size from a wrenching for not getting on her horse fast enough. Along with wrenching her elbow, her captors broke the bridge of her nose in two places. She lost one of her lower teeth, taking a kick, trying to protect her son. Because of her "dawdling," they tied her wrists. Instead of letting her ride, they made her walk, occasionally dragging her behind the horse of the one they called Burns The Grass.

"Don't cry, sweetie; don't cry." Days ago, Lucy lost track of how long she and her children had been prisoners. She pondered grabbing a knife or a gun. She would end the suffering of her children—and her own.

"Try to sleep, Maddie," she whispered to her oldest child. "Maybe we won't have to travel tomorrow. Maybe they'll let us rest." She brushed Jenny's hair back from her face. The little girl was sleeping, but she stopped talking days ago. She had not cried for three days.

Dylan threw up most of the previous night. He spent the day tied to a mule's saddle to keep him from falling off. Lucy did not believe her son would live through the night.

Chapter Fifteen

Annie ran a strand of her long dark hair across Gray's mouth. He wrinkled his nose and wiped his hand across his face but did not wake up. She brushed her hair across his lips twice more and then his eyelids. He swished it away and rolled over. Annie leaned down and blew on his ear. "Graham, Graham, time to get up." She shook his shoulder and repeated his name. "Are you awake?"

"I'm awake. What time is it?"

"A little after six. How'd you sleep?"

"Terrible. I didn't go to sleep until after three. My foot throbbed half the night, and my knees ached the rest." Annie got out of bed and pulled back the drape. "A little cloudy. The weather may start cooling off."

"I thought we might ride the Palominos today unless you don't want to." Gray stood and gingerly put his weight down on his right foot.

"You sure you don't want to take Lena?" Annie watched her husband struggle out of bed. Limping across the room, he looked worn-out. Sitting on a straight-backed

71

chair, pulling his pants on, he was pale and gaunt. Until this summer, Annie never got the impression Gray was fatigued, not when men half his age would be. Now she sometimes caught glimpses of him when he not only appeared tired but aging. At forty-six years old, he was no longer a young man. His blonde hair surrendered to graying around the temples, and a few lines were noticeable around his eyes, usually after hard days of work. But Annie didn't mind. She accepted life's changes and remained comfortable with everything in her life.

"I've ridden Lena a lot this week," Gray said, speaking of the bay mare. "I think I'll give her a day off."

Like her brother, Jean often encountered trouble sleeping. Before daybreak, she slipped into the house and had breakfast half-finished when Annie and Gray came downstairs.

"I swear, Jeannie, you'd make somebody a fine cook. We ought to hire you."

"I cooked for you long enough before Annie took you off my hands."

Trent and Millie tied their horses to the back hitching post and crossed the back porch. "Hi Dad," the girl said, kissing the side of Gray's face. "Looks like rain."

"How's your eye this morning?" Annie asked before telling Trent to help himself to the coffee.

"I'm fine. How's Dad's foot? He's limping."

Annie sighed without looking up from rinsing a medium-sized porcelain bowl over the sink.

Millie peered at Gray and shook her head. "We should take you down to Cheyenne for a decent doctor to examine you." Annie and Jean got quiet when the girl mentioned Cheyenne. Gray stood and slipped his arm around the girl's shoulder, giving her a quick hug.

"Oh, my foot's a long way from my heart. I suppose I'll

survive without you having to pack me down to Cheyenne."

"I don't want you to be a cripple," Millie's voice quivered as she wrapped her arms around Gray, laying her face on his chest.

"Don't worry, sweetheart," Gray whispered, stroking the back of her head. He glanced at Annie and smiled. The smile was more mournful than happy.

Annie embraced Millie and Gray. Glancing at Jean, she mouthed the word "tomorrow." Jean nodded her head. Tomorrow would mark six years since Millie's adoptive mother died, killed by Cheyenne on the way home from Ft. Laramie and treaty talks.

As a little girl and still, as a young woman, Millie clamored for Gray to take her along every time his wanderlust pulled him out of the valley. At about nine, she saddled her pony and tried to follow him. Now, she had not left since her mother's death.

"I'm fine, Dad," Millie said, patting him on the back as she stepped out from between Gray and Annie. "I'm fine," she repeated as she sat at the table. "I think we should go to Casper or Cheyenne before the weather gets bad." She picked up one of the biscuits Jean put on the table. "I mean, we need to leave this valley once in a while." Millie said grace over breakfast, thanking God Nellie was with Him, and she would be with her again someday.

An hour later, the five friends crossed the river and vast meadow behind Gray and Annie's house and headed up the ridge to the high country. They each brought a saddlebag full of food and a bedroll in case the search kept them out overnight.

"I sure wanted to find them down here this morning," Gray said of the missing horses, "but I guess we've no such luck."

"Nope," Millie said. She wouldn't tell the others, but

she was happy the horses had not come in themselves. She wanted to spend the day looking for the horses and would have been disappointed if the trip had become unnecessary.

"We'll make the falls by late morning. I bet we'll find them in one of the two upper meadows," Trent said. He urged his chestnut gelding into the trees.

The waterfalls fell some thirty feet down through a half-moon crevasse into a deep dark pool, where High Meadows' kids skinny-dipped. Thick meadow grass sprinkled with red, white, blue, and yellow wildflowers made the spot breathtaking. Annie sighed at the beauty.

Jean hung her hat on her saddle horn and pushed her blonde hair away from her face. "Going to be another beautiful day. The threat of rain this morning didn't last long."

"We'll have plenty when fall gets here." Millie spurred her sixteen-hand Appaloosa gelding. "Might only be a month away."

"I'm ready. I like the autumn; such a peaceful time," Annie said, thinking about the turning of the leaves and the Indian summer soon to arrive. "I love the bite to the morning air, and we always do a couple of bonfire socials down at the church. Autumn is always a relaxing time of year."

The morning slipped by, full of small talk and friendly conversation. Before eleven, the group rode out of the trees into the lower of two meadows surrounding the river and waterfalls. The crisp mountain air carried what Annie called the breath of fall—a hint of childhood, of memories, of contentment, tinged with a touch of melancholy.

Red and purple flowers still filled the high prairie. Rocky peaks burst from the meadows on three sides. A cow elk and calf, disturbed by the visitors, splashed through the clear river, sending glistening droplets up into brisk air.

"I suppose we should spread out a little and cover the ground as fast as possible," Gray said. "I'll hug this tree line. Annie, you and Jean follow the river. Trent, you and Millie head over to the other side, along the base of the mountains.

Yell out if you find them. If nobody hears you, I guess fire a shot."

As Trent and Millie headed off to the others' right, Millie started to talk about the high country's beauty. "I wouldn't mind building a home and living up here."

"I'm afraid the winters would be long and hard," Trent said. "I doubt Poncho would like all the snow."

Millie patted the Appy's neck. "Poncho's tall. The snows wouldn't cover you up, would they, Poncho?"

"They might cover me up, though," Trent laughed. "You want to keep digging me out."

"Well, if you move so slow the snow covers you, I ought to leave you buried for being lazy."

Trent laughed again. "You wouldn't leave me buried 'cause you like my warm feet at night."

Thirty minutes later, a shot echoed down along the river. "I guess Annie and Jean found the horses," Trent said. "We better head on down."

Before Trent and Millie arrived, Gray came over from the trees. Trent saw two mares and one foal but no sign of the second foal. As they approached, Jean started toward them. "We've got them, but that cat tore up one foal."

"Oh no," Millie gasped, kicking Poncho over toward where Gray was kneeling on the ground.

"Is it dead?" Trent asked.

"No, I think she'll live, but she's not going to be pretty anymore."

Millie found Gray kneeling over a sorrel filly ripped open along her chest with a deep gash over her hip. Startled by Millie's rapid approach, the foal tried to stand, but Gray grabbed her and held her down. "That damn cat!" Millie spat the words out. "That damn cat!"

Annie put her arms around the girl. "Shush. You'll scare the baby. She's going to live. Let's not frighten her."

Trent and Jean returned to the group, and Trent stepped down off his gelding. "I'll swear, she took a clawing."

"She's got a helluva piece of her chest ripped open," Gray said, pulling flesh back. "Have you got anything with you we can use to bandage this up some?"

"A spare shirt, but I doubt it will go around her."

"Well, grab the spare one in my saddlebag, too. If we tie the shirts together, they'll go around her. She needs some sewing, but I guess we don't have anything to sew with."

"I didn't think about bringing a needle and thread," Annie said.

"No one expected you to." Gray glanced up at Annie. "We sure didn't anticipate anything like this."

After Trent got the shirts tied together, the two men spent thirty minutes getting the uncooperative foal doctored and wrapped. "When do you think this happened?" Millie asked.

"Sometime last night," Gray said without looking away from the young horse. "A lot of the blood is caked."

"We'll start to make a camp," Jean said. "I'll look around for some firewood."

"Don't we want to take this baby home?" Millie asked.

"No, she'll be better off resting today and tonight," Annie said. "She'll be stronger tomorrow."

"Somebody needs to kill that damn cougar," Trent said, noticing for the first time how bloody he and Gray were after the doctoring. "He's got a real taste for horses and cattle."

"The cat will be lucky to enjoy another sunrise," Gray said, wiping his bloody hands on the tail of his shirt.

Annie and Jean both recognized the tone of Gray's voice, the tone showing what Jean referred to as her brother's "hell-bent determination."

For the next hour, they prepared a makeshift camp. Gray spent the afternoon stroking and whispering to the injured foal while Annie sat a little way off, watching the gentleness with which her husband handled the young horse.

Gray stroked the mom, telling her, "Your baby's gonna be all right, mamma; your baby will be all right."

The dark bay mare was jumpy about letting others approach her injured baby but allowed Gray to handle the foal. Annie loved Gray's gentleness, a side she often experienced, a soft quality. She found not only in his manner with horses but with her, he was always gentle, always patient. She wished more people benefited from opportunities to appreciate this side of her husband.

About mid-afternoon, Gray sat next to Annie and slipped his arm around her. "I'm going to lie down and try to catch a couple hours' sleep. About dusk, I'm going after that cat."

Biting his words off, he triggered Annie, for a moment, into almost feeling sorry for the cougar. But this beast thrived on killing cattle and horses. They were easier prey. They mostly stayed in one place. There was no need to hunt and chase down a deer or elk.

"Take Trent with you. We'll be okay here," Annie said, not because she worried about Gray, not really, but she would be less anxious if Trent went along. If Gray found the cougar after dark, the danger would be extreme, worse if he didn't kill the cat with the first shot.

About an hour before dusk, Gray and Trent went through the ceremony of checking their rifles and ammunition. The pomp and circumstance going into the hunt's preparation amused Annie. Gray and Trent cocked and uncocked the rifles. Both men squinted down the barrels before blowing into them. They wiped them with their shirttails and applied the precise amount of spit to remove any remaining dust.

"I'm surprised someone so concerned with cleaning isn't more help with the housework," Millie said.

"Never noticed the house being dirty," Trent said. "Otherwise, I'd have hired a maid."

Millie laughed at her husband's reply. "Well, I'm throwing out all the feather dusters."

"Be careful," Annie whispered to Gray as he stepped up on the Palomino mare.

"Don't worry; I'll be fine. That cat will be the one meeting his maker."

"You two stay together," Millie urged as they rode off toward the mountain peaks to the east.

"Any idea where we might find him?" Trent asked.

"Well, Elder Canyon is full of caves and holes. A little creek runs through the bottom for water. He prowls this meadow, but he also likes to head down toward the livestock in the valley. So, I suppose we'll need some luck to find him."

Trent nodded, feigning agreement. Gray might talk about luck, but he seldom depended on chance to accomplish what he set out to do.

"Seven Brothers' Creek runs down into the river about half a mile ahead. We can start hunting where they come together." Gray's Palomino jerked back when they spooked a small fox out of the tall grass. "Easy, Trig. You're fine; a fox won't hurt you."

Cat tracks abounded all around the area where the small stream emptied into the river. "This is a curly wolf huge cat we're after," Trent said after kneeling and measuring the width of the paw print. "These tracks are fresh. I'll bet they're from after sunup this morning."

"Let's leave the horses here and head up on foot," Gray muttered half to himself as he gazed up into the narrow green valley floor wedged between steep rock walls. "Elder Canyon only goes back in a mile or so. We can walk the length before dark."

Trent wasn't afraid to start up the canyon, but he was less than thrilled with the prospect of having to outrun a charging mountain lion with no horse. Something else bothered him. He thought Gray sometimes liked to do things in the most challenging way possible. Trent almost suggested taking the horses, but Gray figured they would be quieter on foot, enhancing their success chance. Rather than suggest taking them, Trent asked if Gray wanted to leave the horses saddled.

"I suppose. Let's pull the bridles and hang them on the saddle horns. If they wander back to camp, the women will figure we let them go."

Trent hoped Captain and Trig would still be grazing along the creek bed when they emerged from the canyon. Otherwise, they would be making a long, dark walk back.

The two men followed the tracks along the stream for about a quarter mile into the canyon, where the cat left the water and headed up the rocky wall.

"We'll not have any more tracks to follow," Gray said. "I hope he doesn't climb too high."

Trent pointed at a good-sized cave and a few sizable holes not far above. "They'd make a livable den."

Gray glanced back and forth across the wall, searching for the easiest way to approach. He shifted his weight to his right foot. Climbing would be the most severe test of his healing. An instant of doubt flashed through his mind, but he said nothing of this to his companion.

Gray Wehr did not allow his fallibility or weakness to interfere with accomplishing something, not anything. He didn't tolerate quitting in others, and he would not put up with feebleness in himself. Gray checked his rifle, assuring himself a cartridge was chambered. "I wish this fella would show himself before we start in a cave," he said. "Not smart, stumbling into a dark hole looking for a cat fond of blood."

Foot and handholds were scarce, and most of the available ones meant stretching and contorting arms and legs to grasp them. The two men climbed for about twenty minutes, finding the going harder than expected. Trent slipped at one point, falling on his knee, tearing both pants and flesh.

When the cat screamed, dusk made vision at any distance difficult. Trent jumped three feet when the growl ripped the still air. "Can you see him?" Gray barked, no longer concerned about sneaking up on their prey.

"Give me a chance!" Trent's eyes darted back and forth through the dark shadows of the canyon. "I can't find him! Hell, he could be right on us, and I doubt we'd know."

Wehr didn't respond to the boy. Instead, he scoured the wall for some kind of movement; a shadow, a flicker of light, anything revealing the cat's location. Above and to the left, another snarl, louder, not more than a hundred feet from where Gray kneeled. Charging down at them, covering twenty feet with every leaping stride, the dark gold-colored cougar attacked—three, two strides away. Gray needed to shoot before the ripping and tearing at his flesh began. Time was up. Feeling the hot breath, he shot his first round from the hip with the cat not six feet away. The wound was not mortal but sent the cat bouncing down the rock face, brushing Gray as he went down.

Trent jumped to his feet, drawing a more precise bead on the target. His bullet ripped the middle of the animal's chest, exiting along his tail. The enraged cat screamed in pain and wrath, flailing side to side, lashing out in crippled fury.

Slamming the lever action of his rifle down and up, Gray seated the next cartridge. This time he took careful aim and shot the cat below his left ear. Trent, although ready, did not need to shoot again. The threat was over. He shook his head in disbelief as the two men started working their way down to the dead predator.

"I guess you'll not rip up any more of our horses." Anger over what the cougar did to the weanling dripped from Gray's voice.

Chapter Sixteen

The long series of sleepless nights drained Susan Carlyle's physical and emotional strength. Cold, lying on hard ground, she wanted the sun to rise, enabling them to start again on her journey back to her childhood home. A trip she hoped would result in the safe return of her family, her precious grandchildren. In the dark, the chances of their rescue seemed remote.

What if Gray Wehr forgot her or refused to help her? What if her old friends resented the way she left the valley— without as much as a goodbye. Worst of all, what if Gray finds the children and Lucy dead? Tears again filled her eyes as she wished so hard the morning light would arrive.

As the eastern sky started turning orange, Susan crawled out of her blankets and placed a few sticks on the almost-dead fire. She ran her fingers through her dry, tangled hair. *I must be a fright*, Susan thought, but no longer cared. "Gabe, are you awake?" she asked as she bent down and touched his boot.

"Gabe. It's getting light. We should get ready to travel."

"Are the others awake?"

"I don't think so," Susan said. "Tom is snoring and hasn't moved."

Gabe sat up and rubbed his head with both hands, disheveling his hair enough to make Susan chuckle.

"Colder this morning," he said, crawling out from under his wool blanket and stretching.

When Susan shook Tom's shoulder, he awoke with a jerk. The newspaperman stood and shivered. "Do you want me to find more wood for the fire?"

"I think we should pack and head out. We can eat some jerky while we ride. If we push hard, I think we can be in High Meadows in two days."

She caught Tom gazing at her as she spoke. Susan often noticed him staring. She knew about his feelings for her. Susan wasn't sure how she felt about Tom. Even before everything happened in the past few weeks, she maintained doubts about being courted, about the possibility of a second marriage. She experienced loneliness, mostly at night, but being lonely might not be the best reason for taking a new husband. Now, Tom's trivial attentions meant nothing.

"Del, roll out of your bedroll." Gabe nudged the boy on the side with his foot. The boy got to his feet, making no fuss.

Susan told the men as soon as they hit Crazy Woman Creek, they would follow it south and west to the pass leading into the Bighorns, the little valley, and the town of High Meadows. "Once we make the mouth of the pass, we'll be about a day's ride from High Meadows."

"Any idea when we will find it?" Del asked.

"I think before noon," Susan said. "Close as we are to the mountains, the Crazy Woman can't be too far."

Gabe pulled an old flannel shirt out of his bedroll. "Better dress warm today, Del. Chilly this morning." Gabe shivered. "I hope the day warms up before we cross the creek. I hate to be chilled and wet." Despite knowing Gabe hoped for a hearty, hot breakfast, something to warm the morning chill, Susan insisted they saddle up and head west.

By mid-morning, the sun shined bright. The temperature warmed enough, Gabe shucked the flannel shirt. Some of the gentle bluffs and hills got higher as the group continued west. Susan decided someone should ride up the crown of the ridge a quarter mile or so away. "You may see the creek from the top," she said, although she thought they might still be an hour or two away from the Crazy Woman.

"I'll go," Gabe said, trying to sound casual. Weaving through the sparse sagebrush, he kept thinking about his wife, about her soft skin, and the hint of lilac in her hair right after she bathed. He thought about their life in Bismarck. Laura said nothing, but Gabe wondered if she didn't miss Ohio. He questioned if Bismarck would ever be her home.

At the top of the bluff, something caught his eye. Hurrying back below the hill's crown, he stepped off, glanced around for somewhere to tie the reins, and crawled back up. He crept a little further on his belly. He counted four men but six horses tethered between two trees. Gabe believed the Indians to be Lakota, a hunting party—he hoped—not a war party.

Gabe lay still but, to his surprise, was not afraid. Their presence was more of an aggravation than a threat. He stayed hidden in clumps of sage for another five minutes before slipping back down the hill. In the entire time, none of the warriors as much as glanced toward the bluff. He stepped into the saddle and started back toward the others.

"We need to swing south. There's a small Sioux hunting party camped on the other side of the bluff," he said before anyone asked why they needed to change directions. "They're a quarter mile or so past the bluff, a half-mile from here. Let's go south a couple of miles and turn back west toward the creek."

"How many?" Susan asked.

"Four men and six horses. Might be more. I couldn't tell. We can ride around them."

Tom Gibbs thought of a flurry of questions. Did *they have Lucy and the children? How did Reed know the Indians wouldn't head south as well and run right into them? How did he know they were a hunting party?* For some reason, perhaps due to the confidence of Gabe's voice, he held his tongue.

"We'll backtrack a mile or so," Susan said, riding off from the others. The three men cast a few blank gazes back and forth and followed Susan Carlyle, none of them making any comment.

They rode back over their trail for about fifteen minutes before swinging south. The terrain grew rougher. They stayed in gullies and coulees, hidden from anyone riding past. In less than an hour, they made Crazy Woman Creek.

"Let's cross and build a fire to dry out," Susan said.

"You're not worried about the Sioux seeing the smoke?" Del asked.

"We've ridden a long way from where your dad spotted those Sioux," Susan said. "I want a hot meal and to ride dry."

Tom Gibbs led his paint horse down into the water. "It's freezing," he yelped.

Susan laughed about how the Crazy Woman was ice cold every time she crossed as a girl.

With the others watching, Gibbs worked to the middle, still not too deep for the horse to walk across. Despite his horse walking, the water flowed up and over Gibbs's saddle.

In a cautious moment, Tom untied his saddlebags containing his writing supplies and some clothes and held them high over his head. He negotiated the entire creek, keeping the bags out of the water. "Make sure you keep anything you want to stay dry up high," he yelled to the others.

Relieved they'd be changing, Del grabbed his reins in one hand and his saddlebags in the other.

"I'm next." Del led Shorty out into the water ahead of his dad and Susan. The chestnut forded the stream without a problem, other than Del being soaked to the chest when he reached the other side.

Susan and Gabe went into the water together. "Easy, Buck, easy," Susan whispered when her stocky brown horse balked at the cold water. "Come on," she urged, pulling his head back round toward the water and giving him a couple of swift kicks in the flanks. The animal started into the water, backed out, fought his bit. "Come on."

Susan kicked and slapped Buck with the reins. The horse lurched forward, crossing the remaining creek in three giant leaps. Susan lost her seat on the first lunge. She grabbed at the saddle horn, mane, rein—anything and everything. Susan went under twice before reaching the other bank, getting soaked from head to toe. *Such language*, Gabe thought, watching Susan bob and splash her way out of the water.

Del broke first. Gabe and Tom strained not to but failed. Susan started laughing at herself when she and the horse made dry ground. Before she dismounted, the horse gave himself a vigorous shake, almost dumping his rider. Del laughed harder.

"Get me a blanket," Susan snapped good-naturedly at Tom. "You two start a fire before I freeze to death." The three men set about their tasks. "I ought to shoot you," she said to her horse.

Chapter Seventeen

Many Cheyenne warriors considered Burns The Grass cowardly. He never showed bravery in battle but gloried in abusing a squaw or child. He slammed Lucy Carlyle against a pinto horse. "You move too slow," he yelled.

Lucy lost track of the days long ago, but she thought it must be weeks, a month, since the capture. She wished they would get to wherever they were going.

Chapter Eighteen

"High Meadows," Susan whispered, pointing at the valley floor when they stopped on a bend in the trail. Long and green, several houses and ranches with both horses and cattle grazing in various herds added to the peacefulness the view invoked. Susan's eyes filled with tears as she scanned the serene beauty of where she grew up—twenty-plus years melted as memories flooded back.

"Are you all right?" Gabe asked.

Susan, looking vulnerable with her face backlit by the morning sun, tugged her horse back, forced a sheepish grin, "I'm scared." She wiped a tear from her cheek, took a deep breath, and sighed. "I didn't expect to be emotional l like this."

Gabe swallowed. "Well, I suppose we may as well head on down," he said. "Where does Wehr live?"

"Their ranch is in the middle of the valley," Susan said, "but let's stop in town to be sure he still lives in the same place." Susan was bold, looking for help here after so many years away. Years passed without her once as much as writing a letter. At this moment, because of her long absence, she worried about asking for Gray Wehr and trembled about telling him what she needed.

Riding down the twisting trail into High Meadows took an hour. Most of the buildings, older now, seemed smaller than Susan remembered. The High Meadows Bank, still the first building on the south side of town, shined with a fresh coat of paint. Susan stopped about halfway down the street, in front of a store with the words *KELLER'S GENERAL MERCHANDISE* painted across the gable. Susan stared at the name, an odd expression on her face prompting Tom Gibbs to ask if something was wrong.

"No," she said, still staring at the sign. "This used to be the Laurie Mercantile."

"Every place changes."

"Yes, I suppose," Susan said. She didn't expect changes here. Susan expected everything about High Meadows to be the same. Foolish, yes, but she still pictured her childhood friends looking as they did when she left, somehow frozen in time and youth.

Until now, Susan planned to inquire at the Baptist church regarding Gray. Now she thought about asking at the general store where new owners would not recognize her. It did not occur to her after twenty-five years; no one would recognize her. "Let's stop here," she said. "I'll go in and ask if Gray still lives here."

"Still lives here?" Del gasped.

Glancing at the three men, the color flushed from her face. She never told them more than this would be the best place to look for Gray. Still, Susan led them to expect Wehr would live here, albeit he might not be home. He might be in Casper, Cheyenne, or Kansas shooting men, not as fast with a pistol. "I won't be long," she whispered, ignoring Del's comment.

Every step across the boardwalk creaked. The shadowy store's only source of light came from two glass windows in the front shaded by the porch overhang extending to the edge of the walk. Rough log beams running across the ceiling, straw-colored and heavily varnished, revived old memories. Susan walked past men's shirts stacked helter-skelter on a table. Two female wax figures stood on each side of a table filled with bolts of cloth; one wore a yellow dress, the other a blue calico. The blue one at least two years out of style, even by Bismarck standards.

"May I help you?" An elderly woman asked while walking down the center aisle toward Susan.

"Where might I be able to find Gray Wehr?"

"He and Annie live about a mile north of town." The mention of Annie took Susan back for a moment, although, as she thought about Gray and Annie, nothing was surprising about them marrying.

"Do you mean Annie Laurie?"

"Used to be Annie Laurie," the woman said, picking up an old yellow cat purring with its back arched up. "She's been Annie Wehr for six years now."

"Are you a friend of Graham and Annie?"

"I am, I guess I should say I was," Susan said, stumbling over her words. Trying hard not to sound confused, she asked, "Do they live in Gray's folk's house?"

"Oh, no. Jean lives there. Gray and Annie are in Annie's house."

"Her folk's house?"

"No, no. Annie built a home about ten years ago. About a mile north, this side of the river."

Susan thanked the woman and started toward the front door before turning around. "Is Gray home?"

"Always," the woman smiled. "He lost his wanderlust. Annie took such foolishness out of him," she laughed. "He hasn't left our valley in years."

Susan walked back out on the rough board sidewalk. The bright sun, a sharp contrast to the darkness inside the store, caused her to misstep, almost miss the first step.

"He lives about a mile out of town," she said, looking

up at Gabe. Reed handed Susan her dark leather reins. She put one hand on her gelding's neck and the other on the saddle horn as she stepped up on the horse's back.

No one spoke on the entire ride to the home of Gray Wehr. A three-ring hitching post stood in front of the two-story white house with black shutters. A stone walk with flowers lining each side ran up to a spacious porch surrounding the house.

"Why don't we wait here for you, Susan?" Gabe said as they rode up to the end of the lane.

"Are you sure you don't want us to go with you?" Tom asked, the words sputtering from his mouth.

Susan hesitated a moment before answering. "No. I should go by myself." She was disappointing Tom, but it didn't matter. It was better for her to go alone. She stepped down from her horse and secured the reins on the hitching post. She started up the stone walk, hesitating only for a moment at the porch. Susan walked across the broad veranda, smiling at the swing hanging toward one end. She knocked on the front door before giving herself any time to lose her courage. After hearing no answer, she tapped a little louder.

"I'm upstairs, Jean; come on in."

Susan didn't want to walk in, although she would have been comfortable walking in twenty-five years ago. Now, Susan wondered whether to go in or knock again. She opened the screen door calling out, "Annie? Annie, it's not Jean." Shuffling sounds came from the top of the wide stairway.

A tall, slender woman stepped out of the second room down a long hallway. As she walked toward the stairs, the light through an upstairs window caught her face. Annie, as beautiful as Susan remembered, looked much younger than her forty-six years. Her hair, still dark brown with perhaps the slightest hint of auburn shining in the morning sun, fell well past her shoulders. Her charcoal dress with a white collar and cuffs evidenced her elegance.

"Good morning. Can I help you?" she asked, starting down the stairs.

Susan Tucker Carlyle struggled for something to say. She wanted to throw her arms around this old friend and weep. "Annie?" she said as Annie reached the bottom.

"Yes."

"You may not remember me."

Annie studied her, then stared at her.

"It's been a long time."

"Susan?" More than twenty years disappeared. "Susan Tucker."

Emotion flooded through Susan. Rushing toward Annie, tears streamed down Susan's face. Annie opened her arms, letting her childhood friend fall into them. Susan emotionally lost control, and Annie stroked Susan's hair. After several long moments, Annie pushed her away, enough to see her face.

"Susan?"

Susan pulled Annie back up against her. Outside, the three men sat on their horses.

"Are those three men with you?" Annie asked, staring through the screen door.

"They're friends from Bismarck. They brought me here."

"From Bismarck?" Annie said. "Come over here and sit down," she said, pulling the distraught Susan toward an overstuffed couch. They sat facing each other, and Annie put her hands to both sides of Susan's face, raising her chin.

Susan, flushed and perspiring, couldn't focus.

"Susan, tell me what's wrong. You need to tell me what happened."

Susan, breathing shallow and rapid, still couldn't speak.

"Susan. Susan, look at me. I want you to look at me."

Susan's sobbing eased a bit.

Annie repeated herself—waited for an answer. "Tell me what's wrong. You tell me now."

The tale was horrifying. "The Sioux raided my son's

ranch outside of Bismarck. They killed Danny and kidnapped his family." She told Annie everything, emotionally at first, then calmly. She explained about asking the Reeds, a father, and son, to bring her to High Meadows and how the third man volunteered to come along.

"When did this happen?"

"About four weeks ago. Like I told you, we sent out a search party, but they couldn't find them. So, I came here," Susan said, crying again, "Gray can find them. He can, Annie. Gray can save them. He has to," she sobbed.

Susan's words chilled Annie's soul. Twenty years passed, more than twenty. Now, she has the gall to ask for such an outrageous thing? How could Susan imagine Annie's husband should—would risk his life for someone without the common decency to say goodbye when she ran away from her home and friends? Without so much as *hello again*, Susan expected Gray to charge off to rescue strangers. People likely dead.

Annie dropped her hands from Susan's face. Annie's countenance, cold and distant, did not go unnoticed.

"I'm sorry. I don't have anywhere else to go to." Susan struggled for composure. "No one else to ask."

For years, Annie lived in terrible fear of some gunman or Indians killing Gray on one of those horrible trips outside their valley home. No. She would not let Gray go, not after she prayed for so long to keep him home with her. "Why do you think Gray can help you?" Susan's answer better be uncontestable.

"I lost my mother, my father, and my brother by the time I turned seventeen years old," Susan said. "My husband died, and now my son is dead. All I have left in this world are those three children and Lucy." She stood and walked across the room toward an enormous mahogany fireplace. Staring at the floor, she spoke again. "They're alive. Gray can save them."

Not good enough! "Why Gray?" Annie was curt, wanting an answer better than how Susan lost many loved ones. They lived in a hard land; many people's loved ones died. Losing their family didn't give them the right to ask something like this. Annie wanted an explanation, a damn solid reason, for why her husband should play the role of rescuer. She wanted no more of him being the provider of everyone's deliverance.

Susan turned her troubled blue eyes toward Annie, someone once close but now little more than a stranger. "Because...because he can kill."

Susan's words made no ally of Annie. She tried to apologize.

"I'm sorry, Annie. I didn't mean that. Gray is," she stumbled for words, afraid she destroyed any chance of finding help. "I mean," she paused, looking at Annie, searching for something she would never recover. "I meant he is the only man tough enough, who is capable..."

"I know what you meant," Annie said. "Exactly." The truth, the sad truth was, she did. Gray was the most competent man Annie knew. She didn't care. The audacity of this woman coming into her home and asking such a thing. She would not have it.

The almost unbearable silence lasted a long time while Annie stood glaring out the front window.

"Graham's not here now."

More quiet. Annie paced. Susan sat with her eyes fixed on the door. Neither said a word.

Angry and trying to avoid an ugly confrontation, Annie went through a swinging door into the kitchen and poured a cold cup of leftover coffee. She hated coffee and spat the bitter brew in the sink.

Indignant, Annie stomped back into the living room to kick Susan Tucker out of her home. She almost did. But, for some unfathomable reason, despite everything within her objecting, Annie told Susan, "I'll send someone out for

Gray."

Annie took Susan into the kitchen and poured her one-time friend a cup of tea. "We've got one old hired hand. I'll go find him and send him for Graham." Numbly, she went out the back door and across the barnyard toward the barn. She slid the heavy door open and walked in. "Sanchez? Are you in here, Sanchez?"

"I'm in the back stall, Senora," Sanchez said.

Sanchez was an old Mexican Gray saved from a Kansas lynching. He brought him home to High Meadows and got him a job as a cook in Nellie's restaurant. Annie and Gray gave him a job working for them when Nellie died. Gray built him a small but comfortable cabin down by the river.

"Sanchez, I need you to go get Graham for me. He's down in the south pasture with Trent. Tell him everyone is all right, but I need him to come back to the house right away. Tell him I'll explain when he gets here." Annie started back to the house but turned to the old man. "Be sure to tell him I'm fine."

Annie went back into the kitchen, where she found Susan had not touched her tea. She sat across the table before remembering Susan's friends still waiting outside. She insisted Susan stay at the table while she went out to bring in the three men—or shoot them.

"I'm Annie Wehr," she said, extending her hand.

"Gabe Reed, ma'am." He shook her hand.

"I'm so sorry we've left you standing out here. Please come in."

She smiled up at the other two men.

"This here is my son Del. And that's Tom Gibbs."

The men dismounted and followed Annie inside the house.

Chapter Nineteen

Trent put his knee on a colt to prevent him from moving. Millie slapped the red-hot brand on him, leaving a smoking W/T emblazed on his rump. Once Trent untied him, the colt jumped up and ran away, rejoining the more than thirty other weanlings.

Wehr led his bay mare into the group and separated a feisty sorrel filly. Twirling the lariat twice before letting it fly, he threw the loop over the filly's head and jerked it closed around her neck. Wehr's horse backed away, drawing the slack out. Trent grabbed the taut rope and bulldogged the little filly. He wrapped three of her feet and laid across her while Millie applied the iron. "I think I'm going to keep her for my own," Millie said as the little sorrel crow-hopped a few times before running off.

"She'd make you a fine horse," Gray said. "So would that bay. Leggy, as she is, she's gonna be a runner."

"Why'd you suppose he's coming out here?" Trent asked, pointing out across the pasture.

Gray and Millie followed the line of Trent's finger, seeing Sanchez riding the old mule he brought with him from Kansas. "I swear, I can't figure who walks slower, him or his old jackass." Gray laughed. The mule stopped twice to graze on the grass. Both times Sanchez yanked the reins and kicked the mule's flanks.

"Why don't you ride a horse?" Millie teased. "You spend all day going a mile on that ol' Jenny."

"She is like me. We are old; we like to take our time."

"You run out of work to do?" Gray asked in mock irritation.

"Hmph, the work, she never run out around here," Sanchez said. "Annie say to come and tell you come to the house. She say everyone is fine, but for you to come to the house now."

"She didn't say why?"

"Tell me, Go get Graham. Say she is all right, but for you to come now."

"Do you want us to come along, Dad?"

Gray thought a moment. "No, I guess nothing is wrong. I'll bet she's decided she wants some furniture moved."

"I will stay here." Trent laughed.

"I'll be back as soon as I can." Gray coiled up his rope and handed it to Millie. "You and Poncho can rope. Sanchez, you slap the iron on 'em when Trent gets them down."

Sanchez climbed off his mule and took the branding iron from Millie. "This is cold. We can't brand with a cold iron," he said as he poked it at her.

"Well, stick it in the fire, you old coot." Millie took a bogus kick at the seat of the old man's pants.

Annie watched out the kitchen window. "Graham's back,"

Tom Gibbs got up, wanting to be the first to see the famous Gray Wehr. The man stepping down off a bay mare carried a no-nonsense air about him. About six feet tall, he wore brown pants and a cream-colored shirt but no gun. Wavy blonde hair flowed out from the bottom of his hat. Gibbs backed from the door as Wehr made his way across the backyard and up the porch steps.

"Annie," Gray said, opening the door but not yet looking into the kitchen. He took off his hat, tossing it on the counter next to the pump before looking up. When he did, he saw four visitors grouped around the oak table. Annie was still standing in front of the window. "Morning," Gray said, stepping into the room and closing the door. He glanced over at Annie, tilting his head quizzically.

A woman struggled out of her chair and studied him.

Annie took a few seconds before speaking. "Graham."

"Annie?"

"This is Susan Tucker."

Gray took a second look at the blonde woman sitting at his kitchen table. She was attractive, yet something about her was sad. Before he realized she was stepping around the table, she grabbed him in both her arms, wrapped him tight. Her face buried in his shoulder, she muttered something about being glad. Her words were so muffled in his shirt he didn't know what she was glad about.

Not a touchy person, Gray didn't appreciate being embraced by strangers, and he considered people missing for twenty years strangers. Worse, she wasn't embracing him; she wasn't hugging him; she was clutching him.

He hugged back—with one arm—and not very long. The woman wanted something, whatever it was she planned to use her femininity to get. When the woman let him go, relief flooded through him.

"It's been quite a while," he muttered, leaning away to prevent any further embracing. "We all wondered what happened to you," he said as he and Susan both sat down.

The statement came across cold and dispassionate.

Annie glanced at Gray and took a seat at the table as Susan spoke.

"After my mom died, I had nothing here."

Her first lie, she had a house, and friends.

"Perhaps I shouldn't have left. Not the way I did, but I was so alone and suffering." Susan glanced at the men with her. "I'm sorry. I guess I forgot my manners. Gray, this is Tom Gibbs, Gabe Reed, and his son Del. They brought me here from Bismarck."

Gray nodded at each as Susan introduced them but said nothing. He turned back to Susan, his face expressionless.

"Gray, I'm here," she said, "because of Danny..."

For a reason understood only by Gray and Susan, the mention of Danny changed Gray's expression.

"I thought naming him Danny was the right thing," Susan murmured, smiling. "Danny, my son Danny, died on August 14th. Indians scalped him, burned him, burned his farm, stole his wife and three children." Susan gasped for breath. "They butchered Danny."

Tears flooded Susan's eyes, making her angry. She did not want to cry. She did not want sympathy for some weak, crying woman. She was not the concern. The concerns were her daughter-in-law and her grandchildren. Because of them, Susan wanted help. She made this journey for them, not her sadness. Susan intended to save the rest of her family. She stiffened, forced herself to regain some composure. "The kids are so sweet—two girls and a boy."

"Who did it?"

"The Sioux. They killed my child and kidnapped my grandchildren."

Gray hesitated, unsure how to ask. In fact, maybe he should not ask. He did. "Are you sure about Sioux?"

"Of course, we're sure," Tom Gibbs said.

"Not Cheyenne?" Gray asked, frostily looking over at Gibbs.

Gibbs and Reed glanced at each other. "I guess we never thought about them not being Sioux." Reed hesitated a moment. "There's been no Cheyenne around Bismarck, and I think Custer going into the Black Hills provoked the attack."

Looking down at the table, Gray rubbed his fingers across the tablecloth. An ivory-colored linen Annie purchased in Casper. "Any coffee left?" he asked, looking over at Annie, who nodded and asked if anyone else wanted any. They didn't. "Maybe so," Gray said about the Sioux. "I've heard nothing about the Cheyenne being so far north or east. Probably they were Sioux. I rather doubt the Custer tie-in. Why would they stop with one small ranch? More likely, a simple random attack on an easy, opportune target."

"I hate the Indians," Susan growled.

Gray, unemotional and detached, frowned at her. "It's a perilous thing…hate." Standing up and walking across the kitchen to the pump, Gray took two swallows of coffee before emptying the rest down the sink. Pumping water into his cup, he swished the water around before sitting the cup upside down. He stared for a moment or two out the back window, looking first at the pasture where broodmares lazed in the afternoon sun. His eyes drifted across the mountain skyline. When he turned around, he leaned back against the kitchen counter. "What is it you want me to do, Susan?"

"By God, he's direct," Tom Gibbs whispered to Gabe Reed.

"I want you to go after them," Susan said, staring straight into Gray's eyes.

Gray turned back toward the window. After an awkward silence, Tom Gibbs rambled about taking out a search party for ten days, leaving the day of the attack.

"Where'd you go?" Gray asked without turning around.

"North," Gibbs said.

Wehr turned back toward the others. "How far?"

"We followed the river up to the lake, turned west," Gibbs said.

Gray thought about the country, an area he had traveled only twice. "How far did you follow them before you lost their trail?" Gray didn't say so but thought it must require quite an effort to lose a trail left by so many horses.

"We didn't follow tracks," Gibbs said weakly.

"What the hell made you go north?"

"The search party leader was confident about it," Gibbs said.

"Experienced man?" Gray sounded indifferent.

"Well, the most experienced," Gibbs said, looking over at Gabe for help. None came.

"Well, let me ask you this," Gray said, shifting his weight off his right foot and looking down at the men. "What makes you think these people are still alive?" Blunt. The question shocked everybody in the room as Gray fixed his hard stare on the men, not looking at Susan at all, as if he somehow held the men responsible for providing a reasonable answer.

Gabe shifted in his chair. "Well, why would they bother to haul them away? Wouldn't they kill them right there? I don't understand why they would kidnap them if they meant to kill them."

"She's a woman," Gray said, looking at Reed, who grew uncomfortable in Gray's glare. "It doesn't mean she's still alive."

"Why would they take the children?" Annie asked.

Gray peeked over at Annie, hoping she would give him some guidance on what to say next.

"How long ago did you say this happened?" Gray asked in a somewhat softer tone, this time looking at Susan.

"August fourteenth."

"What's the date today?" Gray asked, turning toward Annie.

Annie thought for a second. "September eighteenth."

"A lot of time's gone by."

Susan Tucker spoke straight to her childhood friend. "They're alive, Gray." She tapped her chest. "I know in my heart."

The sorrow in her eyes made Gray think she intended

to walk over to him.

To prevent more hugging, Gray limped back across the room and sat down. "I broke my foot last spring. Gets to aching if I stand too long." He crossed his leg, putting his foot on his knee, and rubbing the top of his boot. "Paints His Horse?" Gray asked, looking at Annie. "I guess Paints His Horse went down to the Powder several weeks ago," he said, shifting his gaze toward Susan. "The Lakota are gathering over along the Powder and the east slope of the mountains. He might be aware of a raid like this."

"Who's Paints His Horse?" Tom Gibbs asked.

"He's the chief of the Teton Lakota who live near here. He's a friend," Susan said.

"Do you think he would help us?" Tom asked.

"She told you we're friends," Gray said, his tone and stare both icy.

"I remember the time when you, Danny, and Paints His Horse went off on a buffalo hunt." Susan chuckled to relieve the tension building between Gray and Tom Gibbs. "What were you, ten years old? You lost your horses and walked a half-day home from the other side of Seven Brothers Creek."

Gray smiled, patting Susan's hand, reassuring her about his self-control. "Long time ago," he said. "The horses didn't come home for another three days. Old Crow Dog made Paints His Horse go back looking for his. He stayed out four days before working up the nerve to go home."

"Do you think you can find him?" Susan asked, her voice serious once again.

"I think I know where they might camp along the Powder."

"How soon can you leave?"

Looking down at the floor, thinking about his boyhood, about times he and Danny Tucker shared, Susan's words caused him to look up at her. "Susan, I didn't say I'm going."

Chapter Twenty

On the Wehrs' front porch, Susan Tucker gazed across the valley. "I thought he'd say yes," she mumbled, half in the direction of Tom Gibbs. "I wouldn't have brought you here if I thought he might say no." She bit her lip and peered off at the river, toward where the flow turned south out through meadows behind Annie and Gray's house. The late afternoon produced a few dark clouds up the valley, giving the ridges and peaks to the southeast an ominous appearance.

Tom put his arm around her shoulder. "He'll make the right decision, Susan; I'm sure he will."

Neither Annie nor Gray spoke after Susan and the three men left the room. Annie leaned close to her husband and placed her hand on the back of his neck. She started to speak, but Gray interrupted her.

"I promised you six years ago I wouldn't again leave

this valley."

"You kept your promise," Annie said with the slightest wisp of a smile crossing her lips. "Thank you."

Gray lost himself in Annie's soft brown eyes. His voice grew unsteady. "Do you think I should do this?"

"Graham, I'm not telling you what to do." More silence. "I understand why she's asking, but I don't want you in danger." Annie rubbed her hand across the table, contemplating the problem. She gathered the empty coffee cups, put them in the sink, and turned back toward Gray, staring down the hall toward the sitting room. "Do you think they're still alive?"

"No idea, Annie." He stood and stepped closer to her. "Sometimes, the Sioux make slaves out of captives. I suppose there is that possibility."

"It's a funny thing. After not seeing or hearing from Susan in twenty-five years, she still seems like a part of my life. When I recognized her standing in the foyer, it refilled something in me, something empty inside me. Until she told me why she came back."

Gray put his arms around Annie and kissed the top of her head. "You are the most important thing in the world to me," he whispered. "I'll do whatever you want me to do."

"I don't want you hurt," she said, "I don't want you killed."

The two talked for an hour before Annie went to the front porch as the messenger.

"Graham wonders how well-supplied you are."

A warm breeze drifted from the meadow across the road. "We'll need to pick up some more food," Gibbs said. He squeezed Susan to himself.

"Don't worry about food. I think he's more interested in your guns and ammunition supply."

"We're supplied," Gabe Reed said. "We came

prepared."

Lord, I hope so. I hope so. Annie led her guests back into the house.

Because he did not want to receive any grateful hugging, Gray kept the kitchen table between himself and Susan Carlyle. For a long time, Gray explained in painful detail how they would pursue the Sioux raiding party, including his having absolute say about how they would proceed.

They would take no pack horses; they would hunt for their meat. They would take a bedroll and an extra coat, given the time of the year. Wehr suggested an oilcloth duster. Tom Gibbs said he would ride into town and pick one up, but Gray told him he would loan him a slicker. He asked the men what type of weapons they brought along and told Del he would provide him with a better rifle and pistol than he possessed. The guns came with stern counsel: "How old are you, son?" Gray asked.

"Sixteen, sir, seventeen, in two months."

Gray glanced at Gabe before locking a cold stare on the boy. "What was your name again?"

"Del."

"I want you to listen to me, Del," Gray spoke calmly, but his piercing eyes burned through the young man. "This hoped-for rescue is likely to turn out a waste of time. Our chances of success are poor, and it will be damn dangerous. Succeeding will be repugnant. There'll be nothing well-mannered about this, boy. Rescuing these people will mean killing with no time to think about right or wrong. You hesitate; you'll get one of us killed. I don't want an arrow or a Sioux lance in my gut." Gray leaned toward Del, who turned away. "Look at me, boy!" Gray snapped. "I'm going to ask you this one time. Can you hold up your end?"

The boy squirmed in his chair, his face ghostly white. Gray's voice softened but stayed stern. "Listen, son; this is going to be dirty, bloody business. If I'm asking you to be something you're not ready to be, you need to be a man and say so now. No one will think less of you." Gray motioned at Gabe. "Your dad here, and your mother, too, likely hold a lot of dreams for you. Don't you throw them away trying to prove something you don't need to prove." Gray stopped speaking, sat back in his chair. "Are you sure about making this trip?"

Dear God, Tom Gibbs whispered to himself, the way Wehr is bearing down, I shouldn't be going.

"I'll hold up my end," Del said, looking straight into Gray's eyes.

"I believe you will," Gray said. "I believe you will."

Chapter Twenty-One

Less than an hour after the boy's commitment, the kitchen door opened and closed with a bang. "Don't worry; the door still works," Millie yelled.

"Well, I hope so," Annie called back. "We're in the sitting room."

In her early twenties, the young woman came down the hallway into the arched doorway, hopping up and down on one foot, creating quite a spectacle, trying to remove the stubborn boot and keep her balance. Her dark hair danced along the top of her shoulders.

"I'm not stepping on your new rug; don't yell at me. I don't think there's any manure on my boots," Millie laughed as the boot came off, almost tossing her on the seat of her pants. Looking into the room for the first time, she gasped, seeing guests in the house. "Oh, hell…I mean, oh, Dad, I didn't realize you have company. Damn, I mean, oops." The girl stammered, drawing a scowl from Annie. Face flushing red, Millie, in only one boot, hobbled over next to Gray and burrowed close to him, seeking protection from Annie, who objected to her swearing.

"Well, I guess you do now," Gray laughed. "This is Millie," he said, looking over at Susan and the men.

"This is your daughter?" Susan asked as she stood and took a step toward Millie, extending her hand.

Gray glanced at Annie, smiled at Millie. "Yes, she is. We don't know where she learned to cuss."

His daughter…poets, and minstrels describe how Gray's words affected Millie, but not the common man. Millie worried about being an outsider, never secure about her place in the world. She was accepted, loved, but questioned belonging. Millie trusted, loved Gray, Annie, and Jean, but she wasn't theirs. She longed to be Gray's daughter, not in play-acting, for real.

Millie's one aim before marrying Trent was to be Gray's daughter. She wanted to hug her *dad*. Gray's simple statement, claiming her as his, overwhelmed her. She might cry, something she avoided. Millie cried when Nellie died, but not until darkness allowed her to weep alone. A few tears ran down her face when Gray walked her down the aisle on her wedding day. No crying now, not in front of strangers.

"I'm Susan Tucker," Susan said as Millie reached out to take her hand.

"Millie Thaxton." She hesitated. "I'm not his daughter, but I like to pretend I am." Millie sat on the floor next to Gray and leaned against him. "I'm an orphan." She forced a laugh. "Twice, in fact." Millie gave Gray her sweetest smile. Her eyes were full of bewilderment—or confusion. Gray's eyes revealed only tenderness for the daughter of his heart, if not his blood.

"Well, she may not be the daughter of my blood, but she is the daughter of my heart," Gray said, squeezing her hand.

Millie was outgoing and feisty; most people called her a little firebrand. Inside, though, Millie was different. She wanted to please people, at least those she enjoyed. Deep inside, she wanted to belong, be family, and be someone's blood. Millie wanted that until now. Now she had something better, a daddy's heart. A daddy's heart is better than his blood.

"These are my friends," Susan said, drawing Millie's attention back to the people in the room. "Tom Gibbs, Gabe Reed, and Del Reed."

A funny thought crossed Millie's mind. "What did you say your last name was?"

Susan thought a minute. "I think I said Tucker, but it's Carlyle. My maiden name was Tucker back when I lived here. I grew up with Gray and Annie, and I guess being here made me say, Tucker."

"Didn't your brother shoot your cat?" Millie asked, giving Gray a mocking little grin.

"He did, the little jackass," Susan laughed. "Who told you?"

"Dad here told me one night around a campfire," Millie said.

"Well, he took part in the killing," Susan said good-naturedly.

"Not true," Gray said. "So, put a cork in your story."

"Enough." Annie looked at Millie. "Come on with me. We'll start some supper. You and Trent may as well stay and eat here."

"Are the kids here, or are they still at the birthday party?" Millie asked as she and Annie started toward the kitchen.

"They're still at Martha's. She'll bring them home when the party's over."

When the two women got away from the others, Annie intended to explain the circumstances of Susan Tucker's return, but Millie spoke first. "Gray told her I'm his daughter. He meant to let her believe I'm his," Millie said, pleased and surprised. "Annie, he told her I'm his."

Annie smiled at the girl, touched by the depth of her emotion. "Well. You've been calling him 'Daddy' ever since you started talking. Has he ever told you not to?"

Wrapping her arms around Annie, tears rolled down Millie's face. "I guess I thought he put up with me."

A warm smile spread across Annie's lips. "Millie, you know better. He loves you like his daughter."

"He pretends too," Millie said, trembling.

"He's not pretending, Millie."

"The daughter of his heart. I better show him more respect," Millie said as she laid her head on Annie's shoulder and held her tight. Annie laughed.

Chapter Twenty-Two

Lucy Carlyle sat expressionless as she rocked the child in her arms. Dylan stopped crying an hour before he fell asleep. He stopped breathing an hour later.

Chapter Twenty-Three

A nasty storm raged through the night, passing across the valley and over the Bighorn Mountains summits by first light. Millie Thaxton stood on the porch when Gray, Tom Gibbs, and the Reeds rode up, coming down the steps as Gray tied his chestnut stud to the hitching post. "Keep an eye on my husband," she said as she slipped her arm around Gray.

"He'll do fine. He's a capable man," Gray said light-heartedly.

"Well, you watch out for him."

"Constantly. Don't worry."

"I guess I'll not worry any more than Annie," Millie said.

Trent came out of the barn, leading a tall chestnut gelding. "I thought I might take Captain on this little adventure. He covers a lot of open ground in a hurry. If I need to run away, I'll go quick," he grinned, glancing over at Millie. "You're a fresh sight in this morning drizzle," he said, slipping his arms around her and giving her a slight hug.

"Go if you're going," Millie said, pushing her young husband away.

Trent smiled at her before catching her chin for a quick kiss on the lips. She threw her arms around him, clutching him to her as she trembled.

"You be careful, and you come home to me," she whispered in his ear before a final goodbye kiss. Trent slipped out of her arms and up on his horse.

"We'll be back before you start missing us," Trent said, warmth in his voice.

"No, you won't," she said, patting his knee. Never apart since their wedding, saying goodbye drained her inside.

Gray leaned down from his saddle and kissed the top of Millie's head. "We'll be fine. He'll be fine." He lifted her face. "I promise."

Millie nodded, but her emotions, those she'd tried to suppress all morning, got the best of her. "How do you think five men are going to take captives away from a Sioux raiding party? Assuming you find them," she added, tears rolling down her face.

Gray glanced over at Trent to catch his reaction to the girl's feelings. Stepping from his horse, Trent took the girl back into his arms. "We're not going against the entire Sioux nation. The bunch we're hunting is likely small, not over five to ten warriors, and I doubt they'll be well-armed."

Millie stayed quiet despite wanting to say the fight would be five or ten against two—because the Bismarck men would be worthless.

Trent gave Millie another hug before stepping back into the saddle. The young man moved with self-assurance and ease. His physical grace first attracted Millie to him.

With the sun rising above the mountains' crest and breaking

through the remaining clouds, Gray led the men across the valley. They climbed toward the summits. The first two hours of the journey passed with little conversation.

Tom Gibbs, a prolific talker, broke the silence. "You say you have a fair idea of where to find your Sioux friend?"

"Yep," Gray said.

"How long do you think we'll take finding him?" Gibbs asked.

"Two, three days. Depends on where Paints His Horse is. When we hit the Crazy Woman, we'll follow it north to the Powder. I expect we'll find him about a half-day up the river."

"In case we don't, any other ideas where he might be?" Gabe asked.

"Well," Gray said, looking over at Trent, "if he's not on the Powder, my best guess is he'll be up in the greasy grass along the Little Bighorn. Or the Tongue or the Rosebud. Unless he's somewhere else," Gray laughed, glancing once more at Trent.

"With autumn coming on, we hope they won't be too far north," Trent said.

Del wanted to ask Wehr about some of his adventures. He spent the morning working up his courage. Gray was friendly enough, and not even a pistoleer would shoot a fellow for asking him a question. At least, it was unlikely. Gray hadn't worn a gun until this morning. Now, he was wearing a Navy Colt holstered crossfire on his left hip, not tied down to his right leg like Del thought a gunman would wear a pistol. Del began with a slight hesitation in his voice. "Susan said you're friends with Wild Bill Hickok and Buffalo Bill."

Gray turned around in his saddle. A slight twinkle lit his eyes, and the corners of his mouth twitched in a modest smile. "She said that, did she?"

"Yes, sir, she did," Del said with more confidence in his voice.

"I'm acquainted with both those scoundrels." "Do you know either?"

Del laughed right out loud. Gray might be kidding him. Nevertheless, he was flattered. "Nope. Never met anybody famous," Del said the wrong thing—again. *Never met anybody famous?* What about Gray Wehr, the man he was talking to. "Well, except for you and General Custer," an embarrassed Del said, hoping to redeem himself.

"Well, meeting me sure won't count for much," Gray laughed. "Custer...now he's famous."

"I guess Hickok and Cody are about the most famous men in the west," Del said. "Are they the bravest men, you know?" Again, he said the wrong thing. Del wished he could keep his mouth shut. He must learn to shut up.

Gray pulled his horse back beside the boy. "Well, if I got into a tussle, I wouldn't refuse Hickok's help. Yep, I'd pick ol' Jimmy Hickok to be on my side."

Del's hopes of talking to a famous man about famous men soared. "What about Buffalo Bill?" Del asked, his curiosity and confidence growing. "I guess you don't like him much. Least Susan said you don't."

Laughing and shaking his head, Gray responded. "Now, that is puzzling. It's been twenty-five years since I've seen Susan Tucker. Yet, she can tell you who I like or don't like. Surprising."

Del's soaring hopes shattered. He said something ridiculous. It was a mystery how he could ruin an opportunity so quickly. Del's mind raced for an answer, a way not to lose his chance to talk to an important man. "Uh, well, I'm not sure. I guess somebody told her you don't like him."

Gray laughed again, adding to Del's humiliation. Gray glanced over at Trent, stifling another laugh. "Oh, Cody's all right. I have nothing against Cody. I prefer Hickok."

"So, Buffalo Bill is not as brave as Wild Bill," Del

concluded.

"I didn't say Cody's not a brave man," Gray said, "but he always likes to brag about how courageous he is and about all his conquests." Sarcasm dripped from Gray's voice. Jimmy's better company. Jimmy's a..." Gray paused a second. "He's a humorous fellow. I enjoy sitting across a campfire from him."

Tom Gibbs laughed. "Rumors say Hickok is quite the lothario, engaged in a dalliance or two with Mrs. Custer." When Gibbs mentioned the rumored affair, Gabe's eyebrows raised, irritation shot across his face.

Wehr shook his head and smiled. "Well, I suspect he's tried to 'dally' every female he's ever met."

"A married woman?" Gabe asked, full of righteous indignation.

"A little thing like a wedding ring never bothers Jimmy too much."

"The man lacks honor," Reed said.

"I didn't say he's honorable. I said he's humorous."

Trent and Gibbs laughed out loud. Gabe frowned.

"Have you met General Custer?" Tom Gibbs asked after a moment or two of awkward silence.

"Never had the pleasure," Gray said. "I suppose you're familiar with him, living up in Bismarck, so close to Ft. Lincoln."

"Had a conversation or two with the man," Gibbs said, an exasperated tone in his voice.

"What's he like?" Trent asked. "There are a lot of conflicting tales about the boy general."

"Arrogant. Damn arrogant," Gibbs said. "What do you think about him being in the Black Hills?" the newspaperman asked of Gray.

"The Black Hills, their Paha Sapa, is sacred land to them," Gray said. "We signed a treaty with the Sioux back in '68. Custer's violating that treaty. I can't justify treaty breaking."

"Gold is the justification," Del laughed, drawing a dark

115

frown from his father.

Gabe scowled at his son. "You don't need to be criticizing the government. You haven't lived enough to earn that right."

"I lived through Red Cloud's war," Trent said. "Gold will cost innocent people their lives," he added, harshness echoing in his voice.

"How do you think Sitting Bull will react?" Gibbs asked.

"From what we hear," Trent said, "Sitting Bull and Crazy Horse are both over along the Powder or the east summits of the Bighorns."

"Are you sure?" Gabe asked.

"I'm sure," Gray said. He glanced at Del. The news about Sitting Bull and Crazy Horse being on the Powder upset the boy, who shifted in his saddle. "Those two being on the Powder may save old Hiestzi's hair," Gray said off-handedly.

"He's got over 1,000 men with him," Gibbs said. "Would the Sioux attack so many?"

"I suppose their attacking would depend on the number of Sioux," Gray said. "They might not attack his full force, but I expect Custer's invasion into Paha Sapa will start them raiding throughout the area."

"Do you approve of the treaty with the Indians?" Gabe asked.

"I believe a man should keep his word," Gray said. "So should governments."

Chapter Twenty-Four

"We're in here," Annie called out when the front door opened and slammed.

"Go on in, and play with Kenyon," Millie told her five-year-old twins. Her tan pants and red shirt revealed her intent to work with the horses. When she found Annie and Jean sitting across the kitchen table, both women wore dresses, not a sign they intended to do outside chores. "I thought we should finish branding the weanlings," she said, disappointment clear in her voice and manner.

Annie and Jean winked at each other, but neither responded to the girl. "Do you want some coffee?" Annie asked after a moment's hesitation.

"I don't think so," Millie said. "Aren't you planning on branding?"

"I hadn't thought about it," Annie said. "There's no hurry to finish."

Annie's reply bothered Millie, not because of any urgency about finishing, but because she decided she would survive the day by branding horses.

"Why don't you sit down?" Jean said. "I brought some blackberry pie over, have a slice."

"It's too early in the morning to eat pie."

"Oh, I didn't know." Jean pushed her empty plate to the middle of the table.

"Where's Susan?" Millie asked, sitting down and picking a berry from Annie's plate.

"She went back upstairs to lie down after the men left. I suspect she slept little last night."

Millie stiffened. "Who did?"

Annie put her hand on the girl's arm. "They'll be fine, Millie. They'll be home before you know it."

"I hope they don't find them," Millie said, angry eyes flashing at Annie. Millie motioned toward the upstairs, where Susan Tucker rested. "Why does she think she can come here and ask for such dangerous help?"

After a moment of silence, Annie said, "I guess she doesn't have anywhere else to turn,"

"She's not a bad person. She wants to save her family. I'd do the same thing in her place," Jean said.

Millie almost lost her temper; only the thought of her twin girls playing in the other room held her back. At five, they were the age of Susan's grandson. The idea they might ever be in a situation as horrible as those children was too dreadful to imagine. Perhaps she indeed was Gray Wehr's daughter. She possessed his rigid sense of right and wrong. If she were a man, she would be riding with the other men to pursue the Sioux raiding party.

"Let's go finish branding," Annie said cheerily. "We'll take Sanchez and make him babysit."

"I'll have to go home and change clothes," Jean said. "Unless some sister-in-law might loan out a pair of pants and a shirt."

"Go help yourself." Annie turned to Millie. "It would be courteous to ask Susan to come."

"Fine," Millie said, sounding sincere.

"Los ninós and I will follow, walking," Sanchez said. "You go ahead; we will come behind."

Annie was riding a three-year-old black filly she called Fury. She gave her the name because of her fiery personality as a baby. As a weanling and a yearling, she had been the wildest of colts and fillies in the Wehr/Thaxton herd, always quick to kick or bite. Zack Joseph once asked Gray if he had "been on her back yet?" Gray said no. Zach suggested he be awake when he stepped up the first time.

The wildness in the horse first drew Annie to her, much as Jean said the wildness in Gray drew Annie to him. Now, like her husband, the horse was steady and gentle. "Fury and I will rope," Annie said, more as a suggestion than as any kind of order. "Jean, you and Millie can hold the horses. Susan can brand."

"I'll help throw horses on the ground. I don't want to be the one to brand them," Susan said. "Let Jean brand."

Annie, proficient at roping the weanlings, as skilled as any cowboy, dropped loop after loop over the heads of the colts. The young horses proved to be more difficult for Susan and Millie to wrestle. Jean started to slap the iron twice when a colt managed to escape and delay the W/T singed into their hides.

Annie's rope dropped flawlessly around the head of a good-sized buckskin. Millie ran alongside, grabbing the stout yearling around the front shoulders. The filly pulled at the rope, reared up, pitching Millie six or seven feet. Susan grabbed the young horse by the neck and tried to twist her down. Up from her fall, Millie caught the little buckskin's back feet. Not yet a veteran cow horse, Annie's horse let the rope go slack for an instant, long enough for Millie to take a couple of glancing cow kicks.

"Bulldog the little devil," Jean said. "Throw her down!" she laughed as the little horse broke away again, this time sending Susan Carlyle on the seat of her trousers. "Atta girl, Millie; you've got her now."

Millie and Susan got the feisty filly sprawled out on the ground after being tossed numerous more times. They flopped down over her, Susan lying across her head and neck, Millie spread-eagled, less than lady-like, across the belly and rump. "Hurry," Millie ordered Jean. "Hurry up." Sanchez and the three kids burst out laughing at the spectacle of the women flailing about with the filly.

"Ow! Holy Hell, you branded me!" With Millie jumping up and down, the horse escaped from Susan and kicked her in the thigh. "You branded me!" Up and down, Millie jumped, waving her arm around like a wild woman. Jean dropped the branding iron, and Annie leaped from Fury's back. Both women grabbed at Millie.

"Hold still!" Annie yelled. "Let us see."

"Hold still, my butt! It burns like fire."

Annie and Jean overpowered Millie and got their first view of her forearm.

"Oh, for heaven's sake. You're hardly singed." Jean waved her hand and walked away. "I've been burned worse taking pies out of the oven. I expected the whole W/T branded on you." Jean came back and took Millie's arm. "Lord, the corner of the T is barely there." Jean gave her a playful slap on the back of the head. "No one would even know what ranch you belong to."

Jean was right; the burn was not much.

"I don't care; it still hurts," Millie whined.

"Well, let's go back up to the house. We'll pour some cold water on you and doctor you up a bit with some butter," Annie said, laughing at her young friend.

Chapter Twenty-Five

The day brought no more rain, but the skies stayed cloudy, and the temperatures dropped lower than any day of the still early fall. When Gray called an end to the first day's travel, Del and Trent shot two good-sized jackrabbits, which served as the bulk of the evening meal.

"Have you suffered through many Indian attacks, living out here so isolated?" Gibbs asked Gray.

"We've always been friendly with the Lakota. We've worked real hard at being helpful neighbors."

"I'll tell you," Gabe said, "I'd never seen anything like what they did to the Carlyle boy. I hope I never do again." He paused and threw his remaining coffee out on the ground. "Do you suppose," he looked at Gray, "these people we're after are still alive?"

Gray used a dry stick to stir the fire around before tossing it in. "I can't say, but we'll have our work cut out for us." He picked up his cup and took a drink. "The Sioux will take hostages to keep as slaves. Sometimes they raise child captives as Lakota, treating them well."

"What about Lucy? What will they do to her?"

Gray rubbed his hand across his mouth before answering. "She'll be in for a hard time. The women will most likely make a slave out of her. She'll be in for a lot of beatings." Wehr hesitated, mulled over speaking in front of the boy. "Some men will use her for a whore." Gray took another drink of coffee and unbuttoned his shirt collar. "What does this Lucy look like?"

Gibbs and Reed glanced at each other before Tom answered. "She's an attractive young woman with light red hair she wears long and straight. Beautiful green eyes," he added.

"Her hair may keep her alive; she'll be a novelty." The tone of Gray's voice raised doubts about whether living would be the finest thing. "The problem, as far as finding them goes, is where to search."

"Do you think the Sioux we're looking for will give us any information?" Gabe asked.

"I can't say, but it's our best chance."

"If they can't help, what do we do?" Del asked.

Gray eyeballed the boy, his face silhouetted by the full moon hanging feint in the cloudy sky behind him. He took a moment before responding. "I don't know."

Chapter Twenty-Six

Warmer temperatures and sunny skies greeted them the second day of the journey. Everyone's mood turned more optimistic with the clouds and the threat of rain gone. They hit the Powder River before noon and rode north for three hours before Gray's chestnut stallion started snorting and acting up. He threw his head and danced before whinnying loudly. "Hush, J.L. Don't be talking," Gray said, giving the reins a few quick jerks.

Tom Gibbs pulled his horse a short distance away from the dancing stud. "What's wrong with your horse?"

"I imagine he smells mares. Let's hope from a Sioux pony herd."

Gibbs looked disturbed at the mention of a Sioux herd. "How far away?"

"It'd be hard to say for sure. Somewhere upwind. We'll let J.L. find them."

Del leaned close to his dad, muttered low enough no one else would hear. Fear again pumped through the younger Reed. "Why did I tell Wehr I could hold up my end? Why wasn't I honest? I should have told him I've been scared to death ever since we crossed Sioux land on our way to High Meadows." Gray noticed Del's hands were shaking so badly he wouldn't be able to hold a rifle, let alone aim one.

Suddenly, urgently, he needed to go to the bathroom. Unless he relieved himself soon, he'd flood his saddle. "Can we stop a minute?" Del asked. His timid voice made him sound like a faint-hearted coward. "I need to take a leak." The men stopped while Del jumped from his horse and ran for the backside of a thick bush.

Gray leaned forward on his saddle horn and shook his head. The youngster had some growing up to do. He just hoped his growing happened before they got in the middle of a fight with the Sioux.

The boy remounted, more relaxed, without such an urgent bounce in his step. Trent started up a conversation with him. "If we find Paints His Horse before the evening meal, we'll eat better than we did last night. I wouldn't mind a little elk stew, would you?" Del forced a smile. "Some Sioux women are right fair cooks. Yes, sir, their cooking will beat the dickens out of dry, stringy old rabbit like we ate last night." He gave Del a light slap on the back.

"Let's move out," Gray said. He tapped his mare and led the untested little troop deeper toward the Lakota territory.

A short time later, Gray said, "I wouldn't mention Custer being in the Black Hills." Gray told Tom and Gabe as their horses splashed through a small stream. "If they bring Custer up, don't lie. They hate liars."

"I hadn't considered being asked about Custer," Tom Said. "I guess I need to think better."

Gray's stud began prancing and fighting his reins. He reared, twisted, and started talking. Gray pulled his face around and told him to hush. "When we go up over this rise, I suspect we'll find a Sioux village."

Trent topped the bluff first. A vast Indian encampment spread out before him. "You ever see a camp this size?" he asked Gray. "I'll bet there are over a thousand braves of fighting age."

"Well, let's hope they're not in a hostile mood," Gray said. "Easy, J.L. Calm down," Wehr said, patting and rubbing the side of the chestnut stud's neck.

"Do you think they've spotted us?" Tom asked.

Gray shook his head. "I don't think so."

"What do we do? Do we ride on down?" Gabe asked, with either worry or confusion in his voice.

"It's what we came for." Gray tried to sound detached, unconcerned. "Let's swing over toward the river and on down. I want this horse out from downwind of the pony herd."

"Do you think we should show a white flag?" Del asked, reaching back into his saddlebag for a handkerchief or appropriate cloth.

Gray chuckled. "I doubt they'll think we're attacking them. You're not planning an attack, are you?"

The Indians showed only a passing interest in the five white men as they rode into camp. The women and children scooted back, standing a short distance with the young ones staring wide-eyed. Several braves moved a little closer, but none appeared agitated by their presence.

Three hundred yards into the village, Gray stopped and dismounted. He handed the reins to Trent.

"Guess we'll find out if my Lakota is still passable."

"What did he say to you?" Gabe asked.

"Oh, he hopes he can say 'we're friendly' in Lakota. Sometimes he gets his words confused and ends up saying, 'we're here to eat your livers,'" Trent said, grinning at Del, who took no amusement in Trent's feeble humor.

Gray asked an older man if this was the camp of Paints His Horse. The old brave nodded, talking and smiling. He pointed a long boney finger first toward the middle of the encampment and up and down the river. Gray returned the smile before rejoining the others. "He says Paints His Horse is camped over there. The San Arc are at this end, the Tetons are next, and many Oglalas are at the other end. Sitting Bull and his Hunkpapas are about three miles up."

Trent fidgeted with his reins, rubbing them between his fingers. "He can stay upriver for my part."

Gray stepped back on his stud, and the five men headed to the center of the village, drawing curious stares as they passed through. A ten-year-old boy ran up and hit Trent on the knee with a stick. He whacked Del as well, causing Del to jerk his horse away.

"Relax!" Gray yelled at the younger Reed.

"He's showing off for his friends," Trent reassured Del. "Counting a little coup." The boy whooped and hollered, quite pleased with himself. Another brave young warrior, this one only eight or nine, scurried forward while lifting an aspen switch, but before he counted his coup, his mother ran him down and swooped him up in her arms. Gray smiled and winked at the woman, who shook her head and smiled back.

"Crow Killer, my friend," Gray exclaimed as the men dismounted. The Sioux took Trent's arm at the elbows and made a slight shaking motion. More warriors moved toward the group, smiling and appearing happy to have company.

"Paints His Horse sits in his lodge. I will take you to him," Crow Killer said.

"At least they speak English," Tom mumbled to himself.

They walked up the river a short distance and stopped in front of a lodge. After Crow Killer called out, a smoothly muscled brave opened the flap.

"Paints His Horse," Gray said, taking the Lakota chief by the hand and slapping him on the shoulder. He said a few brief words in Lakota. The chief motioned for the whites to enter the lodge. Four or five buffalo hides were piled to one side. A bow and quiver of arrows lay across the tipi. The red coals of a fire still burned in the center.

Tom Gibbs scribbled a few notes about the inside of the

deerskin tipi and the Teton Lakota chief's appearance before Trent told him to put his pencil away.

The Indian, about Gabe's height, had a "classic Roman nose" and high cheekbones. He wore no feathers or adornments in his dark, braided hair. His eyes were warm and friendly as he embraced Gray and Trent.

When Paints His Horse mentioned "Annie" and "Millie" in English, Gray and Trent nodded their heads and smiled as they replied.

"They're good," Gray said. "Annie backed you a pie, but I got hungry last night and ate it."

Paints His Horse laughed and called Gray a glutton.

After a bit of small talk, Wehr took on a more severe countenance, using his hands to make and emphasize specific points. He used the names "Danny" and "Susan Tucker." Paints His Horse took up the discussion. He shook his head back and forth.

Wehr turned to the other men. "I explained to Paints His Horse about Susan coming back home. He remembers her; he always liked Danny. He says we got into a lot of mischief together. I told him what happened. He's surprised."

"What direction did they go?" Paints His Horse asked.

There was no point in lying.

"We don't know," Tom Gibbs said. "We searched to the north for two weeks, but we didn't find anything."

"We'll eat before visiting the Oglala camp," Paints His Horse said.

They ate their meal sitting outside Paints His Horse tipi. An old woman served elk and a stew brimming with meat.

"This is good," Del said.

"Never had rattlesnake stew before?" Trent asked.

Paints His Horse laughed, patted Del on the knee. "Don't listen to him. He's a grand deceiver."

"You speak English well," Gabe told the Lakota chief.

Paints His Horse smiled. "Wehr's mother taught me English." My mother taught Wehr Lakota. I learned English

127

better than Wehr learned Lakota," he said, with a self-contented smile on his face.

"Well, my mother was a better teacher," Gray said.

"I think I am smarter than you." Paints His Horse laughed.

"Well, not much to brag about," Gray chuckled.

A beautiful sunset painted the western horizon in hues of orange and purple when Paints His Horse and two other braves, one called Running Wolf and the other Fool Heart, took Gray, Trent, and the three visitors into the Oglala village. "We will talk with Tashunke-Witko," Paints His Horse said while giving Gray a cockeyed glance. "I believe you are old friends."

"We met once."

"Tashunke-Witko says you used my name...so he would not kill you."

"It worked," Gray laughed.

After a young Oglala warrior delivered the message that Paints His Horse wanted to talk, he led them to a tipi removed from the others. A small fire in the center of the lodge cast dancing shadows as the men stepped in. Gray noted a tall Sioux, maybe seven feet tall, standing to the flap's left. Next to him stood a man of average height, about five-ten. The huge Indian dwarfed him.

In the lodge's dim interior, the one of normal height appeared to be light-complexioned, with light brown hair hanging loose. White spots about the size of a man's thumb decorated his chest; a smooth stone hung on a leather thong looped over his ear. He was a handsome man except for a nasty scar across his left cheek.

"This is Touch The Clouds," Paints His Horse said, motioning to the Indian giant. This is Tashunke-Witko," he continued, pointing to the other Sioux.

"Crazy Horse and I are old friends," Gray said, referring to their one only semi-cordial meeting six years earlier when Annie suggested he approach the Sioux warrior after laying down his pistol to show himself friendly. Gray greeted Crazy Horse and the three warriors with him, wearing his pistol and carrying a rifle to prove himself dangerous.

The Sioux leader spoke in Lakota, flashing a smile as he finished. Wehr and Trent both smiled and laughed. "He says we have a hard time staying out of Sioux lands," Gray told the men from Bismarck. "He says every time we meet, we're trespassing. He's making a joke," Gray said, smiling at Del. "At least, I hope he's joking."

Crazy Horse motioned for everyone to sit down. Touch The Clouds picked up a pipe propped against a stone next to the fire smoldering in the center of the tipi. "We will smoke before we talk," Touch The Clouds said.

Gray was not happy about smoking. "Be careful not to inhale," Gray cautioned Del. "You've never been sick 'til you've been sick from a Sioux pipe."

While Crazy Horse and Touch The Clouds smoked, Trent glanced at Gray and ran his finger across his left cheek. Gray shook his head, indicating he didn't remember the scar either. Once everyone took a puff on the pipe, Paints His Horse explained why the whites were in the village. When he mentioned the attack happened in Bismarck, Crazy Horse interrupted.

He spoke for a couple of minutes before stopping for Paints His Horse to interpret for the white men who did not speak Lakota. "He says rumors claim soldiers are in the Paha Sapa."

Gibb's eyebrows wrinkled, "Paha Sapa?"

"The Black Hills," Gray replied. Gray leaned toward Crazy Horse and, speaking in Lakota, addressed Crazy Horse and Touch The Clouds. "We live in the Bighorn Mountains. We haven't been out of our valley since we first met. Like you, we heard rumors soldiers entered the sacred Paha Sapa. We did not believe the stories because the treaty of Fort Laramie forbids whites in Lakota land. These men are from Bismarck, the settlement close to Fort Lincoln. They told us whites broke the treaty. I am ashamed. They have no right to be in your land."

Crazy Horse accepted Gray's statement and did not pursue the matter further. Paints His Horse completed the story of what happened to Susan Tucker's family. He stressed this woman who lost her children had once been his friend.

Neither Crazy Horse nor Touch The Clouds knew of any raid or captive whites. Crazy Horse stepped out of the tipi and told a young warrior to find someone, although Gray did not hear the name.

A few minutes later, another Sioux entered. "This is Gall," Paints His Horse said. "He was the last to be in the Paha Sapa, near Fort Lincoln." Gall, a strong muscular man well over 200 pounds, was not a man Gray would want to confront. Paints His Horse told him why the white men came to the Sioux camp.

Gall showed no emotion and did not speak until Crazy Horse asked him about raids and white captives. Gall denied any knowledge of any such activity, but both Gray and Trent spoke enough Lakota to understand Gall questioned why they would help the whites, again bringing up the rumor of whites entering the Black Hills.

Gall's jaw tightened, his body tensed, resentment poured out of his eyes. He spat a single word at the intruders. "Dogs." Gray wondered for a moment if the situation might turn sour.

Paints His Horse stiffened. He rose and glared down at Gall. "These are my friends. They are men of honor, and they are my guests in this camp. You will treat them with respect."

Gall stood, avoided Paints His Horse's glare, and, speaking in more than passable English, turned toward Crazy Horse. "Tashunke-Witko, do you accept these white eyes in our village?"

Crazy Horse did not stand, which Gray took to be a slight insult to Gall. "They only seek help."

Gall repeated the fact he knew of no raid or captives.

He threw the tipi flap back and left, snarling at Paints His Horse, whose temper flashed as he stood and responded. Gall spun back toward his tormentor but changed his mind and stomped off.

"Gall does not like white eyes," Crazy Horse said, matter-of-factly.

Tom Gibbs spoke for the first time. "What about you, Crazy Horse? How do you feel about the whites?" Paints His Horse, calm again, translated Gibbs's words. Crazy Horse studied Gibbs, glanced at Gray, and over at Trent. He again turned to Gibbs before speaking.

"I am born to be free on this land. I want no boundary on where I ride, where I hunt, or where I sleep. The white eyes come into our land, the land of our fathers. They say we can no longer be free; the land belongs to them, we must live in agencies or within boundaries. I will not. Wakan Tanka gave us this land; he did not give the land to the white man. I will not surrender what He gave us. I will not leave my home, where I live free. If men try to take our lands, I will fight."

Crazy Horse waited for Paints His Horse to tell them what he said. He continued, "How do I think of the white man? Casper Collins was my friend. Most white eyes are not like him, or these men," he said, motioning at Gray and Trent. "They do not want to be the friend of the Lakota; they only want the land. You take not only our land. You kill our families. My child died this year of the running face sickness. She was only three summers. This sickness we did not know until you people came. Our medicine men have no cures."

Crazy Horse said a little more, but Touch The Clouds spoke for half an hour. Like white men, the Lakota had their politicians.

Once they returned to the Teton Lakota section of the encampment, Paints His Horse had a tipi emptied for the whites to sleep. Trent brewed up some coffee and was pouring a cup when Tom Gibbs said quite off-handedly,

"Hell, maybe ol' Josiah Park was right."

"About what?" Gray asked, taking an interest in the conversation.

"Do you know that crazy old man?" Gibbs asked.

"I know him. Right about what?" Gray asked again, his irritation unmistakable.

"Ah, the old fool followed Gabe's wife out to the Carlyle place the day of the kidnapping. He was running around hollering something like, 'the Sioux didn't do this; this is white man's work.' He was nothing but a damned nuisance."

Gray's eyes turned icy, his mouth tensed, and he bit off each word, "Josiah Park called the attack white man's work?" The tone of the question and the glare in Wehr's eyes caused Tom to blanch.

"He said something close, but he's a crazy old coot."

"I'll be damned," Gray said, flinging his coffee cup across the tipi, his temper flaring. Enraged, he kicked dirt at the fire as he stormed out of the lodge.

"What the hell is wrong with him?" Gabe asked, brushing dirt and some small coals from Wehr's kick off his pants.

"Do you have any idea how long Josiah Park has lived in this country?" Trent asked, his voice much gentler than his expression.

"A long time, I suppose, but he's crazy," Reed said.

"Crazy?" Trent spat out the words, anger flowing despite his half-whispering. "He may be crazy, but I'll guarantee you he sure as hell knew whether Indians or white men did the kidnapping. We're chasing the wrong people!"

Chapter Twenty-Seven

Maddie smelled of blood, sweat, and dirt, nothing like the little girl who loved to splash on the "flowery water" her mother kept in the drawer in her bedroom. "Mommy, your lip's bleeding again," the child reached up, touching her mother.

Lucy Carlyle put her fingers to her mouth. "They're sunburned, sweetie. I'll be fine," she said, taking her six-year-old daughter into her arms.

"I'll kiss them better," Maddie said as tears welled up in her eyes. "Don't cry anymore, Mommy; Dylan's in heaven."

"Tell that woman to start some supper." Walker stomped through the ratty camp, swearing under his breath. "And tell her to shut her kid up, or I'll slit her damn throat."

Bert Camp spit a tobacco wad out as he started toward Susan Carlyle and her children huddled together. "Git over here; we're hungry."

"Stay here with your sister. I'll go make us something to eat." Lucy kissed the side of Maddie's face. "We'll feel better after a meal."

"Git!" Camp bellowed as he kicked the now frail woman. Camp had ridden with Jack Walker since deserting from the Union Army halfway through the Civil War. "Move yer ass, I said."

Wanted almost everywhere west of the Mississippi River, they now rode with five other men, picked up in bars or jails. Burns the Grass was a renegade Cheyenne, kicked out of his tribe for stealing, Carter Cline was a two-bit thief, Carl and Bob Fox were brothers who reputedly cut their mother's throat. If true, killing her would have been the bravest thing either of the two cowards had ever done. Bill Beachum was a rapist and back-shooter whose speech was almost impossible to understand since a whore tired of his rough manner and bit three-quarters of his tongue off.

However, none of the five would dare to face Walker or Camp. Walker and Camp were different, even from killers. Most killers killed for money or to hide other crimes. Walker and Camp killed out of pure meanness.

"What do you want me to cook?" Lucy became a little mouthy, too tired to care about taking the back of a fist or the butt of a pistol across her mouth.

"What'd she say?" Cline asked.

"Asked what to cook," Carl Fox said.

"Some of the hash and a few potatoes," Jack Walker said.

Maddie started screaming and crying. Lucy spun around to catch Bill Beachum urinating on the child. Though she stopped fighting back weeks ago, having surrendered to the futility of defiance, this was too much. She charged through the camp and leaped on Beachum's back. Lucy tore at his eyes, trying to claw them out. Screaming profanities she'd never uttered in her life, she chomped down and ground her teeth into the back of Beachum's neck, biting out a mouthful of flesh.

The renegade Cheyenne charged her first. He grabbed a handful of hair, giving it a horrible, vicious jerk, shooting burning pains screamed through her head as the hair ripped from her scalp. The pain didn't matter. She was free again. She bit into the back of Beacham's shoulder, and if not for his thick wool vest, Lucy'd have bitten out another chunk of hide.

Bert Camp raced across the small clearing, jerking his heavy colt dragoon out of its holster and crashing the pistol down over the back of Lucy's head. The force of the blow knocked her five feet away from Beachum. She landed unconscious on her back.

Beachum, screaming like a crazy man, went after her. No one understood him because of the missing portion of his tongue, but he yanked a long-bladed knife from the sheath concealed in his left boot. He would have cut the woman to pieces if not for the shot from Jack Walker's revolver.

"Leave her be," Walker screamed.

Beachum was furious. He glared at her.

Walker fired again. "By Gawd, I said, let her be. You take another step, and I'll send you straight to hell."

Beachum whirled toward the shooter, and for a moment, the men stared each other down. Beachum backed away from the woman and sheathed his knife. "You better back off. I'll not have her killed. She's going to bring us a lot of money."

"Money?" petty thief Carter Cline said. "How much do you think we can get for one woman and a couple of brats?"

"We ain't sellin' only one," Walker said. "I figure we'll take around six or eight women and ten pups with us. Some of the Mex like the young ones. They'll fetch a tidy sum."

"Where we gonna steal the rest?" Cline growled. "Hell, it's more'n a month since we took this one."

"We'll take 'em when I say to," Walker spit out through his chaw. "I've not found what I'm lookin' for. We'll take 'em when I do."

Chapter Twenty-Eight

Susan Carlyle's heart sank when Gray, Tom, and the Reeds walked in the front door. "The Sioux don't have them. Whites do," Gray said, glaring into her eyes.

"How do you know?" Susan asked, no demanded.

"Because Josiah Park said so." Gray sat and started pulling off his right boot.

Susan stood dumbfounded, horrified over Gray blaming white men based on the word of a crazy man.

"Did you see Josiah?" Annie asked, sensing something needed to be said to diffuse the tension spreading through the room.

"No. He told these people before they ever left Bismarck!"

"Where's Trent?" Annie asked, with a sudden fear coming over her.

"He went home."

Sick to her stomach, Susan sat on a straight-backed oak chair, hoping she would not pass out. She put her face in her hands for a full minute before looking back up at Gray. "You came home," she said, trembling and crying, "because some crazy old fool claimed it was whites."

The words came not as a question but as an accusation, biting through tears. Susan glared at her childhood friend, so famous for his bravery, for his gun skill, now seizing on such an excuse to run home.

Inescapable anger flashing in Gray's eyes froze everyone. "No, Susan, I came because Josiah Park said it was white men." Gray stood and limped across the room. "I'm going to get some coffee. It's been a long ride."

Tears poured down Susan's face. "I thought he would help me."

Annie watched—dispassionate. Susan jumped up and headed for the kitchen. Annie flew to her feet and followed.

"Damn you!" Susan screamed as she went through the swinging doors.

Gray spun around to face her. "What?"

"Damn you! If you didn't want to help, why didn't you say so!"

"If I didn't want to help you?" Gray's eyes tightened, and his lips parted. "If I didn't want to help you?" He slung the coffee into the sink. "I left my wife and child to go find your family! What the hell do you mean if I didn't want to help?" More anger flushed through Gray's face as he started toward Susan.

"Graham!" Annie snapped, drawing Gray's attention to her. She held up both hands, moving them forward, something she did when she wanted someone to calm down. Gray growled something before turning toward the window.

Annie moved over to Susan and wrapped her arms around her after a moment's hesitation. "Shhh. Shhh. Take a breath. Try to relax."

Tom Gibbs pushed open the swinging door and stepped

into the doorway. Annie held her hand up toward him and shook her head. Clearly frustrated, Tom retreated to the sitting room.

"Calm down now," Annie whispered, her voice tender but also stern. Gray turned back to the kitchen table, came, and sat, his flash temper having cooled as rapidly as it flashed.

"Susan, I told you I would do my best to find them."

Annie studied her husband. She stared expressionless as she listened to Gray.

"I'll keep my promise." Gray left. He went through the sitting room without speaking to the Reeds or the newspaper reporter. He climbed the front stairs, limping, and went into the bedroom, closing the door behind him.

Annie let go of Susan and turned away. She walked over to the window and stared out across the meadow behind the house. The aspen trees down by the river were showing the first hints of yellow in their leaves. Most of the summer wildflowers lost or were losing their blooms. "Days are looking more like autumn," she said, as much to herself as to Susan Carlyle.

Chapter Twenty-Nine

Libbie Custer sensed for the last few days Laura Reed growing disheartened, discouraged. She believed Laura perked up when General Custer came home and told them there'd been little sign of Indians while surveying the Black Hills. But now, Laura was slipping into a blue mood.

"They probably haven't been any place to post a letter." Libbie pointed out when Laura expressed concern that she hadn't received a single one.

"I think I should go to this High Meadows town. Do you think Red Holstein might take me?" Laura asked.

"What a foolish idea. If you make it to, what's the place called, High Meadows? Gabe and Del aren't going to be there. What would you gain? And the trip would be so dangerous."

Laura got up and walked across the General's library. A room cluttered with rifles, sabers, and taxidermy; the hobby Custer picked up after coming west. A stuffed white owl sat perched on the five-point antlers of a buck deer.

Pictures of Custer's two favorite Generals—McClellan and Sheridan—hung on the wall. A picture of Libbie in her bridal gown peered down over the General's desk. Two hounds slept in the sunshine under a window. "It's so hard to stay here, not knowing," Laura said.

"I've spent half my life wondering about Autie's well-being," Libbie said, turning away from her friend. She turned toward Laura as a broad smile crossed her lips, revealing beautiful white teeth. "He always says, 'Watch for our return, Libbie,' and always I do. How I watch." Libbie glanced up at the clock. "Goodness, half-past noon. We should make ourselves something to eat. Autie is eating with the officers, so we'll have the meal all to ourselves."

Chapter Thirty

Jean Wehr tapped on the bedroom door. "Worn out?" she asked, leaning against the doorjamb.

"A bit. Come on in."

Jean closed the door behind her. "Annie says you and Susan engaged in quite a screaming match." She hesitated for her brother to respond, but he did not comment. "Is everything all right?"

"I haven't seen her since I came upstairs," Gray said, "but I imagine Annie smoothed things over for me. She's rather skilled at smoothing."

"Well, the argument wasn't your fault. As I understand, Susan started yelling." Jean eased down on the bed next to Gray, putting her arm around him. "I'm sure you're tired of people expecting you to get justice for them, but you're a brave man. Everyone sees that in you."

"I acted like a jackass, getting so mad over Josiah saying white men were responsible." Gray sat quietly as his sister laid her head on his shoulder. "The old man is crazy. I guess I shouldn't have expected them to believe him."

"Well, you can't do anything now." Jean kissed the side of her brother's face and ran her fingers through his hair before standing up and pulling him to his feet. "Come on; dinner is about ready. Trent, Millie, and the kids are here. It'll be a regular family reunion."

Susan put a platter of fried chicken on the table as Gray and Jean came into the dining room. She sheepishly walked over to Gray. "I was out of line. I want to apologize." Gray smiled and shook his head, indicating no apology was unnecessary.

"The twins and Kenyon are eating in the kitchen, so I guess we're ready to sit down," Millie said.

After Trent said grace, Annie worked at keeping the conversation cheerful. She brought up memories from their childhood. They laughed about things Gray and Danny Tucker got into as boys, and about a few stunts perpetrated by Annie, Jean, Susan, and her mother. "Do you remember," Susan asked, laughing hard enough she had to stop talking and catch her breath, "when Jean and Nellie stole Frieda Parish's mule?"

Jean, her bright blue eyes gleaming, propped her hands on her hips. "We didn't steal the beast. We—borrowed him."

"Old man Cain wanted them hanged as horse thieves," Susan laughed.

"Lord, I'd rather been hung than got the whippin' we got," Jean said, rubbing her backside.

"Whatever happened to Adrian Cain?" Susan asked, wiping tears out of her eyes from laughing so hard.

"Oh, he died, what? Two and a half years ago." Annie said.

"Did he ever get any nicer?"

"Not a bit," Jean said. "Not one bit. Remember when he spat tobacco juice on the front of Millie's dress?"

"You should have seen her," Annie grinned, spooning more mashed potatoes on Gray's plate. "Millie nearly whacked him senseless with a broom. She chased him clear through the middle of town. Whop! Whop!" Annie laughed, making the motion of a swinging broom. "Mrs. Keller scurried out of the general store and called her off."

"I should have beat him to death, the old bastard."

"Millie, I'm going to wash your mouth out with soap!" Annie snapped at the girl with both her eyes and her voice.

"Well, he *was* an old bastard," Jean said, defending Millie.

"That doesn't mean Millie should talk like a drunken cowboy," Annie said. "Cursing doesn't become you as a lady or as a Christian."

Millie glanced at Trent, looking for some help, but he only agreed with Annie. "Well, I don't enjoy swearing," Millie said. "It just helps me make my point." Her whole face broke out in a laugh. "I'll curb my feisty tongue. At least in front of Annie.

After supper, everyone retired to the back porch. "Such a pleasant evening," Annie commented, looking out at the starry sky. "Peaceful and quiet."

Following a few minutes of small talk, Gray started the conversation about renewing the chase effort, a relief because the subject had been hanging somberly over the group. "Since Cheyenne is the closest place we can find any law, I think Cheyenne is where we should head."

Annie had been afraid of that. While she didn't think one direction would be more dangerous than another, Cheyenne confirmed a long trip. Cheyenne lay ten, eleven, or more hard days away. Annie feared the rescue, successful or not, would take a month, at the least.

"I'm still not convinced it wasn't Indians," Tom Gibbs said.

"I am," Gabe said. "The Sioux weren't anything like I imagined. They weren't bloodthirsty savages. They laughed

Rod McFain

easily and were friendly and comfortable to be with. Paints His Horse asked about Gray's family. The same way a white man would."

Gray changed the subject back to where they should search. "If I were getting only one guess, I'd pick south," Gray said. "I wish I knew why they kidnapped them. We'd have a better idea where they're headed."

"White slavery is quite a business down in Louisiana," Del said.

"What do you know about white slavery?" Gabe asked.

Del shrugged. "Not much. Mostly rumors."

"What's white slavery?" Millie asked.

"Selling women into prostitution. An ugly business," Gray said, staring down at his hands. "Happened down in Arkansas a lot after the war."

Almost half an hour passed before someone spoke. Annie broke the silence. "If white slavery's the reason, they would have headed straight south of Bismarck. You should go southeast instead of toward Cheyenne."

"The thing is, Annie," Gray said, "we can make Cheyenne sooner than any other town where we might pick up some news. We can also swing by Fort Laramie. My guess is they've done this deed at more than one ranch. Wouldn't be much profit in one woman and three children."

"If they were kidnapped for white slavery, they'll still be alive," Susan said. She turned to Gray. "I want to go along," Susan said, looking at Gray.

"Well," Gray said in a soft but unyielding voice, "that's not happening."

"They're my grandchildren and my daughter-in-law," Susan said, matching the sternness in Gray's voice.

"True, but I won't discuss this. The answer is no."

"Why? I can keep up. I won't be a burden."

Annie reached for Susan's hand. "Let's you and I go for a walk." Susan got up and followed Annie down the porch steps without objection.

The two women walked past the barn and into the

meadow toward the river. "This is my favorite place," Annie said as they neared the water. "I love the quiet and serenity." Annie sat along the river's edge and pulled her knees up between her arms. She smiled at Susan as she kneeled beside her. Annie let the next few minutes pass, listening to the water's slow flow and babbling.

"Six years ago," she began, "Jean, Millie, Nellie, and I made Gray take us down to Fort Laramie for the treaty talks." Annie bowed her head. "We made Fort Laramie and back to Crazy Woman Creek, where Cheyenne Dog Soldiers attacked us. They killed Nellie." Annie gazed out across the water, where the moon's reflection bounced along on the riffles. "There is no reason," Annie whispered, "but Gray has always blamed himself for her death. He can't let it go." Annie stood and walked a little way down the bank. After a short time, Susan followed.

"We should head back to the house," Susan said. "The dark scares me."

Chapter Thirty-One

"Are you awake?" Gray asked as he slipped out from under the blankets and put his feet on the cold floor.

"I turned and tossed most of the night," Annie said as she rolled over on her back and stared at the ceiling.

Gray leaned over and kissed Annie on the eyebrow. "Stop worrying," he whispered. "I doubt we can find them. We may as well be chasing the shadow of the moon."

"The shadow of the moon. For someone else, but not you. You're tenacious. Once you start, you won't quit. If those men live and breathe on this earth, you'll find them. Like you found Ben Green's son's killer." Annie paused; peered at the sun's light orange glow behind the mountains. "Like you did, Harvey Kehn," she said without turning away from the window.

Gray took a faded red shirt out of his top drawer. As he put the shirt on and began buttoning the front, he made no response to Annie's comment about Kehn, the man who killed her brother and sister. Annie's father solicited from

Gray a promise if he ever found Kehn, he would kill him. Years later, Gray kept the promise. As Annie dressed, putting on pants and an old shirt, indicating she intended to spend the day working with the horses, Gray tucked his shirt in. "If you're against this, I can tell Susan I'm not going."

Annie turned toward the man she loved. His shoulders slumped, his shirt hung loose, evidencing his weight loss over the past couple of weeks. "You're thin."

"Annie," Gray said, "if you tell me not to go, I'll stay right here."

"That's hardly fair." Annie sat in front of the bureau mirror and brushed through her long, dark hair. Gray watched her for a little while before speaking.

"I guess I don't understand."

"Don't understand what?"

"What you meant by 'hardly fair,'" he answered, with confusion in his voice.

Annie spun toward him. "It's hardly fair for you to make me the one who prevents you from helping her. I suppose knowing you would have helped her, except 'Annie wouldn't let me' comforts you." She laid the hairbrush on the dresser. "I understand you are torn between doing what you think is right or staying home with your family, which is also right, but don't put the decision off on me. I don't want to carry that burden. If you're so upset about this, why didn't you come to me and ask what you should do? Why didn't you talk to me?"

Gray turned pale, "I thought I did."

"You thought you did? You didn't come to me and ask to discuss it. You told me, sitting at the kitchen table, before you left to find Paints His Horse, to 'decide'; you put all the responsibility on me. Nothing can be your fault. Susan Tucker couldn't blame you; I'd be at fault." Annie again picked up the brush and turned back toward the mirror. "Well, I don't want to be the one who decides whether those kids live or die, or worse."

She ripped the brush through her hair. Gray thought she

was going to tear her brown hair out at the roots. "Annie, I didn't mean to put everything on you. I thought you were for this." He sat on the bed, "I didn't want to do the wrong thing in your eyes." Annie stopped brushing her hair and studied Gray's reflection. "I don't know what to do."

"Neither do I, Gray. Neither do I."

The two sat for several minutes. Finally, Annie spoke. "Do you think those children and the woman are still alive?"

Gray shrugged, stood, and limped to the window. "If they kidnapped them to sell them into prostitution, they're still alive. If they took them for their personal pleasure, they're dead by now."

"I don't want you to go." Annie turned to face him, exhaled. "But, if we ever intend to grow a worthwhile country out here, someone has to fight for what's right. We won't win the battles if we don't care about each other or help each other. We'd be," she said, dabbing a little perfume on her neck before standing and looking at her husband, "no more than common cowards. I've no regard for a coward." She slipped her arm around Gray's waist. "I just wish Graham, it didn't always have to be you."

Gray Wehr wrapped the woman he loved in his arms. He enjoyed her smell, the soft, warm way she felt. "Why don't we tell her we'll give the search one month? I think that's fair to her."

Chapter Thirty-Two

Burns The Grass slipped back into camp before the dawn revealed his coming. Jack Walker had been awake for two hours and resented how the Cheyenne crept in. Walker did not trust many of the men he rode with; they had little loyalty and would turn on anyone if they thought they'd benefit. But even among men who were not trustworthy, Walker considered the renegade less reliable. When he first picked up Burns The Grass, he had decided he would not hesitate to kill him the first time the Indian gave him any doubt or cause for concern.

"What did you find?" Walker growled, startling the Indian.

"I thought you were asleep."

"Well, I ain't."

"A ranch two hours southwest. Three women and two female children."

"How many men?"

"Two, and a boy old enough to fight."

"Flatland or hills?"

"Plains," he grunted. "You should know the land better."

The Indians crack made Walker's blood boil. "How far from town are they located?"

"They couldn't run for help," Burns The Grass said insolently.

Walker scowled at the Cheyenne. *Damn you. I ought to put a bullet in you, you brash sonuvabitch.* But he would wait until he had no more use for the renegade.

Walker kicked Carter Cline. "Wake up!" He abused Cline because the petty thief was the least dangerous of his gang. Bill Beachum or the Fox brothers might have fought over a kick in the ass.

"What'd you want to git up so early for?" Cline grumbled as he sat up out of his bedroll.

"The injun's back. He found some women I may be interested in." Walker threw four logs on the dying campfire and stirred the coals around with his foot. "Wake the woman up; tell her to cook something. Hey, Camp? You awake yet?"

"I am. We got any coffee?"

"Not hot," Walker said. "The fire will be going here in a minute."

"Let the girls sleep," Lucy Carlyle pleaded with Cline after he jerked her blanket off her. "They can't travel without some rest."

"They'll go when we tell them to," Cline said in an emotionless voice, adding, "or they'll end up the same way that other kid of yours did."

Cline was no taller than she was and didn't outweigh her by more than a few pounds. He was wearing a ratty plaid vest and an old pair of tan pants hanging on him like a gunny sack. A derby hat added to his ridiculous appearance. Lucy thought if given half a chance, she'd whip this runt. She decided if the opportunity came, she would put a knife between his ribs.

Lucy picked through the pack on the old mule carrying their food and blankets as the other men stirred. She pulled out a slab of bacon and almost commented about running low on provisions. No, she'd keep quiet, hope they'd all starve to death.

"If you want those kids to eat, you'd better be waking them up," Bert Camp told her. When Lucy patted the girls, they climbed out of the bedrolls without complaining. Maddie, the older child, did say the morning was cold but neither cried nor made any fuss.

"We'll hit the ranch the Indian found by late morning and be skinned out of the area by noon," Walker said.

"We need to pack some supplies," Camp mentioned offhandedly.

"I'll be glad to have some fresh women," Bob Fox bellowed, so Lucy would be sure to hear. "One female is getting a little stale."

Rod McFain

Chapter Thirty-Three

"I gave you mare a long look when we were in town buying supplies, and I've been paying close attention to her since we've been on the trail," Gabe told Gray. "She's sure a nice animal."

Wehr patted the side of the bay's neck. "I doubt I'll ever own a better one than Lena here."

"We're making good time," Trent said. "We'll hit the Crazy Woman in another hour. Do you suppose those fellas over to the east will ride on in when we stop at the creek?" he asked, glancing over at Gray.

"We'll wait and let them do whatever they plan on doing. We'll have the water to guard our backs."

"What men?" Del asked anxiously.

"They're over on the horizon," Trent answered, motioning with his head. "They've been tagging us for the best part of half a day now."

"I hadn't seen them either," Gabe said. "What do you think they want?"

"Can't say." Gray sounded unconcerned.

"Do you think they mean to do us harm?" Gabe asked.

"Can't say."

"Can you tell how many there are?" Tom Gibbs asked as he peered at the eastern horizon. "I don't see them."

"Six or seven. They're trying not to show themselves," Gray said, glancing to the east.

"Do you think they're the ones we're after?" Del scoured the direction where the men were riding.

"Can't be sure," Trent said. "They're not leading any horses. So, I don't think they are pulling captives."

"What if they never approach us?" Tom asked. "What if they ride on by when we stop at the river?"

"I'll be disappointed," Gray said. "I wouldn't like having them out in front of me and not knowing where, or at least who they are."

"Maybe they're just riding along the same direction we're going," Gabe said.

Gray never understood why some men wanted to ignore it when danger approached. He preferred to confront things on his terms as much as possible to define the rules. Ignoring things rarely worked out. In this land, disregarding potential trouble might get you killed.

"Don't you think they might be riding in the same direction by coincidence?"

"Could be." Gray smiled at Trent. Not much of a smile, a wry little one barely bending the corners of his mouth. "Could also be Methodist missionaries, but I doubt it," he chuckled.

"The question is," Trent said, "what are they doing out here, coming from the north? There's not much there except Sioux land. They've no business there."

"Maybe they're lost," Del said.

Trent sighed. "Why wouldn't they come over and ask for help?"

The Wehr party reached the Crazy Woman River less than an hour later. They rode about a quarter of a mile downriver to a grove of trees, where they tied their horses and unpacked enough food for a quick meal. "Don't start a fire," Gray said. "I don't want them to think we're planning on bedding down here. Hopefully, they'll come on in if they think we're moving on."

"Come on in?" Del said. "I hope they don't come at all."

Trent chuckled and patted the boy on the shoulder.

Gray and Trent ate jerky and sourdough, not showing a concern in the world. Tom Gibbs and the Reeds had no appetite. After about twenty minutes, the riders, seven of them, started working their way down the river bank toward the trees.

"They're sure not in a hurry," Trent said humorously.

"I bet they'd be surprised if we mounted up and rode off," Gray said.

"I think that's a good idea," Del said.

"You recognize any of them?" Gray asked Trent as they got closer.

"Strangers to me."

The strangers rode into their camp and remained on their horses.

"Afternoon, boys," Gray was confident in situations like this. He believed men who came looking for trouble had inherent flaws, which made them vulnerable to anyone who maintained a cool head. Gray had proven to himself he had the ability.

"We wondered if you might have any coffee," the tall ugly man in the center of the group said.

"Sorry, we stopped to eat a little jerky. Aren't even building a fire."

"Well, our bad luck," the same man replied. "We had a cold camp last night. Concern over the Sioux, you know."

"I believe most of them are a little further north," Trent said. "I wouldn't worry much about starting a fire."

"Humph, I guess you're a brave fella," the second man from the left said, shifting in his saddle.

"Suppose you boys would share a little food?" The fat, sweaty man in the middle, the group's leader, asked.

"Well, again, we're sorry, but we've only got enough to get us where we're going," Gray said. "The game out here's plentiful. You shouldn't have any trouble kicking up a meal."

The man doing all the talking put both hands around the saddle horn and leaned forward. "Well, now, you folks is plum unsociable. The Christian thing would be to share your bounty. Don't you think so, Luke?"

"Only Christian thing to do, John."

John was not only tall; he was an enormous man, almost too much for the horse he was riding. He ran his hand over his unshaven, dirty face, pushed his thumb against his nose, and blew snot on the ground. He had a Navy Colt hanging on a strip of rawhide looped around his neck and another revolver holstered on his hip.

"Well, since you aren't willing to share, we'll have to help ourselves."

"Stepping off your horse or reaching for one of those shooters would be foolish," Trent said when John shifted his weight.

"Foolish?" John laughed. "You fellas is outnumbered, and in all humility, well…we're sort of professionals at this." Two men grunted before one spit out a stream of tobacco. "Now you can give us what we want," John said through a smile revealing his tobacco-stained and rotting teeth, "or we can kill you and take everything." He glanced around at his companions. "Hell, boys, if they're generous, we might leave them a few scraps. What'd you think?"

"Well, do you think we should do as we're told? As the man says, we 'is' outnumbered," Trent said. "And he looks like a tough man."

"He's not tough, Trent. He needs a bath. Filth is often confused for toughness," Gray said.

John's face reddened as rage surged through him. "You must be in a hurry to die, mister."

155

Gray didn't as much as flinch. "You'll be dying. The two of us will kill three of you each before the first one has time to hit the ground. Only be one left. You boys might want to think that over."

Two of the other men did. "Oh, hell, John," the smaller one said, "Jerky and sourdough biscuits ain't worth being shot up over."

"Shut up, you yella piece of crap." John glared at Gray with blood in his eyes. "I'm gonna kill you now."

Gray's face turned icy. "Mister, you talk too damn much."

Infuriated, John grabbed the pistol hanging from the rawhide strip. Del wet himself. Gray's Navy Colt cracked.

"Uhhhh," the brutish man moaned as the force of the bullet sent him somersaulting off the back of the horse.

Trent Thaxton fired over the heads of the others. "Now sit still before somebody else gets hurt."

Wehr stepped around the spooked horse, now riderless. He jerked the Colt from the fat man's neck and threw it in the creek. He took the other pistol and did the same.

"Now, the rest of you toss your guns in the river. And be sure you throw 'em way out," Trent yelled. "Rifles, too," he said when two of them hesitated.

"Aw, damn boy, these are new weapons. We haven't had them a month."

"We couldn't catch up to you. Not while John's got such a hole blowed in him," the other one said.

Trent glanced over at Gray, who kind of shrugged. "Well, hand them down here to me." The two men handed the Springfields down to Trent, who unloaded them and tossed the ammunition into the river. He took both guns and drove the barrels down into the soft dirt along the bank. "I wouldn't shoot them until you've given them a thorough cleaning," he said, "or you'll blow 'em up."

"A couple of you climb down and shove your pal back on his horse," Gray ordered.

"Hell, mister, he's hurt bad," the first one down said.

"If we try to ride off with him, it'll likely kill him."

"He was warned," Gray growled. "He's lucky he's not dead."

Three of the men pushed their oversized friend up in his saddle. He slumped down over the horse's neck and groaned as they led him away. "If we come across you again, we'll kill the lot of you," Gray hollered as they left.

Two hours south, Del asked Trent if Gray meant what he said. "Will he kill those men if we run across them again?"

"I'll tell you, boy," Trent said, "Ten years ago, he'd have killed them the first time."

Chapter Thirty-Four

"One man and a boy are out behind the barn. I don't know where the other man is," Carl Fox said, rejoining the others on a bluff about a quarter mile from the ranch house after spending the last several minutes creeping around the homestead trying to locate the whereabouts of the family.

"What about women?" Bert Camp asked. "Did you find them?"

"Must be in the house, but I couldn't sneak up to a window without being seen."

The house was built on one floor, constructed piecemeal. Three sides were log, and the front was a combination of logs and river rock. The windows had heavy wood shutters with crosses cut into each for moving a rifle up and down or side to side. Penetrating the house would be a difficult task if defenders locked themselves inside.

"Those two are fixin' to climb up on the barn," Carl, the larger and older Fox brother, said. "Draggin' shingles up."

"Now, won't this be easy," Walker quipped, wiping tobacco spit from his chin. "Camp, you go find a spot to shoot. Let us ride down a couple hundred yards from the house, then knock those two off the roof; the rest of us will charge the house. We'll take 'em before they know what hit 'em."

The men slipped back down the bluff to the little stream where they left Carter Cline guarding the horses and the Carlyle's.

"Cline, you stay here with the woman and her pups," Camp ordered the little petty thief.

"Why don't you leave one of them brothers or the damn Indian? There might be something in the house I'd be interested in. Or, hell, tie 'em up, and we can all go."

"'Cause I told you to watch 'em," Camp snarled. "And if I tell you to do something, by gawd, you will."

Cline did not respond; he walked over and sat on a fair-sized rock next to where Lucy was sitting with Maddie and Jenny. When the others mounted and rode off toward the little homestead, Cline stood and gave Lucy Carlyle a hard kick. "You give me any trouble, you whore, and you and them brats'll die sufferin'."

"You won't kill us," Lucy said, scooting out in front of her children. "If you did, Walker would kill you."

Cline started to kick the woman again but instead said, "You ain't worth the effort." The woman was right. If Walker or Camp decided he abused her more than suited them, they might run one of their long-bladed knives through his middle.

Camp found a little ridge about two hundred yards from the barn, a perfect place for him to hide. As he slipped down behind a clump of brush, he checked what the two homesteaders were doing. *You fools. You should've looked around the area, not just go to work putting shingles up. A lot of good a new roof is to dead men.*

He glanced over at Walker and the others. They were getting close to the house, closer than Camp would have liked. He flipped up the rear sight on his repeater, a rifle taken from a cavalry lieutenant who likely purchased the weapon at his own expense. Having adjusted the site, he eased his grimy finger to the trigger.

Camp took as much pleasure in killing as other men would in their most significant accomplishments. Jack Walker would kill a man, woman, or child if they had something he coveted or if he thought there might be a profit. But Bert Camp—he killed for pure enjoyment.

The rifle cracked, breaking the stillness of the beautiful fall day. The man did not hear the shot; he dropped over dead, half of his head missing. His son didn't grasp what happened. A tow-headed boy about fourteen, he jumped at the loud noise. When his father fell face-first on the roof, he plain froze.

Bert Camp remembered fear doing this to people before. Man or woman, brave or cowardly, Camp had seen people paralyzed by dread. A damn stupid reaction, in his opinion. But he always enjoyed toying with scared men—or children.

Camp chuckled out loud. "Sit still, boy. I'll have a little fun." The killer took careful aim and put his second shot only two inches from the boy's foot. The helpless boy lurched away when the bullet ripped a hole through the shingles.

"Where you goin', boy?" Camp muttered as he aimed again. This time, he shot the youngster's kneecap. He screamed a terrible, animal-like scream as the impact knocked him over to the left. Grabbing his leg, he lost his balance on the barn. As he slid down, Camp laughed to himself. "He's gonna fall right off."

The boy was close to the edge when he realized what was happening. He grabbed for something to stop himself.

There was nothing to grab. The burning pain in his left knee and the momentum of sliding down the steep roof would have prevented him from holding anything anyway. Nothing could be done. His fall was almost graceful. His arms stretched out like he was going to fly.

He hit on his feet, crumpled hard probably breaking both ankles, and for a moment or two, did not move. Camp first thought the drop killed him, but the boy began lurching around like some crippled animal. "Hell, boy, wiggle around so I can blow your blame head off. I'll fix you so that damn Indian won't have any scalps today."

The suffering young man struggled and agonized for another full minute before Camp decided he wasn't going to oblige him with a clear head shot. Camp aimed for the middle of the boy's back and squeezed the trigger. His body hurled forward before he died, face down in the dust.

When Bert Camp's rifle split the morning, the others charged the house. The front door swung open as Bill Beachum jumped from his still running mount. He shot the man coming out. The bullet went clear through him and lodged in the door facing. Jack Walker and the Fox brothers burst into the house where the women and children became hysterical.

"Shut up!" Walker bellowed as he cuffed one of the terrified women across the face. "Shut the hell up!" The other woman slapped and clawed at him as he fought to subdue her. "Git them other females!" he ordered the Foxs.

Another woman grabbed a huge kitchen knife as Bob Fox hurled himself at her. She slashed at him, cutting a deep gash across his forearm and chest. He unleashed a barrage of profanity as he tackled the woman. "I ought to slit your throat!"

"You don't cut her!" Walker shouted.

"She sliced me!" Bob, the smaller of the Fox brothers,

wrestled the weapon from the little woman, unable to put up much of a fight. He drew the knife back, but before plunging the blade forward, a bullet sang past his ear.

"I told you not to cut her!" Bob Fox spun toward Walker, who had his dragoon aimed right at his chest. "Don't cut her!"

Fox threw the butcher knife across the room and shoved the crying woman out of the cabin. Carl Fox and Walker dragged the other two women out. "Git those kids," Walker yelled at Beachum and Burns The Grass as he finished scalping the dead man on the porch. "There's two girls and a boy. Kill the boy."

"No! Don't hurt him." One woman screamed as she fought to free herself from Walker's grasp. "No! No!"

Walker cracked the side of her head with his revolver, and she lost consciousness. "Burn this place down," Walker ordered the younger Fox as he and the other men threw the unconscious woman and frantic children up across their saddles. Bob Fox stared at Walker. "I said, burn the place," Walker repeated with his cold eyes bearing down on the cut-up man.

Fox started the fire.

"Go git some of those horses out of the corral," he snarled at the Indian. "We sure ain't gonna ride double."

Chapter Thirty-Five

"There's a little stream about an hour from here," Gray said. "It'll make a suitable place to spend the night." The late afternoon temperature was dropping, common on the plains at this time of year. Gray reached back and untied a brown duster from behind his saddle. "I think tonight's going to be a little nippy," he said to Trent as he slipped on the coat.

"Makes you wish you were home in a warm bed," Trent said.

An hour after supper, Tom Gibbs and the Reeds fell asleep in their bedrolls. Gray and Trent sat next to the fire, drinking up the last of the evening's coffee. "Do you think we've much chance to find these people?" Trent asked in a somber voice.

At first, Gray did not respond. He stretched out his legs and pressed down on his knees, something he did when they ached. "I hope we find them. I'd like to take what's left of Susan's family back for her, but this bunch needs stopping."

Gray ostensibly made the journey as a favor to the Carlyle woman, but he carried a strong sense of right and wrong. Wehr believed in what they were building out here,

163

far away from civilization back east. He thought they were doing something worthwhile for the country, and some things were worth fighting for. Men like the ones they were chasing needed dealing with, and Gray figured handling them was up to the people with a stake in the land.

"I hope the sheriff in Cheyenne knows something."

"Millie says you were close to Susan's brother," Trent said.

"I suppose Danny was my best friend when we were kids," Gray said, choosing his words. "Danny, he didn't always make friends easily. Sometimes he had a little trouble getting people to like him." Gray thought back to the childhood mischief he and Danny carried out. "When we were eight or nine years old, he was a rough customer, and he didn't have any qualms about beating somebody up. He bloodied my nose," Gray laughed. "But by the time we turned twelve or thirteen, Danny wasn't as big as most of us. He took a few paybacks for a couple of years."

Trent glanced over at Del, flailing about in his bedroll. "I think he's been having nightmares. "Getting scalped every night."

"I guess I was kind of the one kid who stuck with Danny. Later on, he got sickly." Gray remembered back. His friend would be bedridden for weeks at a time. He kept losing weight and struggled to catch his breath. "One Sunday morning, his mother went in to wake him for church and found him dead in bed. Not long after, I left High Meadows for the first time."

The town folks said Gray had wanderlust. Whatever it was, Gray came and went for twenty years. A time when he proved himself more than competent with a gun.

Del moaned again. Gray stood and walked over to where Del was tossing and moaning in his sleep. He bent down and shook the boy's shoulders. "Del, Del, wake up a minute." The young man jerked and sat halfway up. "You must be having a nightmare," Gray said, smiling at the boy.

"Indians were chasing me. Sure was real."

Chapter Thirty-Six

"We should make Cheyenne by tomorrow night," Trent said, "if we don't freeze first."

"I doubt we'll freeze to death this time of year," Gray said.

For the past two days, the weather had turned ugly. Dark rainy skies refused to give way to any sunshine. Hoarfrost covered the brush and grass the last three mornings. Instead of warming up as the day wore on, it grew colder.

"I hate the thought of cold weather. I guess I'm just cold-natured. Worse, I don't think Laura can care for the cattle if winter hits before we're home," Gabe said to Del.

Del shook his head. "Now there's something new to worry about. I'm already scared of being shot, freezing to death, or being swept down the Powder River."

Wehr stepped up the pace of the group's travel over the

previous few days. He was now riding at a trot or light lope as much of the time as the horses could bear, something displeasing to Tom Gibbs, whose horse had a stiff trot and disagreeable canter until he stretched out to a full gallop.

An ache deepened in Gibbs's back with each passing mile and more demanding pace. He thought once or twice of asking Wehr to slow down to a walk for a while. He did not comprehend the necessity of trotting. Lucy and the children had been missing for such an extended time. What difference would an hour or two, or a couple of days, make at this stage of the rescue?

But Wehr did not ease up. He turned dogged in his pursuit of Cheyenne as if he thought any news of the kidnapping might blow away on a strong wind. Lena, his bay mare, loved the fast pace.

She ran on and on, never breathing hard. Like Pegasus, she flew through the sagebrush and over gullies. Sundance, Trent's bay gelding, was equally energetic. Shorty, Del Reed's chestnut, also enjoyed the rapid pace, much more than his rider. Gibbs continually spurred his paint to keep from dragging behind.

In the late afternoon, from the crown of a hill, they caught a glimpse of the Powder River. A slow, chilly rain had been falling for the past hour, soaking men and horses.

"Let's push right on across," Gray said. "We'll start a fire on the other side if we can find any dry wood."

"I'm already wet and miserable. It can't get much worse," Del said.

Gray's *if* was troublesome to Tom. Did he mean if they couldn't find firewood, they would continue riding? The afternoon was freezing, and the sun would be down in another hour, meaning the temperature would drop still lower.

"Isn't she the horse you had the accident on, 'cause she wouldn't cross water?" Tom asked, hoping Wehr might think about the problem and stop for the night on this side of the Powder, a foolish action since they'd be getting wet again in the morning.

"I was trying to make her go through a bog," Gray said. "Lena, she's a river crosser."

Del's eyes bounced up and down the river's edge. The current was not menacing, not the way he feared, no boiling rapids, just murky water meandering through miserable weather. His courage took a slight jump.

Gray and Trent urged their horses out into the water, with neither animal raising any fuss. Del did not want to be the last man in, so he gave his chestnut a fair-sized kick. "Come on, Shorty." Shorty leaped in, with Gabe and Tom following along. None of the five men had any trouble crossing, much to Del's relief. He would have no more icy rivers to cross before making Cheyenne and a dry, warm bed.

"Let's put a cover up and build a fire before these wet clothes freeze hard," Gabe said as he shivered. "I've never been so cold in my life."

Gray and Trent unpacked the tarp and sat up a lean-to while the other three gathered the driest wood they could find. Within an hour, the men stripped off their outfits and put on dry ones. They huddled inside the makeshift shelter, hoping a stiff wind would not rob them of it. "Kick my butt, and call me Charlotte." Gray looked around. "Isn't this a pleasant place to spend an evening?"

The rain turned to sleet at about two in the morning and continued until two hours before dawn. All five men were more than pleased for the sun to rise.

"We'll sleep in beds tonight," Gray said, smiling at Del, "unless you'd rather camp outside of town."

Del assured Gray a bed would be fine with him.

Gabe had not been careful enough about getting his spare clothes into a spot where they would stay dry, and now he wore a pair of damp pants, which chaffed his hind end raw by the time they stopped for a noon meal. "What time do you expect us to hit town?" Gabe asked.

"Sometime around dusk, I'd guess," Trent said. "We can make Cheyenne faster if you want to pick up the pace a little."

"Sundown will suffice," Reed said.

Dark came more than an hour before the five men rode into Cheyenne and checked into one of the local hotels. Each enjoyed a hot bath and headed to bed.

Chapter Thirty-Seven

Gray knocked on Trent's door at almost ten in the morning, irritated about sleeping so late. "How long you been up?" He asked when Trent came to the door.

"Couple of hours, I suppose."

"Why'd you let me sleep if you were up?"

"Well, no one else is up, and I promised Annie not to let you wear yourself out." He added with a bit of a laugh.

"I'm sure you did," Gray grunted. "Well, it's past time for breakfast, but I wouldn't mind some coffee. We may as well let the others sleep. They'll only be of limited help if they're alert and might get us killed if they're not."

Trent and Gray sat and drank coffee in the hotel dining room until almost eleven-thirty. "I swear, I guess those boys are never going to wake up," Gray said as he pulled out his pocket watch.

"I'll go up and roust them," Trent said, "I'll probably be politer about it. Fifteen minutes slipped by before Trent came back down.

"What'd you do, catch a catnap?" Gray asked in a tone

that could have been joking or irritated.

"The Reeds are heavy sleepers. Took a lot of pounding on the door."

Another half-hour passed, contributing to Gray's irritability before the remaining three men came down the stairs.

"You boys had eaten yet?" Tom Gibbs asked.

Gray cocked an eyebrow at him. "A bit late for breakfast. Let's head over to the sheriff's office and find out if he's going to be any help."

The office was about halfway across town, and Gray's humor didn't improve when they found the door locked.

"We could try the Blue Moon," Trent said.

"I guess I don't have any better idea."

"What's the Blue Moon?" Del asked.

"A saloon," Trent said. "Will we have any trouble keeping you out of the whiskey?"

Del laughed and shook his head. "Naw, I'm a beer man, myself."

"Any specific reason for going to that saloon?" Tom asked.

"We might know the barkeep," Gray said.

The saloon was about a third of the way down a street full of bars and gambling houses. "Hell, this ain't much different from Bismarck," Tom said.

The barroom was dark inside, and their eyes took a few minutes to adjust. An oversized picture of a large female hung over the bar.

"I believe she's new," Trent said. "I don't remember her from before."

The place stunk of beer and cheap whiskey; a pall of bluish smoke drifted under the ceiling. The bartender, who spoke with an Irish accent, likely tipped the scale at three hundred pounds.

"What'll it be, boys?"

"What's your recommendation, Pete?"

The fat man's eyes furrowed. "Well, by dogs, old Gray

Wehr." Pete stuck out a hand the size of a grizzly bear paw. "Good to see you," he said, giving Gray's hand a vigorous shake. "I see you're still traveling with this boy." He slapped Trent on the shoulder hard enough to knock him off balance. "You're looking healthy, boy, not as skinny as you used to be."

"Home cooking," Trent laughed.

"So, what brings you down here? Your women throw you out?"

"No, not yet," Gray said. "They may when we get back."

"Well, where's your whiskey drinkin' friend? What was his name, Zach, weren't it?"

"Oh, we left him home this time. He's not cut out for the work we're pursuing."

"Sounds like dark business," Pete said, laying down the rag he had been wiping glasses with.

"Pete," Wehr said, "any stories about a killing up in Bismarck pass through here? They killed a kid in his early twenties and kidnapped his wife and children."

Pete rested his burly arms on the bar. "Nothing about Bismarck. Dakota's a long way off, but something similar happened at a couple of remote ranches around here. Men were scalped and murdered, women and young kids taken, the places burned to the ground. Sound like the same bunch?"

"Close," Gray said. "Any idea who the scoundrels might be?"

"Jack Walker is what most people figure. If it is Walker, he'll be with a man named Camp." Pete spat a stream of tobacco juice at a spittoon. "If that's true, Gray, they're mighty sinful men."

"Hey, how about a little service down here?" A cowboy at the other end of the bar held up his empty glass.

"Wait a minute. I'm busy." Pete turned back to Gray. "They also say a renegade Indian is with 'em. He's likely the one doing the scalping. 'Course, I wouldn't be surprised if

Walker himself is cuttin' their heads open."

"Pete!" the cowboy yelled again.

"I told you, I'm talking to these men. Come around and grab a bottle." The puncher stepped around and picked out one; satisfied, he and his friends headed back to their card game. "Damn customers, they're more trouble than they're worth. What's got you after these fellas?"

"The boy they killed in Bismarck was the son of an old friend."

"The sheriff might be a little help. Probably not. You stop by his office?"

"We came from his place," Trent said. "All locked up with a sign on the door saying he'd be back mid-afternoon."

"Yeah, he's got him a recent widow he likes to delight at noontime. He ought to put up a note telling where he is. Everybody in town is gossiping about them. I can tell you where to locate the dove's house if you want to go find him."

"We're not in that much of a hurry," Gray said. "I kind of hate to interfere with a man's lunch pleasure. We'll eat something ourselves and head back to the sheriffs a little later."

"I can feed you right here. Got all sorts of sandwiches in the back room, even got pickled eggs."

"I thought we might head over to Annabelle's," Gray said. "The café still runnin'?"

"The café is, but a new woman runs the place. Annabelle died, oh, I guess, three years ago."

"Well, I'll swear," Gray said. "I'm sorry. The woman had a big heart."

"Everything about ol' Annabelle was big," Pete laughed. "Eat lunch here. I owe you. I never had any more problems with Bill, not after you whacked the side of his head. You and Trent'll both be free. 'Course I'm forced to charge your three friends here; they weren't part of your work."

The men went to the back room. Tom Gibbs ate three eggs, washing them down with a glass of beer. Del Reed almost got sick watching him.

Dan Taggert, the sheriff, showed up at his office at about half-past two. "I know you," he said to Gray. "I heard you were dead."

"Dead?"

"As a doornail. The story was some gunman backshot you in Colorado. 'Bout a year ago."

"Not hardly. I haven't been to Colorado in over six years. Who told you I was dead?"

"Oh, I couldn't tell you for sure. One of those rumors that sort of drifts by."

"Well, if it floats past again," Gray said, "I'll appreciate you putting a stop to it. I find it a little unsettling."

"Well, you're lively enough. What can I do for you?"

Gray sat in a chair across from the sheriff's desk.

"Well, you are shaken up about your killin'."

"What?"

"When a man's upset enough, he has to sit down; I call him shook."

Trent started laughing right out loud.

"Oh, shut up," Gray said to Trent. "I'm sitting down 'cause I've got a bum foot. Now, do you have any information or not?"

"What are you lookin' to find out?" Sheriff Taggert asked, leaning back in his chair and putting his feet on his desk. "You ought to elevate your lame foot. It'll reduce the swelling."

"They killed a young fella up in Bismarck," Gray said, a bit irritated. "They kidnapped his wife and children, burned his place to the ground. We understand something similar happened around here."

"About two months ago," Tom Gibbs said.

"Been short of two weeks since the killings down here. I suspect Jack Walker. Ever hear of him?"

"Nothing good about him," Gray said.

"You're damn right; nothing good about him," Taggert said. "He's a mean S.O.B., and he's done this kind of thing before. From what I understand, he hauls hostages south where he sells 'em for a right tidy sum."

"What's the law doing about him?" Gabe asked.

"The law? The law in this country is too scared to go after him, even if they could catch him in their jurisdiction. I can't blame 'em either. None of us would be a match for a man like him." Taggert turned away from Gabe and back at Gray. "You better be skilled if you go after Walker."

"Where down south?" Gray asked.

"Anything I would say would be speculation, but maybe down around Louisiana. Them Cajuns, they're an immoral bunch. And New Orleans is nothing but a horde of Frenchies, gamblers, and thieves."

"How many captives did they take from the two ranches around here?" Gabe asked.

"I believe seven. Two women and three girls in their mid-teens. Two young children, both girls."

"I doubt they'll travel too fast having women and children in tow," Trent said. "If we push hard, we might catch up to them before Boulder."

"Boys, if you start after these men, I'll take the liberty to give you one piece of advice. You kill 'em before asking them to surrender."

Gray paused outside the sheriff's office. "I don't think they'll head to Boulder. I think they'll move east, away from the mountains." He stepped off the porch and on Lena. "It's backtracking, but I think we should swing through Yellow Bird. The place is a haven for men like Walker. If we don't find out anything there, we may as well give up."

Yellow Dog, a pitiful excuse for a settlement, never amounted to much more than a few poorly constructed buildings. The town stayed in existence only because of its remote location on the Platte River, providing the only shelter for about four days in any direction. Given its location, the tiny town might have prospered if its residents were not so tolerant of gamblers, drifters, and other malcontents.

Chapter Thirty-eight

Jack Walker's outfit now had fourteen hostages in tow.

"We got too many kids. They require constant watching, and the little brats are more trouble than they're worth. We ain't never gonna make the Arkansas River if we stop every thirty minutes for one of them blame brats to crap," Carter Cline said. "We oughta leave 'em. Hell, they won't be worth anything. Why do you want to drag them along?"

Weary of Carter Cline and his constant bellyaching, Walker contemplated doing him in. He would have shot him days earlier if he didn't need all the men to guard the captives. "They'll bring some money," Walker said. He gave Cline a hateful scowl. "Some is more than none." Walker glared at the children who were riding double, huddled together against the wind. "Any more of you have to answer nature's call? If so, you better go now; otherwise, you'll ride wet and dirty." One of the teenage girls they kidnapped north of Cheyenne slid off her horse and headed for the far side of a tree.

"I figure we pick up two or three more women and head for Nebraska," Walker said to Bert Camp. "We'll make a fair profit."

"A fair profit? Camp snorted. "It's all profit. That's how I like doing business.

Walker, aggravated, twisted around in his saddle. "Damn Indian oughta been back by now." Walker, displeased with the renegade's behavior, leaned toward Camp. "I'm gonna kill that petty thief and Cheyenne when we make the Arkansas River," he whispered at Camp. Camp glanced over at Cline, rolling a cigarette. "Two hours 'til dark," Walker said. "If we run across a homestead, we'll sleep indoors for a change." Walker pulled his pistol out of his belt and aimed at the tree hiding the young girl. He fired one shot, hitting the trunk on the left side and sending bark flying. "Hurry up! You've been long enough."

Walker led his band of malcontents and hostages at a stiff pace until dark fell. Having not found any ranch or homestead, they would have to spend another night sleeping outside. The Fox brothers went off looking for something to shoot for supper while Bill Beachum started gathering firewood. He ordered the woman named Meg Brown to pack every stick and limb he picked up.

Captivity grew easier for Lucy Carlyle after the kidnapping of the others. While the persecution hadn't stopped, with more women, the abuse became less frequent. Beachum, who abused Lucy the hardest, took a liking to Meg, and although not proud of her feelings, Lucy couldn't help but hope Meg survived and continued to draw some of Beachum's attention.

Carl Fox, who shot most of the food, threw a couple of dead jackrabbits at her. "Skin 'em!"

"With what?" Lucy asked.

Fox stared down at the battered woman. He reached down to his boot and pulled out an old skinning knife. He turned it over in his hand several times before tossing it in Lucy's lap. "Here," he half-grunted, "but be damn sure you only cut rabbit. Otherwise, I'll slit your skinny white throat."

Lucy studied the knife. If she was quick enough, she might stick Fox before he could react. If she weren't, though, he would kill her, and Maddie and Jenny. Lucy picked up the rabbit and cleaned the evening meal.

Carter Cline came walking past the Carlyle girls on his way back from tethering the horses. "What are you looking at?" he snapped at Jenny. The little girl who had not spoken for weeks tried to huddle down in an old torn blanket. He snarled at her and gave her a hard kick. "Worthless brat!"

Lucy Carlyle flew into a blind, fiery rage. Leaping to her feet and shrieking, she held the knife over her head as she charged Cline. The dingy thief only got halfway turned around toward her before she struck the first blow. The blade glanced off his collarbone and across his throat. With blood spurting all over her, she stabbed again but hit his breastbone without enough force to penetrate his chest.

"What the hell?" Jack Walker hollered, scrambling to his feet. "Somebody git hold of her!"

Bill Beachum was the closest, but he couldn't stop her from slashing Cline with the knife two more times, once cutting a deep gash from his shoulder to hip. The last effort skipped off one of his ribs and into his side.

Beachum struck Lucy on the back of her head with his pistol and sent her sprawling to the ground. Still full of fight, she whirled back toward Cline, only to be kicked hard in the chest by Beachum, a bull of a man, who caught her under her chin with another blow from his revolver. Lucy's jawline burst open with blood splattering across Beachum's face. Beachum now turned back to Cline, who crumpled into a pile next to the fire.

"How did she get a knife?" Walker asked. "How the hell did she have a knife?" he bellowed again.

"I gave the damn thing to her," Fox said, not cowering down to Walker. "She needed something to clean the rabbits with."

Walker crushed Fox across the face with the back of his right hand. "You dumb sonuvabitch. I ought to kill you." Fox reached up and rubbed the back of his hand across his mouth. He licked at the blood on his lip, but he did not reply. Walker was dangerous, but Fox didn't think Walker would kill him over Carter Cline. He was dependable, and Walker couldn't afford to lose too many men. "You damn fool," Walker said as he stomped away to examine the damage Lucy inflicted on Cline.

Without a word, he walked up to Cline and ripped the runt's shirt open, revealing the slashes through his chest and torso. Lucy was close enough to view the results of her attack. She had not killed him, but she hurt him. She thought he might bleed to death. She hoped he would die painfully.

Cline was blubbering like a child, the gutless little coward.

"Shut up!" Walker yelled.

Cline pulled his shirt away. "Look how she's cut me up! The whore cut me up."

"You're right about that," Walker said. "You'll be no account now. Hell, you never were, to begin with."

"I'm gonna kill her," Cline said, still sniveling.

"You ain't killing anybody, you piece of crap."

Bert Camp peered at the deep, nasty gashes. "He's a bloody mess. He'll be worthless for a couple of weeks or more if he lives at all."

Walker shook his head at Cline and growled something at Camp. "Beachum," Walker said. "Drag this runt away and finish what she's started. He's no damn use to us now."

Cline's blubbering turned to uncontrollable sobbing as the dirty little man thrashed in Beachum's grip, pleading for his worthless life. But the begging did not affect Beachum or any of the others, except Fox. He gave her the knife, but he had no say in the matter and no way to profit by getting involved.

Lucy enjoyed Beachum dragging the petty thief, screaming and crying, away from the campsite. He was taking him a long way because the bawling grew fainter. When a single gunshot split the chilly night air, a sense of satisfaction settled over her. She wasn't afraid when Jack Walker threatened to kill her if she ever did something like that again. The lack of fear in her eyes dissatisfied Walker.

"Did you hear me, woman? Do it again, and I'll slice you crotch to throat, right after you watch me cut open them pups of yours."

Lucy scooted away, her expression convincing Walker she understood his threats. Understood but no longer feared.

Chapter Thirty-Nine

It amazed Tom Gibbs how little sleep Gray required. He understood how someone as young as Trent pushed so hard without wearing out, but Wehr was middle-aged, older than he was, and the pace wore him out. The days warmed up after leaving Cheyenne, but the nights were getting colder. Gibbs wished they would find a ranch where they might offer at least a night in a barn and a hot meal. Sleeping in a hayloft, though unpleasant, would be a welcome treat compared to the cold, hard, and often wet ground.

On their third day out of Cheyenne, they found one of the burnt-out ranches Pete and Sheriff Taggert mentioned

"Looks like the same work to me," Gabe said.

Gray, who didn't talk too much, became quieter, more intense. The depression and self-doubts, which haunted him returned to torment his sleep. Trent recognized the distress in his friend but doubted anyone else would. When the time

came, Gray would push aside any self-doubt, all worries, and he would act. He would do what was necessary.

Trent stopped his horse on the top of the knoll and studied the modest ranch. A sizable stream ran behind the house, and a well-built barn stood off to the left. Trent turned back toward the others and waved his hat back and forth.

"The rest of you stay here," Gray said after they reached the crown of the hill. "I'll ride in and find out if these folks can tell us anything."

"Why don't we all go?" Tom asked. "They might give us a hot meal."

"Is that what you'd do?" Gray asked Gibbs. "If you lived out here all alone and some of your neighbors had been killed and kidnapped, and five strange men come riding in, you'd offer them dinner?" Gray stopped, waiting for Gibbs to respond, but the newspaper reporter said nothing. "I'd be more inclined to shoot you."

Gray untied his faded bandana and wiped some of the day's sweat and dirt off his face before starting Lena down the knoll. He studied fifteen or twenty nice-looking horses grazing off to the south as he rode to the little homestead. Two men were chopping wood when Gray approached. "Afternoon," he called out, thinking the men were poor in their observation skills, letting someone ride right up the way they did. Gray's voice startled the younger man, who jumped. "Easy," Gray said, "I didn't mean to scare you."

The older man, about Gray's age, glanced over at the rifle leaning against the side of the house, measuring the odds of getting to the weapon before the stranger pulled his gun. "You're welcome to pick up your rifle if you'll be more comfortable," Gray said. He sat his horse in a relaxed manner. His shoulders slumped, unthreatening. "My name is Gray Wehr. I mean you no harm."

"Gray Wehr, you say, I heard of you. I wouldn't have

much chance of reaching my weapon if you didn't want me to." He stared for a moment or two before walking over toward Gray and sticking his hand out. "Name's Charlie McClain," he said as Gray leaned down to shake his hand. "We're a little spooked around here. Been some harm done to some ranches in this area."

McClain's handshake was firm, in fact, hard, something Gray always thought indicated an honest man. "Step on down; let your mare rest her back awhile."

Gray stepped down and nodded to the other man, who continued to keep his distance. "My son, Tom," McClain said. The young man did not walk over any closer.

"The trouble you mentioned," Gray said, "You mean ranches burnt?"

"Most people figure the Cheyenne are to blame; they've been getting' ornery. Bold, too. Roman Nose, he's the problem. The Sioux, though, haven't been around much. I guess they're stayin' on their lands up north; 'course, rumors have them raiding over in Nebraska." McClain walked over and lifted a dipper full of water out of a wooden bucket sitting in the barn's shade. "Others suspect a white man named Walker. Ever hear of him?" He asked as he offered the dipper to Gray.

"Some," Gray said before taking a drink of water. "I guess he's capable of such things."

"Well, Indian or white, they're a vicious bunch," McClain said. "They burn the places down, murder the men, and carry off the women. Some children are taken. They kill some of them. Fine folks too," he added, almost as an afterthought.

"Who do you suspect?" Gray asked, not because Charlie McClain's opinion mattered much, but out of idle curiosity.

"Well, you hate to think a white man would be so cruel," Charlie said. "But in my experience regarding meanness, the Indians got no monopoly on such business."

"I've seen a lot of mean white men," Gray said. "I'm

sure these are white."

Surprise showed on McClain's face.

"There are four men with me," Gray said. "They're waiting up on the hill in front of your place. We've been after the ones who've been doing this."

McClain's head jerked around. "This bunch needs chasing, but what's got you after them? You relation to one of those families?"

"No, not these folks, but this started up around Bismarck. They burned out the family of an old friend of mine. We're trying to get her daughter-in-law and grandchildren back for her."

"How long you been chasing them?"

"Couple of weeks, I suppose," Gray said, not worried about being precise.

"So, is it Walker?" McClain asked.

"Well, I can't say for sure, but it's white men. The sheriff in Cheyenne thinks Walker's the one."

"How many men you say you got with you?"

"Four. If you have no objections, I'll wave to them to come down."

"Go ahead."

Trent and the others started down the hill toward the ranch. "Maybe they'll offer us a hearty meal." Gibbs was obsessed with having a filling meal

Del snickered. "You practiced gluttony in Casper. I'm surprised you don't weigh 300 pounds."

"I guess I burn my food off faster than most people," Tom said. "Some people get fat, eating hardly anything. Other people like me; we can eat all we want and never gain an ounce."

Trent knew people like that. His father ate enormous amounts and didn't gain weight. Millie tried to put a little meat on him, but he stayed slender, no surprise in his case. He had little appetite.

Gray introduced his traveling companions to the McClains. The fact that McClain was a widower visibly disappointed Tom. So much for getting a fine meal.

Charlie McClain did extend an invitation for Gray and the others to eat a meal and spend the night, but Gray turned him down, reasoning they would make Yellow Dog by dark or right after. He thought they might pick up some news about Walker or whoever they were after.

Disappointment sucked some energy out of Tom when Gray first said they would push on, but the opportunity of doing a bit of gambling at Yellow Dog held some allure for him. He enjoyed poker, more if the competition wasn't too skilled, and they generally weren't in places like Yellow Dog.

As the five men remounted to move south, Gray surprised the three men from Bismarck by asking McClain if he might have any horses for sale.

"Well, sure, what would you want to do? Pick him up on your way home?"

"No, we'd want to take him now. The paint Gibbs is riding concerns me; I'd like him a little better mounted."

The comment about his horse dumbfounded Gibbs. To him, a horse was a means of getting from one place to another, nothing more.

"Well, I suppose we can make a trade, some cash and the horse," Charlie said.

Despite not liking the pinto, Gibbs was offended by Wehr thinking the animal was of so little value and because Wehr did not ask him if he would like a new mount. But Tom didn't say anything. Instead, he pondered Wehr's observation skills. Gibbs had given no thought to how well or poorly anyone in the group was mounted.

When the men went out to the pasture to pick Gibbs's fresh horse, it became clear Gray and Trent would make the selection without as much as asking the newspaperman's opinion. After looking through the herd, they settled on a stout gray gelding. "He'll hold his own traveling hard or fast," Gray said. "He's got a deep chest and a solid hind end."

Gibbs wondered if they were buying him a horse or a woman.

ther, Gray said. "It's not a deep place and we did find
end
Gabe wondered if they were buying man a horse or a
woman.

Chapter Forty

Yellow Dog. Gabe wondered how the place, only a saloon, two cheap hotels, and a couple of houses for sporting women, stayed in existence. "Do people live here full time?" Reed asked.

"Some," Gray said. "Fifteen or twenty, I suppose."

"People with families?" Gabe asked.

"I don't think you'll find too many families here." Gray chuckled. "Yellow Dog sort of thrives on the business of travelers."

Del laughed hard at Gray's response.

"We'll take care of the horses. Go find rooms in one of these fine hotels," Gray said, smiling at the boy. "Trent and I'll wander through some of the other establishments and see if we can find out anything to put us on the right trail."

"What do you want the rest of us to do?" Gabe asked.

"Do whatever you want. We'll be here all night."

Gabe didn't think Yellow Dog would offer much he wanted to do—and less he would like his son to do. He decided he and the boy would spend the evening resting in their room, a sparsely furnished affair with a lumpy mattress. Del fell asleep early, leaving Gabe sitting alone thinking about Laura. Never separated for so much time, he ached to hold her. The separation bothered him since they left Bismarck, but the sorrow was more intense this night. Until now, it had been a sense of loneliness. Tonight was foreboding.

Trent glanced back and forth across the saloon. "Do you recognize anyone in here?" he asked Gray.

Wehr shook his head.

"What kind of food are you serving?" Gray asked when the barkeep came over.

"Nothing fancy, beans and tortillas."

"I guess we'll each take a plate and a couple of cups of coffee."

The bartender went over and spooned up the beans on tin plates. He tossed three tortillas on top. "You want anything in this coffee?"

"Black will do," Trent said.

"I didn't mean milk. Do you want whiskey in here?"

"Black," Trent repeated.

"Suit yourself."

"You know anything about a fella named Jack Walker?" Gray asked when they got their meals.

"Why would you be looking for Walker?"

Gray pondered his response for a moment. "Been some ranch burning and kidnapping going on. A lot of people think Walker's behind the raids."

"What if he is?"

"I want to catch up with him," Gray said, pushing his fork around in the beans.

"Seems a damned foolish idea to me."

"I can't argue with you. Still, I'd appreciate any help."

The bartender continued to wipe a shot glass with the bar rag, not inclined to pass out information, not the kind to come back and hurt him. Jack Walker would not react well to having someone set on his trail.

Gray took a sip of coffee. He wanted to spit. "Well, it's robust. On second thought, you can put a little milk in this."

"We don't have any." He sat the shot glass in a stack to his right. "You must be interested in the people from one of those ranches."

"Listen, friend, if you don't know anything, or you're unwilling to help, say so. Don't stand and dance me around."

"Like I said, I figure you've something personal in retrieving somebody he took. I'm wondering if you're man enough. I don't want Walker coming after me. Mad I put you on him."

"Well, a man needs to make his own decisions." Gray picked up his plate and coffee and sauntered over to an empty table, with Trent following. They sat down and started on their suppers, which were not bad.

"A little cornbread would be enjoyable," Trent said. "Course, cornbread would be too much to hope for."

A couple of drifters walked in and ordered beans and whiskey. Little else happened over the next half-hour. Gray and Trent finished their meals and sat sipping coffee, keeping an occasional eye turned toward Tom Gibbs and his poker game. Men shuffled out, and more wandered in. After the bartender woke a drunk at a table in the corner and sent him off looking for another place to sleep, he started over toward Gray and Trent. "You want any more to eat?"

"I think we're fine," Gray said. "Your beans are tasty, though."

The man waved his bar rag at a pesky fly before sitting next to Gray. After a little small talk, which Gray found uninteresting, the man looked off across the saloon. He yelled to a bent-over old man sweeping the floor with a worn broom, turned back to Gray, and spoke in a subdued voice.

"A drover who passed through here yesterday saw Walker and Bert Camp two days southeast of here. Bill Beachum and some others are with them. He said they had a mess of kids and women in tow. You be damn sure no one finds out where you got this information."

Trent nodded his head. "We appreciate this."

"Well, the puncher said Walker's movin' slow. Determined riders might catch him and his bunch in two, three days. My guess is they'll stick close to the river." He stood and wiped the rag over the table before picking up the empty plates. "I'll warn you to be careful. Camp's handy with a rifle; they say he can pick a man out of a saddle at long distances." The bartender picked up a couple of whiskey glasses on his way back to the bar.

Chapter Forty-One

Kenyon Wehr came bouncing into the kitchen, where Annie stood washing the lunch dishes, and Millie sat folding laundry. "What are the twins doing?" she asked the sandy-haired four-year-old.

"They're sleeping," he said, not pleased.

"Sleeping?"

"Yes, and I wanted to play."

"I'll bet they'll play after they wake up," Millie said, smiling at the boy. "Maybe you should take a nap too."

"I don't need one. I'm a big boy."

"They're the same age you are."

"They're girls."

"Oh," Millie said. "I forgot."

"No, you didn't," Kenyon shot back.

Millie laughed at the little boy and again started folding the laundry. "How soon do you think Trent and Dad will be back?" she asked, looking up at Annie.

"Graham said he'd give the search a month, then come

home."

"If they ride away from here for a month, it'll mean another month to get home," Millie said, concern showing in her voice.

"I suppose, but I hope not," Annie said, pausing from washing a glass.

"Why do you call my daddy 'Dad'? Are you my twin?" Kenyon asked, big eyes staring at Millie inquisitively. Annie turned around, grinning. She raised her eyebrows and smiled broader.

"Do you think I'm your twin?" Millie asked, smiling at Kenyon.

"No! You're too old. You are my aunt."

"Yes, I am." Millie picked up the boy and sat him on her lap. "I'm your aunt." She gave him a sizable, loud kiss on the cheek.

"So, is my Daddy your Daddy?" he asked again.

Millie was in over her head. "Are you going to help me out here?"

"Nope," Annie said. "You're on your own."

"Thanks."

Millie tickled the boy. It didn't work. He asked again.

"Well, he's not my real daddy."

"Why do you call him Dad?"

Annie turned back toward the sink, trying to muffle her laughter. Millie hesitated a moment, rubbing her hand back and forth across his knee. "Well...when I was a little girl, I didn't have a daddy of my own, but your daddy treated me nicer than anybody else. I liked to pretend he was my daddy, so I started calling him 'Daddy,' and he let me. For me, he became my real daddy."

"Did he spank you?"

The laughter burst from Annie, drawing a glance from Kenyon before he focused on Millie. "Only when he could catch me." Millie brushed the boy's hair back away from his eyes. "Do you mind me calling him Dad?"

Kenyon puckered his lips and squinted his eyes as he

thought about Millie's question. "I don't mind. He's a good daddy."

"Uh, oh, I think Nellie's awake in the other room," Millie said. "You better go ask if she's ready to play."

Millie got up and walked over next to Annie, kissing the side of her face. "Did I do all right?"

"The truth is always more than all right." Annie's attention turned to the meadows behind the house. "A storm's rolling up the valley. I hope winter doesn't come too soon."

Chapter Forty-Two

As time passed, Laura found Libbie Custer's companionship helped relieve her loneliness. She left her house more often, crossing the river and visiting Fort Lincoln. Libbie always maintained a bright outlook on life and could convince Laura her husband and son would return unharmed. Laura relished Libbie's company when General Custer went on some scout or military maneuvers. Better than going to the fort was having Libbie come to her home. The two would spend hours in "women talk," covering everything from eastern fashion to cooking to the benefits and perils of living in the "Wild West."

"Lord, I want some news," Laura said. "Even a rumor circulating the saloons would be something."

"Now, how would you be privy to any rumors passing through the saloons? You aren't frequenting saloons, are you?"

Laura managed a slight laugh as she sat across the kitchen table from Libbie, thinking about all the work around the house she should be doing. But why keep a clean home with no one around to enjoy it? "I wish I knew this Gray Wehr," she said, her mind far away. "I might rest better. All I know is what Del claimed about him being a famous gunman."

Libbie poured herself another cup of chamomile tea. "Well, I haven't met Wehr, but I am a friend of 'Wild Bill' Hickok, and he talks about Wehr. He speaks highly of him. I believe you should take comfort in Bill's opinion."

Hearing Libbie mention "Wild Bill" Hickok had a titillating effect on Laura. She was aware of the innuendos and rumors Libbie was a little closer to Hickok than polite society would smile on. "What's Hickok like?" Laura asked, wondering if she was making idle conversation or hoping Libbie might reveal something a bit more exciting.

Libbie Custer did not give any indication Laura might be preying about something beyond the limits of her business. "Well, he is a delight to gaze upon. He is tall, lithe, and free in every motion." It mesmerized Laura as Libbie exaggerated her arm movements and embellished her facial expressions. "To see that man on a horse—every muscle is perfection. And such an elegant dresser. I recall the last time I was around him; he wore top-boots, riding breeches, and a dark blue flannel shirt with scarlet insets in front. A loose neckerchief left his fine throat free."

Libbie snuck a glance at Laura. "Of course, I can't remember all his features, but he has fearless eyes and a courteous manner. But most striking," she sighed, tapping on her chest, "at least to some people, are the two Navy Colts resting in a red sash around his waist." Libbie took a sip of her tea. "Now, as far as this Gray Wehr," she said in a more disciplined voice, "Wild Bill says Wehr is a competent man. I believe he once told Autie that Wehr would be the best possible man to stand with you in any time of trouble."

"Well, I hope your 'Wild Bill' Hickok is right about Wehr."

"Why, Laura, he isn't *my* Wild Bill."

Chapter Forty-Three

Light snow dusted Yellow Dog before the sun came up. "This won't last long," Gray said. "It's a sunny day; this will melt in an hour."

The snow didn't worry Del Reed; snow only makes you cold and a little wet. What Gray and Trent found out in the saloon last night bothered him. They might be as little as two days behind the kidnappers.

Traveling fast, they would catch them in perhaps as little as three or three and a half days. Del, convinced that would be the extent of his life, snorted out the sour burning bile erupting into his mouth and nose. He wanted to hug his mother.

"Any towns or ranches will be close to the river," Trent said. Gibbs and the Reeds listened as the two men discussed the direction the rescue party would head. "They'll stick to the river on into Nebraska. At least, I think they will."

"Well, let's follow the river." Gray turned Lena away from the hitching rail. Tom made a mental note of Gray's doing what the younger man thought best. Still, he believed

Wehr agreed; otherwise, he would chase his own instincts.

Gray kept the group traveling in a trot and a light lope throughout the morning. Surprised by how much easier this new horse rode, Tom Gibbs was grateful Gray got rid of his paint.

Twice Trent pushed his bay into a gallop, moving out in front to scout. Both times, he came back without finding anything of importance. Tom wondered what Trent was scouting for. He didn't ask and neither did Gabe or Del, but he believed Trent might be looking for Indians or signs of Indian presence. A rumor circulating Yellow Dog claimed a few Cheyenne and Sioux bands joined together to raid along the Wyoming and Nebraska border.

By early afternoon, the southwestern sky filled with ominous-looking rainclouds. Black clouds covered the sun by mid-afternoon, leaving only a more silver spot to show its whereabouts. "Make sure your oilcloth coats are handy. This one is going to be a dandy," Gray said.

Del pulled his coat on and his hat down. "We get nasty late fall and early winter storms in Bismarck. But there, we've got a house with a hot stove and two roaring fireplaces. At night, I crawl under heavy quilts. Out here, we're going to catch the storm's full force without the benefit of walls to block the wind or a fire to keep us warm."

"How far do you suppose we are from that old buffalo hunters' shack?" Trent asked,

"A couple of miles, but I sure hate to cower down. We'll lose time and distance between Walker and us."

"I doubt they'll be able to travel much either," Gabe said. "Not with women and kids."

Gray shook his head. "They're two days ahead of us. This storm may not hit them."

Within minutes, the weather cut loose. Its first assault, a terrible blast of wind, blew Tom's derby off, spooking

Gabe's horse.

"Whoa! Whoa!" The horse whirled around twice and crow-hopped a time or two, but Reed regained control of the animal before being thrown.

Tom's tan hat caught in the sage for a moment before a second gust sent the derby straight up twenty or thirty feet. It flew out over the Platte, dropping about two-thirds of the way across. The soaked bowler bobbed once or twice, got caught in the current, and soon swept away.

"Let's run for the shed," Gray hollered, urging his bay into a lope. A few drops started falling, but the wind gusts were so hard most of them blew away instead of hitting the ground.

Before the men covered a quarter mile, a gale began pounding down in blinding sheets. Strong winds propelled the raindrops enough to sting the men's faces and any exposed skin. The horses lowered their heads and ran with them bent away from the blustering sky.

Both Gabe's and Del's horses bucked when they objected to being reined in a direction they did not want to go. Del gave up directing his chestnut and let him charge along in the group. The boy leaned down over the horse's wet neck and strained not to fall off as icy rain swept down the back of his collar.

The buffalo hunters' shed was an awful disappointment. Three adobe walls offered little protection, with only about one-third under a leaky excuse for a roof. Water poured through at least a dozen holes, and rickety gables rose off the sides every time a powerful gust whistled through. "Let the horses huddle against the south wall," Gray yelled over the stiff wind and pounding rain. He and Trent tied a couple of ropes together and strung them for a makeshift corral. "Drag some wood back under the roof," he told Gibbs and Gabe.

By the time they shook their coats out and put them back on, the rain became sleet, making a miserable situation worse. They built a small fire and crowded into the corner, offering the driest refuge. "Settle in, boys; this is going to last," Trent said as he piled more sticks on the flame. And last, it did; for three hours past dark, hail and driving rain pounded their leaky domicile. The storm turned to snow, dropping a white blanket over everything in sight. Gray and Gabe fell asleep. The other three men sat close to the flames.

Tom took a pencil and tablet out of his saddlebag and scribbled notes about the trip for an hour. He tried to describe Gray without sounding too much like a dime-store novel while keeping the description exciting enough to catch eastern publishers' attention.

> *Gray Wehr is a man who is both everything and nothing like his reputation. He is gentle and easy-going around family and friends, smiling and laughing. He is cautious about strangers but undeniably dangerous to anyone who challenges him. When confronted, he is cold and bold. He is not a man I would want to anger.*
>
> *Still, he has warm, friendly green eyes, around which a few crow's feet can sometimes appear. Since the beginning of our trip, he has grown a mustache and chin beard. Dressed in a deerskin jacket over a red shirt and wearing shotgun chaps, he would be quite a dashing figure to women.*

"How long have you known Gray?" Del's question to Trent drew Gibbs's attention away from his writing.

"Most of my life, I suppose. My folks owned Sutler's Stores at some forts out here before the treaty closed them. Gray drifted in and out, and my dad and I delivered supplies to High Meadows. We've been horse ranch partners for almost six years now, since right after Millie and I married."

"Ever seen him in a tussle?" Gibbs asked, glancing over to be sure Gray was asleep.

Trent also took a quick peek. "A couple. You're not planning on starting one with him, are you?"

"Not by a long shot. My momma didn't raise any

fools."

"You ever been with him during a fight?" Del asked.

"Couple of times."

"They say he killed Harvey Kehn," Del said. "Is that true?"

Trent didn't enjoy answering the question. He lifted his hat and brushed his sandy hair back. "Yeah, he did."

This piqued Tom Gibbs's attention.

"I was with him," Trent said unemotionally, maybe unintentionally.

"What?" Del leaned forward with wide eyes.

"Would you mind telling me about it?" Gibbs asked, hoping Trent would not turn sullen. Trent stared into the fire, then began speaking about the night by the river...

"Leave the horses here," Gray whispered.

We tied the bays to scrub oak and slipped toward the campfire. When we crept up to within fifty or sixty feet, Gray stopped in a clump of willows. He motioned for me to kneel. "The one in the middle is Kehn. The half-breed is Crow. I don't know who the other one is. You watch the third one; I'll handle Kehn and Crow."

"Are we going to walk right in?"

"That's as good a way as any," Gray said, standing up, "unless you want to shoot them from here."

I didn't want to shoot at all. I'd never heard of Crow and didn't know much about Kehn, except he was a ruthless killer.

Harley Blaine was the first to notice us walking into camp. "Who the hell are you?" he asked.

Kehn raised his head, squinting his one useable eye to identify the intruders. "Well, I'll be damned, it's that son of a..." he leaped to his feet in mid-sentence, grabbing his gun. Before he cleared the leather of his holster, Wehr's Colt fired. The forty-five-caliber bullet tore a gaping hole in Kehn's chest, spinning him around. Wehr's next shot hit Crow in the belly, exiting through his kidney, as he tried to pull his hunting knife. Gray plugged Kehn two more times

*as the killer crumbled to his knees, swearing and still trying
to return fire.*

*While Gray was shooting Kehn and Crow, I put two
slugs into Blaine, one in the jaw and the other in the chest,
leaving three men lying dead in the span of a few seconds.*

*Of the three murderers and rapists, only Blaine got off
a shot as he fell. Kehn was trying to shoot back when he took
the last two bullets. Gray gave all three bodies a swift kick.
I assumed he was making sure they were corpses.*

"Let's unsaddle their horses," Gray said.

"What do you want to do with the saddles?"

*"Leave 'em and turn the horses loose," he said, cutting
a halter with a knife sheathed on the back of his belt.*

"Aren't we going to take the horses with us?"

*"I've no use for stolen horses," Wehr said as he kicked
dirt on the fire.*

*I almost asked Gray how he knew the horses were
stolen but realized the foolishness of the question. While
looking around the campsite, I found a pile of scalps next to
Crow's body. There must have been a dozen.*

*Wehr walked over to me. He picked up some scalps and
sorted through them. "All women and children," Gray
muttered in disgust. He tossed the hair back down on the
ground. "These were some mighty brave men." He spat on
the ground. Gray took the guns off the dead men, unloaded
them, and flung them into the river. "Damn!" Gray shouted
as he let the pistol go. "Somebody needed to shoot this trash
years ago." Wehr breathed heavily as he stared into the
darkness. Trembling, he shook his head. "Hickok had a
chance once. Instead, he dragged him into some cow town
locked him up. Two days later, Kehn killed a deputy with
three kids and escaped.*

"Are we going to bury them?" I asked.

"They've done nothing to deserve burying."

"Not much more to tell." Trent glanced at the
newspaperman. "Kehn was a vicious man who got easier
than he deserved."

Chapter Forty-Four

Since the night Lucy Carlyle cut up Carter Cline, the captives, except Meg and Rennie Brown, acted like they were afraid of her. This puzzled Lucy; she thought cutting up one man, even the runt of the litter, should please them. And because he ended up dying due to her work, they had one fewer tormentor. The women avoided her in camp, though, and swept their children up like mother hens if one of them strayed too close to Lucy.

"What's the matter with them?" Lucy asked Meg Brown when they nestled up around a small fire Camp allowed them to build.

"They're scared."

"Of me? Those men are who they should fear."

Meg glared at the gang of killers. "I guess they're afraid that they might be hurt worse because you fought back."

"How could life be any worse? I don't know how."

"Tonight's gonna be colder than a whore's heart," the older Fox brother said. "I'm grabbing one of those new women to hunker down with."

Bill Beachum mumbled something to Fox. "What'd you say, you damned simpleton?"

"He said to leave the fair-haired one alone. He wants her." Bert Camp was the only one in the group who understood much of what Beachum muttered.

Walker assumed Camp must have better hearing than the others because he sure couldn't understand anything Beachum said.

"I didn't want that skinny blonde," Fox grumbled. "She ain't got enough meat on her to keep a man warm. I like more woman than her."

Camp started to tell Fox to be a bit more careful about messing with Beachum, but he decided to let them settle their own battles. There wasn't anything wrong with Beachum, other than missing part of his tongue. Camp figured Beachum would best both the Foxes in a fight. And since he somewhat preferred Beachum to the Foxes, he would avoid any brewing trouble.

Lucy Carlyle drew Jenny and Maddie up close to her when Fox started across the camp. Other than the dead Carter Cline, Fox was the most likely of any man to kick the children, although you couldn't put such meanness past any of them. They all took sick pleasure in hurting people, especially defenseless women.

"What are you looking at?" Fox asked as he passed by Lucy. "I ain't interested in you tonight. You can lie alone and cold." Fox grabbed one of the teenage girls they captured at the last ranch they raided. He yanked her up so hard her feet left the ground. The girl began crying as he took her away from the other women. Her sobs drew her a vicious backhand to the side of the face.

Camp sat next to Jack Walker and offered him some whiskey he kept in a metal flask inside his coat. "You figure on pickin' up more?"

"We've got enough for this trip. They're too hard to control." Walker sucked a long swig on the liquor. "Besides, we're short-handed after what the Bismarck woman did to Cline." Walker took another long drink. "Remember the little crap town right before we cross into Nebraska? I thought I might try to pick up a man or two when we ride by. You can escort these fine women around the edge; I'll go in alone."

"Trey Long frequents the place. He's dependable."

Chapter Forty-Five

Susan Carlyle sat in front of the mirror, studying her face. "I look old."

Annie was sewing in the room's corner. "You do not. You're quite attractive."

Susan glanced at Annie. "You're not looking at me."

Annie laughed. "I see you every day; I don't need to. You're an alluring woman. Ask Zach Joseph."

"I don't want to ask Zach Joseph," Susan said with a laugh of her own. "Or any other man."

"What about Tom Gibbs?" Annie asked.

"What about Tom?"

"He's smitten."

Susan didn't reply. Everyone in Bismark knew Tom was smitten, but she hoped those in High Meadows had not noticed. "He wants a wife," Susan said, trying to sound disinterested. "And I happen to be the most available."

"I suspect it's a little more," Annie said, not looking up from her darning.

Susan gazed into the mirror, reflecting on what being

married again would be like. "Are you happy here?"

Annie studied her house guest. "Well, I'm content."

"Is there a difference?"

Annie laid her sewing down on her basket and smiled at Susan. "I think contentment is better. It's being satisfied with what you have, a quiet happiness. What Paul described as 'the peace of God.' At least to a degree."

Susan turned back toward the window, thinking about how different her life had been from Annie's. In the best of times, the happiest ones, her future was precarious. And here sat her friend talking about her life having the peace of God. "Did anyone miss me?"

"Of course, we missed you. We wondered why you ran away, why you left."

The night her mother died, Susan was staying with Nellie Bascomb. She died in the middle of January during deep snow and frigid temperatures. The two young women were sharing an enormous feather bed. They laughed and giggled until after midnight, when Nellie's father yelled for them to shut up.

In the night, Nellie's mother came in carrying a coal oil lamp. Its glow distorted her face, but the way she said "Susan" was terrifying. "Susan, the doctor is downstairs. Your mother passed away. I'm so sorry." Within a week of the funeral, Susan disappeared from High Meadows.

"My parents' deaths reduced me to the town orphan. Everybody pitied me, and I didn't want pity." She turned back toward the window, intending to give no more precise reason for her leaving.

Annie did not push people to reveal things they did not want to discuss, a trait making her a trusted confidant to so many of her friends. Half of the females in High Meadows considered Annie their "best" friend. In reality, that status belonged to Jean and Millie. "Annie." Susan said after several minutes of silence, "after Gray brings Lucy and the children back, do you think people would mind if we stayed here? I mean, in High Meadows, not in your house."

205

"You'd be more than welcome; you should know without asking." Annie got up and walked over to Susan, sitting down next to her and slipping her arm around her waist. "Do you want to stay in High Meadows?"

Susan thought about the question. "I'm thinking about staying, a lot."

"Annie! Annie!" Millie's voice sounded terrified. "Annie! Sanchez is hurt! Where are you?"

"We're up here." Annie and Susan rushed out into the upstairs hall. "What's wrong?"

"Sanchez is hurt. He needs help!"

"Where is he?"

"He's in the back pasture. He's hurt bad! Hurry!"

"Calm down! We are going to hurry," Annie half-shouted, trying to force Millie to regain some composure. "Susan, ride into town and fetch Doc Hollins and Jean." She grabbed a coat from the hall tree and pushed Millie out the door.

"You don't have a horse ready," Millie stammered as they ran down the front steps.

"Poncho can carry us both. Now climb up." Annie struggled to get up on the big Appy behind Millie. "Let me stick my foot in the stirrup." She swung up behind the girl, and Millie kicked the tall gelding as she whipped the reins across his rump.

The horse covered the distance in long, flowing strides. Little time passed before Annie saw Sanchez lying on the ground on the south pasture's far side. Millie skidded the stout horse to a stop. "What happened?" Annie asked for a second time as she slid off Poncho's rump.

"He shot himself with that damned old rusty pistol."

Annie bent down over the old man. Small and frail, he weighed nothing. Annie eased him over. Blood soaked the front of his shirt. Not bright red, but a dark brownish-red—not a positive sign. Annie took off her coat and put it over the old man. His skin was ashy gray, either the result of blood loss or the cold. He slipped in and out of consciousness.

"I'm hurt, Señora. I think I am hurt bad."

"Shhh. Shhh. Lie quiet. Doc's coming. He's on the way. Bring the blanket off your saddle," Annie said, looking up at Millie.

"He's going to be all right, isn't he? You can help him, can't you?" Tears filled Millie's eyes as she questioned Annie. She wept over the old man. She spent almost every day with Sanchez in the restaurant before Nellie died. Now she was losing him. The old man was fading away, disappearing into the dank cold ground. "He will be fine, won't he?"

Annie stood and took her young friend by both arms. "Listen to me, Millie." She took Millie by the chin, trying to catch the girl's eyes with her own. "Quit talking and start helping me. Now, bring me your blanket," she said in a reassuring voice. Millie's gaze drifted again toward Sanchez. The girl froze—didn't move. "Go get the blanket!"

Poncho wandered off, forcing Millie to run him down. The thin blanket was only three feet by four feet, so she handed Annie her coat.

"How long do you think it will take Hollins to come?"

"A little while. Do you have matches to start a fire?"

Millie checked the pockets of her pants and shirt. "No, none." She started crying.

"I'm upset, too, but you crying won't help me, or Sanchez. If you cry, we may both fall apart, and we need to help him. Now gather up some dry kindling; he'll have matches on him somewhere."

Millie's mind stopped; her body refused to respond. Tears choked her trembling speech. Sanchez was going to die.

Annie had enough. Her eyes blistering, she shot Millie a hellish scowl. "Millie. Bring some wood!"

"From where?"

Annie's slap spun the girl around. She pushed her toward clumps of sage.

Annie found matches in his right shirt pocket, and they soon built a small fire. "Lie down on the other side of him. We'll keep him as comfortable as possible."

The two women lay beside him, trying to shield the wounded man from the stiff wind kicking up. They tried to keep their friend warm for were torturous minutes. "Where in the hell is Hollins?" Annie muttered half to herself. It was the first time Millie ever heard Annie swear.

Twice, Millie slipped away to gather more firewood. The sun hung low in the late afternoon sky, dropping the temperature. Worse, a light rain started to fall.

Finally—the rickety old buckboard came bouncing across the pasture. Susan and Doc Hollins sat on the seat. Doc Hollin's wife bounced around in the back, and Quint Swain was riding along.

Millie charged the gray-haired doctor. "What took you so long?"

"Mrs. Swain's broken wrist needed setting," the irritable doc said. "Other people get hurt you know." Hollins clambered down out of the backboard. "What happened to him?"

"He shot himself."

Doc Hollins pulled the blanket and coats back to examine the wound. "How did he manage this?"

"It was an accident."

"I hardly suspected he shot himself on purpose. Not many would shoot themselves in the belly."

"He tried to hammer a nail into the fence post with the butt of his pistol," Millie said. "The thing went off."

"Went off? The old fool must have had it cocked."

"Well, let's lay him up in the wagon," Annie said as the town doctor stepped away from Sanchez, not intending to assist in carrying him. Quint Swain picked up the old man's shoulders while Annie and Millie took his feet.

"Be careful with him," Millie demanded as they hoisted

Sanchez into the back of the buckboard.

"Dorothy, you drive," Hollins commanded his wife. "Annie, you sit back here and hold him quiet," he said in a bossy tone, making no effort to help. Hollins's wife slapped the reins over the two horses, and with a jerk, the rickety wagon creaked into motion. Annie never realized the pasture was so rough. The springless wagon bounced and bumped so high Annie wondered if it might flip over. With limited success, she cradled Sanchez in her arms to absorb the shock of the jarring ride. Two splinters went deep into her hand when she grabbed the old seat after one nasty jolt.

"God almighty, woman, watch where you're driving. This Mexican's got a bullet in his stomach."

"Can I help you?" Susan, sitting next to the doc's wife, asked, looking back at Annie.

"I'm trying to keep him from bouncing," Annie said without looking up. Susan eased herself over the seat and into the back of the buckboard, where she slid down along the other side of the wounded man. Neither woman spoke as Susan tried to hold him stable.

The drive to Millie's house, closer than Annie's, took forever. The drizzle started falling harder, and Sanchez's moaning kept getting louder. He lost consciousness when they loaded him into the wagon, which Annie considered a blessing. "Be easy with him."

The back stairs leading up to the porch were slippery from the rain, and Millie twice thought Doc Hollins was going to slip and fall. She cared little about the doctor but was frantic they might drop Sanchez.

"Stick him into a bed," Doc Hollins said as they entered the house. Millie pulled the covers back and fluffed two pillows for his head. "Shove them under his head! They don't need fluffing up."

Once Sanchez lay on the bed, Annie took Millie into her arms and eased her away.

"Somebody, bring some water," Hollins ordered as he opened his black doctor's bag and removed a pair of scissors with which he cut the old man's shirt open. "Dorothy, you stay here and help me. The rest of you get out. I don't want you in the way."

Millie protested, but Annie guided her out into the hallway. "Come on; let's go downstairs."

Susan met them on the way back up the stairs with a washbowl full of water. "This was the first thing I found," she said, looking at Millie.

"Can I do anything?" Quint Swain asked.

"I don't think so. We appreciate your help getting Sanchez in the house."

"I guess I better head on back home. You sure you don't need me?"

"I don't think so," Annie said, smiling at the man. "We'll be fine."

"Would you like me to stop and send the preacher over?"

"Yes, please," Annie said as she walked with him to the back door.

"Do you think he'll be all right?" Millie asked when Annie came back into the living room, where she and Susan sat on a couch. Annie pulled a straight-backed rocker over in front of her young friend.

She leaned forward and took Millie's hands. "Sanchez is an old man, Mille." Annie began searching for terms not too harsh, nevertheless, words to prepare Millie for what Annie thought might be imminent. Gravely wounded sounded too hopeless—Annie didn't want to destroy the girl's hope, but she didn't want to embellish it either. "I'm afraid he's hurt bad. We need to put him into God's hands."

"They say if you're gut shot, nothing can be done," Millie said without looking at Annie. "If it could, I doubt Hollins can help him."

Annie decided not to respond to the girl. Nothing she could say would change the outcome; people die, and the inevitable would happen no matter how hard loved ones hoped against them dying.

Chapter Forty-Six

The operation, for the most part, failed. Hollins said the bullet was too deep for him to remove. He insisted "jabbing around" would kill the old man. Doc Hollins and his wife left about ten while the preacher stayed until past midnight. Annie, Susan, and Jean spent all night.

"He's still asleep," Jean said as she came into the kitchen. Sanchez was not sleeping. He was unconscious; however, "asleep" sounded more reassuring and less worrisome to them all.

"I wish Trent and Dad were here," Millie said as she poured coffee for the other three women.

"They couldn't do anything."

"I still wish they were here."

"I'll go up and sit with him again," Susan said, wondering if Millie and Jean, both worn out, might be about to have crosswords. When Jean was younger, she could be abrupt, sharp with people, and Susan wanted no part of any spitting contest or catfight about to erupt. Of course, she did not know Millie well, but she sensed Millie to be feisty.

A clay pitcher and bowl sat on the bureau next to the bed where Sanchez lay. Susan poured some water into the bowl and wet a small hand towel to wipe the little man's almost colorless face. She hung the towel up and pulled the light green blanket down to Sanchez's waist. Since the bandage showed no sign of blood, Susan assumed Jean changed the bandages. She tucked the sheets around him.

Looking at the old man with his thin gray hair mussed against the pillow, Susan couldn't help but think back to when her father died, less than a year before her mother passed. He lingered for almost two weeks, never being conscious for more than a few minutes at a time. He didn't recognize anyone; he mumbled incoherently and lost consciousness after only brief periods. The whole affair became difficult for the family.

Susan stared at Sanchez. His skin was pallid. "You fight, old man. If you're going to live, you do it; and somehow, you let these people know you're going to. But if you're going to die, die now."

Doc Hollins didn't show until almost four in the afternoon, making Millie furious.

"How's the old man?"

"He hasn't woken up yet," Annie said, stepping between the doc and Millie.

"Is anybody with him?" Hollins asked as he started up the stairs.

"Jean is," Annie said. "We've not left him alone."

Doc Hollins' visit with Sanchez lasted less than ten minutes. "I changed the bandage. Be sure you keep the wound clean. If anything changes, send someone after me."

Millie tried to go after him right then, but Annie again got between them. "Stay here." Annie whirled and followed the town doctor out the front door, slamming it behind her.

"That's all you have to say?" she half-yelled at the doctor as he went down the steps.

"What else do you want me to say?"

"You might give us some idea of how he is doing or tell us what you plan to do for him," Annie said confrontationally.

"You don't think much of my skills, do you, Mrs. Wehr?"

"I think little of your compassion," Annie shot back, her dark brown eyes flashing.

"The old man is dying, and neither I, nor you, nor anybody else can do anything," Hollins said, turning his back and continuing down the stairs.

Chapter Forty-Seven

After breakfast, Jack Walker left Bert Camp with instructions to head southeast until mid-afternoon, then wait until he caught up. By the time he got back, he hoped for another man or two. The ride into Schuster Flats, a worthless two-bit settlement on the Wyoming and Nebraska border, took Walker two hours.

At one time, the town had the potential to prosper, but Sioux raids throughout the vicinity discouraged settlers from making the place a permanent home. Snow, which fell and melted the day before, changed to a slow rain now muddying the streets. As Walker stepped off his poorly fed gray horse, the sound of a heated argument caught his attention. When he turned toward the yelling, he saw Trey Long, the man he came looking for. Long was drunk. Only ten o'clock in the morning, but the man was falling down intoxicated.

Two men were accusing Long of cheating at cards. The bigger man, a light-skinned Negro, kept waving a pistol at Long and threatening to send him to hell. The smaller man also appeared to be drunk. He unsheathed a bowie knife and started screaming for his money back.

"You'll not be getting a red cent! And neither one of you can take it!" Long bellowed back before tripping over his feet, falling in the mud. He righted himself to his knees. "You wait 'til I git a gun. I'll blow yer damn heads off."

Walker slid the repeating rifle he stole at the ranch closest to Casper out of the scabbard. He stepped around the back of his horse, leveled the weapon, and shot the Negro. Walker levered another cartridge and killed the second man. Long, so blind drunk he didn't know where the shots came from swayed back and forth, glassy-eyed, trying not to fall again. He failed. "Who the hell are you?"

"Ya dumb sonuvabitch, who do you think I am?" The raw morning wasn't quite cold enough to freeze the muddy streets, so Walker splashed and sloshed his way to Long.

After puking, Long squinted at the man now standing over him. "Walker? What are you doing here?" Long gave up on getting back on his feet. He sat like a hog in half-frozen slop.

"Savin' your worthless hide," Walker growled as he pulled the filthy Long up to his unsteady feet.

"What's going on out here?" The voice came from a man with bright red hair running toward them from the north end of town. "What in the world? Those men are dead."

The man wore an old, tarnished badge stamped SHERIFF in all capital letters. "Those two tried to murder Long," Walker said, looking the sheriff in the eye. "If I hadn't rode up, they'd have shot him dead."

People wandered out of poorly maintained buildings to see what all the shooting had been about. "Ben," the sheriff yelled at a man standing down the street, "find a couple of men to help you drag these two off. Be quick." He demanded when the man did not move fast enough. "You ought to come down to the office and write a report."

"Long needs looking after," Walker said, "and I told you what happened."

"Well, a little later," the sheriff said weakly, turning and heading back off without waiting for a reply.

"Put yer arm around my neck, you drunken sot," Walker half-dragged and half-carried Long back into the saloon.

"I don't want any more trouble here." The barkeep shuffled toward the two men coming in the door, waving his hand for them to turn around and leave.

"Shut up. Git some coffee over here." Walker dumped Long into a half-barrel chair. "Sober up, you cur!" he yelled as he cuffed Long across the face. "How long has he been like this?"

The bartender grunted, sat down a pot and two cups. "What? Drunk? Two days now. He's drunk half the time or more. He drinks, plays poker, and starts fights when he loses. This time, he picked on somebody who wanted to fight back. He's lucky that half-black buck didn't kill him before you showed up."

"Drink this." Walker half-poured coffee down Long's throat.

"In all the times I've seen coffee poured down drunks, it's never done a bit of good," the barman said. "The only thing that's going to sober him up is sleeping it off."

Walker grabbed him by his shirt and jerked him close, enough of the bartender's unsolicited advice. "Where's he stay?"

"He's got an old place out behind the hotel. Take the alley south." The shaken bartender squirmed. "You want some help getting him home?"

"I'll manage." Walker lifted the drunken Long by his shirt. "Git up, git on your feet." The whiskey and the heat coming off a potbellied stove were putting the man to sleep. With a lot of struggling, Walker got him to his house, an old shack. Walker tossed him down on the bed, and Long began sleeping off his drunk.

Walker went back down the street for his horse. He tied him in front of Long's shanty and searched for some sign

Long might own a horse. With no animal around, Walker assumed he would either need to buy or steal one. The man was more trouble than Walker thought he was worth.

Walker let him sleep until two o'clock and rousted him out of bed. Long was not yet sober, but close enough to have his wits about him. "I need a couple of men," Walker said, as Long stumbled around the shack in an old pair of torn long-johns trying to find some coffee to put on the fire. "I figure you and one more."

"What's the work?" Long scratched himself before throwing a few fresh grounds into a pot of stale coffee and setting it on the stove.

"Why? You gittin' picky these days?"

"I'm not picky. I'm curious. The type of job might make a difference in who I select to come along."

"I didn't realize this here boom town was so full of specialists."

Long ignored Walker's sarcasm. "Well, I can think of two or three we can choose from."

"Selling women down in New Orleans."

"Always good money in the sale of females. You got the females?"

"I got the first bunch, but we can make steady work of this."

"Ever hear of J.D. Pratt?"

"No."

"Pratt would be good for this kind of venture. He's left-handed."

Walker thought about Long's remark. "Now, what the hell does that have to do with anything? You think a left-handed man is more reliable?"

"Well, no, why would a left-handed man be any more reliable or competent than a right-handed man? Just never met many left-handed men." Long filled his cup. "You want some of this?" he asked, holding the pot out toward Walker.

Walker glanced around for a cup. He picked up an old metal one and wiped it out with the tail of his shirt.

"Some people can use either hand with the same skill," Long, still shaky, poured coffee in the cup, all over Walker's hand, and the floor. "They call them ambidextrous. Never met one, though."

"Hellfire, Long! I don't give a damn if the man shoots with his ass. Is he available?"

"Hell, I can't speak for his availability. I'm only recommending him."

Walker was growing frustrated with Long's ridiculous conversation, but he remembered the man had always been like that. Camp found him humorous and enjoyed his company. Walker thought his constant babbling about idiotic topics tedious. He would have been more aggressive in handling another man whose behavior was so irksome, but Long, when sober, and he was almost sober now, was a dangerous man.

"Would it be too much trouble to find out if this fella is available?"

"No. We can go now," Long said, picking up his beat-up, old tan hat.

Jack Walker took a drink of the coffee, coughed, and hacked. "That's awful," he said, spitting bitter brew out on the floor.

"It is a little stiff." Long laughed as he took another swallow.

J.D. Pratt was in a poker game when Walker and Long located him. He was playing for a sorrel horse, said to be a hardy animal. Walker figured if Pratt didn't need a horse, Long would, so after glancing at Pratt's hand, a King High Straight, he sat while the hand finished. Pratt's opponent, holding three Aces, did not take the loss well. He cussed and offered several alternative payments to allow him to keep the gelding. Pratt turned them all down.

"Let's take a walk, J.D.," Trey Long said after the arguing subsided.

"Sure, I'll show you my horse," Pratt enjoyed milking one final bit of amusement out of the former horse owner's disappointment.

"Can we use the women while we're on the way to New Orleans? I don't care much for kidnapping women who won't be available to me," Long said.

"Help yourself all you want."

"I'm wondering about one other thing," Pratt bent down to inspect the shoes on his new horse. "Is anybody chasing after you, a posse, or some damn overzealous relative? I'll want a little more incentive if I'm gonna fight somebody off every couple of days."

Pratt's questions irritated Walker. "No one is following us," Walker spat tobacco, "but, by Gawd, if you're of such a worrisome nature, this ain't the job for you."

"I like to be aware of what I'm gettin' into," Pratt said without looking up, further irritating Walker.

"Well, I'll tell you what; when we go back, we'll send somebody scouting to make sure we're alone. I wouldn't want you to lose any sleep worrying we're bein' chased." Walker snorted, determined now to ignore the smart-ass Pratt.

"I'd sleep much better."

It turned out Trey Long had a horse, a sounder one than Walker's gray mount. An hour later, the three men were on their way to meet Bert Camp and the rest of Walker's gang.

Chapter Forty-Eight

Something was wrong. Gray could not settle his mind on what, but something was amiss. He shook his head at Trent. "They've given us the slip. We should have caught up with them this morning."

"Maybe they're riding hard," Gabe said.

"They're dragging too many captives to be traveling fast," Gray said. "Somewhere, Walker's switched directions. This is a clever bunch. They probably figure somebody's chasing them, so they changed course." The realization galled Wehr. He assumed the kidnappers would follow the Platte to Kearney, turn south until they hit the Arkansas River. Now he didn't know where the bunch was going, except they left the Platte.

"Well, New Orleans is a long way from here," Tom Gibbs said. "We'll pick up their path again."

Picking up the trail was not the issue. Time was. Gray was unhappy about being away from home.

"Any ideas where they might head?" Gabe asked.

"They'll head south."

"Let's go south," Reed said.

"South is a sizable place."

Gabe flushed at Gray's cutting remark.

"My guess is they'll head toward Horse Creek," Trent said, "skirt Pine Bluffs and head into Colorado."

"We went through two years ago," Del said.

"How big?" Gray looked both at the boy and his dad.

"Larger than Yellow Dog, but not much."

"I remember three or four remote ranches," Del said.

"They'd be easy pickings," Gabe said.

Outlaws are a greedy breed. They would not pass easy pickings. "If they're familiar with the country, you might be right," he said, looking at Trent. "If they don't, no telling where they may head."

"Walker knows the area," Trent said.

"Horse Creek sounds like the best idea to me," Tom Gibbs said.

"I guess if we find raided ranches, we're right," Gabe said.

"A devil of a way to be right," Gray said somberly.

They rode south for the next three hours with little conversation because Gray again sat a stiff pace and kept them riding an hour past dark. "How far do you think we are from Horse Creek?" Gray asked.

"Never been right in this spot," Trent said, "but my best guess is we're still to the north, half a day."

"If that's the case, I suppose we may as well stop here."

"Does your bay ever wear out?" Gabe asked when Gray sat down at the campfire. "My horse is done in, but your animal acts like she's ready to run another ten miles."

Gray, always more than willing to talk about his horse, smiled and laughed. "She is a goer. Never owned one like her."

"Where'd you get her?" Del asked.

"Annie bred her." Gray's eyes shined with pride for

both Annie and the bay. "The stud she came out of died of colic. A top-quality stallion. Annie took a long time getting over him dying."

"You've made quite a life for yourself in High Meadows," Tom Gibbs said.

Gray expected Gibbs' statement was leading up to something else, something he would not be willing to discuss. Gray stirred the fire with a stick before looking up at Gibbs. "Listen, Tom," he said with the hint of a smile on his lips, "I don't want to be in some newspaper. If given a chance, I would have lived my life differently. I don't enjoy talking about the past."

"Easterners find men like you interesting. You're considered heroes. They admire the lives you live out here, and they respect how you make something out of an unsettled frontier."

Gray frowned and shook his head. "No desire to be admired or thought of as a hero,"

"I think what you're doing now is heroic," Del Reed said, his boyish innocence showing.

Gray laughed. "You're here too. You're a brave man. Del's the one you ought to write about."

Chapter Forty-Nine

Jean Wehr came down the stairs a little after seven. Annie and Millie busied themselves in the kitchen, preparing biscuits and gravy for breakfast. "Sanchez is gone." Jean slipped her arm around Millie.

Chapter Fifty

Libbie Custer threw the book on the couch." That's a foolish decision! I won't let you go."

"Well, I'm a grown woman. I don't need your permission."

Laura's response took Libbie aback. "Well, if you're determined, I'm going with you." Libbie had no intention of any such thing, but she thought the possibility might yank Laura back to reality.

Laura cocked her head and stared at her friend. "Fine. Be ready in the morning; I want to be on my way."

"Oh, for heaven's sake, I'm going back to the fort and bringing Autie back. He'll put a halt to your foolishness."

"He can't stop me. I'm not in the Seventh Calvary,"

Libbie flopped down on the living room couch. She shook her head and tried to think of something to say to make the woman listen to reason. Laura never acted so bull-headed. Starting off across Sioux land in late fall, when Indians or weather might kill you, was suicidal.

"Who are you going to take with you?" Laura, even when acting irrationally, wouldn't start alone. Libby snickered at her friend, turned flippant. "Red Holsten?"

She did. Laura's face gave it away. The woman intended to cross Indian land with Red Holsten, a good-for-nothing troublemaker.

Libbie threw her arms in the air. "He doesn't have any better notion of where High Meadows is than you do, and you have no more idea than I do, which is none. The Bighorn Mountains cover a lot of territory."

Libbie started to curse Holsten's character but cursing Red wouldn't help. She spent the next few minutes pacing around the house, groaning, frustrated beyond words. How could anyone as intelligent as Laura Reed contemplate such foolishness?

Libbie thought of another approach. "Besides, what's your husband going to think about you taking off on a long trip with another man? I don't think he'll be happy." Libbie detected a sensitive spot. "People will talk. Don't think they won't."

"I want to search for my family. I hardly think that should set chins wagging."

"Searching...with another man!"

Laura walked to the front window and stared at the. The gray, dreary day added to her blue mood. *How concerned about gossip would other women with missing husbands be.*

Libbie sensed Laura's resolve weakening. "Laura, I keep telling you; if you're lucky enough to make this High Meadows place, which I doubt you would be, Gabe and Del won't be there. What would you gain?"

"Information about where they went."

"Laura, the people in High Meadows won't know any more than you do. The best thing is for you to stay right here where you're safe." Libbie stood and walked over to her friend, slipping her arm around her waist. "Laura, I appreciate what you are going through. No woman's husband goes off into danger more than mine. I understand how difficult waiting is," she said, giving Laura a slight hug. "I guess, Laura, it's the price a woman must pay for being wed to a brave man."

Laura glanced up at Libbie but didn't immediately reply. "I suppose you're right. Will the time get any easier?"

Libbie hesitated for a moment. "No."

Libbie stayed with Laura for another hour before she left to catch the mid-afternoon ferry back across the river to Fort Lincoln. "You're doing the right thing. When they're home, you'll agree waiting was the right thing."

Chapter Fifty-One

Melancholy took over long before the tears began flowing. The sadness always started the same way, a tremendous emptiness, followed by a terrible omen of loss. Laura slumped down next to the front door. She forced herself to rethink the plans. Laura would give herself one more chance, one last opportunity to convince herself not to do this. Sadness, helplessness overwhelmed her, and tears began falling. Wailing, she curled up on the hardwood floor, sobs shaking her body. For such a long time, she wept. Once she cried herself out, she fell into a light slumber.

The nightmares started. They came every time sleep came—always the same. Gabe and Del being unimaginably tortured in the murderous hands of the Sioux. Gabe raised his bloodied face, calling her name. Del's head hung down as he cried out for Laura. Not the groans of a young man, but cries from his childhood, screams of a defenseless little boy. The nightmare slashed through her soul, brutal and lurid. They screamed out in pain and sorrow. They begged for her to come, set them free, to save them.

Waking but not at all rested, weary and empty, Laura

227

wrapped a heavy shawl around her shoulders and headed into Bismarck. At first, she intended to harness a team to the old wagon, but she changed her mind and made the short walk on foot.

The nighttime temperatures warmed up little, and patches of frost still hid in the shadows. Her high-button fashionable shoes provided no protection from the damp cold, and she wished she had taken the time to pull on a pair of boots. With no idea where to begin her search, she assumed any of the saloons would be as good a spot as any.

Laura had never been inside a saloon, not even one of the high-class "Ale Houses" back home, often frequented by couples when the husband wanted to treat his wife to a meal out of the house or a traveling entertainment show.

When Laura stepped into the first of the many saloons Bismarck offered, she doubted the wisdom of her decision. The floor, slick with tobacco spit, squished under every step. Cigar smoke hung so thick her eyes burned. The place stunk, reeking of body odor from unwashed men, beer, and whiskey, far from the aroma of the lilac water Laura often left in an open container in their sitting room.

"Can I help you, honey? You look a little lost." The raspy voice belonged to a red-haired saloon girl sporting enough rouge to last Laura three or four months. Her eyes, swollen and bloodshot, she was at least twenty pounds underweight, skin and bones. Laura guessed the girl in her early twenties, but her thin and drawn face aged her beyond her years.

"I'm looking for Red Holsten," Laura said, trying not to sound unnerved by the surroundings.

"Red? I don't believe I've seen him around here today. Are you a friend of his, honey?" The sad state of the girl's teeth, stained by tobacco and whiskey, some rotted, caught Laura's attention.

"I need to speak to him," Laura said, not wanting to classify herself as a friend of Holsten, or anyone, frequenting a place like *The Trooper House*. Laura assumed they named the saloon to draw the business of enlisted men from Ft. Lincoln, a clientele with a considerable thirst.

The rouge-cheeked gal's eyes ran up and down Laura, making her more uncomfortable. "'Cause you don't strike me as a friend of Red's."

"As I said, I want to speak with him for a moment."

"Well, as I said," the saloon girl's abruptness insulted Laura, "I ain't seen him around today." She turned with such verve her skirt, a green satin affair, swirled out like a can-can dancer's. She sashayed back toward the center of the noisy room, yelling at a regular, "Clancy, ol' boy, are you of a yearning to buy me a whiskey?"

Laura lost interest in searching through stinking, fly-infested saloons. Standing back on the sidewalk, the day was dreary and gray, still cheerier than the inside of *The Trooper House*. For a moment, her heart hurt for the rouge-cheeked girl.

Laura started up the street, trying to think of another way to locate Holsten. Red having no job other than some occasional gold mining, eliminated going to his place of employment. She thought about how to find the man and decided to check Willy Tyler's tobacco shop, where Laura visited once or twice with Gabe when he needed to replenish his supply of pipe tobacco. She cared little for the tobacco store, but at least Willy was a decent man, and a half-drunken saloon strumpet wearing a green satin skirt wouldn't accost.

When the little bell over the door rang, Willy looked up from rolling a leaf of tobacco into a long cigar. "Why, Mrs. Reed, I didn't expect you to stop in. With Gabe out of town, I didn't figure you to run short of tobacco."

"The tobacco supply is fine," Laura said, smiling in acknowledgment of the little joke. "Willy," Laura said, ill at ease in the shop but not as uncomfortable as in the saloon, "Where I can find Red Holsten?"

"Red Holsten?" Willy raised his bushy eyebrows.

Her searching for Red was going to shock everyone.

She tried to think of some reason to need Red, not sounding contrived or bringing a series of questions. "I need a bit of work done, but I'm not strong enough."

"Well, if an ox is what you want, Red oughta meet your need." He gave the tobacco leaf one last roll before licking the edge. Putting the cigar into the display case, his demeanor turned more formal. "If you can wait for a little while, Mrs. Reed, as soon as I close up, I'll be happy to come and give you a hand, only be a little more than an hour."

"I don't want to put you out, but you're kind to offer."

The shopkeeper's eyebrows raised at her rejection.

"And besides, I think Red needs a little money, and I'll pay him for the work."

Willy didn't speak for a minute. "Try the livery. He likes to play checkers there in the afternoon. If he's not there, he's getting drunk somewhere, and you'll be wasting your time trying to find him before breakfast, which he eats around nine o'clock at Carson's Café."

"Thanks, Willy. We'll be in for tobacco when Gabe gets back."

A colossal mud puddle flooded the entrance of the Bismarck Livery Stable and Blacksmith Shop, leaving Laura no alternative but to tiptoe through, muddying her high-button shoes. She found the owner, a hairy man named Otter Elliot, bent over, shoeing a contrary, white mule inside the front door. His colorful reference to the animal's heritage shocked Laura and embarrassed Otter when he glanced up.

Despite the chilly day, sweat poured down the man's grimy face. Laura thought him small for a blacksmith. Not meeting many blacksmiths, she expected they should be burly men with massive hairy shoulders and chests.

"What can I do for you, ma'am?" He stuttered. "Other than stop my swearing."

"I'm looking for Red Holsten."

"Red? He's in the back playing checkers with my kid. Go on back." Otter wiped his arm across his face and sighed. "I better be more careful about my conversations with mules in the future."

"Well, hello, Laura," Holsten said when she stuck her head in the back room. Most men would have spoken to her as Mrs. Reed.

"Can I speak with you a minute, Red?"

"In private?" he asked.

His tone was way too familiar. Laura almost said yes, but changed her mind, deciding if Red agreed to take her, the news would spread through Bismarck within the hour. "Red," she said, surprising herself with the boldness in her voice, "I want you to take me to High Meadows. I want to find Gabe."

Holsten appeared confused. "I thought your husband went back out looking for Lucy Carlyle."

"He did. They're going to High Meadows to pick up another man."

"I never heard of High Meadows." Holsten jumped two of his opponent's black checkers, giving a satisfied grunt. "Where is it?"

"In the Bighorns."

"The Bighorns," Holsten blurted out. "Hell, woman, that's the other side of Sioux territory. You want us scalped?"

"I want to find my husband." Laura's eyes cut through the man.

The iciness of the woman's expression took Holsten aback. "Well, I can understand. But damn, woman, the Bighorns are a long way off."

"I thought you might be man enough to help me. I guess I was wrong." Laura spun on her heels and started back through the barn.

"Now wait a minute here," Holsten yelled, jumping up, knocking his chair over backward. "I didn't say I wouldn't take you."

"Don't you raise your voice to me!"

"I just said those mountains are a long way from here." He scratched at his heavy red beard. "Did you say they was picking up another man?"

"In High Meadows. He's sort of famous, I think. A gunman, I believe."

"What's his name?"

Laura wanted to smile but didn't. She sensed having this ox of a man about where she wanted him. "I can't remember." Laura put her hand to her chin—deep in thought. "Ray? I think his name is Ray." More hesitation. "No, Gray," she said as if some revelation, an epiphany, came over her. "Gray something."

"Wehr? Gray Wehr?"

"I think so. Yes, I'm sure." Laura feigned disinterest. "When do you want to go?"

Victory—she wanted to dance a little jig. "As soon as possible. I can be ready tomorrow morning."

Red, not a quick thinker, scratched his head—again. "Would you oppose taking someone along? I can ask Hank Potts. Two men might make for a safer trip."

"I would appreciate help from anyone willing."

"I believe Hank would go," Red said, nodding his head. "But we can't go for free. We'll try not to charge you too much, but I'm afraid we need paid a little something."

Red's sudden entrepreneurship caught Laura by surprise. "How much would you want?"

"Well, now, I'm not sure. Let's say two dollars a day."

"Two each?" Laura gasped.

The shock on her face caused Red to lose his nerve. "No, not apiece." He muttered. "Together."

"One dollar each per day," Laura said deliberately. She hesitated, looking first at Red, away, and at him again. "All right. A dollar a day each, but I can't afford anymore."

"No, ma'am, a dollar a day. No more."

"Be at my home in the morning."

"Right at daylight." Red smiled as he shook her hand.

Laura tiptoed back across the mud puddle and headed for home. *How easy to make a man do what you want.*

Chapter Fifty-Two

"To the Bighorn Mountains!" Hank Potts exclaimed. "Across Sioux land? Have you lost your senses?"

"I have no intention of going across the Indian territory," Red said. "The woman will give up after three days out on the cold ground. We'll ride her around in circles another day or two and bring her back home. We'll tell her 'cause she cut the trip short, she needs to pay us ten dollars each. Hell, we'll make easy money," Red laughed.

Chapter Fifty-Three

The men made Horse Creek about noon.

"It'll be hard to make Pine Bluffs today unless we push well into the dark," Gray said.

"Are we going to ride late?" Del asked.

Gray glanced over at the boy sitting to his left. Del's eyes sagged, his mouth drooped, showing his lack of enthusiasm for riding half the night. "No, we'll make a camp and go into Pine Bluffs tomorrow." Gray turned his attention to Trent. "I'm going to ride down the creek and look for any place where a lot of horses crossed in the last few days. Keep straight south. I'll catch up with you at camp tonight."

"Will you be able to find us at night?" Tom asked.

"Build a roaring fire, and I'll find you. Keep an eye on these three," he said, slapping Del on the shoulder before turning his bay and heading her down Horse Creek.

He crossed a mile or so downstream to ride the south bank where the riders would come out. Although Walker and his band were likely to head west, Gray wanted to send

Trent in the other direction. He also thought of sending Trent on this scout since he believed Trent's skills exceeded his own. However, his own had always been good enough to gain employment with the Army. Back then, Bill Cody bragged about his tracking. He claimed to be better than Gray or J.B. Hickok.

Hickok always pointed out scouting required more than the ability to follow a track. Instinct was more valuable, and Hickok and Gray possessed more than Cody. Still, he believed Trent would have done a better job, and he would have sent him, except he didn't want to answer any more questions from Tom Gibbs and the Reeds. He didn't dislike the three men; he loathed constant conversation.

Gray did not push his mare. Naturally a fast walker, they covered a lot of ground with Lena setting her own pace. Wehr's knees, old adversaries, and the foot broken in the spring ached. He thought of stopping to rest a few times, but not in pursuit. Little slowed him down in a chase.

After two more fruitless hours and a brief encounter with a surly badger, Gray decided to turn back and find the others. The increasing futility of the search for Walker and his gang depressed him.

The surrounding countryside didn't help, either. Except for a few birch trees a half-mile or so upstream, nothing but old scrub brush and dry gullies lay in any direction. What leaves the sparse bushes carried in the summer had fallen off. "I swear, Lena, this is a lonely country." He stopped the mare and stepped off. "Let's have a drink and head back."

The horse meandered out into the creek and splashed some water around with her nose. "I'm a tired old boy, Lena. How about you?" He squatted down at the edge of the water. The day, sunny earlier, turned cloudy and contributed to Gray's gloomy mood.

Gray let the bay stand in the water until she came out on her own. "I guess you're ready to go." He stepped back up into the saddle. Mounted, he took one more glance around the area. His eyes settled on a flat spot in the bank a hundred yards down the creek, an easy place to cross, worthy of a quick inspection before heading back.

"Well, kick my butt and call me Charlotte. I believe we've found where they crossed." He stepped down off the horse for a closer look.

They weren't brand new. Gray judged them at least two days old, but determining the exact age of the tracks was, in his opinion, an imprecise business. Some old-timers claimed to tell within minutes. They would declare, "they made those prints about ten, Wednesday morning." Gray always believed such trackers were full of crap.

Lena whinnied and jerked back a step or two. "Easy. What's the matter?" Gray reached out to rub the front of her face. The horse crow hopped. "Whoa." Before stroking the horse's face again, something rumbled in a clump of bushes off to the right. Gray drew his pistol in case he and Lena stumbled on some predator, most likely a bobcat or another badger.

"Stand, Lena." Gray dropped the reins and started toward the brush. As he approached, the moaning increased, a terrible sound, not crying, but a pain-filled moan. He scoured the bushes to find the source of the noise, nothing. Then he realized the groans came from a gully beyond.

The moans got louder, bringing back dark memories of men suffering on Civil War battlefields, a place where Gray remembered bloody, desperate wails, cries, and weeping. But this was different, not as deep, not as throaty. This moaning was more childlike; still, the sound was the same, the echo of dying.

When Gray reached the lip of the gully, he holstered his pistol. He found a young girl about ten years old, wearing a pale blue dress, or what they left of one.

So much blood covered her. He laid his hand on the ledge for support and jumped down into the ditch. The girl screamed when Gray landed beside her, a ghastly scream, not what anyone would expect from a child. Unsuccessful the first time, Gray tried to touch her. She shrieked and jerked away, her bloody, dirty body convulsing.

"It's all right, sweetie," Gray said, although he doubted the girl was coherent enough to understand him. Gray reached for her again. This time, he moved fast, pulling her into his arms. The child went out of control. Fighting and flailing, she inflicted a nasty scratch along the side of Gray's neck.

He tried to hold her without being so forceful as to injure her further. She screamed and fought him with every ounce of her strength, kicking and striking out with her tiny fists. Almost as fast as she flew into the rage, she went limp, slumping in his embrace. Gray thought he scared her into passing out. He laid her on the ditch bank, climbed up, and picked her up into his arms.

He started back for the creek. "Lena, stand, girl," he said to the horse, concerned she might smell the blood on the child and bolt. "Easy, Lena." The bay backed up a step or two but did not panic. Gray left the girl on the bank and picked up the horse's reins. He tied her to the largest bush in the area before going back to care for the injured girl.

Gray kneeled over her the unconscious girl. Someone shot her in the right shoulder. The bullet entered her back, further angering Gray. Judging from the nasty way her foot twisted, Gray thought she had a broken ankle. Besides the gunshot wound and ankle, she had taken a severe beating. Her face cut, bruised, and swollen so much on the left side, Gray suspected her cheekbone was fractured.

Gray went back to Lena, took a towel out of his saddlebag, and undid his bedroll. He covered the girl with the blanket before wetting the towel in the creek to wash away some of the crusted blood. Someone savagely whipped her with a quirt. The beating tore a gash over her left eyebrow, revealing a small portion of bone.

Gray, not a squeamish man, having seen some terrible sights in his life—men shot, scalped—seldom backed away, but this abuse sickened him. He sat back for a moment, wondering what to do. The child had not been lucky enough for the bullet to go all the way through. The girl was going to die if he didn't remove it and stop the hemorrhaging, but he was no doctor.

"Dear God," Gray whispered, "what do you want me to do? What do you want me to do?" He held one of his spare shirts over the wound for thirty minutes, hoping to at least slow the continuous blood loss. Before the beating, she had been a pretty child. Her blonde hair hung almost to her waist. She had long eyelashes curling away from her eyes.

The bleeding slowed, either from the pressure he started applying or because the girl was running out of blood. Gray stood and built a fire. He turned the still unconscious girl on her stomach. He pushed the blanket back away from the child's upper body and cut the remaining top of the dress away before tucking the blanket in everywhere else around her.

"Father, If I shouldn't do this, please stop me." What did he expect? A flash of lightning? A deafening roar of thunder?

He needed to probe the wound and find the bullet. That much he knew from seeing field operations during the war, but surgeons had medical instruments. Some removed bullets with the patient awake without the man hollering.

But other times, more often, men screamed and jerked in terrible agony, requiring two or three soldiers to pen them down. This was not a man, not a battle-hardened soldier. But a helpless child without the benefit of an experienced doctor wielding a medical probe.

Gray had no such instrument. He tried to find the bullet with his finger. The chunk of lead ripped through the shoulder blade, leaving a hole larger than his thumb through the bone and torn the muscle. Like a little tunnel, the bullet's path took a definite downward turn. A little further, deeper probing, the bullet was almost straight across from the girl's armpit and right below the skin.

The girl slipped into a more profound state of

unconsciousness. Gray rolled her to her side. Pushing on the lead with his finger, a lump rose. "Lord, I think I can cut this out from the front." That encouraged Gray since he lacked medical instruments to extract it from the other side.

Laying the child down, he hesitated for a brief time before holding his bone-handled knife, a good-sized hunting knife, not a surgeon's scalpel, over the fire.

Gray moved around to the other side of the girl. He picked her up and tried to cradle her against his chest while slipping the longest finger on his left hand back into the wound. This time, the girl jerked and made a deep moaning sound. Gray held her for another few minutes while she settled back down.

He could pin her down, perform his surgery, but he did not want to cut any more than necessary. He desired to push on the bullet with one hand and make the incision in the exact location with the other.

Again, he slipped his finger through the wound and pushed the slug. This time, the girl regained consciousness, although only for a moment. She screamed and thrashed in his arms. Gray squeezed her until he feared he might hurt her.

As she quieted, he loosened his grasp and laid her back down on her back. Gray let her lie still for a few minutes, hoping she would relax more into her state of unconsciousness and because he so dreaded what came next. He listened to the child's raspy breathing—more like a weathered and dying old man than a child. He again took the girl into his arms and held her, rocking her like a restless baby fighting off sleep. She was so small, much smaller than when struggling and thrashing in the gully.

Gray studied her features. She had a pug nose and dark eyebrows, much darker than her blonde hair. Her skin was white, Gray assumed, from the loss of so much blood. Once or twice over the next few minutes, she stirred a little but did not wake up.

During the war, field surgeons prayed for God's

guidance over their hands, a prudent thing at this moment. Gray leaned over the girl. He changed his position, placing one knee over her arm and the other on her chest. The slug was much harder to find than when pushing from the back. Found.

The girl's soft skin was easy to cut. His first incision went down into the muscle. One more time, a little deeper. He tried to pinch the piece of lead between his fingers. His cut wasn't long enough, but he did not want to slice her anymore.

He struggled to flip the bullet out with his knife; he failed. His second attempt wrestled a painful moan from the child. Before resorting to more cutting, he would try once more.

This time, he bent down and put his mouth to the wound. Pressing his fingers around the opening, he sucked, much like someone trying to suck the poison out of a snake bite. The slug moved and slid between his teeth. Gray spat out the bullet and a fair amount of salty-tasting blood. He wiped his sleeve across his lips before sitting again.

Gray lay on the ground. He needed to bandage the child, stop the bleeding, but he must lie down. *A minute or two,* he thought; *otherwise, I'm going to pass out.* As he lay still with his left arm across his face, doubt haunted him. *Did he do the right thing? Or did he help to kill the girl?*

Gray forced himself up. He went over to Lena and got his last spare shirt out of his saddlebag before taking a mouthful of water from his canteen, swishing it in his mouth, and spitting. He thought himself the first person to remove a bullet by biting the patient, something so ridiculous he almost chuckled.

When he returned to the limp child, he found the bleeding worse. Wehr panicked. He knew only one way to stop the hemorrhaging, but did he have the courage?

Distressed but convinced the girl would die otherwise, he broke open several bullets and sprinkled gunpowder on both sides of the wound. He took a burning stick out of the fire, touched the black powder.

The child's shrieks rent his heart. Gray grabbed her into his arms. Her cries were horrible, animal-like sounds. Why did he set the powder off? If she had bled to death, at least she would have died peacefully, not in this beastly agony.

Minutes passed like hours before her screaming and fighting subsided. She lived, slipped back into an unconscious existence, a place where Gray hoped she would find some peace and rest. Gray bandaged the girl, wiped tears from his eyes, and rocked the now precious child back and forth.

Chapter Fifty-Four

"Where do you suppose he is?" Del asked, no longer trying to hide his concern.

"Don't know," Trent said, "but if he's not here by the morning, I'll head back up to Horse Creek and find him. You three go on into Pine Bluffs and wait for us."

"I'm not sure we can find Pine Bluffs," Gabe said.

The comment frustrated Trent. "You ride straight south; how can you miss a town?" he asked with irritation.

"We've never been there from here, Trent. I'll admit we're not as competent out here as you and Gray," he said in a defensive, harsh tone of voice. "But we're doing the best we can." Reed tossed his tin plate, still half full of stew, down on the ground. "I'm nothing but a farmer from Ohio, and I guess I wasn't too successful at that. I lost everything. I've sure as hell got no business trying to rescue somebody else. I couldn't even save us. That's the reason we had to move out here. And her father provided all the money for our home in Bismarck. I can't save anyone."

Del got up from the fire and walked off into the darkness. "The boy's ashamed of me."

Trent was not sure what he witnessed, but he had seen similar behavior in other men. Self-doubt swallowed many admirable men who provided well for their families.

Other men, even Gray, were subject to sudden bouts of despair or discouragement. "The doldrums," according to Millie. Gray tried to hide his misery from everyone when the hopelessness overwhelmed him, but Annie and Jean always spotted it. Millie would know something was wrong. "Sometimes, I think he needs to be alone," she told Trent.

Annie attempted to talk with him but always found Gray reluctant. Jean said the "blues" sometimes hit her mother, and she thought Gray inherited the problem.

"He's a good boy, and he's not ashamed of his father," Trent told Gabe as Del walked off into the darkness. "It's none of my business, but I think the boy he is speaks well of the man you are. 'Course, as I say, none of my business." Trent picked up the tin plate. He scooped up another ladle of stew and handed it back to Gabe. "You better eat this to help keep you warm through the night."

Del came back into camp, his arms loaded down with wood. "I thought we should make a blazing fire in case Gray's looking for us."

Chapter Fifty-Five

By what Gray judged, or at least hoped, to be the middle of the night, the girl, so small lying on the hard ground, seemed to rest. She awoke several times but didn't speak. Sometimes she would stare up at him or peer at the fire. But she would only moan for a while and fall back into her sleep or unconsciousness. When her fever broke, her breathing got easier. He thought some color returned to her face.

Clear and full of stars, the night turned cold. Gray breathed on the girl's hands and face, trying to warm them. He made sure he kept the fire well-fueled. Still, he feared despite his best efforts, she was going to die.

Could a child so small possess enough will to live? Living through such experiences of horror required a strong will to survive. Especially if she watched her entire family butchered, the way these men who captured her butchered.

He wondered how long it had been since the girl ate. Did the bastards starve as well as beat her? Besides the other things going against her, Gray only brought jerky with him.

Nothing fit for a sick child. Maybe he'd find a rabbit or something to shoot when the sun came up. A hot meal would give her enough strength and will to live. At least Gray hoped so.

He expected Trent would come looking for him at daybreak, hopefully with food. Gray's partner would push hard and show up by early afternoon. In the meantime, they were in for a long, chilly night.

Wehr fell into a light, dream-filled sleep. In the first dream, he rode Lena across an open plain. They were chasing something, but what or who. His hat flew off as the horse pushed harder. He pulled back on the reins to check the horse a bit, but she would not give.

She stuck her nose out and pinned her ears back. The sky turned dark and smoky, but the animal would not relent; she would only run. When Gray woke up, he realized the light wind shifted, and the smoke from the fire was drifting right into their faces.

The second dream was worse. A group of women and children off in a hazy distance reached out toward him, crying for help, but he'd lost his bay mare. On foot, he limped to them. Barely able to walk, he couldn't reach the desperate women and children no matter how he strained.

He was failing them. Regardless of how he tried, he couldn't run to their aid. He hobbled his way forward on crippled feet and knees.

The slightest mist of rain woke him. The little girl was still in his arms, and when he looked down at her, her eyes were open. "Well, hello."

The child stared at him without responding. Until her eyes blinked, Gray wasn't sure she was alive. "Are you cold?" He tried to pull his coat up around her a little tighter. His movement scared her, and she jerked away. "I'm sorry. I didn't mean to scare you. I want you to be warm." He smiled at the girl, but she didn't react to him. "Let's put a little more wood on our fire," he said, reaching over and picking up a couple of branches. "That'll help," he told the blonde child as he kneeled and kissed her forehead.

She was burning up. Wehr cursed himself for falling asleep. He would have realized the fever was returning and stopped it if he had stayed awake, although he didn't know how.

The girl's eyes drooped shut. She was dying. Out of fear, he shook her. She opened her eyes again, and a flood of relief roared over Gray. When she closed her eyes this time and drifted back to sleep, he did not panic.

He put more wood on the fire. Perhaps if he got her warm enough, the fever would break. He pulled the blanket up tighter and wrapped his coat around the outside. He held her in his arms and breathed on her face and neck, hoping his breath would somehow crack the malaise.

Another hour passed before the girl broke out in a sweat. Gray loosened the blanket and tried to dry the girl with his neckerchief. Two more times in the next three hours, he repeated this process, and Gray thought he was going to lose the child each time.

"Who are you?" Her voice was so small Gray struggled to hear. He had not noticed she again opened her eyes, and her voice, quiet and frail, startled him. "Who are you?" she asked again.

"My name is Graham. I won't hurt you, sweetie. I'm going to help you." The girl turned her head toward the fire. The bruise on the right of her face kept getting darker, causing Gray to assume someone hit her right before they left. He brushed her matted hair back from her face. "Would you like a drink of water?"

"Promise you won't hurt me."

"I promise." Gray cradled the girl, hoping she would live through the rest of the night. If she made it through the frosty night, she would live—maybe. And, if she lived, Gray would find and rescue any of her family still be living, giving her at least part of her life back.

Chapter Fifty-Six

Trent woke before daylight to leave camp at first light. "Stay right here," he said to the others. "If we're not back tonight. Don't worry. We'll be in sometime tomorrow."

"Don't you think we should go with you?" Tom asked.

"No, Gray may show up here in an hour. If he shows, tell him if he wants to head on into Pine Bluffs, I'll catch up with you." Saying nothing else, he turned the bay gelding and retraced the same ground they rode in on yesterday.

The child slept for two hours before she woke up, crying and confused. The darkening bruise on her face had turned almost black, but the swelling around her eyes had gone down. "Shhh, shhh," Gray whispered as he tried to comfort the girl, swaying back and forth as he held her. The girl again fell asleep a little while later but did not sleep long.

"My foot hurts," she cried. "Hurts bad."

"I know, sweetie. When the day warms up, I'll try to help you. Let the sun warm up a little." Gray wasn't waiting for the morning to heat up. He was hoping Trent would show up to assist in setting and splinting the leg.

"I don't remember your name."

"Graham, Graham Wehr. Can you tell me your name?"

"April. My mom called me that because April is the month my birthday's in."

The girl was better, but Gray still had a disquieting sense she was far from out of danger. "That's a pretty name," Gray said, believing keeping the girl talking might help keep her mind off her agony. He wanted to check on her shoulder, but since she had mentioned no pain there, he didn't want her scared by what would not be an encouraging sight.

He decided if she fell asleep again, he would try to sneak a look. "All I've got to eat is some dry old jerky. If I knew I was going to find such a beautiful little girl, I'd have brought along some cake or at least a little candy," he said, smiling as he rubbed the side of her face. "Would you like a little water?"

The child nodded, her eyes drooping; she was slipping into unconsciousness again.

"Stay right here by the fire. I need to go over to my horse for a canteen." Trying to stand after holding the girl in his lap all night proved quite an experience. His knees, back, his entire body objected.

April took four sips, tiny sips, and drifted back to sleep, this time into a more peaceful rest. After about half an hour, Gray checked the girl's shoulder. She stirred and moaned when he moved her but did not wake up. Given the severity, the wound was not bleeding nor more inflamed than reasonable.

Gray wondered how severely the ankle was broken. The girl wore a high lace-up black shoe, which Gray hoped would provide support. Her foot twisted to the outside, but not as much as he first thought. Once she stopped struggling, the break didn't appear too bad.

Gray thought about setting the ankle while the girl slept but decided not to. That would be a terrible way to wake up, and she might start thrashing about, causing herself more injury.

Gray took advantage of April's sleep and left to gather more firewood. He did not go far enough away to lose sight of her, which limited the availability of wood. After tossing the newly gathered sticks on the fire, Gray laid down next to the girl. Again, he slipped into a shallow and unwelcome slumber.

Gray didn't wake until almost mid-morning. April was still sleeping. He believed the more she slept, the better she would travel. It would be a long day into Pine Bluffs, but Gray thought it best to make the trip all at one time. He wanted to get her to a doctor as soon as possible, if Pine Bluffs had a doctor.

The sun shining and the warming temperatures lifted Gray's spirits. His spirits rose again when Trent rode into the little camp. "Did she say anything about how long ago they left her or about how many there are?" Trent asked after Gray told him about finding the girl and cutting the bullet out.

"Not yet. I haven't tried to make her talk any more than she's done on her own." He bent down and pulled Trent's blanket back up over the girl's shoulders. "I wish we'd had yours' last night. The air got crisp out here."

"I saw a few antelope about half a mile from here. I ought to slip back and shoot her a decent meal."

Trent found the antelope close enough Gray heard the shot. They spent the next hour skinning and butchering. Trent scoured the area for more wood, and before April woke up again, roasting meat wafted through the camp. They also cut up a few chunks of meat to make some soup in case the child couldn't chew solid food.

Another hour slipped by before April stirred and awoke. Although Gray didn't think as severe as during the night, the fever returned. She cried more this time, saying her shoulder and ankle hurt more than before she fell asleep.

Gray urged her to eat. She managed two spoonsful of the soup. "Millie gave me a vial of laudanum," Trent said in a half-whisper. "She sent it in case someone got injured or a bad headache." Laudanum was a wildly popular painkiller used by doctors for everything from headaches to busted feet.

"I sort of hate to give her that stuff," Gray said, thinking back to when Doc Hollins dispensed the nasty liquid to him liberally when he broke his foot. Gray spent the better part of a month in a stupor and then struggled to stop its use.

However, after some mild arguing from Trent, Gray decided the medicine would be preferable to having the child in such pain. "Sweetie, do you think you can take a little of this? It will make some of the throbbing go away." Gray gave her a teaspoon of the vile-tasting liquid. She gagged for a moment, and he wondered if she was going to get it down. When she managed to swallow, he gave her another spoonful of antelope soup.

Minutes later, she fell asleep again. Gray decided to examine her ankle. He got the shoe unlaced with no reaction from the girl, but when he slipped it off, she jerked violently. Gray leaned down over her, trying to calm her.

"It hurts," she wept. "My foot hurts worse than my shoulder."

"I think it's broken. If you let me touch your foot, I might help a little. If we put your shoe back on and tie it up snug, we might make it feel better."

"All right."

The child's pain caused Gray to lose his nerve. "Let's wait a little while, sweetie." April again fell into a restless sleep. "Let's give the laudanum a little longer," Gray said, glancing at Trent for some reassurance regarding his medical work.

"Maybe we should give her another dose before you

try to set her ankle. I doubt you'll turn her into an addict."

Thirty minutes later, the child woke up again. With trepidation, Gray gave her another spoonful of the laudanum. "Let's wait a while."

April stayed awake and, in fact, got a bit talkative. "I think she's a little drunk," Trent laughed. Gray didn't much appreciate the poor attempt at humor.

"Let's try to look at your ankle," Gray said to the child.

"My feet doesn't hurts so much anymore," she said, slurring her words. Gray gave Trent a half-dirty scowl.

"The only thing is, honey, this may hurt."

"My mama says I'm a tough little chicken."

Trent chuckled at the child's response. "How old are you, April?"

"Ten. I'll be eleven on April ninth."

"Well, you are a brave girl."

"Now I want you to lie back, and Trent's going to hold you so you don't jump too much when I fix your foot." Gray started untying the shoe. April flinched.

Once he slipped the shoe off, he could feel her ankle twisted out of its socket. "I don't think her ankle is broken," he said. "Just out of joint. Are you ready?" He glanced up at Trent, who nodded his head. Gray gave the foot a terrific jerk to the right. POP. The joint snapped back into place.

April lurched off the ground, thrashing her way out of Trent's grip. "Hold her! Keep her down." Trent re-established his grasp on the hurting and scared child.

April didn't stop crying for half an hour. Gray almost wished he had left her foot alone, but there was no sense worrying now. And that was not Gray's way, anyway. Once he got her shoe back on and laced up snug, she felt somewhat better. A little later, she went back to sleep.

"Did the other three head down to Pine Bluffs?"

"They were afraid they couldn't find it."

"Couldn't find a town?"

"Didn't think they could find it," Trent repeated. "I

told them to stay put, and we'd pick them up."

"I swear," Gray said, shaking his head. "Well, I'm taking this child to Pine Bluff's on a straight line from here. You can cut over for them up. I'll meet you in town. You can find the town, can't you?"

Chapter Fifty-Seven

Red Holsten and Hank Potts rode up in front of the Reed house two hours before sunrise.

After raining the day before, the sky stayed cloudy as the three passed through Bismarck. The ferry crossing took only a few minutes, and Laura and the two hired men were three miles away when daylight broke.

"Looks like rain again today," Potts said, sounding discouraged.

"You won't melt," Red said sharply.

"I ain't afraid of melting. I just hate to ride wet."

"Take a shot of this," Holsten said, pulling a flask from the inside of his coat.

The presence of whiskey surprised Laura. She didn't expect the men to bring liquor on a dangerous journey, an abysmal decision. And now, here they were, drinking with the sun barely up. "I'd rather you not drink while you're riding," Laura said.

Holsten got haughty. "It'll take the chill out of the

morning air."

"Well, I'll not have men I'm paying getting drunk," Laura said.

Holsten gave her a nasty glare, and she expected trouble.

"All right, Missy, all right. We'll save it for the nighttime. You won't object to a shot or two before bedtime, will you?"

Laura did not want them drinking whiskey any time, but she doubted she could stop them entirely, so she looked for the best compromise. "As long as you don't make yourselves drunk. I won't put up with drunks."

"No ma'am. No drunks," Red said.

"And you may call me 'Laura,' or 'Mrs. Reed'," she said, looking Red straight in the eye, "but I would prefer you not use degrading names like Missy."

Hank Potts chuckled at Laura's statement. Red was less amused.

Within the hour, a depressing rain started to fall. Laura tied an old scarf over her head and rode with her face down. "If you weren't such a strict task woman, I'd offer you a sip of whiskey. It'd take the chill off," Red said.

"I'm fine. The rain's not miserable enough to justify drinking."

"I expect we'll be safe from the Indians while it rains," Red said. "Nobody'd be riding around out in this weather if they didn't have to. I 'spect they're all hunkered down in their tipis around a warm fire."

"I hope it pours the entire trip," Potts said. "I guess I'd rather be wet than scalped."

About noon, Laura told the men she carried some cornbread and honey butter in her pack if they wanted to stop for a meal. The rain still pounded too hard to build a fire, not displeasing Laura, since she wanted to be traveling again as soon as possible.

Chapter Fifty-Eight

April slept most of the day and throughout the night. "How are you feeling this morning?" Gray asked as he knelt beside her.

"My shoulder hurts, but my foot doesn't hurt as much."

"Can I look at your shoulder? We need to wash it a little and change the bandage."

Gray slipped down the arm of one of Trent's spare shirts, which April now wore. "I have some salve in my saddlebags," Trent said.

The dark gray residue from the gunpowder scared the girl. "Why is my skin so black?"

Gray wasn't about to tell the child he set her on fire. "I used some black medicine to stop the bleeding." April didn't ask anything else.

"Let's rub some of Trent's salve on your wound," Gray said, smiling at the girl. April nodded before pulling the shoulder of the oversized shirt back up when Gray went over for the balm.

"Do you want to give her a little more Laudanum?" Trent asked in a half-whisper.

"I'll put some of this on her. We'll try to ride with her. If she gets to hurting too bad, we'll give her a little," Gray said as a compromise.

Gray rubbed the girl's wound with the ointment and used another of Trent's clean shirts to make a bandage. "Let's dab a little of this on your eyebrow, too," Gray said, dipping his finger back in the dark brown glass jar. "You've got a cut here, too."

"Fox hit me with a quirt," April said, reaching up.

Gray caught her hand before she touched her eye. "Let's not touch it, sweetie; we don't want you to bleed." Gray smeared her eyebrow with the ointment. The brow needed stitches, but he didn't have any needles or thread, and not being life-threatening, he would not put the girl through stitching, anyway. He would leave the sewing to the doctor he hoped to find in Pine Bluffs.

He debated asking her about the man who beat her. The name Fox meant nothing to him. He decided not to question the girl about the men; there would be enough time after seeing a doc.

"How would you like to take a ride on my horse? Do you think you're strong enough?" Gray asked after finishing his doctoring. "We want to take you to Pine Bluffs where someone can take better care of you." April tried to stand, but Gray picked up the wobbly child and carried her to Lena.

"She's a sweet horse."

"She is," Gray agreed as he lifted her into the saddle and stepped up behind her. "Are you comfortable?" The girl nodded her head.

For a while, April got talkative. She told them she lived on a lonely ranch. She talked, bravely, Gray thought, about the men taking her and her mother after killing her dad and two brothers. Since the girl volunteered this information, Gray asked her how many men. "Five. But Maddie's mommy stabbed one of them. One of the other men shot him 'cause he was going to slow them down. Walker, he's the leader, left and brought two more men back."

"Does Maddie have a sister named Jenny?"

"Yes, they're little kids," April said, giving them the first actual confirmation they were after the right men. "But the men still hit them. They didn't care if they were little."

Gray looked over at Trent, who shook his head.

They rode in silence for two or three miles before Gray realized April was crying. He patted her on the leg and kissed the top of her head. "Do you think anybody will try to help my mommy?"

The bay mare took only a few more steps before Gray answered her. "Trent and I are going after your mom." April cried harder, and Gray squeezed her close to him. "We'll bring her back to you," he whispered before kissing her above the ear.

An hour later, April spoke for the first time since Gray's promise. "My arm hurts bad, Graham. It burns a lot." The child, hot to the touch, was complaining about being cold. She started shivering, and chills shook her slight frame. Gray wrapped the blankets tighter around her.

Chapter Fifty-Nine

"Hello!" Gray pounded hard on the front door of Pine Bluffs' only physician. "We need a doctor out here!"

"It's almost midnight. Who's we?" The female reply was impatient and not friendly.

"I have an injured child out here."

"What's wrong with her?" An elderly woman cracked the door open just enough to peek through. Seeing April, she let Gray in. "What happened to her?"

"She's been shot," Gray said, laying the girl down on a small couch next to an old hall tree.

"Thomas! Thomas, wake up. A man has a hurt little girl down here." The woman hurried up a dark, narrow staircase.

Soon, the woman came back down the stairs. "He'll be down in a minute. The old goat would sleep through a war. Let's get her in the exam room," she said, starting down the hallway and pointing to a door off to the left. A worn leather examining couch stood in the middle of a room full of instruments. "Lay her right here," she said as she picked up a blanket to put over the girl and lit two coal oil lamps.

The lamps gave an odd, almost eerie glow to the room. The light created deep shadows, denying Gray any peace in the room.

"How did this happen?" The voice startled Gray, causing him to jump. The doctor, a man in at least his seventies, slipped too quietly into the room. The expression on the doctor's weathered face convinced Gray the old man blamed him for the girl's condition.

"She was kidnapped from a ranch," Gray said, as much to remove the blame as to explain the situation. "I found her yesterday up by Horse Creek."

"Jack Walker took us," April said, speaking for the first time. "They hurt us," she said, starting to cry.

"Lie still, child." The old doctor pulled the blanket back and the shoulder of the oversized shirt down. "Who did the cutting?"

"I did," Gray said, shuffling his feet and staring at the floor.

"It's a lucky thing you ran out of gunpowder. What were you trying to do? Burn the child alive?"

"I didn't know any other way to stop the bleeding."

"Hmph. Did you think about a bandage? Rosie, bring me something to clean this girl up with." The doctor took a bowl of soapy water and a jar of ointment from his wife. He glanced at Gray. "You're a little pale. If you plan on passing out, go to the other room. I don't want to be stepping over you."

"Thomas! Leave the poor man alone," Rosie told her husband as he busied himself with cleaning the wound.

"Does this hurt?" he asked, looking at April.

"A little."

"Did you give her anything for pain?"

"I gave her a little laudanum. I hated to, but we didn't have anything else."

"Why would you hate to give the child painkiller? You'd rather she be in misery?"

Gray's shoulders slumped, his head dropped as he backed away, wanting to disappear. He didn't respond to the old doctor. He tried to do the right thing for the girl, but everything he did must have been wrong.

"Don't you let Doc Boone bother you. He likes to annoy people," she said, giving Gray a warm, almost motherly smile.

"I hope I didn't hurt her."

Doc Boone gave Gray another cockeyed glance. "Oh, I suppose you saved the girl's life," he said. "You did a Christian thing. But cut down, in the future, on your use of gunpowder. Cauterizing is one thing. Setting off an explosion is another."

Chapter Sixty

Laura sensed their presence in the pale morning light. They were shadows at first. Soon, she made out several horses and men moving around the camp. Without warning, they jerked her to her feet and pushed her away from the smoldering campfire. Another man grabbed her around the chest and throat. And while she couldn't see it, or feel it, she sensed the knife being held under her jaw.

Hank Potts, sleeping next to the fire, took a terrible kick in the back, causing him to scream out in both pain and surprise. The boot knocked him three feet across the rough ground. "Oh, God! Don't kill me!"

When Pott's screams woke Red Holsten, he burst from his bedroll. He cut through a brush pile and tried to climb up a steep bank. A horsehair rope looped around his neck and shoulders before slipping tight and jerking him over backward.

The next instant, a Sioux warrior mounted on a black and white spotted pony pulled him back across the gully.

The Lakota dragged him only a short distance, fifty feet, into a rocky area to Laura's right, an aggravating way to start a morning.

The Sioux holding Laura pushed her down toward Hank Potts, who had taken another hard kick to the middle of his chest. He lay clutching sagebrush as if the scraggly brush offered some protection.

Laura cut her palm when she landed on the ground. She started to cry but choked back the pain, afraid a scream might result in retaliation from the Indians. A kick, like the one Hank Potts got—or worse.

Several still mounted Sioux slid off their horses and rummaged through the camp, scattering the packs' contents. Selective about what they took, they grabbed ammunition, food, an extra coat Holsten brought.

They threw a photograph Laura packed of herself and Gabe into the fire. The warrior who kicked Hank Potts pulled his knife before kicking Potts a third time, this time square in the face. Potts flopped on his back before the Sioux jumped on him, pinning him down.

Hank tried to fight back, but the brave slashed the top of his head and ripped his scalp off. Potts was still screaming and writhing on the ground when the warrior stood and waved his fresh scalp and hair back and forth.

Laura leaped to her feet to run, but two warriors grabbed her and turned her back to Potts. One of them jerked her hair and forced her face up when she attempted to turn away from the brutal torturing of Potts.

Three more Sioux ripped off his coat and shirt. Two held him down while the third sliced open his arms and plucked out his eyes. At first, his screams were ghastly, but Potts only moaned weakly when a Sioux grabbed his jaw, shoving his head back before cutting his throat. Laura squeezed her eyes shut, but she couldn't shut out the echoes of Potts's dying shrieks.

Red Holsten, barefoot and shirtless in a circle of five Lakota, begged for his life. He wasn't making any of his brash talk about what he'd do if they found Indians. He was whimpering like a puppy. The Lakota kept pushing him back and forth between them, almost like school children would do when bullying a weaker child.

Two of them used stone war clubs to hit him whenever the others pushed in their direction. A heavy-set warrior raised his club and beat Red over the head. Once his brutal work satisfied him, he smashed Holsten's skull and brains to a bloody jelly.

The Sioux believed a man entered the next life the same way he left this one. These men would now be no threat to them in the spirit world and would forever regret their intrusion into the sacred land of the Lakota.

Two warriors still held Laura while the other Sioux talked in rapid, excited voices. With the other men dead, Laura thought they might be arguing about her future. She assumed some wanted to kill her while others wanted to take her captive. Which fate would be worse?

A young brave with black and yellow paint on his face brought a horse over to the men restraining her. The younger Indian tied one end of a rawhide thong to Laura's ankle before handing the other under the horse's belly to one of the other warriors, who jerked the cord tight, tying the rope to the other foot.

After scavenging the camp one last time, the Sioux got back on their horses and started northeast, deeper into their sacred Paha Sapa.

Chapter Sixty-One

J.B. Hickok wiped the white gravy out of his mustache. "So, Doc Boone says the child will be all right?"

Gray nodded. "He says with rest and decent care; she should be fine, except for a nasty scar on her shoulder. These over-easy eggs are a little hard this morning," he muttered as he forked up a mixture of eggs and sausage.

"Well, I suppose a scar is a small price to pay for escaping."

"She didn't escape," Gray said between bites. "She busted up her ankle, and they decided she was too much trouble. Lord, they shot the child and left her to die."

"That's sure a bunch in need of killing," Hickok said.

"Well, I wouldn't turn down your help," Gray said, casting a long glance at Hickok.

"I can't, Gray. I told you a woman is waiting for me."

While disappointed, Gray didn't act so in front of his old friend. Hickok had always been an independent sort, impossible to talk into anything he didn't want to do. Still,

Gray thought his reason was weak.

A woman should accept a man sometimes having responsibilities needing immediate attention. A faithful woman should wait; Annie waited enough for him.

The two men finished the rest of their breakfasts in silence before Hickok spoke to him.

"There is another reason. I'm not sure I'd be of much help to you."

Gray couldn't disguise the disbelief on his face.

"I don't see too well these days." Hickok ran his hand over the rough, old wooden table, brushing a few of the crumbs of toast on the floor. "I'd need to be awful close to shoot a man. Sometimes I experience short periods of near blindness. They never last long, but they sure shake a man."

Sad for Hickok, Gray couldn't imagine living the life both he and "Wild Bill" led and ending up blind. "Have you seen a doctor about this?"

"Enough to cure every illness," Hickok laughed. "Not one of 'em gave me a decent answer. Several of them told me to wear dark spectacles in bright sunlight. What a sight."

Gray chuckled at the image of "Wild Bill" Hickok walking around the street in his frock coat, polished knee-high boots, red sash around his waist, long hair blowing in the breeze...and wearing a pair of dark-colored spectacles.

"Oh, I'm not blind yet. I can still read a hand of cards. Some doctors say my eyes may not get worse." Hickok wiped his mustache. "Course, you don't need to be spreading this information around." He hesitated. "I'd rather every gunman west of St. Louis not have a reason to come looking for the old blind pistolero."

"I imagine I can keep my mouth closed," Gray said. "There's Trent," Gray said, glancing over at the café door. "You remember Trent Thaxton, don't you? His folks ran the Sutler Store down at Ft. Laramie. I found this old horse thief wandering around the hotel lobby this morning," Gray told Trent.

Hickok smiled at Trent and slapped him on the

shoulder. "Sit down. You're wearin' a healthy color, boy. Gray tells me married life agrees with the both of you."

"You should try it," Trent said as a redheaded girl of about fourteen poured him a cup of coffee and asked what he'd like to eat for breakfast.

"Why, Jimmy's thinking of that exact thing. He's on his way up to Cheyenne this afternoon to dazzle a member of the fairer sex."

"Who's the lady?" Trent asked.

"Agnes Lake, a widow of five years," Hickok said, a curious grin on his face. "Ever hear of the woman?"

"The circus performer," Trent said.

"Circus owner now. Quite a woman. World-famous as a horsewoman, tightrope walker, dancer, lion tamer."

"Why would such a woman be interested in you?" Gray joked.

"In me? I'm the only man who's more famous than she is."

The three men laughed about Hickok's success with Agnes Lake and ladies in general until the redheaded girl brought Trent a platter full of biscuits smothered in gravy.

"Boy, you eat all that, and your poor horse won't be able to carry you." Trent's breakfast caused Gray to ask if he woke the other three in their party before leaving the hotel.

"Of course, I woke 'em. I know what you think about men sleeping in."

Gray asked what time in the night he and the others arrived.

"About two o'clock this morning," Trent groaned. "When I got back over to the spot where I left 'em, they weren't even saddled up. I swear they had everything we brought unpacked. It took us an hour to break camp."

"The Reed boy is going to be thrilled to meet you," Trent said. "He's asked Gray about you a dozen times or more."

"Young men are always enthusiastic about making my

acquaintance." Wild Bill spoke with mock pomposity as he blew a smoke ring.

"Because boys aren't mature enough to have sound judgment," Gray said.

Almost thirty more minutes passed before the Reeds and Tom Gibbs showed up. The delay would have aggravated Gray had he not been so enjoying the company of his old friend.

"Del," Gray said, standing up and putting his hand on the boy's shoulder, "this poor excuse for a man sitting here is J.B. Hickok."

Chapter Sixty-Two

Hickok kept all five men amused with stories and tall tales for the next hour, many involving Gray. His babbling got Gray thinking back about his life. Since his marriage, he worked to convince himself his earlier wildness was something to regret. Still, Gray enjoyed the memories. When they were about thirty, Annie once tried to pin him down about why he kept leaving their beautiful valley home.

"For the adventure, Annie," he told her, knowing full well from the emptiness in her eyes she did not understand what he was trying to describe.

As the clock approached noon, Hickok decided the day was mature enough to embrace its first whiskey. The stories improved over the next hour, and according to Gray, occasionally skirted the truth.

"Has anyone escaped from you?" Del asked, still taking in every word the famous gunman and marshal said with absolute amazement.

The question sobered "Wild Bill." "Only two, son, only

two." Hickok leaned over the table and lit his second cigar of the morning. The redheaded girl came back over and asked if anyone wanted anything else. Trent wondered if she wished they would leave, but only four other people were in the place, and they all pulled their chairs up to listen to Hickok's tales. "And you can take this down, Mr. Newspaperman," Hickok said, pointing his fresh smoke right at Tom Gibbs. "Only two. One was that damned John Wesley Hardin."

Gray remembered the incident. John Wesley Hardin was a Texan, which didn't sit well with Hickok. He was also one of the most obnoxious men and vicious killers who ever lived. Harden once followed some Texans he had a disagreement with up to Sumner City, Kansas. He killed the man and headed on up to Abilene, where he gunned down another man for no reason at all. The killing infuriated Hickok, the town marshal.

"Hardin cut out when he found out I was looking for him. Yellow S.O.B. I spotted him when he first rode in, but I was trying to cut down on my killing, so I didn't shoot him."

Del's eyes grew round as the story went on. Gray figured Del wasn't sure whether Wild Bill meant the remark or was being funny.

"I should have shot him. A man who would kill a fella for snoring too loud doesn't deserve any benefit of the doubt."

Hickok paused long enough to finish another whiskey, which went down in one gulp. "By the time I got on his trail, he'd snuck off in the dark. He tells people I didn't show when he called me out." Hickok flicked the ash off his cigar. "I ever run across him again, I'll put his little story to rest."

"Who was the other one?" Tom Gibbs asked, pausing from scribbling down his notes.

"Harvey Kehn," Hickok said.

Del studied both Trent and Gray. Neither showed any kind of emotion on their faces.

"Another mean cur," Hickok said. "He murdered, raped, and tore up this area for near fifteen or twenty years."

Gray sat back in his chair and turned toward the window, staring at the empty street.

"I guess you still don't enjoy talking about him," Hickok said,

"Not much," Gray said, drawing a sip of his now cold coffee.

"Well, if I'd done what I should have, I'd have saved a mess of lives, including a boy deputy. Not killing Kehn got my deputy killed, widowed his wife, and left two babies orphaned." Hickok pushed back his chair and stood. He poured another whiskey and drank it, again, in one swallow. "I've got hit the trail. You take care," he said, looking down at Gray. "And say hello to your sister. She's a handsome woman."

Discouraged, Wehr shook his old friend's hand. His melancholy would have deepened had he known they would never see each other alive again.

Chapter Sixty-Three

The Sioux showed no kindness toward Laura, riding her hard all day tied on the back of an unsaddled horse with a sharp backbone. But they didn't harm her, either. They all but ignored her. When they stopped for a brief time to eat, she sat alone after being tossed a piece of unrecognizable meat.

The same warrior led her horse all day. He was the only one of the Sioux not wearing a shirt. Laura wondered why, on such a cold day, this man rode shirtless. His back was painted black, his chest red, yellow spots adorned his face. He wore a half-dozen feathers braided into his raven black hair.

He would turn and glance at her, but he never spoke. He probably didn't speak English. Still, she wanted him to say something to her. Perhaps the tone of his voice would give some clue about what would happen to her. But no one spoke to her, not the brave leading her horse, not anyone. They rode deeper into Sioux land.

By late afternoon, black clouds building all day burst into driving icy rain. The shirtless warrior wrapped a blanket around his shoulders. Laura was wearing only the light coat she slept in when the Sioux took her. The rain soaked her, leaving her freezing.

An hour after the storm started, the one riding out front turned his horse and rode back next to Laura. He pulled his knife, and for a moment, she thought he was going to kill her. Instead, he cut the rawhide strap binding her hands. "Wear this," he said, tossing a black and red blanket at her. Laura, so shocked he spoke to her in English, almost dropped the blanket. The Sioux said no more and trotted his horse back to the front of the procession.

As the late afternoon grew darker, Laura shut her eyes and tried to sleep while riding. Impossible. Besides, staying awake was better. If she went to sleep, she might fall off her horse. The Sioux might think she was trying to escape, do to her what they did to Red and Hank, or worse.

Laura was afraid and didn't expect to be free again, but she was not ready to die, not yet, and never this way. She heard many stories of what the Sioux did to female captives, horrifying, but not dying. As long as you weren't dead, you still had hope.

The English-speaking warrior came back after another hour. The rain all but stopped, and Laura was less uncomfortable. "You want go?" he asked, looking at her. At first, she wasn't sure what he said. When she did not speak, he asked again. "You want go?"

"What?" Laura said, still unsure she understood him.

"You want go?"

"Go?"

"Go, you go." Was she being given her freedom? "You need go; we stop. No go, we ride."

Laura realized she was not being released. She was being offered a chance to go to relieve herself.

Chapter Sixty-Four

They arrived at the Sioux camp deep in the night, or Laura thought it was late. Laura grew more afraid, perhaps because she had gotten used to the pace of the day, of not being talked to, and of not hearing the men speak much to each other. But the camp wasn't quiet. Children ran amok; the commotion scared her.

Laura's presence created more excitement. Several women spoke to her in Lakota. She couldn't understand them, but they were not friendly.

"You get down," the warrior who led them to the camp said. He cut the rope tying her feet together. He reached up and yanked her off the horse. A stooped-over old woman jabbed Laura twice with a sharp stick, which hurt something awful. Laura cried out, but when she did, the man who pulled her off the horse gave her a fierce backhand to the face, knocking her down.

"Shut up," he said before reaching down and jerking her back to her feet. The stooped-over old woman now gave her some vicious lashes with the switch. They stung, raising red welts, despite Laura trying to protect her face as the woman whipped her several more times. The warrior grabbed a handful of Laura's hair and half-dragged her to a medium-sized tipi, where he lifted the flap and shoved her inside.

With no fire, Laura struggled to adjust her eyes to the darkness. The tipi was almost empty. *Probably only for prisoners. The Sioux equivalent to jail.*

After pushing her into the tepee, the same man returned. He brought a few pieces of wood and built a small fire. He tossed a few more sticks on the ground and left without saying anything.

Laura fell asleep for a few minutes, a restless, dream-filled sleep not lasting long. When she woke up, the fire was almost out. Earlier, she had been afraid to use the wood, but now she was so cold she put some smaller sticks on. The fire was so close to being out she had to blow on the coals to ignite the sticks.

She felt awful, much worse than before she fell asleep. She had a swollen eye and headache from the punch taken from the English-speaking Sioux. She realized for the first time how hungry she was. She had not eaten the piece of meat they gave her earlier. Now she would eat anything, including dog, which Laura thought the meat might have been.

Sitting cold and dark, a greater fear overcame her, a level of anxiety she kept at bay most of the day. Now panic haunted her. She wondered if she might be better off dead.

At first, the talking was a little distance away. A minute later, the voices were right outside the flap. They were females, but Laura remembered everything Libbie Custer told her about how Indian women abused captives.

Libbie claimed Sioux and Cheyenne women used female hostages as slaves, treating them much worse than the Southerners treated blacks. Libbie called Sioux women the cruelest people on earth. Of course, Libbie Custer rather disliked most Indian women. Laura believed because of all the rumors of her husband's dalliances with them.

When the flap opened, five women came in. The old stooped-over woman was not with them, which relieved Laura. One woman, who appeared to be in her early twenties, was eye-catching. Her hair hung loose. The other four wore braids. Laura wondered if hair meant something significant, perhaps a sign of marital status.

The one standing next to the attractive one said something to her. "I don't understand," Laura said, trying not to sound scared. The woman spoke to her again, this time in a much harsher voice. Laura shook her head, "I'm sorry, I don't understand."

The women attacked her. They hit her with their fists, and one of them drew a stream of blood when she scratched Laura's face. They tore at her clothes. First, they pulled off her coat and her blouse. Three of them held her down while the other two stripped off her trousers. Once they took her clothes, the pretty one spat on her. Another kicked her before they left.

Laura curled up and sobbed uncontrollably as she lay naked in the Sioux lodge.

Chapter Sixty-Five

Gray decided to spend a couple of extra days in Pine Bluffs because he wanted to monitor April's progress. He figured three or four days of hard riding south would put them right back on Walker's tail. He declared to the others once they started back after the gang, he intended to push at a brutal pace.

"I wish I could go with you," Doc Boone said as he bandaged the girl's shoulder.

The comment surprised Gray, not only because the man was so old, but because he felt Boone cared little for him.

"Anybody who would do this to a child needs stopping," the doctor mumbled while brushing April's hair back to see how much swelling had gone out of her face. "And I suspect you're the man who can stop them."

"I am. And I damn well intend to."

Trent found Del sitting alone in the hotel lobby, not much of a lobby. The whole affair was only two old wooden chairs, one on each side of a rickety table, and a six-month-old copy of a St. Louis paper.

"You look a little lonely," Tent said to the boy in a cheery voice.

Del forced a weak smile.

"Where's your dad and Tom?" Trent asked.

"My dad's asleep. I don't think he can sleep at night. I think Tom's upstairs writing a newspaper story."

"If you want to drag along with me, I thought I might go scout around for information about the men we're chasing."

"Nothing else to do. Where are you going?"

"There's a saloon down at the end of the street. I thought I'd wander in." Del's face blanched. "You don't need to have any whiskey," Trent laughed. "It's never agreed with me either. We'll ask a few questions."

The two men walked out into the street, muddy from a warm sunny day melting the early snow from two nights before.

"You think we might find out anything if we asked at the general store?" Del asked.

"We might ask. But I doubt we'd find out much. The information we're looking for comes from men who are more likely to frequent a saloon than a church or a general store," he said lightheartedly.

"Aren't you afraid Walker could have friends hanging around in a saloon?" Del asked.

Trent shrugged but didn't answer.

A weather-beaten hand-painted sign hung over the door, *Saloon*. It was a filthy place. Not as well kept as the Blue Moon in Casper. Dirty glasses and turned-over whiskey bottles cluttered almost every table. A kicked-over spittoon spilled its contents into a stream running in front of the bar, only a broad board laid across three barrels. Del stuck close to Trent.

The barkeep had only one hand. "Couple of beers,"

Trent said when the bartender started their way.

"He's a little young to be having a beer," the man said, motioning toward Del.

"He is," Trent said through a friendly grin, "but I didn't think you'd keep any sarsaparilla."

"Hmph," the barkeep grunted before heading to the other end of the bar. When he came back, he slammed a beer in front of Trent and one in front of Del. "We're out of milk. Don't let yer pup git sick in here."

The man caught Del looking at the stump where his hand should have been. "Argument with a bear."

Trent paid the man for the beers before glancing around the dark room. One card game was underway in the far corner, and two cowboys sat at a table next to the window, nursing a bottle of whiskey.

"I'll find out if they know anything," Trent said, starting across the saloon. Del followed along, forgetting the beer and having to go back. "Mind if I ask you a question?" Trent asked, walking up to the table.

"Depends on what the question is," the older man, in his mid-fifties with a salt and pepper beard, said. Trent explained Jack Walker's kidnapping spree.

"We're from Nebraska," one of the cowboys, a hard-looking man in his late-thirties, said. "Haven't heard of anything like you're describing."

"Well, thanks anyway." Trent turned to leave, with Del following.

"Boy," the younger cowboy called out.

Del turned around.

"You're a might young to be pullin' on a beer."

Del didn't respond, just gave the man an awkward smile and started back toward the bar.

"Hey, I'm talking to you. Don't turn your back on me," the cowboy said, now with a nasty tone to his voice.

Del turned toward the man. "You can have this one. I haven't taken a drink." He reached out to set the beer down.

"I think I'd rather you drink it, wouldn't you, Bill?" The

cowboy turned toward Del. He leaned back and put his feet up, holes in both boot soles.

"Hell, Dan, I want him to drink it all in one swallow."

Dan pressed his thumb to his nose and blew snot on the floor. "Go ahead, boy; pour your beer right down. Pour it right on down."

Trent stepped back toward the two cowboys. "I don't think he's thirsty, boys. I don't think he likes beer much."

"A man who doesn't like beer shouldn't be carrying one around. It's a waste of beer. You wastin' good beer, boy?" Dan asked.

"Listen, fellas, you don't want to mess with this boy," Trent said with an exaggerated smile. "He might not look like much, but he's a regular terror when he gets mad."

"Oh, I can see he is. I'm shakin' in my boots."

"I'm not lying to you," Trent said. "You rile this boy, and he won't fight fair. He'll hit you, kick you, bite you, scratch you; hell, he'll club you with a thorny stick." Trent, no beer drinker either, still had a full beer in his hand. He stepped in between Del and the cowboy named Dan. "You'd be better off letting this dog lie."

"Is that so? Well, I believe I'll find out for myself." Dan rose from his chair. Dan was not quite to his feet when the heavy mug caught him square on his right ear. The handle broke off in Trent's hand while beer and the rest of the mug flew across the room. Dan didn't fall right away. He wobbled back and forth for a moment or two before landing face-first on the table, which flipped over, dropping him flat on the floor.

"Sit still!" Trent yelled at the other cowboy. "So help me, I'll knock the fire right out of you."

"I don't want none," he said, holding his hands up. "None at all."

"His head's gonna be ringing when he wakes up," Trent said. "I'd try to find him a bed to rest in."

"He can pay for the glass," Trent said to the bartender, motioning at Bill. Del sat his still full beer down on the bar and followed Trent out of the saloon.

Trent glanced over at Del as they walked down the street. "I swear, I don't know why I let you talk me into going in a saloon."

Chapter Sixty-Six

After attending too many funerals in her life, Susan didn't want to attend Sanchez's. Not going, however, would have offended both Millie and Jean, so she went along.

The Baptist preacher, a man named Haggerty, preached a traditional funeral sermon. He told the mourners that because Sanchez followed Christ as his Savior, all those who accepted Christ would meet him again.

The minister surveyed the congregation. "With every eye closed, and every head bowed, I want you to search your hearts and consider what scripture says: 'for all have sinned and come short of the glory of God. There is none righteous, no, not one. The wages of sin is death, but the gift of God is eternal life through Jesus Christ our Lord.' 'Behold, I stand at the door and knock,' Jesus said, 'if any man hear my voice, and open the door, I will come into him,'" The pastor's voice became more soothing: "'For whosoever shall call upon the name of the Lord shall be saved.'"

He moved toward the front of the platform. "If you died

today, would you be where Miguel is? Salvation is so simple. I invite you to pray this prayer with me and secure your eternity. 'Father, I confess I am a sinner, and believing the Lord Jesus Christ died on the cross for my sins and was raised for my justification, I do now receive and confess Him as my savior.'"

Millie sat weeping between Annie and Jean.

During the week since the funeral, Susan decided to stay in High Meadows. She wondered how the Reeds would accept the news she would not return to Bismarck, at least not until the spring when she would go back and put her business affairs, such as selling the home, in order.

Her staying would upset Tom, but she wasn't interested in a future with him, so he would not benefit if she returned to Bismarck. Susan would be forever grateful to the newspaperman, but not enough to marry him and take him to her bed every night for the rest of her life.

How Lucy and the children would react worried Susan, but why would they want to return to Bismarck? The place would be full of horrible memories. Susan believed Lucy and the kids would be far better off staying right here in High Meadows with her. She refused to think they might not be coming back.

"My only concern," Susan said, as Annie washed the last glass before handing it to Susan to dry, "is, will the old memories haunt me?"

"If you're going to run every time someone dies, you'll never have a home," Annie said in a sympathetic but stern voice, staring Susan right in the eyes. Annie's eyes, so soft and beautiful, also revealed determination, a determination convincing Susan to stay in High Meadows.

"I suppose the only other concern is, how am I going to make a living?"

"What did you do in Bismarck?"

"I took in a little sewing," Susan said, "but I didn't need much. Adam built our house before he died, so we had no mortgage. Danny also raised cattle and most of our food, so we didn't have many expenses. Life will be a little different here."

"Your folks' old house is still standing," Annie said. "No one ever moved in. A few people would have bought the place, but they had no one to buy from."

"I wasn't sure if, after twenty years, I had any claim to the place."

"Why wouldn't you?" Annie pulled the plug and let the dishwater run down the drain and into the backyard. She scrutinized Susan sitting at the kitchen table. "Why haven't you gone out?"

Susan thought about Annie's question. She didn't answer. She thought about going one or two times since she came back. When she first arrived, though, she thought only of persuading Gray to go after her family. Later, she became involved in the lives of her old friends, Annie and Jean. It had not been important to her to go out to the old "homestead," as her father always called their acreage.

"I'm afraid to. I faced a lot of sorrow in that house."

Annie sat down across the table from her old friend. "Susan, it wasn't all sad. I remember many good times. You were saved in that house. Plenty of pleasant memories are waiting. If you want, I'll go along."

Susan did not respond. She glanced at Annie, turned away, glancing in several directions.

"We don't need to go right away," Annie said, seeing Susan's reluctance, "but if you ever want to, and you want some company, I'll be happy to go."

Annie walked over to the back door. "The sky is getting dark. I ought to let the yearlings out of the corral and back into the pasture before the rain starts." She took her oilcloth coat off the coat tree standing on the other side of the door. "You want to come along?"

Susan, lost in memories of her old life, didn't realize

what Annie said. "What?" she asked, somewhat embarrassed.

"I asked if you wanted to go help turn the yearlings back out into the pasture," Annie said, pulling on her coat. "Looks like rain, and I don't want them standing around in a muddy corral."

"Sure, let me pull my old boots on."

By the time the two women got back to the house, a slow drizzle was falling. They hung up their coats and went into the sitting room, where Annie put a couple of small logs on the fireplace.

"I like the fall," she said, almost as much to herself as to Susan. "I enjoy sitting here in front of the fire on gray afternoons like this one," she smiled as she sat down in the wing-backed chair next to the mahogany mantle. "If a storm builds up today, we'll be able to watch the black clouds move right up the valley," she said, motioning at the massive window on the west side of the room. "Millie should be back with the kids before too long. I thought we'd ask her to stay for dinner, the night if the weather turns too bad. She gets lonely with Trent gone."

"Would you like a cup of tea?" Susan asked. "I think I'll make some."

Susan left the room and went to the kitchen. Annie thought Susan was upset and decided to give her a few minutes alone. The tea making took too long, and Annie was about to check on her friend when Susan came back.

"I put two teaspoons of sugar in." She began to cry when she sat on the couch closest to Annie's chair.

For the past several days, Susan had difficulty controlling her emotions. She was apt to weep any time, although, until now, she managed to hide her weeping from Annie or anyone else around. Now tears were flowing. This angered Susan because the tears wouldn't help; crying would change nothing, only make her weak in front of Annie.

Annie moved over next to her. She slipped her arms around her as Susan turned and laid her head on her shoulder. "Let the hurt out," Annie whispered, rocking her friend back and forth.

Soon, the rain came down hard. The wind whipped enormous drops across the windows in waves. "I'm sorry, Annie," Susan said, her words choked back by tears. This was the first time she had spoken since mentioning the sugar in the tea. Annie let her slip out of her arms. "I had no right to ask Gray to find them," Susan said, sounding almost as if pronouncing judgment on herself. "I had no right."

"I'm praying he won't be hurt," Susan said, turning back toward Annie with tears again flowing. "Please forgive me. I'm so sorry."

Annie took her back into her arms.

She whispered to Susan, "Everything will be all right. Graham will be fine, and he'll bring your family back." She squeezed Susan a little tighter. "Gray always keeps his promises."

Susan let the tears fall.

Annie almost cried with her. But Annie didn't cry much.

Chapter Sixty-Nine

Gray left his hotel room well before dawn, making an uninvited visit to Doc Boone's to say goodbye to April. Rosie, not Doc Boone, answered the door. April lay awake in the guest room bed when Gray slipped his head in. She rolled on her right side, her jaw clenched, rubbing her shoulder.

Gray promised her burning was part of the healing process. He sat with her and stroked the still child's hair for more than half an hour. "April," he said, leaning over and kissing her forehead, "What did you say your mommy's name is?"

April moaned as she eased over on her back. She struggled to take a breath. "Carolyn."

"I'm going to leave now, sweetheart. I'm going for your mommy."

After saddling all five horses, Gray tethered them in front of the hotel. At dawn, he woke the other men. For the first time, Gray wore a forty-five caliber Colt tied to his right thigh.

After little conversation over breakfast, Gray spoke pointedly to the three men from Bismarck. "From here on, we'll ride from sunup 'til close to midnight. I intend to catch these reprobates within a week." He stood and tossed a couple of silver dollars in the middle of the table. "Keep up, or I'll leave you."

"Hell, Wehr, you can't capture them by yourself," Tom Gibbs said, in a voice filled with frustration and perhaps a little fear, too.

Gray, who started toward the front door, spun around to face Gibbs. "Capture them? Capture them? You think we'll capture these men?"

Gibbs shifted from one foot to the other.

"Let me tell you something, Mr. Newspaperman; we won't be *capturing* anybody. Do you think they're going to surrender to us? This is killing you're getting into." Gray's temper heated. "If you can't stomach killing, head north."

Chapter Seventy

In the morning light, Laura rubbed the welts from whippings at the hands of the stooped-over woman during the past few days. Some bright red; others a dark purple, a few bled. The back of her legs, the favorite target for the hateful old witch, hurt so much she could hardly sit, so she lay on her stomach for relief.

After being naked for more than a day, they gave Laura an old deerskin dress. She received little to eat, though they forced her to carry water and firewood all day. One man abused her some, but not for a couple of days.

She woke later in the day. At least, she thought so because of the noise around the camp. The fire died overnight. Perhaps the women withheld wood, hoping she'd freeze to death. She curled up over the barely warm embers, wishing to disappear.

Laura fell back into an uneasy sleep. A Lakota brave woke her—not gently. He pushed her out of the tipi hard enough she stumbled through the doorway and landed face first in the dirt. The warrior jerked her to her feet, half-dragging her across the camp to one of the larger lodges, a fancy one with a red and yellow stripe around the top and some crude drawings of mounted hunters chasing buffalo on the sides.

The brave shoved Laura down outside the flap and stepped inside. The old, hunched woman rushed her with a willow switch. She began whipping her. Laura hunched down, trying to protect her head and face. The old woman screamed or spat at her with every burning lash of the branch.

The one who dragged her from the other tipi came back out and shoved the hateful old woman away. They yelled a few sharp words back and forth before he motioned for Laura to go inside.

A good-sized fire warmed the lodge. Laura stared at the ground, not wanting to commit some offense by looking at someone she shouldn't.

"I am Rain In The Face." The man's English startled Laura. "You are in Lakota land, where you do not belong. The treaty forbids you entering."

Rain In The Face wore a deerskin shirt with beadwork covering the front. Long fringe hung from the elbows to the wrists, clearly a man of importance. "Sit." Laura sat across from him.

"Why are you in our land?"

The quality of his English surprised Laura. His speaking English didn't mean he would not kill her, but it eased her fear, a little.

Laura shuddered. Her voice cracked. "I'm searching for my husband."

"Your man wasn't one of the men my warriors found you with?"

"No, they were helping me find him." Laura looked into Rain In The Face's light brown, almost tan eyes for the first time.

"Where are you from?"

Will my answer influence my fate? "Bismarck." She shifted her eyes away from Rain In The Face's stare.

"Where is your man?"

Laura told the story of how Gabe went looking for men who kidnapped a friend's children. She said her husband and three others left for a town in the Bighorn Mountains. She wanted to find him.

Laura did not tell the Lakota leader Sioux did the kidnapping. When first brought to the camp, Laura expected Lucy to be in the camp. From the reaction of these warriors, she was not.

Rain In The Face picked up a bowl containing a few scraps of meat in some kind of stew. He reached across the fire and offered her the food, an almost tasteless porridge. It needed a little sugar and cinnamon sprinkled on the top, but even without it, Laura ate, grateful for anything.

The Lakota argued back and forth for several minutes. Laura wished Rain In The Face would tell her why, but he ignored her. Occasionally one of the Indians would mutter *"wasichus,"* the word for "white men." The conversation stopped for a short time. Rain In The Face studied Laura.

"Hietze, Custer, I don't like him. I dislike all Custers." The Sioux leader crossed his legs. "You like Custer?"

"I don't know him well." Not at all would sound like a lie, given she lived in Bismarck. "I know his wife," she added when the Sioux's eyes caused her to wonder if he believed her. "Libbie…Mrs. Custer, is my friend."

"Mrs. Custer." Rain In The Face grinned at the other warriors. "Mrs. Custer does not like me."

The Sioux again talked among themselves. "Some think we should keep here you as a…" Rain In The Face searched for the English word "…slave. Many Coup thinks you should die." He let his words sink in. "I do not want a fight the soldiers from Ft. Lincoln." Rain In The Face stood and pointed at a man two warriors to his left. "This is He Dog. You are fortunate. Tomorrow, he will take you home. You tell Custer I showed you this mercy."

Chapter Seventy-One

Once they crossed into Colorado, Jack Walker, lazy and wilting, slowed the pace. Bill Beachum and the Fox brothers enjoyed sleeping late and having a few whiskeys before the day started, making them meaner.

Stopping earlier in the evening gave the men time to drink before dark, making them more abusive. Of course, they sometimes passed out early, leaving the females a little peace.

Lucy Carlyle and the two Brown women tried to stay awake at night, hoping Walker and his entire crew might fall asleep. Lucy said they could steal the horses and run. Rennie wanted to slit the men's throats and escape.

The opportunity did not arise. Walker, Camp, Long, or the renegade Cheyenne never slept at the same time. Long and Pratt, the two men Walker brought back from Schuster Flats, proved brutal with unquenchable appetites for women, especially Pratt. He liked to "soften a woman up with a beating," he would sneer before having his way.

Lucy sat by the campfire, rocking Jenny. The child stopped speaking the first week of being captured. Now she blankly stared straight ahead. She seldom blinked her eyes, and her expression never changed. Lucy accepted the child's mind being gone, but she would still whisper her name as she rocked her, humming little songs and telling her she would be all right. "Maddie, do you want to slip under here with me?"

Camp tossed Lucy a patchwork quilt belonging to Carter Cline. Since Lucy's cutting him up led to his killing, Camp called Cline's death the fruit of her labor. The gift irritated Carl Fox, making him more abusive to Lucy. Lucy wondered if Camp gave her the blanket, intending to make Fox more brutal. She didn't care; she intended to keep it. It might prove the difference between living and freezing.

Fox, drunk and carrying a half-full bottle of whiskey in his left hand, headed across the camp after midnight. Lucy wanted to run but running would be pointless. He would catch her and make life worse for her. She slipped out from under Jenny, wrapping the old blanket tighter around the two girls.

Fox yanked her to her feet and dragged her from the fire before slamming her down on the rocky ground. She squeezed her eyes shut while he tore at her tattered dress. Fox, too drunk to last long, passed out. Lucy pushed him off and crawled back to Jenny and a weeping Maddie.

"Hush, sweetie. I'm all right. Momma's all right." Lucy stroked the blonde hair of her older daughter, kissing her face and the top of her head. For a long time, they sat with Lucy, thankful for two children to hold.

One woman kidnapped at the last ranch the men raided tried to escape. For her trouble, Bill Beachum stuck her with a skinning knife. The blade went in below the shoulder, puncturing a lung. The woman, not yet twenty years old, moaned on the other side of the fire, a gurgling, strangling sound—the death rattles.

Chapter Seventy-Two

"Take her clothes if you want to," Jack Walker growled at the woman. "She don't need 'em anymore."

The young woman died from her stab wound during the night—a blessing. The men would have killed her this morning, anyway. Death came easier in the night.

"Head south 'til you find the Platte," Walker ordered the renegade. "Take a few canteens to bring some water back in."

The women started making preparations for the day's ride. Days became routine—odd. How could such misery be customary? Perhaps, she thought, through the strength of the human soul, the unquenchable yearning to survive.

Most of the prisoners had given up all hope of being rescued. Some of them talked about the desire to die, thinking being dead would be easier than being alive and held by Jack Walker.

The country got less rocky; the terrain flattened out, with the Rocky Mountains rising off to the west. The sun was shining for the first time in days, warming the air, making for a beautiful fall day, except for being a captive of Jack Walker.

"You women hurry up! I want to make some time while this weather holds."

Hours passed as they traveled at a steady pace. Lucy rode with Jenny in front of her. The girl's matted, soured hair stunk. Lucy always enjoyed shampooing the girls' hair, hair that shined when rinsed with brook water. She now wondered if her children's hair would ever shine again.

About mid-afternoon, Burns The Grass returned. Lucy and the other women hoped every time a man left, he would get lost or die. They always came back. Burns The Grass filled all the canteens and rode back to report the water still two hours away.

Each of the men took drinks but offered none to the captives. Lucy didn't care about not being given any water for herself. She had grown accustomed to riding all day without a drink, being allowed water only when they stopped at night, but thirst twisted through her girls and the rest of the children.

In the whiskey since mid-morning, Trey Long and Carl Fox were both better than half-drunk. A few prairie dogs drew their attention, and they started taking turns trying to pick them off with Long's Navy Colt. Neither man hit one, but they kept shooting, missing, and blaming the wind, sun, or their horse stumbling.

Camp spat a stream of tobacco, wiped his mouth with his sleeve. "You two put that gun away. You're too drunk to shoot anything, 'cept your blame foot, and I'm tired of listening to all your noise."

"Hell, ain't nothin' else to listen to out here," Long said, "and I want to keep my shootin' eye sharp in case I need to plug a damn redskin."

The Cheyenne stared at Long, a squinty-eyed, hard stare, but didn't say anything.

"Whatsa matter, Indian?" Long taunted. "You not

tough enough to live like your own kind? You like sleeping in a white eye's camp? Eatin' white man's food?"

Burns The Grass pulled his horse to a stop and raised his rifle, but Bert Camp, riding next to him, cuffed him across the face. Camp whirled toward Long and pointed a long finger at him. "Shut the hell up."

At first, Lucy Carlyle thought Long might challenge Camp, and she hoped so because one of them would kill the other, but Long backed down. The renegade, however, remained ready to fight.

"You need to be hit again?" Camp barked, turning his attention to the Cheyenne. "We're not having any fighting."

Burns The Grass did not respond; he kicked his horse and rode out a little way in front of the group.

Lucy figured Long would end up scalped by the Indian before too much longer.

Jack Walker led his mount over closer to Camp. "That son of a bitch, I'm going to kill him before we deliver these women."

"Long's drunk. He started in on the Cheyenne." Camp said. "Can't blame the damn Indian."

"I may end up shooting both of them." Walker sneered.

Chapter Seventy-Three

Still hurting from the whippings she received in the Sioux camp, Laura rode in pain for two days, her horse led by a young warrior of no more than fifteen or sixteen years of age. In some ways, he reminded her of her son. The Sioux was a more serious boy, not laughing much, unlike Del, who laughed easily.

Laura could not picture this boy slipping up behind his mother and hugging her as Del did. Still, an occasional "motherly urge" came over her, the desire to tell him to put on a coat or to push his hair back away from his face.

She wondered for a moment, no, she hoped, a Sioux mother might have the same compassion toward her son if they captured him.

At night all three warriors, He Dog, the young man leading her mount, and a third warrior from the group that had taken her captive, built a fire and went to sleep, posting no guard or sentry. They didn't bother to tie Laura up.

If she wanted to run away, they would not stop her. She

thought of running but decided to stay because Rain In The Face said they would take her home. She did not know if she trusted him or whether the warriors would do as he told them. Unfortunately, she doubted she could find her way home alone, leaving her no choice but to go along.

They did not mistreat her. They gave her food whenever they ate and a blanket to keep her warm at night. The one thing they did not do was talk to her. She was not sure if they didn't understand English or didn't want to communicate with her. She didn't speak to them either.

Laura caught occasional glimpses of the river, which encouraged her to think they might be close to Ft. Lincoln. The younger Lakota led Laura's horse up, and much to her relief, the fort sat below them at the river's edge.

He Dog slipped off his horse and walked over to Laura. He raised his hands to help her down. Laura leaned over, and he eased her to the ground. He went back and swung on his pinto pony. The three Sioux did not speak; they turned their horses and headed back in the direction they came.

Laura stood for a moment, watching them. Should she say thank you or wave to them? They didn't as much as turn or glance at her. Laura waited two or three minutes, looking down at Ft. Lincoln. The post seemed miles away, too far away for her to walk.

A few men wandered along the river bank. They appeared unconcerned about being outside the protective walls of the fort. Would they be so apathetic if they knew Sioux warriors rode less than a mile away?

Chapter Seventy-Four

Laura Reed started down with fear and emptiness overtaking her. An enormous sense of loss and guilt gripped her. *Why now?* She thought. *I'm free now; I'm safe.*

As she approached the fort, tears filled her eyes and ran down her cheeks.

Every step brought her pain. The ground was cold, still covered in many spots with a heavy frost from the previous night. The Sioux did not return her boots or offer her any moccasins, so she walked barefoot down the hill full of sharp rock, goatheads, and thorns. By the time she made the gate, both feet were bleeding.

Two privates ran to her aid. "For the love of Pete, ma'am." the older one, a career soldier in his fifties, stammered as he put his arm around her shoulders to help her stand.

Laura did not respond. She stared straight ahead, weeping.

"Go find an officer, Jenkins. Hurry, man!" The private

yelled when the other trooper made no move to leave. "Let's set you down over here on this old bench," he said, leading Laura toward a roughhewn log. Three more soldiers gathered around. "Ma'am, can you tell us what happened?"

Laura's shoulders slumped further, her eyes bounced to and away from the soldier, who had a wrinkled but kind face. "I'm hurt."

"Bring some water." The private directed a young cavalryman in the center of eight or ten troopers. "Can you tell me your name?" he asked kindly, kneeling on one knee in front of Laura.

"Laura, Laura Reed." Her eyes followed the soldier. She feared if she took her eyes off him, all the soldiers might walk away and leave her sitting alone, helpless. Silly, but she was still as frightened as in the Sioux camp.

The young man returned with water, which the private held up to Laura's lips. "Why don't you try to take a drink, ma'am? Easy now," he whispered as he tipped the canteen up.

Laura took a sip or two, but most of the water ran down her mouth and dripped off her chin on the deerskin dress.

An officer, a young and green second lieutenant, pushed his way through the group of men. "Good Lord, she's a friend of Mrs. Custer. I've seen them together several times."

The older private replied. "She came walking up to the front gate. I can't get much out of her."

"McCreedy, go find Col. Custer. Tell him one of his wife's friends from Bismarck is here. Tell him she's in poor shape," he added as the trooper ran off. The lieutenant leaned down, asking Laura what happened.

"We tried to cross Sioux land. We shouldn't have gone."

He again offered her water, and this time Laura drank two or three swallows.

"Should we take her over to the infirmary?" asked one private in the crowd, a southerner.

The lieutenant glanced at several enlisted men seeking their guidance in the matter. "Maybe we should wait for the Colonel." He bent over and spoke to Laura. "You're hurt, ma'am? Would you like us to take you to the post-hospital?"

"Let me wait for Libbie."

The private came back a few minutes later, leading both George and Libbie Custer. Laura sat disheveled, her arms wrapped around her knees, blank eyes staring at nothing.

"Dear Lord, what happened to you?"

Laura stood and stumbled toward Libbie, who took her into her embrace.

"Let's take her home."

Custer, Libbie, and Laura eased toward the Custer home, with Laura limping on her bloody and swollen feet before Colonel Custer picked her up and carried her the rest of the way. Once inside, Libbie again asked Laura what happened.

"You were right, Libbie. I shouldn't have gone."

Chapter Seventy-Five

George Armstrong Custer, Son of the Morning Star. Hiestzi. Panther Who Attacks At Dawn. The Boy General. Autie, his wife, called him. Custer stood almost at attention as Laura told Libbie the Sioux captured her two days from the fort. He stiffened more when Laura related the deaths of Red Holsten and Hank Potts.

Libbie glanced up at her husband with sorrowful eyes, shook her head, hoping he would hold his tongue. Custer was stern, military, and almost patientless but not a cruel man. He also idolized Libbie. He would never hurt or anger her. Neither was he a fool about reading the feelings of women.

"Perhaps, I should leave the room for a few minutes. Laura may be more comfortable without my presence. Call for me as soon as I can help." He turned and left the room.

Once alone, Libbie, sitting next to Laura on a leather couch, toughened. "I told you not to do such a foolish thing," she said, not speaking in anger but still sternly, much as a mother might talk to a child who gave her a horrible scare before being found safe.

Laura broke. Tears poured down her face. "I never meant for them to be harmed. I wanted Gabe and Del. I wanted them home." She sobbed, her voice choking as the sobbing overcame her. "I had to stop the nightmares of Gabe and Del dying."

Libbie rocked her back and forth; for a long time, neither woman spoke. Laura took comfort in the silence. Custer stuck his head in once, but Libbie motioned him away.

After a few more minutes, a gentle rain started to fall. The slow rhythmic pattern of the rainstorm made the shadowy room more comfortable.

"Red died so hard, and Hank…" Laura couldn't continue.

"Shhh. I've got you. You're safe now; you're fine now, Laura," Libbie said as she held her friend close.

"Libbie, one of the Sioux raped me."

Laura felt Elizabeth Custer shudder, leaving her speechless.

The rain fell harder before Laura spoke again. She pulled away from Libbie. "How am I ever going to live with this? Those men are dead because of me. I'm no longer clean for Gabe. How am I going to face him?"

Libbie wiped tears from her eyes before looking up at Laura, now standing. "We all make mistakes. Some of them bring terrible consequences, but we go on. You're going to go on. Your husband and son need you. You're going to go on." Libbie stood but did not reach out to Laura. "Let's get you a bath and some decent clothes."

Chapter Seventy-Six

"There are three cowboys camped about two miles ahead," Trent said, returning from a short scouting trip. "I didn't approach them since they outnumbered me."

"I'd be curious if they've seen any sign of the people we're looking for," Gray said. "Evening," Gray called out as they approached the campfire.

"Howdy." came the reply.

"Mind if we come on in?"

"Come ahead. But we'll be more comfortable seeing your hands."

"Understood." Gray urged Lena forward. He held an advantage over the men, riding in from the near dark while they stood around in the fire's glow. "Gray Wehr. Any objection if we step down?"

The men stepped a little closer together, which helped Gray relax. Experienced fighting men would spread out, not group up to become easy targets.

"Did he say 'Gray Wehr'?" One of the men asked

"He sure did. I thought he was dead."

Gray stopped Lena, still a little distance from the men, and again asked permission to come in.

"Come ahead," the tallest fella in the group said. "Come on in."

Gray walked in, leading his bay a little way in front of the other four. He stuck his hand out and shook the hand of each man. "Hope we didn't startle you."

"Not too much," the man standing closest to Wehr said, "but I guess we should pay a little more attention."

"You may not remember me, but we met once about eight or ten years ago," the third man said. "You were with the cavalry, chasing around after Red Cloud. I was a sergeant under Lt. Collins. They sent me out on a couple of scouts with you and Charlie Reynolds. My name's Marion Morris."

"Sure, I remember you." In reality, while Gray remembered scouting with "Lonesome" Charlie Reynolds and a few troopers, he didn't recall this man.

"Where're you headed?" Trent asked.

"Down to Cheyenne," Morris said. "We're going to pick up about fifty head of horses, push 'em up to Ft. Robinson and sell them to the Army. What brings you down here? I thought you stayed up in the Bighorns someplace."

"We're after Jack Walker," Gray said. He explained what Walker and his gang had been doing before being asked to sit down around the fire.

"You boys run across any burned ranches or men with a bunch of captive women?" Tom Gibbs asked.

"No, and I believe we would have noticed." The tall man poured everyone a coffee before asking Gray how confident he was about being on the right trail.

"I'm certain," Gray said. "I mean to catch them within the week."

"How many men do you reckon are in this bunch?" the second man asked.

"According to a child we found, a little girl they shot and left for dead," Gray said, "about seven of them."

"Any idea how many captives?"

"From what the girl said, at least a dozen, maybe close to twenty."

"I doubt if they can push so many reluctant people very fast."

"This may have nothing to do with the group you're after," Morris said, "but when we rode through Schuster Flats, people were talking about two killings last week. Some fella shot a couple of bar dogs, then left with Trey Long and J.D. Pratt. You ever hear of those two?"

"Of Long," Gray said.

"Pratt's cut out of the same cloth," Trent said. "He caused some trouble at Ft. Laramie, the winter of '67. He sliced up a soldier in a fight over a card game. They stuck him in the stockade for three months. Heard nothing about him since."

"Can't say if Walker and his bunch had anything to do with the Schuster Flats murders, but they'll outnumber you if they did." Morris glanced at Del. "I advise caution when you approach them."

Chapter Seventy-Seven

"Wake up!" Jack Walker kicked the renegade Cheyenne sleeping curled up under a buffalo hide. "Git up!"

Burns The Grass rolled over and sat up. "What?"

Ever since J.D. Pratt mentioned a posse back in Schuster Flats, the thought of being followed chewed at the back of Walker's gut. He doubted anyone was coming, but struggling through a restless night, he decided to make sure.

"I want you to scout our back trail a ways. Find out if anybody's following us." Walker said. "Ride back a half-day. You can catch us tonight."

The order did not thrill the Indian, which he showed by being slow getting out of his bedroll and readying his horse. By the time he left, Walker was seething with anger. He meant to finish off the red son of a bitch as soon as they got to the Arkansas River.

"You think somebody's on our trail?" Camp asked Walker after the Indian's departure.

"No, but we ought to check." Walker broke off a chaw

306

of tobacco, sticking the wad in the side of his mouth before offering a piece to Camp. He ran his fingers through his greasy, thinning brown hair. "That damn red-haired woman who cut Cline, I'm thinking about killin' her youngest girl. She don't talk; hell, she don't even cry. She just stares straight ahead. I think she's gone crazy. Nobody'll pay anything for a touched kid."

Camp spat tobacco toward where Jenny lay by her mother. Lucy Carlyle sat between her two girls, with one arm around Maddie while she stroked Jenny's face. "I'll tell Beachum to kill her. He don't like the Bismarck woman. He'll enjoy finishin' her kid."

Chapter Seventy-Eight

She smiled as Gray stroked her long hair. He ran his fingers along her face and down her throat.

"You're a beautiful woman in this morning light."

Annie's body jerked as she woke up from a fitful and tormented sleep. She slid her hand over the empty side of her bed, sighing as she settled her head back into the pillow. How she wished the dream was true. How she longed for her husband to come home, touch her hair and her face. How she needed to hear him call her beautiful.

She took her time getting dressed and sat for another ten minutes brushing her dark hair in front of her dressing mirror. When she walked over to the window, the sun was shining.

Some Indian Summer would be a pleasant change from the damp and chilly fall they experienced so far. Annie opened a jar of cold cream and rubbed some across the backs of her hands and into her red, chapped knuckles. "You're not as young as you used to be," she said to herself as she stared into the mirror. "You may start getting old if you're not careful."

Susan Carlyle stood in the kitchen cracking a couple of eggs into a skillet when Annie came downstairs.

"You're up early today."

"It's after eight," Susan said, "but I guess I have been sleeping in."

"You're probably exhausted. I'm sure you needed the rest."

"I brewed some tea this morning," Susan said, sounding like she might want to change the subject. "Do you want coffee? I'll start some."

"No," Annie said, walking over to the cupboard for a cup. "Tea will be fine."

"What do you want for breakfast? I'll cook."

"I'm not very hungry."

She and Susan sat talking about nothing in particular for the next few minutes. "I'm riding over to Jean's; do you want to come along?" Annie asked, a little tired of the idle chatter.

"No, I think I'll go into town and talk to the Kellers about the store. I don't want to lose my nerve."

Annie had been encouraging Susan, worried about her financial stability if she moved back to High Meadows, to speak to the Kellers about the general mercantile. In their late seventies, they were getting too old to run a business, and Mrs. Keller told Annie several times over the past year if offered a "reasonable" price, she would sell and settle into an overdue retirement.

Mr. Keller first balked at selling, saying once a man retires, the only thing left for him is dying. With his declining health, he was becoming reconciled to hanging up his shopkeepers apron.

"Do you want me to come along?" Annie asked, wondering if Susan would like her support in bringing the topic up with the present owners.

"No, go on over to Jean's. I should be woman enough

to make my deal; otherwise, I may not be enough woman to operate the place."

Annie laughed at her friend. "Oh, it's not too hard. High Meadows is a captive bunch of customers."

"I guess it would take a poor business person to go broke when you're the only store in town."

Annie headed out to saddle Fury, finding the filly in a frisky mood. Not out of her stall for the past three days, she kicked up her heels when Annie walked up with a bridle. "You take a few runs around the corral. Run out some of your excitement before I climb up on your back."

The mare bucked, ran, and pranced for twenty minutes before she settled down enough Annie believed her ready to be ridden. The black took a couple of playful bites at her after Annie went in the pen.

"Quit. I'm not Graham, and I don't want bit." Annie patted the horse's chest. "Graham lets you get away with bad habits." Everyone yelled at him, but he didn't care. They told him one of those babies was going to take a chunk out of him someday or kick him a swift one.

"They're playing; they won't hurt me." They never did. If they pushed him too hard or got too rough, he raised his voice, and they would immediately quiet down, making Gray laugh. "See, they never hurt me." Annie gave up arguing the point with him.

Annie brushed the horse before laying a red blanket across her back. "Your coat's getting thick. Are we in for a hard winter?" She set the saddle on and reached under her belly for the cinch. The two-year-old jerked back a step. "Oh, standstill. Nobody's going to hurt you." Annie turned Fury away from the fence and stepped up on her.

At Jean's, Zach and Ethan Joseph sat on the corral doing nothing, Zach Joseph's favorite pastime. For years, he had been Gray's best friend and carried quite a torch for Jean. Jean, however, declined his offer of marriage, and since, Zach drifted away from them. He remained close, but not like before Jean's rejection.

"What are you over here for?" Zach called out to Annie. "Are you and Jean planning on baking me a couple of pies?"

"Of course. Why else would I ride over here?"

"Make me a peach one, will you?"

"Now, where do you think I'd find peaches this time of the year? We plan on fixing custard and mincemeat."

"Well, you can leave me out of your serving plans."

Annie laughed at Zach as she started up the steps to the front door. "Anybody home?"

"Upstairs!" Jean hollered. "I'm glad you came over," she said when Annie came up and found her sister-in-law trying to wrestle a heavy bureau from one side of the spare bedroom to the other. "Give me a hand, will you?"

The two women huffed and pushed on the chest, which had a will of its own, intending to stay in its corner next to the old oak writing table. "What's in this thing?" Annie asked after they got the piece moved across the room.

"Clothes. The blame thing weighs about as much empty. You should have seen Graham, Paxton, and my Pop hauling the monster up here. Mom kept telling them to remember, 'skin heals, and furniture doesn't.' Pop almost took an ax and turned it into firewood."

"Well, it would smolder the whole winter." Annie laughed.

"I ought to burn it when it snows."

Once they relocated a few smaller pieces to Jean's satisfaction, the two women went downstairs, and Jean brewed some tea. "It's been two days since I've seen Millie; how's she holding up?"

"She's lonely, but why wouldn't she be?"

The tone of Annie's voice caused Jean to turn around from her brewing. "How are you doing?"

"I'm not sleeping," she confided to her friend. "That's an enormous bed when half empty." Jean set a cup of tea and a sugar bowl on the table. Annie put two teaspoons in hers. "Dreams and nightmares wake me up all during the night. I keep hoping for some kind of letter or something."

"Well," Jean said, "They are both capable. I'm sure they'll be home soon, and likely, they'll bring Susan's family with them."

Jean's optimism lifted Annie's outlook. At least a bit. Although Gray frequently slipped into blue moods, he always responded to Annie's occasional sorrow by taking on the most charming ways. Millie, too, often raised Annie's spirits. The girl's spunk and love for life naturally delighted Annie.

Chapter Seventy-Nine

Del Reed never wanted to leave the Dakotas, and now he didn't want to depart Wyoming. Colorado meant getting farther away from home and taunting death. Short of declaring himself a coward, he couldn't turn around and head for home. He would just get lost. He probably couldn't find his way back to Pine Bluffs.

"I never expected to miss my ma so bad," he whispered to Trent. The men started posting a guard, and although Trent's turn, Del, unable to sleep, sat along with the traveling partner he had become most comfortable with. Trent didn't criticize Del, though he made some significant blunders on the trip, the worst falling asleep on his watch.

Del had slumped across a boulder, and his snoring woke Trent. Trent crawled out of his bedroll and sat the remaining hour. He told Tom he and Del traded shifts. Del remained grateful for Trent's keeping the secret.

"It's natural for a fella…to miss his mother."

"I doubt anybody else is missing their mother," Del

said, embarrassed about confiding something so personal.

"I believe we all miss somebody. We worry they're all right, safe. Our women depend on us."

Del doubted his mother depended on him, but he did her. He hadn't worn a well-washed shirt or eaten a dumpling since he left Bismarck. "My ma, she makes the best apple dumplings. I like 'em a little undercooked, kinda doughy. I'd give about anything to eat one of those for breakfast today."

Trent smiled at the boy. It was odd what men missed most about being away from home.

"Well, I don't think there are any apple dumplings, but if you pour a little honey on one of those hardtack biscuits, they're not too bad." Trent paused, contemplating his thoughts, "I don't miss big things when I'm away, but little things, like the smell of fresh bread or listening to my dad fiddle out a tune on the front porch."

In another hour, the other men awoke to the sizzle of bacon frying over the fire, making Del hungrier. He made a bit of a hog out of himself at breakfast.

"We should hit the South Platte mid-day tomorrow," Gray said. "It might be smart if you or I," he continued, looking at Trent, "push on up ahead and scout the river east and west. We might find where those boys crossed. If one of us rides hard and late, we can still sleep a few hours, rise at first light, and search up and down the riverbank."

Trent told Gray he'd be happy to go since Gray went down Horse Creek. Gray agreed, although he preferred going himself, not because he didn't think Trent capable; he wanted the time alone.

Trent stuck an extra box of cartridges in his saddlebags and swung on his bay. Trent's horse, a runner, enjoyed the fast pace. They didn't run across anything more than an occasional jackrabbit or coyote for the first four hours. Trent figured if he found nothing before meeting up with the others, Gray would leave the three Bismarck men in camp while they scouted up and down the river.

With the weather rainy until today, the flat plains were soft, and hoofprints would be deep and long-lasting. Once they crossed the gang's tracks, he figured they would catch up in three or four days at the outside. He hoped sooner.

Neither he nor Gray held a personal interest in the captives until they rescued April. Gray may have cared a little more than Trent did because he grew up with Susan Tucker Carlyle. But finding a child so beaten and abused started a fire in Gray's gut.

Every day, the hostages took new beatings. Likely, some would die at the hands of their captors. The sooner they caught them, the more lives they would save.

At noon, Trent let Sundance graze and to himself eat a piece of jerky and a hardtack biscuit. After starting back on the trail, he crossed a track headed south, a lone unshod horse. From April's information, a Cheyenne rode with the group.

Trent didn't know whether the renegade rode an unshod pony or a shod horse he stole from a ranch. If Walker sent someone snooping along their back trail, Trent thought it would likely be the Indian.

Riding across such flat country was risky but a risk worth taking. The Cheyenne would lead him right to Walker. Trent followed the lone set of tracks.

A couple of hours later, he found where the man stopped to eat. He had not made a fire, but a few scraps of meat lay around, meaning the man wasn't far ahead; otherwise, some scavenger would have made a meal out of the remains.

By pushing his horse hard enough, he might catch the man before dark—if he wanted to. If he did, and the rider turned out to be the Cheyenne or another member of the

Walker gang, Trent would end a life.

Killing the man would leave no one to trail back to the rest of the outfit. He decided if he caught him before making the South Platte, he would kill him; otherwise, he would wait at the river for Gray and the others.

The man dying today or living another twenty-four or forty-eight hours made little difference, although, on second thought, killing him as soon as possible might save a captive from another round of abuse at this man's hands. He pushed Sundance.

Chapter Eighty

With no warning, Bill Beachum shot Jenny Carlyle from across the camp. The coward.

Beachum shattered Lucy's cheekbone when she charged him after watching her daughter die. He hit her squarely with the butt of his Springfield rifle. Except for the gun being an old single shot breach loader, he would have killed her instead of bashing the side of her face.

Meg and Rennie dragged Lucy away from Beachum and grabbed Maddie, who went hysterical seeing her sister die and her mother crumple from the blow with the rifle.

Jack Walker screamed at Lucy. "You didn't have enough sense to stop trying to run. If you had, one or both of your pups would still be alive." He poked a dirty finger in her face. "You've been nothing but a damn headache. One more escape try, or trouble of any kind, and I'll kill you."

The thought of dying no longer concerned Lucy, but the manner Walker described scared her.

"I'll slice off the skin of your last kid. While she's still

317

alive, I'll choke her. I'll cut off her fingers and shove them down your throat until you strangle on them."

Even if Lucy had the strength to fight again, she wouldn't. What tortured Lucy most, though, was concern she'd die from the previous beatings. Dylan died not from a single beating but a series of thrashings. Lucy feared the same thing happening to her. An almost constant ache burned dull and deep in the right side of her abdomen. Once or twice, she threw up small amounts of blood, causing her to wonder if she might be bleeding to death inside.

The fear of what would happen to Maddie terrified her most. Maddie would face a horrible death if her mother died. Lucy made Meg Brown swear if she died, Maddie's end would come swiftly.

Burns The Grass rode into camp after dark. "Five men follow us," he told Walker.

The news set Walker on a tirade. Profanity and everything he could grab flew all over the camp. He flung the coffeepot and two cook pots out into the darkness. He kicked over the spit on which a jackrabbit was sizzling, dripping grease into the fire and causing loud popping sounds. He cussed everything from the dark to the distance to the Arkansas River.

J.D. Pratt pulled his navy colt ready to shoot Walker. Camp jerked the gun out of his hand. Walker took the last drops of rage out on one of the newest captives, kicking her before slamming her face down into the dirt as if trying to drown her.

"Let her go," Camp screamed as he tried to pull the madman off the woman. "Let her go. Hellfire, won't be anything left of her to sell," he cursed at Walker after he got him off the woman and shoved him to the ground.

Walker lunged at Camp, but the smaller man yanked his pistol out and pointed the gun right at Walker's face.

"Come ahead, damn you; come on."

Walker didn't. Only a fool charged into a cocked Navy Colt.

The Fox brothers picked up the equipment Walker flung all over the camp. The Indian headed off into the dark for the coffeepot and the two cook pots. Bill Beachum sat down close to the fire and dealt himself a hand of solitaire. Long and Pratt, the new gang members, drifted to the opposite side of the camp and whispered back and forth between themselves.

Bert Camp walked over to them. "Don't think of skippin' out. Walker'll kill you both, and if he don't, I will. We've got our damn hands full keepin' these women in tow, and I don't plan on being short-handed." Neither man replied.

After Walker calmed down enough to be approached, Camp sat down beside him. He removed a whiskey flask from his pocket and took a long draw before offering some to Walker. "Tomorrow morning, I'll double back on them sonsabitches. I'll hide in the outcrop of rock we rode through and pick off two or three of them. I'll take the damn steam out of 'em."

"Who in the hell do you suppose they are?" Walker asked, pulling on another shot of whiskey.

"Who knows?" Camp said, unconcerned. "Likely some do-gooders or relatives. They'll give up when a few of them take a belly full of lead."

That night, Lucy Carlyle cried her remaining tears. The left side of her face was swollen so much her eye had almost disappeared. She was vomiting from swallowing her blood. Rennie Brown begged the men to give Lucy a little whiskey to dull some of the pain. Trey Long laughed at her and spat in her face before dragging her off for his amusement.

Chapter Eighty-One

Laura Reed woke up sobbing, as she did every night. Most nights, she couldn't go back to sleep. When she did, she slept only for a short time before the nightmares would return. Red Holsten and Hank Potts would repeatedly die at the hands of the Sioux. Laura believed a lifetime of haunted nights would be her payment for the terrible thing she had done.

Chapter Eighty-Two

Before dark, the single set of tracks Trent followed ran into the trail of fifteen or more horses, easy to follow, with only a quarter moon. Once he reached the South Platte, he stopped and pulled the saddle off his horse. He spread out his bedroll and sat on the bank eating the last piece of dried beef he brought along. The night was clear, so the temperature was dropping.

Trent thought about keeping a cold camp but decided not to freeze all night. The men he was after already crossed the river and were at least a full day ahead of him. He built a decent fire and curled up in a blanket. Sleep came fast and deep. The sun was high in the sky when Trent woke around eight. He and Gray agreed to meet at a bend only four or five miles to the west. He didn't need to rush. Gray and the others wouldn't arrive until around noon.

He walked down to the riverbank and washed his face and hair. On the way back, a rattlesnake sang out at him. Trent debated making breakfast out of him.

Mountain men and buffalo hunters claimed the rattlesnake was "right tasty," but after living his whole life without eating snake, he wasn't hungry enough to start now. Buffalo hunters also said a raw heart or liver cut out of a fresh kill and eaten while still warm made a fine meal, so he put little faith in the menu recommendations of hunters or mountain men.

He gave the rattler, which he held nothing against, a wide swath. Once saddled, he crossed the river, finding the tracks heading straight south, confirming Walker was bound for the Arkansas River.

After coming back across the South Platte, Trent made the bend where he was to meet Gray. Much to his surprise, Gray and the other three showed up about an hour later.

"You made good time," Trent said.

"We've been in a full run most of the morning," Tom Gibbs said. "At our pace, I'm glad this is a sizable river; otherwise, we might have ridden right across without noticing."

"I found their trail about four miles east of here," Trent said after giving a courteous laugh to Gibbs' humor. "I suggest we ride down and have some lunch. I skipped breakfast," he mentioned off-handedly.

"How long ago do you think they crossed?" Gray asked.

"A day, a day and a half back. They didn't camp here. I checked both sides. The place where they waded across is shallow. I found the track of a rider by himself. He led me to the other trail. So, they may have sent somebody back to check on whether they're being followed."

For the first time since starting, Gray's face bore a trace of doubt. Not worry, not a deep concern, just doubt.

Except for getting their feet damp, crossing the South Platte presented no problems for the men. Their quick noon meal consisted of a few biscuits and dried beef. About mid-afternoon, they discovered the campsite, most likely used by Walker and his gang the previous night. The plains of southeastern Colorado allowed for fast travel, and they put almost twenty miles between themselves and the river before Gray called an end to the day.

"Do you think we'll catch them tomorrow?" Gabe asked when Gray sat down next to him.

"With luck." Gray scooped up his last fork of whistle berries. "I'm sure tiring of our menu," he said as he laid his tin plate down in front of him. "A little of Annie's fried chicken would sit well."

"I'd settle for a hot platter of chicken and dumplings," Trent said.

"These beans aren't that awful." Gray laughed. "I think I'll go check on our horses," he said, standing up after stretching out his bad knees.

"Why's he checking the horses?" Del asked after Gray left the campfire. "None of 'em are making any fuss."

"We picketed those horses almost two hours ago," Trent said. "He can't stand being away from his mare for so long."

"He has a particular affection for the animal." Tom chuckled. "Most men have less interest in their wives than he has in that horse."

Gray slipped down the picket line, whispering to each horse as he moved along. He picked up their feet to check for stones or anything lodged in their hooves. He paid particular attention to both Lena and Sundance. Convinced all was well, he returned to the fire.

"I guess you'll think we're incompetent by my asking this," Gabe said, as Gray poured a cup of coffee and sat down, "but I was wondering what we do when we find this bunch."

Gray studied the older Reed but did not respond. Instead, he took off his tan hat and brushed some dirt away. He took a drink and looked at the campfire before glancing around at the three Bismarck men. "What you can't do is lose your nerve. You hesitate—you'll die."

He paused again. How do you instruct a man to kill? He killed others, but almost always in reaction to the other man's aggression. "If we're close, shoot with your pistol. Don't take time to aim. Point your revolver at them. Gutless wonders scare when somebody's shooting at them."

Del stared at Gray. "You think they're cowards?"

Gray's green eyes glanced down at the fire before focusing on the boy. "These men are cruel, Del." The lines around his mustache deepened. "Means not the same as being brave. Most mean men are gutless once in anything resembling a fair fight."

Gray said nothing, but he was not confident either the Reeds or the newspaperman would hold up well in a fray, not because he thought them cowardly, not because he didn't think they would make a respectable effort, but because of their inexperience. He didn't enjoy depending on inexperienced men in a gunfight.

"They may try to run," Gray said, looking each man straight. "Don't let them. Men of this cut need to stopping; letting them escape won't accomplish what's needed."

"You want us to shoot them in the back?" Gabe asked.

Gray stared at him for a moment before tossing his coffee at the fire. "I want you to shoot them wherever it's convenient."

Chapter Eight-Three

"You think we'll catch them today?" Trent asked.

"I hope so," Gray said. "Not only do they need to be stopped and those women and children freed, but I'm missing home."

From the sound of Gray's voice, Trent sensed something else on his mind, but he did not pursue it. Gray would talk in his own time. "His time" came sooner than Trent expected.

"When the fighting starts, you watch yourself," Gray said. "An incompetent man makes mistakes, gets others killed, no matter how honorable his intentions." Gray finished rolling up his bedroll. "You and I'll flank these men. We put them in a crossfire, and they won't be able to concentrate all their attention in one direction."

Gray looked over at the other three men before continuing. "It'd be best to kill Walker and Camp first. But since we can't identify them, shoot the man nearest you. I'll drop the one closest to me and any who appear to be a threat to those three," he said, motioning toward the others with his head. "I suspect you and I," he said, looking at Trent in the eye, "will have to account for every one of them. We'll be lucky if our men hit anyone."

Gabe, leading his horse while eating the last piece of the hardtack, rejoined Gray and Trent. "I didn't sleep much. This is my first attempt at a mission like this."

"I wouldn't worry much about falling asleep." Trent half laughed. "Gunfire tends to keep a man awake."

"Especially shots aimed at him," Gray said, slapping Reed on the shoulder and assuring him he would handle himself all right.

Del Reed's saddle spun under the horse and dumped him on the ground when the boy stepped up on his gelding. Shorty didn't take kindly to having a saddle dangling under his belly. He lit into a bucking fit and didn't stop until he rid himself of the annoying tack. Gray grabbed the horse's reins and led him back to Del.

"I forgot to tighten the cinch up."

"Are you hurt?" Gray asked, trying not to laugh.

"I think he stepped on me a little, but I'm all right."

"I guess your dad needs to give you a lesson in saddling a horse," Gray good-naturedly said as he reached out and pulled the boy's hat down over his eyes.

"Apparently," Del said.

After two hours of hard riding, Gray gave the horses a brief rest. Everyone loosened their cinches a bit, prompting Gabe to remind his son to remember to tighten his.

Tom Gibbs wiped his face with his neckerchief before taking a long drink from his canteen. "A blind man could track this bunch. Why didn't they make some effort to cover their trail?"

"What would they do?" Trent asked.

"Well, I don't know," Gibbs admitted, "but something."

"I doubt they can sprout wings and fly," Tent said.

Gibbs let the matter drop. Instead, he asked if the tracks

were any fresher than yesterday.

"We're cutting the distance," Gray said. "I guarantee you."

"I'm anxious to find where they camped last night," Trent said. "I want an idea how far ahead of us they still are."

"I guess we've rested these horses enough."

"Don't forget the cinch," Trent said, smiling at Del.

Gray soon put them into a full-out run, a pace Del's tall horse favored.

"Too bad your horse is gelded," Trent told the boy after the pace slowed up. "He'd pass some fine traits along."

"I think so too, but the previous owner cut the horse before Dad purchased him. I'd like to be a horse rancher. We're raising some cattle, but mostly we're farming."

"Well, you're young," Trent said. "You can raise horses."

Gabe first spotted the place where Walker and his gang made camp under a group of junipers and a few medium-sized boulders. "I'll swear," Gray said as he stepped off Lena. "This bunch ain't got enough sense to find a stream to camp next to. We've passed, what, five or six in the last two hours?" he asked, looking up at Trent, still sitting on Sundance. "And they stop here, in nothing but rock and dirt."

"I bet they stopped here 'cause of the junipers. They likely wanted a little shade," Tom Gibbs said.

"Why would you need shade at night?" Del asked, drawing a chuckle out of both Gray and Trent.

"They're a messy bunch," Gabe said. "Garbage all over."

Trent kicked at the campfire. "The coals are all dead." He bent down and ran his hand over the blackened earth. "Cold. That's disappointing," he said as he glanced up at Gray.

Several broken whiskey bottles littered the ground, causing Gray to wonder if these men carried anything else in their packs. Looking around a little more, he found a pool of dried blood. "They hurt somebody."

Gabe wandered off to the other side of the junipers. Gabe was standing in one place, and Gray assumed he must be relieving himself. He meandered around the area a little more, rummaging through the few items left. None were of any value, nor did they offer any clues about how long ago they abandoned the camp.

As Gray started back toward his horse, Gabe still stood near the clump of small trees stiff as a dead man. "You all right, Gabe?"

"I found who they hurt."

He sounded so defeated. No one ran to his side. They wandered toward him, almost mindlessly.

Tom Gibbs spoke first. "Jenny Carlyle."

Gabe bent over and vomited.

Trent grabbed Gabe's arm. The man almost collapsed. Gray walked over to the child lying fifteen or twenty feet away. One wound killed her. A bullet entered her breast bone and passed through her. Dried blood caked both sides of her dress. Gray picked up her small body and carried her past the other four men, saying nothing.

Back at the abandoned camp, he lay her down and took the blanket off the back of his saddle. He knelt and started to put the cover over the small body, hesitating for a moment to take in the child's delicacy. Even in death, her blond hair matted in blood and dirt covering her eyes and face, she looked innocent. Gray tenderly pulled her hair loose and pushed the locks back. He ran his fingers over her eyes, shutting the lids over the empty blue pools.

Gray remembered Susan Tucker at about the same age. So much resemblance. He laid the blanket over the girl's face.

Trent came back over, leaving the other three men standing where Reed found the body. "I'll try to find something to dig with." Gray sat down, putting his head between his knees. In all the brutality of the war, he encountered nothing compared to the evil in the men they were pursuing.

Theirs was far beyond common cruelty or viciousness. These men held an utter disregard for life. They not only enjoyed killing, but they also basked in murdering the most defenseless, making them despicable cowards. "When I catch you boys," he whispered to himself as he sat next to Jenny Carlyle, "you'll wish you had a millstone tied around your neck."

The closest thing to a shovel or a spade with them was the small Dutch oven Tom kept in his saddlebags. For the better part of an hour, Trent dug out the shallowest grave to place the child in. Finding rocks on the prairie to cover her body enough to keep coyotes and varmints out took longer. During the digging, Gray washed Jenny's face, arms, and hands before folding them across her chest.

"I'll make some kind of marker," Tom said. He broke off a couple of juniper branches and tied them into a cross with a strip of rawhide. "Lord, we can't put her name on here. I don't like not leaving her name."

"We ought to say a few words over her, I guess," Gabe said. Tears pooled in his eyes. "I don't believe I can. Do you think you might, Gray?" he asked as the tears swelled out of his eyes.

Gray never spoke over a grave before, but he knew several scriptures. Raised in a Christian home, he became one himself at only eight. Annie was also particular about them memorizing God's word.

Gray held his hat over his heart with both hands.

"The Lord is my shepherd; I shall not want. He maketh to me lie down in green pastures; He leadeth me beside still waters. He restoreth my soul; He leadeth me in the paths of righteousness for His name's sake. Yea, though I walk through the valley of the shadow of death, I will fear no evil; for thou art with me. Thou prepares a table before me in the presence of mine enemies; thou anointest my head with oil; my cup runneth over. Surely goodness and mercy shall follow me all the days of my life; and I will dwell in the house of the LORD forever."

A peace, a calmness, softened Gray's voice. "Father, this is an innocent child. We're thankful she is with You. I pray for those who are yet captives. I pray the words of the Psalmist will safeguard them. God, we pray Your hand of protection might be around them. Almighty God, I ask You to lead us to their aid. I ask for Your strength and Your courage. In Christ's precious name we pray."

"Amen." The four other men said when Gray finished, "Amen."

"Wrath is coming, boys; wrath is coming," Gray muttered as he walked away from the little grave.

"And who shall stand against it?" Trent whispered to himself.

Chapter Eighty-Four

Annie put two more logs on the fire before sitting down on the couch next to Jean.

"So, you're going to be the new owner of Kellers' store?" Millie asked, smiling at Susan.

"You be sure you give me your business."

"Right," Jean chimed in. "Millie's a cash customer. 'Most everybody else in town will want you to give them credit."

"I hope Lucy and the kids like High Meadows."

Why wouldn't they," Jean responded. "I defy you to find a prettier valley."

"Would you toss me that quilt?" Annie asked Millie, pointing to a dark blue and gold one she and Jean made together as a Christmas present for Gray several years before he and Annie married.

"You're sure cold-natured," Millie said as she opened the quilt and covered Annie, now curled up with a forest green pillow in her lap.

"I think I got chilled out in the pasture this afternoon," Annie said, pulling the comforter up around her. "You want in here, too?" she asked Jean.

"I'm not cold; you must be coming down with something."

"I'm not catching anything," Annie protested before scooting her stockinged feet under Jean's legs. "You can get my feet warm," she smiled, shuffling them back and forth a little.

"I envy the bond between you three," Susan said. "I have friends in Laura Reed and Libbie Custer, but not like this. Your friendship is one of genuine love."

"I guess Lucy is about my age," Millie said.

"She's twenty-four," Susan said, "but an old twenty-four."

"I'm twenty-three," Millie said, getting up and pouring herself a cup of cocoa, her second in the last ten minutes.

"Is the pot empty?" Annie asked.

"Another cup, or a little more. Anybody want more?" The three women declined, and Millie sat back down in the straight-backed rocker, pulling her feet up underneath her. "I don't know if I'm an old twenty-three or a young twenty-three."

"You're a young twenty-three," Jean laughed.

"I think I've been insulted." Millie chuckled as she winked at Susan.

"I wish Lucy were high-spirited, like you," Susan said.

"Oh, no, you don't," Jean said as she pulled some of Annie's quilt up over her knees.

"I didn't think you were cold," Annie teased.

"Lucy grew up fast. Her father loved the whiskey, and her mother paid a heavy price for his drinking. Lucy is the oldest of seven kids, and a lot of responsibility, far too much, fell on her shoulders. Her father ran off and left them right before her thirteenth birthday. A few years later, a rumor floated through about someone stabbing him in a saloon in Tennessee. Lucy doesn't know if it was true."

Susan got up and walked over to the fireplace mantle. She picked up a little glass figurine and traced her fingers across its face. "I remember when your dad gave this to you," she said. "Lucy's been a sweet wife to Danny, but I think she was a little lonely in Bismarck. Not too many young people lived there."

"I'll be glad for the company of a young woman," Millie said, mischief in her voice. "Not many people my age around here, either. I'm forced to spend most of my time with old people."

Annie flung the dark green pillow at Millie. "A privilege denied to many."

Susan laughed at the antics of the two women. She sat down on the floor between Annie and Jean. She leaned back against the couch and put one arm across Annie's knees. "Being back here awakens some pleasant memories. Welcome images."

Annie touched the side of the woman's face. For a brief time, no one said anything. "Everything that made my childhood sweet and the rest of my life so…so warm and wonderful is still in this valley," Annie said. "My dad's kindly wisdom, my mother's and Jean's mother's inexhaustible imaginations, Gray's sense of justice and his tender heart. I have a friend closer than any sister," she said, smiling at Jean. "And we've got Millie and a lot of memories," she said, looking at her young friend across the room as a few tears welled up. "High Meadows is a peaceful place to be, Susan."

Chapter Eighty-Five

"If I'm shot out here, I sure hope it's during the warm part of the day," Gabe whined. "I think a bullet would hurt a lot more in the cold."

"I'm not interested in getting shot, hot or cold," Tom Gibbs said, pulling his coat up around him to prepare for standing his turn.

With only a couple of hours of sleep remaining, Gabe threw all but two of the last logs on the fire before dragging his bedroll so close to the flames he was in danger of setting himself ablaze. He had never been so miserable. Slumped over, he was freezing, missed his wife, and inadequate for the job facing him.

Back in Bismarck, the weather would be colder than in Colorado, but he had a warm feather bed to crawl into, with Laura next to him. He would be eating not only decent but delicious food, and he wouldn't be lying here, unable to sleep because of worrying about being shot.

He should have told Susan Carlyle he wasn't the man she needed, or led her to High Meadows and gone home, leaving the pursuit and capture to Gray Wehr, a man used to doing this kind of work.

Gabe didn't, and now he lay here chilled on hard ground. In two hours, still, an hour or more before daylight, he would crawl out of his bedroll, saddle his horse, and start across the plains in search of what must be the cruelest damn men on earth.

Gibbs wandered around the outskirts of the camp, a habit at the beginning of each of his shifts. He didn't expect to find anything, but he might fall asleep if he didn't move around a bit.

As he walked, Gibbs mulled over how he would write up the rescue story. This tale would be major news in papers in the West, but more important to Tom, in the great eastern cities.

He envisioned making trips to Chicago, Philadelphia, Boston, and New York. In the finest clothes, he would dazzle sold-out audiences with his account of the capture and rescue. *No, not capture.* There would be no capturing; Wehr made that clear. His speeches would detail the historic deliverance and the dealing out of justice on the vicious outlaws.

As he circled the dark camp, Tom debated with himself whether he should refer to the Walker bunch as "outlaws" or "criminals." Easterners would call such men "criminals," but the more romantic western term would be "outlaws." He settled on "The Infamous Jack Walker Gang Brought To Justice" as the headline for the first story.

Chapter Eighty-Six

At sunrise, Bert Camp started back for a rocky little bluff along the Arikaree River. Walker wanted him to take someone with him, perhaps one of the Fox brothers. Camp refused. He planned to kill the "damn pursuers" from a distance. He considered himself a fine rifle shot and didn't want some "poor shooter" mucking up his work. The younger Fox brother took offense about being called a poor shot.

"You may not be bad if you're close," Camp said, "but you couldn't hit a buffalo more than fifty yards away. I intend to shoot those sonsabitches from a long way off. I'll enjoy seeing how damn surprised they act."

With Fox still arguing about the quality of his shooting, Camp climbed up on his horse and headed north toward the Arikaree. Walker and the others got the women and children heading south for the Arkansas River.

"Don't travel too hard," Camp told Walker. "I don't want to chase you for more than a day to catch up."

Camp rode for two hours at a stiff pace. The renegade Cheyenne figured the men Camp wanted were a little more than a day back, meaning they would hit the Arikaree River about noon. Camp wanted to be hiding in the rock bluff before they arrived. He'd be shooting at them from the open plains if they crossed, making a much fairer fight.

In truth, the plains would give the other men the advantage because they outnumbered him. So, Camp planned to be set up all cozy in the rocks to kill a couple of them, hopefully three, and ride back to Walker. The group chasing them would turn and run after a few got lead in their bellies. Those who survived the shooting would drag back to wherever they came from, licking their wounds.

Gray pushed at a hard pace, something he promised them when they left Pine Bluffs. With Trent only, he would not have stayed in camp long enough to eat breakfast, but the Bismarck men might be more alert on a full stomach, so he allowed them to satisfy their appetites before starting.

"We'll rest the horses for a while," he said, reining up in a thick patch of cheatgrass. He stepped off Lena but stood still for a minute because of his stiff knees. Once his knee straightened out, he hobbled around a little, working out some other kinks, especially between his shoulder blades. He ran his index finger and thumb across his mustache and down the chin beard growing under his lower lip. The mustache was still a dark blonde; the beard bore a touch of gray.

"Since they may suspect someone is after them, do you think they will move faster?" Del asked Wehr after Gray overcame his aches.

"A little. But with all the captives they're pushing, they won't be able to go too fast."

"Why do you suppose they shot Jenny?" Del asked.

Innocence still shadowed Del's boyish face.

Understanding some men were plain killers lay beyond his way of thinking. "They're born killers, Del, the way another man might be to furniture building or another to excelling at numbers. Killing comes naturally to some. I can't tell you why a man would kill a child. There's a viciousness in them regular people can't understand."

Gray untied his canteen from his saddle and offered Del a drink, which the boy took. "You sure you don't want anymore?" Gray asked when Dell handed the canteen back. He rather suspected Del being out of water since he didn't take his off his horse when they stopped.

"Susan will hurt when we don't bring Jenny home," Del said, sounding defeated.

Gray sighed and nodded his head. "Susan's seen a lot of death. I hope we'll take the rest of her family back for her." He put Lena's reins back up around her neck and stepped up on her back.

"I'm not as scared as I have been," Del said.

Gray wasn't smiling, but a reassuring countenance warmed his face. "Any man who's not afraid facing danger is a fool, but a strong man will do what has to be done. You're brave, Del, and don't you let anybody tell you different."

Chapter Eighty-Seven

Camp arrived at the bluff over-looking the Arikaree, not a high bluff, twenty or twenty-five feet above the water. The jagged boulders would provide suitable cover. The other side was flat, with no place for the riders to hide once Camp started picking them off. Also, the river would be between him and his targets, so they wouldn't be able to charge him, even if they were brave enough.

He'd shoot a man the far right first. Most shooters would pick the middleman, causing the men to separate in at least two directions. Hitting an outside rider would make them all go the same direction—away from the first victim. Camp took pride in his skill of killing at a distance. He considered himself an expert.

He spent the next few minutes picking the exact place he would shoot. He selected a position behind a medium-sized boulder with bushes in front. The brush was small enough not to interfere with his firing but heavy enough to camouflage his presence. Kneeling behind the rock, he had an excellent spot.

Camp wiped his weapon down with a rag from his saddle. He raised the site to accommodate the long-range. He thought about taking a little practice, but there was nothing to use as a target. Not being in eyesight didn't mean they wouldn't be within earshot of the shooting. Shots would put them on their guard. Regardless, Camp didn't need any rehearsal.

Waiting would be the hardest part. Camp wished the men would hurry and come along. Waiting bored him, tested his patience. He hid a flask in his saddlebags but decided not to indulge himself.

Not only might drinking affect his shooting, with the day warming, the liquor might put him to sleep. How annoying that would be, to come all this way, fall asleep and let his targets ride right on past. So, he left the whiskey alone and amused himself by whittling on a sizable stick. Camp, not a proficient enough whittler to make much, not an animal or a statue or anything artistic, but anyone could carve a crude whistle. So, he passed his time while waiting to kill— sitting up on the bluff, whittling a whistle.

The bullet struck Gabe in the center of his chest, causing him to slump backward off his horse. Gray yanked his Winchester out of the scabbard and jumped off Lena before the echo of the rifle shot disappeared. "Get out of here!" He grabbed the headstall of Del's chestnut horse and spun him around in the opposite direction before giving him a resounding slap on the rump. "Get them out of range!" he screamed at Trent.

Tom jerked his horse around and lashed the reins across both hips. Del went into a complete state of confusion. He pulled back on his horse before Trent grabbed the bridle and charged back across the plains. "Come on!" Trent yelled as he kicked his bay gelding.

Wehr only glanced once at Gabe. The man was dead. Another glance, this time at the surrounding area, confirmed to Gray his terrible situation, on foot, with nowhere to hide. The only possible shelter, a poor one, was Gabe's body.

The ambusher shot again at the men, now close to being too far away. A foolish thing for the bushwhacker to do because, while Gray couldn't see the shooter, he had an idea of where he was hiding. As fast as he could work the lever on his Winchester .44-.40 rifle, Gray put four rounds into a clump of brush at the top of the bluff.

He took a glance toward his mare, only to be distressed as she followed the other horses. He took two more shots at the bushes.

"Do you see those boulders sticking up?" Trent shrieked at the other two. "Shoot at them. Now!" Trent bellowed when neither of the Bismarck men obeyed. Once the two started firing, wildly, Trent tore back across the open plains toward Gray, lying behind Reed's corpse.

Gray shoved five more cartridges into his rifle. As soon as he thought Trent had come back within range of the shooter, Gray raised up and again opened fire on the clump of brush.

Trent charged in a dead run back to Gray. He leaned down, extending an arm, which Gray hooked into his left elbow. Trent yanked Gray upward as Gray leaped toward the back of the horse's saddle. For a moment, Gray didn't think he would make it up behind Trent. His age and recent injuries didn't make such a daring rescue any easier. Gray realized he would never succeed while trying to hold .44-40. He let the rifle drop and grabbed at Trent's back.

The whole attempt lasted only seconds. Gray didn't have a decent seat, but at least he was on the horse. Trent kicked the bay back toward Tom and Del, who, for some unfathomable reason, quit shooting. They stood in a small wallow, watching Trent and Gray charge away from the river.

Once the shooting ended, Bert Camp stuck his head up into the cover of the brush. All four survivors were out of range. With no more chance to kill, Camp scooted back down to his horse. He would expose himself for a stretch of several hundred yards, but with the opposition so far away, Camp didn't consider this too dangerous.

He shoved his Winchester back into its scabbard and climbed up on his sorrel. Nervous from all the noise, the animal balked at starting up the trail. Camp gave the beast two hard kicks. He'd have about a fifty-foot climb before reaching the top, where he would turn left before having to cover the open ground.

Del's eyes revealed he knew his father was dead. Gray started to speak to Del when Tom asked why the man quit shooting. "We're out of range," Gray said. "He's gonna run."

"I want him!" Del shook violently.

Gray did not respond to the boy. He turned back toward the bluff. A rider, a silhouette, appeared on the bluff's crown. "Gimmie your rifle!" Gray shouted as he reached up toward Trent. Trent tossed it to him, and Gray swung up on Lena.

Gray and the bay charged toward the river. As soon as Gray thought, or at least hoped, he might be within range, he slid the horse to a stop and jumped off. "Whoa, Lena, whoa," he yelled as he pulled her around to rest the Henry across the saddle.

Gray squeezed the trigger, and his horse jerked back from the noise. "Easy, Lena," Gray said as he tugged on her reins. He again rested the weapon on the saddle, although the mare would not stand as still this time. "Whoa, Lena." Gray took another shot at the rider, who, when shot at the first time, kicked his horse into a faster gait.

His target's horse slid on the way to the top of the embankment. Gray lowered the rifle. "I'm shootin' at you! By hell, I'm shooting!" He doubted the man heard him, but he hollered.

Trent followed Gray toward where Gabe's body lay. He stepped off Sundance and picked up Gray's Winchester. Gray, limping, led Lena to where Trent was waiting. "That was damn foolish, riding right up toward the bluff," Gray said, sounding both frustrated and discouraged. "We thought they might send scouts on their back trail. When we saw those bluffs, we should have moved downriver, away from this open ground."

Trent stood for a moment without responding. "I'm gonna cover Gabe with my blanket. I don't want Del to see him like this."

Chapter Eighty-Eight

The blanketing turned out to be useless. Del pushed it back, kneeled over his dad, whispered something. A moment later, he put the blanket back in place.

"Let's bury him on the other side of the river," Gray said. "I don't want to be caught out here without cover again."

"Do you think they're still around?" Del asked.

"No, not likely."

After some difficulty catching him, Trent brought Gabe's horse back, and he and Gray lifted the body up and over the saddle. After tying him on, the four men waded their horses across the Arikaree. A time or two, Gabe's face went under the water, not bothersome to a dead man, but the dunkings upset Del.

A narrow trail led up the bluff from a flat area, fifty or sixty feet wide on the other bank. Once the men made the top, Trent searched for a grave spot. He selected one far enough back from the rim to be out of the rocks but close enough to see the meandering river and the open plains. People usually wanted to bury their folks with the best view.

Grave-digging without a shovel proved arduous, taking over two-thirds of the day to dig a suitable one. Gray said words over Reed. Gibbs should have handled the task, but Tom privately backed out, mumbling about not knowing what to say.

Gray wondered how a man could write newspaper stories but not utter a few thoughts about a fallen friend.

After the brief funeral service, Gray gathered wood for a fire. He thought about going after the shooter, but this close to dark, with two inexperienced men along, trailing him would be a chancy proposition.

Trent's rifle cracked through the dusk. A few minutes later, he came back to camp carrying a good-sized sage hen. "She didn't jump and fly. She surrendered," he said as he sat down next to Gray and began plucking. The bird wouldn't make much of a meal for four men, but neither did beef jerky. Del and Tom left to care for the mounts.

"How's Del doing?" Trent asked.

"I doubt the reality has set in," Gray said. "Death coming unexpected and violent puts most people in a daze."

Gibbs and Del took a long time minding the horses. By the time they wandered back to the fire, roasting sage hen wafted through the camp.

"Smells good," Del said as he poured a cup of coffee, the first one Gray remembered him taking.

"I'll be glad when this business is done," Tom said after they ate. "I guess a man wouldn't go far before he gets to Kansas."

"Not too far," Trent said.

The clear night's temperature continually dropped, causing Del to think more about his cold-natured father. He had yet to cry for him, but now he was going to whimper like a child.

He bit his bottom lip so hard he wondered if he'd bite through.

He ran his lower teeth through his bottom lip once when he was only three or four years old. He'd fallen and hit his mouth on a table. He still wore a small scar.

"Ma is going to miss him."

"Yes, she will," Gray said, patting the boy's knee. "Yes, she will."

The young man stood and ambled off into the darkness. Tears built up in his eyes, blurring his vision. He wiped his shirtsleeve across his face to blot them up before using the sleeve for a handkerchief. Del was grateful for the full moon. If the night was any darker, he might stumble right off the bluff. If he did plunge off the edge, he hoped no one would tell his mother how he passed. How embarrassing to find out your son died in such a foolish way.

"Are we gonna keep riding right down their trail?" Tom Gibbs asked as the three men sat around the fire.

"It's the best way to catch them," Gray said, without giving much thought to Gibbs's question.

"Well, he may keep picking us off," Tom said.

"Do whatever suits you, Tom, but I'm going after them." Gray's words were harsh, though he didn't mean them to be. "It'd be hard to pick us off on the flat open plains, between here and the Arkansas River. We'll still keep a sharper eye out. If we approach anything looking like cover for an ambush, we'll circle around."

A full hour passed before Del walked back from his father's grave. Gray spent the time worrying about doing the right thing, something he didn't often do. He considered fretting about right and wrong a waste of time. Life seldom offered second chances. Tangling yourself up in lengthy debates with your own heart and conscience gained you little.

He believed in making a choice and following through. He regretted many things in his life but found no point in letting them eat at him. A man should make his decision and live with the results.

He couldn't help being concerned, though, leading a boy into such dangerous work after this day's events. So, when Del sat down, Gray was direct. "Listen, Del, maybe it would be the best thing for you and Tom to head on home. Your mother's going to need you, and I believe Trent and I can handle this matter. We'll be sure Susan gets her family back."

Del looked across the fire at the other men. The boy paused for only a moment before choking the words out. "If you think I'm going to turn tail and run for home, tell my ma those bastards killed her man, and I didn't do a damn thing...you don't know me."

Chapter Eighty-Nine

Bert Camp coughed up dark brown blood most of the night. He was dying. His chances of living would be slim if he got to a doctor but non-existent out in the wilderness. He'd never ride with Jack Walker again.

Walker would show no sympathy for a wounded man, anyway. He would do what he did when the woman cut Cline up; have him killed. Walker was a pal when you were strong and ready to help him raid and destroy, but he'd be no friend to anyone all shot up and dying.

Camp decided to die here, in his own time. Walker might assign his killing to the damn renegade Cheyenne. At least out here, he'd die with his hair, whereas the Indian might scalp him while still alive.

So, when he came upon a small gully, he stumbled off his horse and crawled down where he hoped to shoot the man who did this to him. Yesterday, when he started shooting, he figured the men would turn tail and run, but any man who shot back like that man did wasn't about to quit. They'd be along, and Camp planned to kill one more before saying hello to the devil.

Chapter Ninety

Life was carefree—a long time ago. To a six-year-old, too long ago, with too much hurt in between, to remember joyful times. "Are they going to kill me, too?" Maddie asked, riding along with her mother.

Lucy Carlyle's life had become unbearable; two children and a husband lost, a third child in constant danger. Still, she maintained a determination to survive. Her grim tenaciousness turned bitter after Jenny's death. She would live, at least until Jack Walker died. He'd die for what he did, die by her hand, by the law's hand, or by the hand of God. She did not care who made him pay, but she intended to be there.

"They will not kill you, Maddie; they won't."

"They killed Dylan," Maddie paused, "and Jenny," the child said, her voice reflecting the horrible abuse she had taken and witnessed. Now, living required too much hope for a child.

Lucy started to tell her six-year-old the men would not hurt her anymore, but she might be lying. She might not be quick enough to stop them from hurting Maddie again, but they would not steal this daughter from her.

"Camp oughta been back by now," Walker said, guiding his horse over to Carl Fox.

"You ought to send the Indian back looking for him," Fox said. "The Arkansas River isn't that far. We'll make it with or without Camp."

"I'm not sending anybody after him," Walker said. "I ain't his wet nurse. We'll quit early today," Walker said, aggravated Camp hadn't shown.

"If we're being chased, I'll bet they picked him off," Fox said. "Send somebody back to find out."

"By Gawd, I told you nobody's goin' back!" Walker screamed in a sudden flash of anger. "If he don't show tonight, we'll push out before sunrise and press hard for the Arkansas. If any woman or brat can't keep the pace, we'll kill 'em. A couple of killin's and the rest'll move their hind ends."

Walker called off the travel and made camp in mid-afternoon. Pratt shot an antelope and ordered several women to clean and cook his kill. They skinned the hide back from the chest and shoulders and cut out chunks of meat. Within an hour, the antelope haunch roasted over a sizable fire.

Bill Beachum cuffed one woman captured south of Casper across the face.

She cried out, "I can't understand you! How can I do what you want if I can't understand you?" She held up her forearm in front of her face to block a second blow.

"Hell, woman, nobody can." Carl Fox laughed. "You have to read his mind, which ain't too hard, dumb as he is."

Beachum spun around at Fox, pulling his hunting knife as he did.

Fox jerked his gun and pointed the Navy Colt right at Beachum's chest. "Come ahead, you damn dummy. Your knife's no match for this pistol. Come on, now. Come on."

Beachum shoved the blade back into its sheath and turned away. Fox danced a mock jig at him as he left.

"You better be careful with him," Trey Long said. "He'll jump you some night while yer asleep and cut more'n your tongue out."

"I ain't afraid of him." Fox snorted.

"I wouldn't underestimate Beachum. But suit yourself," Long said.

About sunset, Rennie Brown sat down next to Lucy. "People claim Colorado is beautiful," she said. "Apparently, those people never passed through here."

Lucy thought about that. Who cared?

"I guess it's pretty in another part," Rennie said. "Wyoming is like that. Gorgeous in some parts. Plain ugly in others. What's the land like up around Bismarck?"

"I suppose Bismarck is pleasant enough," Lucy said. "It's a rugged, unsettled place."

"Someday, I'd like to live in a civilized place. Someplace sophisticated and educated. I guess it'll never happen."

Lucy couldn't think of such things as the future. Any future was too much to hope for.

Rennie kept talking, but Lucy stopped listening. Her heart and soul moved to another place, a sunny warm meadow where Dylan and Jenny ran and laughed. She and Maddie were there, but not really. They could observe, but they weren't with the other two. Dylan and Jenny danced to Ring-Around-the-Rosie, but something separated them—Lucy and Maddie could watch but not join in.

"Would you keep Maddie for a few minutes?"

Rennie slipped her arm around the child and kissed the side of her face.

"What do you want?" Walker asked when Lucy Carlyle, who had not been allowed to clean meat or cook since she cut Carter Cline, walked over to where he sat, sipping on a flask of whiskey.

"You killed two of my children. I don't want you to harm Maddie anymore."

"Now ain't that sweet." Walker smirked and took another drink. "You don't want your little girl hurt."

"You've hurt us enough," Lucy said, with a strength in her voice to set Walker back a bit. "I'll do whatever you want. Don't beat my child anymore."

"You'll do anything I want regardless," Walker said.

"But now I'll be willing."

Beaten black and blue, lips swollen and cracked, her face no longer shined.

"I don't give a damn how willing you are." Walker spat a chew of tobacco out, splattering her bare feet. "You'll do what I want."

"Yes," Lucy said. She kneeled in front of him. "I'm begging you; please leave Maddie alone. She won't be worth as much if she's beaten anymore."

Walker laughed at Lucy. "By Gawd, you're a nervy one, ain't you?"

Thinking of no response, Lucy bit her lip to fight back tears. She touched and then rubbed Walker's knee. "If you don't hurt her, I'll be the best woman you've ever had."

Chapter Ninety-One

Gray thought letting Del sleep was one kindness he could offer, but the sun was almost up. He woke the others, and they broke camp.

"We may catch them today," Gray said as the men finished saddling. He could see his statement rattled Tom Gibbs, but Del showed no emotion at all. He stared at Gray, his boyish face brutal. "If we do, they may put up a fight at first, but like I said, men like this are cowards. When a few of them are dying, they'll start begging for mercy. The hell with 'em."

Gray pushed away some of the fringe on his chaps and tied down the well-worn brown holster carrying his Colt. He stepped up on his bay, fixing his stare on Tom Gibbs, standing with a blank expression on his face.

"If they throw up their hands and beg," Gray's eyes burned into both Tom and Del before continuing, "kill 'em." Gray paused for a brief time, during which the other three men climbed on their horses. "They're murderers…and worse. You let them live; one of those women, one of the children, or one of us will pay. They deserve what's coming. Don't you hesitate." Gray turned his horse south, saying no more on the subject.

Thirty minutes later, Trent stepped down off his horse. "There's blood here," he said, kneeling. "You plugged him."

Gray didn't think he hit the man at all. He fired off a long shot without the benefit of time. "I hope he bleeds out."

"Well, man or horse, something's bleeding," Trent said, looking up at Gray. "The blood is dark, so I guess you walloped him."

Gray took a minute to survey the land in front of them. He did not intend to ride into another ambush, but the plains were stark, except for ratty sagebrush and clumps of dried grass. Smelling blood, Gray moved the men forward in a lope.

Chapter Ninety-Two

Bert Camp climbed off his horse at the first outcrop of rock. Not much of an ambush site, but he didn't have many miles in him and no hope of getting back to Walker and the others. Besides, Walker wouldn't help him. All shot up, he'd be no use to Jack Walker.

Walker would have no interest in him, only his gelding, guns, and anything else he thought would be useful. Walker would kill him or leave him to bleed to death.

Camp couldn't ride too much farther, not without falling off and dying. He wanted to take at least another shot, another chance, at killing the man who killed him. He'd shake the grim reaper's hand behind this stack of rocks, but not yet, not until he killed one last time.

When Camp tried to dismount, he lost balance and fell against his mount. The nervous animal spooked and ran away. Making matters worse for Camp, his rifle still hung on the saddle, and the horse left, leaving the wounded killer with only a pistol. More bad luck.

Now, Camp sat scrunched up behind a few rocks and a scrubby bush on a sunny but chilly day. The loss of so much blood made him colder. If the men didn't come along soon, he'd be dead when they arrived. "Come on, you sonsabitches. Come on."

The rocks protruded well out of rifle range. They weren't much. A couple of small boulders, sitting out on the empty plains, but a man might hide behind them.

Gray sent Trent and Del circling off to the left with instructions not to ride into shooting distance until they circled behind the little piece of poor cover. He ordered Tom Gibbs on the same path, except to the right.

"What are you gonna do, Gray?" Gibbs asked.

"I'm going straight in. He needs somebody to shoot at."

Gray eased Lena toward the little pile of rocks. Close enough to be in rifle range, he pulled out the Navy Colt on his hip and kicked Lena into a full-out charge.

Bert Camp had almost bled out, making staying conscious, much less alert, challenging. He passed out at least twice. He wallowed in his own blood, unaware of the presence of the men, until Wehr's attack. He dragged himself up. The charging bay horse was well within pistol range when Camp snapped off a wild shot.

Gray returned the fire, pop, pop, pop. Almost on top of Camp's ambush site, the bay mare left the ground in a smooth flowing motion, jumping the rocks and over Camp. Gray next fired straight down as he and Lena sailed over the killer.

The bullet hit Camp in the chest, ripping open a gaping hole as the slug penetrated and passed through a lung. Gray spun the horse and fired his last two shots into Camp, with the first one finishing the job of killing him. At the sound of the first shot, Trent charged his horse forward, but by the time he made the area, with Del coming right behind, the shooting was over.

Del leaped from his chestnut's back before the gelding came to a complete stop. He pulled his pistol, almost dropping the heavy weapon in excitement. Del ran on foot toward Camp's body, but Gray grabbed him before the boy began firing. He wrapped the boy in his arms. "It's over, Del. Over," he kept repeating. After the boy's body relaxed, Gray let him go.

Tom, the only one still mounted, held his pistol in his hand but not cocked and ready. "He's done," Trent said, looking up at Gibbs. "Bert Camp," Trent said. Camp, not a burly man, small honestly, looked mean, even in death, with his eyes staring straight up.

"I guess he's the one who killed my dad."

"He's the one."

"I want the rest," Del said, shaking so hard he struggled putting his weapon back in its holster. "I want every damn one of them."

Tom kicked around the little ambush spot for a few minutes. Trent assumed he was mulling over his newspaper account in his mind.

"What do you suppose happened to his horse?" Gibbs asked.

"I guess he ran off," Trent said, bending down and turning Camp over on his side. "Here's where you hit him yesterday," he said, pointing to a bloody wound in the dead man's side. "He wouldn't have lived long if we hadn't caught up with him."

"Probably why the horse got away," Gibbs said. Neither Gray nor Trent responded. "Well, we better bury him," Gibbs said after a moment or two of silence.

Trent glanced at Gray. He had been in this situation

with Gray six years ago, standing over Harvey Kehn, Crow, and Harley Blaine. He asked Gray the same question: "Aren't we going to bury them?" This time, Trent answered. "He's done nothing to deserve burying."

Chapter Ninety-Three

Mid-afternoon came without catching the killers, disappointing Gray. Dealing with this bunch was going to be dirty, bloody business. He wanted to finish. "I suspect they know we're after them," he said to Trent. "Camp's probably overdue, so likely they're running."

"You think they'll send anyone back to check on him?" Tom Gibbs asked.

"No," Gray said. "I think they'll run as hard as they can for the Arkansas River. They board a boat…we may never catch them."

"Will they have a boat waiting?" Del asked.

"No. A lot of boats haul supplies up and down the river. Commandeering one won't be much of a task."

"I doubt they can make the river before we get 'em," Trent said. "The Arkansas's at least two, or three, days away."

"If we don't find them before nightfall, we'll make camp, and one of us will go look for them, come back for the rest of us," Gray said, looking at Trent.

Although they pressed hard the rest of the day, they failed to catch Walker before dark. They found a few scraggly bushes along a dry creek bed and made a night camp.

For dinner, they cooked up a couple of grouse Gray shot. It was hardly a feast but better than a piece of jerky or the prairie dogs they ate the night before. "I hope those killers carry some food with them," Trent dryly commented. "I'm a little tired of our menu." Everyone but Tom got a slight laugh out of Trent's humor.

Gray and Trent decided Trent would find Walker and the captives. He would find their campfire and come back with the news of how far ahead they were.

Chapter Ninety-Four

Lucy seldom thought about her life in Bismarck or Danny because, when she did, her soul ached. Dwelling on the past numbed her. She could not afford to be dulled, not while she still had one baby left to protect.

"Come here, Maddie," she said, lifting the blanket wrapped around her. The child slipped under the worn old quilt and scrunched up against her mother. As the night air turned colder, Lucy sat thinking about escape. Two men were talking. They believed someone was after them. Maybe the pursuers killed the long-overdue Camp.

Lucy wondered for days after her capture why no one came, why no rescue party overtook them and carried her and her children back to safety. But when Dylan died, so did all expectations of being rescued.

Did she dare hope again? Might be brave men somewhere in the dark, not be too far behind. Perhaps, if she escaped, if she and Maddie escaped, they might make their way back where they came from and find the people looking for them.

Should she wait for them to arrive? She might have a better chance waiting than trying to slip off in the dark. Walker told her what he would do if she tried to escape or caused more trouble.

The challenge was deciding. Any decision meant risk. If she left, they'd likely capture her, which would result in death, horrible death for both Maddie and her. If she did not run, though, they would make the Arkansas River in only a day or two. Once on a boat, no one would ever catch up with them. If only a rescue party was coming.

Chapter Ninety-Five

"Where's my Bismarck woman?" Jack Walker's brutish words sent a terrible chill through Lucy. Not once after she promised him her pleasure, if he left Maddie alone, had he come looking for her.

Since she lay a distance from the fire, she hoped to go through another night without his abuse. Lucy counted on him grabbing someone more convenient or perhaps drinking himself to sleep, something he did many nights. She wondered if he took more joy in a woman who didn't promise submission.

"I said, where's the Bismarck woman?" The woman Walker snarled at cowered down. Lucy thought she told Walker she didn't know. Whatever she said resulted in Walker giving her a stiff backhand across the face.

"I'm over here," Lucy said, slipping out of the blanket, hoping she would save Maddie and perhaps another innocent woman a beating.

"Come 'ere," Walker said, sounding like Lucy should

want to go to him. "Let's see how good you keep your promises."

"You stay with Meg," Lucy said. Maddie crying as she walked away sickened her.

"Come here, Maddie," Meg Brown said. "You sit here with Carolyn and me." Weeks ago, Maddie learned to take protection wherever offered, in the arms of someone a stranger two months earlier, who would hold her as they would their child.

As Lucy walked away, she looked back to see Maddie tugging the dirty blanket around her shoulders and walking toward the other two women. Meg's daughter was with them, and Lucy watched Maddie put her arms out for the little girl, two years older than herself, to slip into the cover with her. Carolyn Ross wrapped her arm around the two girls as she wept again over her child, April.

Chapter Ninety-Six

Trent drank two more cups of coffee. "Use caution," Gray said.

"You bet," Trent laughed as he pulled on a wool sweater. "I should have brought Annie's Christmas scarf along. And a timepiece. What time is it, Tom?"

Gibbs took out his pocket watch and turned the face a little to catch the flicker of the campfire. "Quarter of eight."

Gray looked up at the sky. "Only a crescent moon. A dark night is to your advantage."

"You sure you don't want me to go along?" Del asked as Trent picked up his saddle and started toward his bay horse. Trent glanced over at Gray.

"Nah, why don't you stay here with Tom and me?" Wehr said.

"Frankly," Tom Gibbs said, "I don't quite understand why we're not all going. It doesn't make much sense to me for one of us to go. He'll need to come back for the rest of us."

Gibbs' reasoning was sound, except Gray was not comfortable having two inexperienced men traveling in the dark, not when they might ride up on the killers at almost any time. If Walker kept a cold camp, and with any judgment at all, he should be, they could stumble right in, unaware.

"I think we should all go," Del said. "We might catch them while they're asleep."

Trent set his saddle down on the ground. Gray ran his fingers through his hair and across his mustache. "We'll do this my way," he said, almost whispering.

Tom shifted from one foot to the other before speaking. "I think Del is right about this. I think we all should move on them. Gain the advantage of hitting them in the dark."

"I told you back in High Meadows, I decide," Gray said. "You should learn to listen."

Tom started to speak again, but Trent cut him off. "I should scout alone," he said. "One man rides a lot quieter. I can slip up on them. Four of us can't."

"You don't think we're capable, do you?" Del blurted the words out, sounding both embarrassed and angry. "You still don't think we're capable." For a moment, palpable, almost touchable, tension hung over their camp.

"No, I don't," Gray said with no emotion in his voice; no anger, no condescending tone, no frustration. Wehr glanced at Gibbs before fixing his stare on Del, his green eyes piercing right into the boy. "You're not skilled enough to hit them at night. Trent and me, that's what we'd do, but fighting in the dark is a tricky thing. You two will need every advantage, and one advantage, maybe the only one I can give you, is daylight."

Gray scoured the black plains. He thought of all the death he'd known. Sometimes, in the war or other fights, dying came violently. Other times, death slipped over its victim lying in a bed waiting. Either way, he hated death most when the end came in hiding in the faceless dark.

"I don't intend for your mother to lose her husband and her son. I understand this is personal for you, Del.

Otherwise, I'd leave you behind, and the two of us," Gray said, motioning to Trent, "would finish this tonight." Gray started to walk away, turned back. "We'll take them tomorrow. All four of us."

Tom Gibbs motioned for Del to follow him back to the campfire. Both men sat before Gibbs poured them coffee.

When Gray returned to the fire after a brief discussion with Trent, he poured himself the rest of the coffee. "Better try to sleep a little. Trent may not be too long." Neither man responded to Gray, he figured, because he wounded their feelings. Too bad. Gray'd rather them be alive with hurt feelings than dead.

Trent eased his horse away from the camp before maintaining a light lope for the better part of two miles. When he slowed the bay down to a walk, he did so because a strange emotion flooded over him. An uneasiness never experienced before, not scouting for the calvary, not when he once got himself lost in Sioux territory north of Ft. Laramie when the Sioux were raiding at an increased pace.

The sense of foreboding grew so intense he stepped off his bay, leading him off into the dark plains. He knelt, listening to the night for the next several minutes. Silence. No one came or went.

Later, he walked Sundance back to the trail. He took another few minutes inspecting the area, lighting a match to give himself a little light.

"I guess I'm getting old and spooky," he said to the horse as he climbed back in the saddle. For a moment, he thought about pulling his rifle out, but he decided against the precaution since any efficient shooting in the pitch darkness would be well within pistol range.

The night air grew cooler. Trent untied his duster from behind his saddle, buttoning the front, including the top button around his neck. As he started again, he sang an old hymn to himself, hoping it's comforting words would relieve him of the eeriness he had not yet shaken.

The singing did not work. Trent again stopped his horse, sat, and listened. Still, nothing unusual about the night. A coyote howled, the wind rustled some leaves; nothing else disturbed the silence.

Later, a dim orange dot flickered far ahead. There was no doubt what the glow signified. Trent swung out to the east, deciding to ride a broad circle until he was south of the campfire. He would sneak up and find out as much as possible before going back to the others.

In about three-quarters of an hour, he made the far side of the orange glow. Once close, he counted three fires burning, none sizeable, but three separate fires.

He took the rope off his saddle and hobbled Sundance. Not his first choice, but with little grass around, he didn't want the horse to wander off searching for something to nibble on. "You behave yourself, Sundance, and stay put."

When he got within several hundred yards of the fires, he crouched down and crept along. He laid down about two hundred yards away and crawled on his belly, edging twenty or thirty yards from the campsite. The light from the three fires made seeing easy enough. Several bodies, Trent guessed, the women and children, slept off to the left. More bedrolls were scattered opposite the fires and three more off to the right.

It was perilous, but Trent crawled a little closer. He wanted an accurate count of how many men they would face. Crawling was a slow business and painful. Twice he put a hand down into some kind of thistle or thorn bush. A goat head penetrated his knee with pain sharp enough he jerked over on his back and slapped at the thorn—careless. "Be quiet," he whispered to himself over his lapse.

The group's horses grazed across the camp, too far away for an accurate count in the dark. Backing away, he caught the sight of the sentry beyond the captives, or at least the group of bedrolls Trent assumed to be captives. He was a heavy man carrying a rifle, a clumsy man.

Trent picked his way back to Sundance faster than he crept up on the campsite. He thought about circling the campfire and chasing off the little horse herd on the way back, but he decided against it. No trees to tie tether lines or a rope corral meant they hobbled the horses. The riskiness and potential consequences of running them off outweighed the benefits. Walker might panic and start killing women and children. Trent concluded he would be wiser to go back for the others.

Chapter Ninety-Seven

"We can be on them in two hours," Trent said as he stepped down off his horse. None of the three men slept. "I got up as close as I chanced. They've got about twenty captives. One guard wandered around the camp."

"How many in the gang?" Del asked.

Trent shook his head as he answered. "I can't tell you."

Gray, wearing a bone-colored, band-collared shirt he picked up in Pine Bluffs, was buttoning the front of his dark wool vest. "What time is it?"

Tom Gibbs carried the only timepiece. "One-thirty."

"We can be there before daylight," Trent said.

Gray stiffened, as if about to give Tom and Del a stern lecture or detailed instructions, but he didn't. His eyes tightened, his mouth bent down. "At last."

Trent kicked dirt on the fire and bridled the other three horses while the men put their gear together. Gray ran his hand along Lena's neck. "You ready to go for a little ride?"

"I ought to write that down," Tom mumbled to himself.

"Go for a little ride indeed."

The four men rode in an easy lope, saying little, Gray and Trent plotting out attack plans, thinking about how they would keep the Bismarck men alive…and out of the way.

Gray tried to anticipate how the two men would react in the fight. Cowards wouldn't be any help, but they would at least stay out of the way. Gray doubted either would act cowardly.

He worried whether they would be wise. Once they got to the camp, he and Trent would devise a plan. They would assign two novice men roles. Would they keep their heads and carry out their part, or would they start shooting wildly? Would they shoot too soon, from too far a distance, which would give the killers more opportunity to grab hostages as shields, killing some? Gray turned over in his mind how best to use Del and Gibbs.

Del thought of his father. He kept hearing the bullet slam into his breast—a dull thudding, much like dropping an enormous stone into soft mud. Over and over, the sound echoed, not the crack of the rifle, the thud before his dad slumped backward. Del wondered if you hear the shot killing you.

Red Holsten, to scare the other men, kept saying you don't on their ill-fated excursion north looking for Sioux. How would he know? He'd never been shot dead. And what a waste of time the trip had been.

That squandered time might have caused his father's death. Had they gotten on the right trail, to begin with, instead of chasing the wrong people, the killers would not have made Colorado, and Bert Camp would not have been hiding on a river bluff.

Del mentioned that to Gray the morning after they killed his father. Gray had been reflective, subdued in his answer.

"We'd change a lot of things in our lives," Gray said, "but the past is gone. No matter how much we want to change the past, it's gone beyond us."

As they rode, Del's mind grew more set, not only on rescuing women and children but on revenge. He would shoot fast and straight. The others better be quick. Otherwise, he would kill every single one of those reprobates. He would go home and tell his mother the men who made her a widow paid a stiff price and paid at his hand. He was no longer afraid.

"There they are," Trent said as he reined his horse back.

A dim orange glow glimmered along the horizon. "Camped right out in the middle of nothing with a fire," Gray said, glancing over at Trent.

"Three fires."

"How far away are they?"

"Farther than it looks out across the plains. Two miles—maybe."

"You'd think somebody who figures they're being pursued, and they must have some idea, or they wouldn't have sent Camp backtracking, would at least keep a cold camp," Gray said.

"I wouldn't call anything they've done smart," Trent said. "They left two children behind, making no effort to hide either. They didn't bother to check if one of them was dead."

"I guess what they lack in brains; they make up for in brutal," Tom said.

"Let's step down here and think this through a little," Gray said. "How are the three fires laid out?"

Trent drew three circles in the dirt. "The captives, or the most bedrolls, are over here. A couple more here and two or three over here. The horses are over on this side."

"Only one sentry?"

"One, when I saw them," Trent said, standing and brushing the dust off his knee. "I guess the worst thing against us is no cover. There are a few thistles and a little scattered brush but no gullies or rocks."

"You still don't think we should take them in the night?" Tom asked.

Gray sighed, and this time tensed up. "Tom, I told you; fighting in the dark is tricky business. You think you'll be able to tell who you're shooting at?"

"What if we charge them fast? Tear right into the middle of them before they're ready," Del said.

"Listen to the night," Trent said.

"I don't hear anything."

"And that's the problem," Gray said. "They'll hear us a mile or more away."

Wehr thought for a minute or two, looking off at the distant campfires, wishing he and Trent were alone. For a moment, he considered telling Del and Tom they'd be staying behind. He thought he might talk Tom into staying, but he doubted Del would because he wouldn't.

"All right," Gray said as he knelt where Trent drew up the camp." We're up here to the north of them. We'll swing around to the left and hit them right about sunrise. We'll put the sun right in their faces. Trent, you and Tom will stop first, and Tom, I want you furthest out. Del," he said, looking at the boy, "you and I will go farther around. You'll stop here. I'll go another fifty or sixty yards further. Let's hope," Gray said, "they drag their asses up about sunup." Wehr stood and pushed down on his left knee before speaking again. "Trent, I guess you're the only one who may recognize Walker. If you can pick him out, kill him first. Otherwise, each of us will take the man closest to us."

Tom slid his pistol up and down in his holster. Shifted from one foot to the other. "Who shoots first?"

"I will," Gray said. "Soon as I shoot, the rest of you open up." Gray spat on the ground before continuing. "I think they'll run in among the women or head for their horses. Kill them before they do either."

Chapter Ninety-Eight

The four men took twenty minutes to ride up within a mile of the campfires. They led the horses another quarter mile before Gray whispered to the others. "Leave the horses here. Tom, you and Del hobble your two. Trent, we'll leave ours ground-tied. One of those scoundrels gets mounted; we want to be after him."

"What if they don't stir at sunup?" Del asked.

"I want to keep the advantage of the sun," Gray said. "If they're not getting up, I'll kill the sentry. You boys start in on the rest as they jump up. Aim right at the middle of their bellies," he said, glancing at Del. "You can miss a little in any direction."

"Do we yell for them to surrender first?"

Gray rubbed the back of his neck, drew a deep breath, let it out before speaking through clenched teeth with forced restraint. "Don't be an ass."

"Make sure your weapons are loaded," Trent said, "and shoot with your rifles first. When they're empty, don't reload. Switch to your pistols."

Gray regained his composure. "Well, I suppose we may as well slip into our spots. We'll still have close to an hour of dark to wait out, so stay awake."

Tom's face broke into a nervous but broad grin, his first smile since they left Horse Creek. He gave a little laugh before he spoke. "Well, *hoka hey,* I guess." Trent and Gray both chuckled.

"You'll be fine, Tom," Gray smiled, wishing he hadn't called the man an ass.

Gray and Del continued after Trent and Tom dropped off. "What did Tom mean? '*Hoka hey'*?" Del asked Gray a few minutes later.

"It's Lakota for a good day to die."

"Wonderful," Del half-laughed.

Gray patted him on the shoulder. "You do what I told you." They sat for a moment, looking off at the fires, now not so far away. Gray studied the boy's face for a short time. "Your dad was a fine man. It took courage to come after this bunch." The young man shuffled his feet, kicked at the dirt. "Del, what we're about to do isn't murder."

"I never expected to be involved in something like this, but..." Del hesitated, trying to express himself, "but I don't think the Lord is mad about what we're about to do. I don't think this is a sin."

Gray assumed Del was worrying about dying or thinking about his father—a lack of attention to his current state of affairs he hoped wouldn't get the boy killed. Del wondering about the Lord's view of their undertaking surprised him. "Are you a Christian, Del?"

"Yes, sir. I am.'"

Gray and Del crouched, circled the campfires, edging ever closer. "You stay here. As soon as I shoot, you open up." Gray edged away.

About fifty yards around the camp, Gray found a place and settled down to wait. He studied the killer's camp, lit only by the now-flickering campfires and the bit of moonlight. One man wandered around aimlessly, the Cheyenne. "I'm about to send you to your happy hunting ground."

As Gray waited for the sunrise, his thoughts returned to Horse Creek and his discovery of April.

A young girl about ten, eleven years old, she was wearing a pale blue dress, or what was left of a blue dress. She was covered with so much blood he wondered how any could be inside her.

Until he found the child, this trip had been a favor to an old friend. Finding April made the search personal.

She raged again and tried to jerk away. He reached for her again. This time he was quick, pulling her into his arms. She went out of control, screaming and fighting him with every ounce of her strength.

"Wrath is coming, boys. You keep sleeping. Wrath is coming." In all the violence Gray had seen in his life, this was the first time he had ever *wanted* to kill.

Chapter Ninety-Nine

At first, a faint, silverfish glow crept into the eastern sky, a bit lighter than the night. Then a blush appeared, orangish then, turning red. A few minutes later, a red ball rose barely above the horizon. The rising sun made it hard to distinguish things. Gray struggled to make out objects. "All right, boys; hell is on its way."

Three men, silhouettes really, walked around the camp. One of them stopped and gave one of the bedrolls a spiteful kick, sending Gray into a rage as he jumped to his feet. "Damn you. You'll do!" He jerked the rifle to his shoulder. The shot split through the red early morning with a loud echo, flinging the man backward.

Trent had been looking for Jack Walker ever since the slightest amount of light appeared, but not finding him, Trent shot the Cheyenne walking guard below the left eye, leaving him staggering after he was dead.

Gray snapped off his second shot, killing another of the first three he located. Del and Tom were up and shooting.

377

Both missed their first shots, aimed at the same man, but Del hit him with his next, high in the thigh. Del didn't kill him, but his bullet put him on the ground.

The women and children screamed. Some ran; others cowered under their blankets, yelling in a blind panic. Lucy Carlyle, however, was alert. When shot, Fox fell not fifteen feet from her. She pounced at him, jerking loose his Navy Colt, still in its holster because Fox died so fast.

Walker was shooting wildly with his pistol when the bullet struck him dead center in his back. He spun toward Lucy before dropping to his knees with his arms dangling at his sides. He tried to lift the pistol, but Lucy shot again. With his lips moving to curse her, Walker clutched at the bloody hole in his belly. Before he raised his head, she fired a third time. Lucy cocked the heavy revolver and fired a fourth shot. She cocked and shot again.

When the shooting stopped and all the cruel gang, every one of them, was dead, Trent and Gray walked into the ratty camp full of beaten hostages. "I doubt these poor women will ever forget this," Trent muttered.

Gray holstered his Colt and walked toward the closest captive, a beat-up girl of eighteen or nineteen. "Which lady is Carolyn Ross?" At first, the girl was too scared to speak. She pointed toward a woman sitting with two others and their children.

Gray kneeled beside her. "Carolyn?" The savaged woman did not answer. "April," Gray said, trying to smile as tears filled his eyes. "April is safe in Pine Bluffs." Disbelief flashed across the woman's face. "She's a tough little chicken," Gray said, reaching out and touching her elbow. Passions burst out of the woman. She grabbed Gray and sobbed into his wool vest. Gray stroked the back of her hair as he rocked her.

Trent struggled to take in the full horror of the abuse of these women and children.

One woman was on her knees, squeezing a child. "What's your name?"

Gray leaned over and ran his hand along her child's face. "Gray Wehr."

Lucy Carlyle turned toward him. "I know you…sort of."

Gray stood and held both hands out to the red-haired woman. "Let's take you home."

Del Reed stood a few yards from the others. The Navy Colt Wehr loaned him hanging from his finger. "Gray, Gray!" Gray followed Trent's line of his sight to the young man swaying side to side, like a young sapling shifting in a light breeze.

Gray started toward him.

"Mr. Wehr? Gray? I think I'm hurt." Del lost his balance, sinking to his knees. Gray caught the boy around the shoulders as he slumped forward. "Can you help me? I think I need to sit, to rest a minute." Gray still held him in a kneeling position when Del raised his eyes and smiled up at Trent, not a cheerful smile, but a foolish one, as if something embarrassed him. "My belly kinda hurts."

"Don't talk now," Gray said, laying the boy down. He pushed Del's coat back and opened two of the buttons on his shirt. Trent shook his head. Dark red blood bubbled from the bullet hole through the bottom rib.

"I sure would have liked one more of my ma's apple dumplings," he said. Blood oozed over his lower lip. "I guess I won't get one, though."

Del's coughing sent a terrible chill through Gray. Every cough caused him to lurch up off the ground, the part of dying Gray hated the most. The one doing the dying was so helpless. Why did they go in such a manner? Why couldn't they close their eyes and drift away? Why couldn't death come peacefully?

The ratting coughing continued for several minutes, tearing the life from this boy's body, although Del slipped into unconsciousness, which Gray hoped meant he was no longer aware of the pain of this world. One more seizure as the young man took his last breath. Gray glanced at his face to make sure his eyes were closed. He wiped Del's now lifeless face.

The red-headed woman broke free from Tom's hold, sank down at Del's side, and rested her head on his chest, crying.

Chapter One Hundred

"I figured it was going to be you," Doc Boone said as he opened the door. "You're the only one set on pounding on my door in the middle of the night." Gray gave the old doctor a light pat on the shoulder as he let them in. "This must be Mama," he said.

A sheepish smile slipped on and off Carolyn's mouth as she and Gray stepped in.

"You've had a rough time," the doc said, reaching up to stroke the side of Carolyn's face, a face still swollen and bruised.

Carolyn flinched at the doctor's touch, but not because he hurt her. Flinching had become her immediate reaction to anyone or anything coming toward her face.

"Now, now, young lady, no one here is going to hurt you, but I can examine this a little later," he said, patting the small of Carolyn's back. "Your daughter's up in the last room on the left," he said, motioning up the narrow staircase. "I imagine she's asleep. Go on; go on up," he urged when

Carolyn stopped.

"You didn't retrieve her any too soon," Boone said in a quiet voice as Carolyn reached the top of the stairs.

"No, none too soon," Gray agreed. "I wish we had been quicker."

Mrs. Boone came half-way down the hallway with an oil lamp. "Right down here, dear," she said. "The child's asleep. I checked on her an hour ago."

Carolyn followed the elderly woman down the rest of the dark hallway. When Mrs. Boone opened the door, she stepped aside for Carolyn to pass by. April lay in the middle of a medium-sized featherbed. Her blonde hair shone in the lamplight, like a halo on the pillow. Carolyn hesitated, staring at her little girl, so peaceful in her sleep.

The flannel nightgown Mrs. Boone gave April was sizes too big and made her young child smaller. Carolyn Ross stood in the dim light. For the briefest of moments, watching her child was enough. Tears ran down her cheeks when she walked across the room and sat next to her daughter. She reached out and touched April's face and her hair. As she leaned down to kiss April, Mrs. Boone eased the door closed.

Chapter One Hundred One

Fresh snow glistened in the mid-day sun, causing the twins to squint when Millie brought them out on the front porch. "Run around the house and grab the sled," she said as they started down the steps.

"You'll pull us to Aunt Annie's?" Heidi asked excitedly as the two girls came back with the sled dragging at the end of a four or five-foot rope.

"All the way to Annie's."

"I remember the ride home from the Crazy Woman after the Cheyenne killed Nellie," Jean said, her eyes downcast. "The longest day of my life. Sometimes sad things take forever."

"I was hoping they'd be home before the first snow fell," Annie said, gazing out the kitchen window at the glistening snow. "The pass is always nasty after the first one."

Jean pushed her chair back from the table. "I wish

Susan wouldn't shut herself up in that room so much." She picked up her coffee cup, meandered toward the sink. "I guess taking over the mercantile next week will bring her out."

Annie sighed as she thought about Susan. "I'm afraid she's given up on getting her family back." The words rankled Jean, working the pump handle to rinse her cup.

"I resent her giving up," Jean said. "You should resent it more."

Annie turned toward her friend. "I guess some people can't help giving up. I suppose all their hope gets used up."

"Is your hope used up?"

"No. Graham and Trent will be back. But like you said, sad things can take a long time."

"What about Susan's family? Do you still have hope for them?" Jean asked.

Annie thought about the question. "I don't know." Jean's face registered surprise at her response. "Maybe it's harder to hope for strangers."

"Lord, Annie, sometimes you're too philosophical for me," Jean said with a half-laugh before her demeanor changed. "Susan makes me angry when she acts like she's giving up. My brother is in danger."

"They'll be back. I have faith," Annie said. "Millie and the twins should be here soon. Let's go out to the front room."

When the two women reached the foyer, they found Millie and the girls finishing up a vigorous snowball fight— Millie on her knees, arms over her head as the twins pelted her with handfuls of snow, all laughing infectiously.

"Hit her once for me!" Jean yelled after opening the door. "Shove some down her neck."

"Oh, no, you don't!" The girls jumped on top of their mom, trying to follow Jean's orders.

"Don't get Aunt Annie's floor wet." Millie pulled the boots off the snow-covered twins and brushed the remaining snow from their coats. "She'll skin us."

"She'll only skin you," Nellie, the more exuberant one, said.

"I'll skin all three of you." Annie chuckled, picking the girls up and giving them a thorough tickling." Kenyon is up in his room playing; why don't you go on up?"

"The day's warming up," Millie said while hanging her coat on the hall tree. "I don't think the snow will last the afternoon."

Jean tied her blonde hair back with a ribbon she picked up from Annie's sewing basket. "I hope not. I don't enjoy tramping around in the slush."

Millie walked over and squatted down in front of the fireplace. She rubbed her hands back and forth above the small fire. "My husband better get his tail-end back here before I start chopping wood. If I expected he'd be gone this long, he wouldn't have escaped without filling the wood bin."

Annie was looking out the front window. "Millie," she said, in a quiet but authoritative voice, a voice which quieted the younger woman. "I think," Annie hesitated, a reassuring smile raised the corners of her mouth. Her eyes shined, "I think you should come over here."

Millie sat for a moment then walked to the window. "Oh, dear Lord," she cried. Her words still hanging in the air as she shot for the door.

Jean went running after her, stopping on the porch. "You don't have any shoes on!"

Annie wiped the tears from her eyes and started toward the door. She stayed at the edge of the porch, suppressing a chuckle as her young friend flew stocking-footed across the yard.

"Susan! Susan! You better come down here!" Jean screamed.

Millie jumped into her husband's arms yards before they got to the gate. Trent swung his leg over Sundance's head and slid down into her waiting arms.

Annie reached out for Jean's hand as the two stood

together on the porch smiling at Gray and the other riders, a group larger than Annie expected. Women, crying as she went down the stairs.

"Have you ever seen a prettier bay mare?" Jean asked, smiling at her closest friend.

"I don't believe so."

Gray stepped down. He walked toward Annie, his smile warming as he approached. Annie hurried down the front steps, meeting him halfway across the yard. Gray took her in his arms, holding her tight, relishing the smell of her perfume.

"It's been a deadly autumn, Annie," he whispered, "a deadly autumn."

Chapter One Hundred Two

On the day Tom Gibbs arrived back in Bismarck, the town buzzed with talk of more gold in the Black Hills. Rumors spread of no less than a dozen wagon trains heading into the sacred Sioux land from as far away as St. Louis. In the uproar and excitement, the treaty of 1868 was all but forgotten.

Forgotten, too, was Tom himself. The typesetter finishing the headline for the next edition, *More Gold in Hills,* frowned at him. "I doubt he'll take time for you," the pressman said as he picked up the first sheet through the press. "He's awful busy."

"He will. You may have to change the headline when I tell him about the rescue."

"The rescue? Oh, oh, you mean the Carlyle woman, you and those other two, the...the Reeds went after."

"Lucy and the three children," Tom said. "Three small children."

"He might print something, I guess," the man said,

wiping the ink from his hands with an old towel, once white. "I'll go find out if he's got some time for you."

Tom sat waiting for ten minutes while three other reporters, now full-time men, hurried in and out of the office with Editor painted on the door in bold gold letters bordered in black. After another five minutes, Tom got off the old bench and went back into the cold, windy day.

He stood in the chilly air before pulling the collar of his tweed coat up around his face. He took a deep breath, turned, and walked down the dirt street toward Laura Reed's home.

Tom should have gone when he rode into town instead of stopping at the newspaper. Perhaps he hoped he would find someone to go with him and help him break the news to Laura.

No matter now. He would go alone. He would do his best to control his emotions, as he tried when Susan Carlyle told him she wanted to stay in High Meadows, and now, although she might someday feel different, she was not ready to take a new husband.

He failed to hold his emotions in check in before Susan. He feared he would fail with Laura as well.

So much death in the past three months numbed to the work of the grim reaper. Should he put his hands on Laura's shoulders and whisper, or ask her to sit down? Should he tell her because of Gabe and Del, Lucy, and one child are alive, or just tell her, your husband and son are dead?

The walk to the Reed ranch took longer than he expected. He stopped before starting up the steps, trying, he assumed, to gather strength. He tapped on the door. The front porch needed painting. He would come and do it for Laura.

Tom didn't know how long he had been standing at the door when he realized no one answered his tap. He knocked again, louder. When the door opened, Libbie Custer, not Laura, stood before him. For a moment, relief flooded through him. "Mrs. Custer."

Libbie's weary expression indicated he would not have

to tell her he brought bad news. Somehow, perhaps because she was the wife of a soldier, she knew.

Libbie glanced back into the house for Laura. Not seeing her, she took Tom by the arm and led him into the living room. "Laura is upstairs napping."

"Gabe and Del are dead," Tom said, his voice hoarse.

Libbie sat staring off toward the entryway and didn't say a word for several minutes. "I think you should let me tell her," she said, squeezing Tom's hand.

Tom nodded.

"She'll want to talk with you a little later," Libbie slipped her arm around Tom's shoulder. "Let me talk to her first."

Tom again nodded, unable to force himself to raise his eyes from the floor. "I, uh, I have a letter here from Gray." His hands shook as he handed her Gray's letter. "Maybe you should read it. I don't think he'd mind." Libbie took the note, only folded over, not in an envelope. She read silently. The words Gray had penned had been engraved into Tom's mind.

Mrs. Reed,

With intense sorrow, I write these words to you. I hope you will one day find comfort and pride knowing your husband and son gave their lives to save those of others.

Because of their sacrifice, seventeen women and children live today. I do not have the words to express their gratitude and thankfulness. Del and Gabe will always live through their lives—and mine. They were men I am proud to have ridden beside. Without their pursuit, there would have been no salvation.

May God comfort you in your loss.

Graham Wehr

1874

Libbie Custer stood and took Tom's hands. She leaned down and kissed the side of his face. "I'll go on up now."